VALENTINE

Also by Tom Savage
and available in Beeler Large Print

THE INHERITANCE

VALENTINE

TOM SAVAGE

BEELER LARGE PRINT
Hampton Falls, New Hampshire, 1999

Library of Congress-Cataloging-in- Publication Data

Savage, Tom, 1948-
  Valentine / Tom Savage.
    p.   cm.
  ISBN 1-57490-243-1
        1.Women Novelists—Crimes against—Fiction. 2. Stalking
  victims—New York (State)—New York—Fiction.
  3. Greenwich Village (New York, N.Y.).—Fiction. 4. Large
  type books. I. Title.

PS3569.A832 V35 1999-
813'.54—dc21   99-050157

BEELER LARGE PRINT
is published by
Thomas T. Beeler, *Publisher*
Post Office Box 659
Hampton Falls, New Hampshire 03844

Typeset in 16 point Adobe Garamond type,
Printed on acid-free paper and bound by
Sheridan Books in Chelsea, Michigan.

For Suzy & Marcia

PROLOGUE
FIRE

WHEN HE WAS CERTAIN THAT SHE WAS DEAD, HE GOT up and walked over to the window. He stood there, naked in the dark, gazing down at the front yard and out at the black shapes of the large evergreen trees that ringed her property. The porch light cast a dim yellow glow that winked on the thin coating of frost on the grass. It was freezing outside, but the little bedroom was warm and cozy. Warmer now, he mused, after the lovemaking.

He chuckled softly to himself and reached out to brush his fingers against the delicate white lace of the window curtains, remembering. Lace. Lace curtains, lace tablecloths, lace doilies on the coffee table and the spinet piano in the living room at home. His mother's lace.
Now, all these years later, he grasped the curtains in his large hands and yanked them from the rod. He tore at them, mauling, ruining the fine floral pattern, hearing the soft, satisfying tearing sounds as he ripped them to pieces. When they were destroyed beyond repair, he dropped them to the polished wood floor and stepped on them, feeling the rough material under his bare feet, crushing it with his toes. His chuckle rose in volume as he bounced up and down on his soles, defiling the pretty, clean lace. He kicked the limp, dead curtains away from him and closed his eyes as the thrill coursed slowly through his body. Then he opened his eyes and turned around.

A second, greater shock of pleasure suffused him as he peered through the darkness at the naked figure on the bed. She lay sprawled on top of the satin quilt, arms and

1

legs splayed, her lovely face and dark red hair partially concealed under the pillow he had used to smother her. From this angle, it almost looked as if she had been decapitated. But no: that was not the agenda. Her end would be very specific. He had planned it that way, long ago.

His gaze shifted from the still form on the bed to the little clock on the bedside table. Six minutes after midnight. He smiled to himself, thinking, I could barely wait.

At the stroke of midnight, as she lay gasping with spent pleasure beside him, he'd risen to straddle her, planting his knees firmly at either side of her waist. He'd leaned down to kiss her softly on the mouth, and his lips had traveled slowly over to her ear.

Then he had whispered his name.

He'd straightened up quickly, looking down with great satisfaction as the name registered and her expression changed. There was a frozen moment as she stared up at him, her green eyes widening in surprise. Just before she could will herself to move, he'd smiled down at her horrified face and crooned the last words she and all the others would ever hear.

"*Happy Valentine's Day!*"

He'd brought the pillow swiftly down over her face. She'd struggled briefly, as the others had, her screams muffled by the crushing pressure. The thrashing and moaning had gone on for nearly a full minute, oddly simulating her own thrashing and moaning of moments before, when he had been inside her. Then she had shuddered and lain still. He grinned in the dark, thinking, how very alike they are: the act of love and the act of dying.

He stood next to the bed, staring down at her. He

remembered another time, the first time he had stood like this, naked before a woman. The music; the pink, heart-shaped candy box clutched to his chest; his long, pale, skinny arms and legs shivering in the cold room; his mind numb with longing; and the thick, rigid thing standing straight out from the curly nest between his legs. He'd waited there in the dark, desire and fear and anticipation mingling in his blood, rooting him to the spot.

Then, in one swift, blinding moment, the lights had come on.

He would never, ever forget that moment. Because of it, he had waited several years for this moment, and for other moments like it.

Smiling at the irony of his action, he reached over and switched on the dim, pink-shaded bedside lamp next to the candy box. The soft glow illuminated the room, the bed, the woman. Just enough light, he thought. Enough light for what I have to do now.

He went over to the chair in the corner where he'd left his clothes. He stepped into his underwear and socks, then jeans, shirt, sweater, boots, scarf, gloves, cap, and leather coat. Then he left the bedroom and descended the carpeted stairs to the ground floor. He walked across the living room to the porch and down the front steps. His boots crunched on the frosty grass as he went over to his car. He opened the trunk, picked up the two large red plastic containers, and carried them back to the porch.
Leaving one container on the floor just inside the front doorway, he carried the other back upstairs to the bedroom. He unscrewed the cap and stood next to the bed, looking down at her, committing the sight to permanent memory. Then he raised the plastic can above the bed and poured, soaking the sheets and the pillows and the satin spread and the still figure in the middle of it

3

all. He sprinkled the rest of the room and made his way back down the stairs, keeping a steady stream behind him. When the container was empty, he dropped it on the floor and went to get the other one. He worked his way through the house, dousing the kitchen and the dining area and the main room, whistling under his breath. He'd made his way back out of the house and down the front steps before he stopped short, smiling, as he realized what he was whistling. It was the song he'd heard for the first time on that cold, terrible night long ago, when all the lights had come on.

"My Funny Valentine."

It had been playing on the stereo that night, he remembered, as he had played it for her tonight. Sarah Vaughan . . .

His high-pitched, elated laughter filled the chill midnight air as he emptied the container in a little pool on the bottom step. He tossed the plastic can through the open front door, into the center of the living room. Then he got in his car and started the engine. In this weather, it would take a few moments to warm up. When the car was idling smoothly, he got out and went back over to the base of the steps.

He pulled the book of matches from his pocket and stared down at it, feeling the power. He was breathing heavily now, panting with the excitement of it, his breath forming puffs of smoke. Despite the subzero temperature, he was aware of the thin trickles of sweat under his layers of clothing. Yes, he thought. It was worth it, all the years of waiting, of dreaming, of fantasizing, for this. This moment. Now.

He tore a match from the book, lit it, and touched it to the others. He stared, fascinated, as the chain reaction shot across the tops of the matches, erupting at last into one big, glorious flame. He closed his eyes, savoring his final, thrilling moment of expectation. Then, with a grin, he dropped the burning matchbook into the puddle on the bottom step.

The car had reached the first clump of trees that concealed the house from the road when he stepped on the brake and turned to look behind him. The entire downstairs was already in flames. As he watched, there was a sudden burst of light in the bedroom. From this distance, he could just hear the faint shattering sounds as the heat inside the house and the freezing cold outside caused the bedroom windows to explode, and the glittering crystals of glass rained down on the lawn. Then the roof caught, and a magnificent pillar of bright fire shot up into the night sky.

Three down, he thought. Three down, one to go.

He drove through the wood and turned onto the country lane that would eventually lead to the highway, keeping the car at a slow, leisurely, unsuspicious pace. By the time his car melted into the traffic heading toward the city, he was singing.

"My Funny Valentine."

He smiled, thinking about the last name on his list. He stopped singing to whisper the name under his breath, over and over until it rose to a murmur, and the murmur to a shout, filling the car, ringing in his ears, resounding through the frozen night. . . .

JILL

CHAPTER 1

THURSDAY, JANUARY 29

"JILLIAN TALBOT!"

She glanced up sharply, lowering the steaming mug to the table in front of her, bracing herself. Here it comes, she thought as she produced the automatic smile and peered through the gloom at the enormous shapes approaching her. She'd chosen the darkest, most quiet corner of the coffeehouse to avoid just this eventuality. But there's no hope for it, she realized. Here we go again.

The shapes came out of the darkness and formed themselves into two rather hefty middle-aged women in fur coats. Perfectly nice women, Jill was sure, but she couldn't help her own involuntary cringe as she watched them coming toward her. The larger of the two was waving at Jill as she barged across the room. The slightly smaller, blue-rinsed model trotted dutifully behind her, an apologetic smile on her friendly face.

"Now, Phyllis," this one bleated as they arrived at the table, "I'm sure Ms. Talbot is very—"

"Nonsense, Schatzi!" the bigger one boomed. "I just want her autograph. Hello, Ms. Talbot. I'm Phyllis Beamish, and this is Charlene Miller. We saw you on the *Today* show yesterday morning, you know, in our hotel? We're here on a culture tour with our women's group. That's what we call it, anyway: Broadway and museums and—"

"Yes," Jill interjected, the blank smile frozen in place. "How nice. Welcome to New York, Mrs.—uh—"

"Beamish. I've read every one of your books, and I can't

7

wait to read the new one. *So* exciting, they are. I was wondering"—she fished in her purse and produced a battered, leatherbound book and a pen and thrust them at the seated woman—"could I possibly—"

"Of course." The two women stared down at her as she found the first blank page in the dog-eared volume and quickly scribbled her name.

"Thank you *so* much," Mrs. Beamish beamed, taking back the book and returning it to the purse. "We were just enjoying a quiet cappuccino in this *authentic* Greenwich Village coffeehouse before we meet the others at the World Trade Center, and what do you think we find? An *authentic* New York celebrity! And I said to Schatzi . . ."

The smile on her face remained, but Jill Talbot's mind went briefly elsewhere, wandering away from the table and the two women and the café. She thought of her home three blocks away, and of everything she would need to make dinner: Nate was coming over as soon as he was finished for the day at his studio. In all the months they'd been seeing each other, she'd never once made a meal for him. Not a full meal, at any rate: toast and coffee, or Chinese takeout ordered in. But tonight she would surprise him with her culinary skills, cultivated from years of watching her mother and helping her in the kitchen. Galician soup, followed by fusilli pesto and a salad of mesclun greens with lemon herb dressing . . .

". . . and I just *loved* your first book! I bought copies for all my friends—when it came out in paperback, of course. . . "

Wine, Jill thought. Pinot Grigio, Nate's favorite, would be perfect with the pesto. She thought about that because it was as good a way as any to get through the Beamish speech: she had no way of knowing how long this woman would be prattling.

" . . so it's almost as if I know you, if you see what I

8

mean," Mrs. Beamish concluded. "The way everyone who reads your books knows you. As they say, a writer belongs to the world—or is it an artist? An *artist* belongs to—oh, well, whatever. It was lovely meeting you, Ms. Talbot. Come along, Schatzi, we've taken up enough of her time. Good-bye!"

"Good-bye," Jill said, blinking away the odd feeling of having just returned from an out-of-body experience.

"Very pleased, I'm sure," Schatzi whispered, smiling, before following her friend away.

Jill sank back in her seat and reached for her coffee mug, the vacuous grin slowly fading. This was the part she would never enjoy: signing autographs and enduring the praise of complete strangers. Oh, well, she decided, there are worse things. Like no praise and no requests for autographs. I'm one of the lucky ones.

She sighed, gazing down at the wirebound notebook and pen on the table next to the cappuccino. More notes: she was halfway through her fifth suspense novel, and the fourth had just this month hit the bookstores. The paperback edition of her third, *Murder Me,* had been the big Christmas title for its publisher last month, and it was holding its own on the *New York Times* bestseller list. Six weeks from now, she was scheduled to leave on a whirlwind publicity tour of several major cities around the country, and at the moment her life was a seemingly endless cavalcade of polite signings and polite cocktail parties and polite televised chats with pretty blond women on morning talk shows.

"Well, Joan, my new book is called The Mind of Alice Lanyon. *It's about a young woman who's clairvoyant, and she's receiving psychic messages from a stranger, a woman who turns out to be dead. The woman was murdered, and she's apparently trying to communicate the identity of her*

9

murderer."

"Gosh, that sounds exciting, Jillian! I loved your last novel—the one that's now out in paperback—Murder Me. Tell us about that."

"Well, Joan, Murder Me *is about a New York policewoman being used as bait by the FBI to find a serial killer. . . ."*

She smiled now, remembering. *Well, Joan . . . yes, Joan . . . of course, Joan . . .* A vapid conversation, and it made the books sound rather silly. But it really wasn't so bad—well, it wouldn't be so bad, if she could only get used to being in the public eye. But that, she knew, was the problem. She would never get used to it. For a well-known writer, Jill craved nothing so much as anonymity. *Thank you, Joan. . . .*

Several couples and groups were arriving in the cavernous, oldworld café. A glance at her watch affirmed that it was five-fifteen. This place—the nineties equivalent of a singles bar—would soon be filled with people on their way home from work. She stood up quickly, put on her gray wool coat, and pulled the matching stocking cap down over her short, dark brown hair. She collected her notebook and gloves from the tiny marble-topped table, glanced at the bill lying there, and searched her bag for her wallet. She always overpaid here because George, the waiter, was an as-yet-unpublished novelist. The fact that he was at least forty-five, more than ten years older than she, embarrassed her so much that she frequently left twice the price of the coffee on the table. She did so today, reminding herself that George was probably a very talented writer, and she was very fortunate to have been published in the first place.

A light flurry was adding itself to the carpet of snow on the ground as she emerged from the coffeehouse into the

10

bustling, bright reality of Sheridan Square and made her way down Seventh Avenue toward home. She was thinking about dinner again. She had gone only a few steps when she slipped on a patch of ice and nearly lost her balance. She dropped her notebook, and she would have fallen had it not been for the hand that was suddenly there from behind, to steady her with a firm grip on her arm. She had a fleeting glimpse of a man's black glove, and of the black sleeve of a leather coat. She leaned down to pick up the notebook and brush the snow from it, and by the time she turned around to thank her Samaritan he had hurried away.

Everyone was hurrying, she noticed, placing the notebook in her bag, which hung from her left shoulder. She was jostled several times by people rushing in and out of the subway entrance at Christopher Street. Others dashed to curbs, hailing cabs before the snow really started coming down and all the taxis magically disappeared. She smiled to herself as she looked around at the activity on the avenue. Not I, she thought. I live just around the corner, in the heart of the Village, and I work at home. I don't have to worry about subways and taxis.

This had not always been the case, she remembered. Her relative freedom was a recent innovation. A New Yorker from birth, some of her earliest memories involved one form of urban transportation or another. Waiting at curbs in front of the Central Park West apartment building she grew up in, clutching her mother's hand while her father—and, later, her stepfather—hailed a taxi. Shuttling to and from high school on the bus with two girlfriends.

When she'd returned to the city from college twelve years ago, her first job had been a nine-to-fiver at a famous publishing house here in Greenwich Village. She'd still

11

been living with her mother, who was by then divorced and already beginning to display the first signs of her illness. So every day, for nearly four years, Jill had taken the Seventh Avenue line all the way down to Houston Street, a half-hour each way on the train, while she worked her way up from copyeditor to associate editor. She learned a great deal about publishing, not to mention men: her first real, adult affair was with a recently divorced senior editor. And every night for those four years, when she'd finished her publishing homework and gotten Mother to bed, she would sit at her computer in her tiny bedroom and write until nearly dawn. Her first three manuscripts were locked away in a drawer: she knew, instinctively, that they weren't good enough to show anyone.

After four years with the first publishing company, she was wooed by another one in the midtown area with the promise of full editorship. She was not advancing anymore where she was, and her romance with the senior editor had cooled, so she accepted the offer. This had lasted three years, until she realized that editing other people's books, though rewarding and often educational, was keeping her from her original dream of writing and publishing her own work. She handed in her notice, found suitable replacement editors in the company for her small but talented group of authors, and went home.

Her fourth attempt at a manuscript had been her first suspense story, *Darkness.* She wrote it in the few moments she had had to herself, when her brief, ill-fated relationship with a corporate tax lawyer wasn't distracting her. She smiled now, remembering Ted and his proposal of marriage—a normal, safe existence. But she was nearly finished with the novel by then, and she knew in her heart that this thing she could do—writing—was essentially more important to her than anything else, certainly Ted. She knew as only a creative artist can know, that *Darkness* would be accepted for publication, and she wasn't the least surprised when it was published, and when it was successful. Because of *Darkness,* she would never again be dependent on public transportation.

And because of Mother, she thought, crossing Bleecker at the intersection and turning into Barrow Street, where she lived. She remembered the day three years ago, a few months after the publication of her first novel, when she had finally come to the realization that the doctors were right: Mother belonged in a nursing home, where she would receive the round-the-clock care and attention she obviously required. It had not been a pleasant decision, but at least the home—okay, *hospital*—in Port Jefferson, Long Island, had pretty green lawns and a view of Long Island Sound. That's what Jill told herself, anyway, when she took her mother there and came back to town to see about selling the apartment on Central Park West where she'd lived her entire life. Saying good-bye to that place was easier than she'd anticipated: her mother was no longer there, after all, and it held too many unpleasant memories of her stepfather.

And then the move here, to the lovely corner of Barrow and Commerce, just in from Hudson Street. To a new setting for her new career, in another part of town. To her beautiful penthouse atop the seven-story corner building, with the tiny elevator and the north-facing picture window affording a view of the taller uptown buildings, and the side windows from which she could see the Hudson River three blocks west. From her east windows she looked down on the quiet, Y-shaped cul-de-sac itself, formed where the end of Commerce Street joined Barrow. The little Cherry Lane Theater was here, one of the oldest off-Broadway theaters still in operation. Across from it were the Twin Sisters, two identical little two-story houses, side by side, with the tiny communal garden between them. They were built by a ship's captain years ago for his two daughters who, for reasons nobody really remembered, refused to speak to each other. Some business about a man, it was rumored, whom both sisters had loved, and who apparently ended up marrying neither of them. Even so, the two women had never forgiven each other, and they had lived out their whole lives there, next door to each other, in isolation and silence. Jill remembered staring at the two houses when she was first told their history, thinking how bizarre it was, and how oddly romantic. This little haven she now called home had been the site of deep passion, if lifelong sibling animosity could be regarded as such. . . .

The snow was falling more heavily as she crossed Bedford Street and came into her block. Everyone on the street had disappeared. The dark of the storm had intensified the natural dark of approaching evening, and the bitter chill of the wind blowing across Manhattan bit sharply into her face. She was alone here now, alone in the snow and the gathering twilight. She paused on the sidewalk in front of the Twin Sisters, rubbing her gloved hands briskly on her cheeks to soothe the numbness.

The sensation came upon her suddenly, and for a moment she wasn't sure what it was. Something odd, different, about the way she was feeling. Something in the air around her. She stood on the corner, staring up at her own building on the other side of the snowy street, slowly lowering her hands from her face to her sides. It was on the back of her head, her neck, and between her shoulder blades. An intensity, a warmth that cut through the chill, tingling on her skin. She was acutely aware of her hair, her

14

wool coat, the tug of the shoulder bag, her clothes, the soft snowflakes; everything that was touching her. And something else; something that was not touching her, but was there just the same. She closed her eyes against the panic that coursed through her. Then she took a deep breath, opened her eyes, and turned around.

There, on the far corner of Bedford, perhaps fifty yards away, stood the lone figure of a man. He was all in black, Jill noticed: jeans and stocking cap and leather coat and gloves. He was standing quite still but through the snow she could not make him out clearly. He was tall, well over six feet, and slender. The cap covered his hair and much of his face, and just as she turned around, he turned his face away to glance up Bedford, as if he were looking for a particular address. After a moment's hesitation, he walked off in that direction, disappearing from her view.

She stared at the now empty corner where he had been standing, then she looked swiftly around at all the other corners and stretches of sidewalk visible to her. She even scanned doorways and windows, looking into the front windows of the nearest Twin Sister behind her and over at the little restaurant on the ground floor of her own building. Nobody, anywhere.

She shook her head absently and clutched her purse more tightly. What on earth? she thought. I could have sworn. . . .

No, she decided. It's silly. But for a moment there, she was positive that someone had been watching her. She could still feel the lingering residue of an intense stare, aimed directly at the back of her head. Ridiculous: the only human being in sight had been that man, who was apparently looking for a building. . . .

Shaking her head again and smiling at her own fanciful imagination, Jill crossed the little street and walked up to her doorway next to the entrance to the restaurant. She got ready with the first of the two keys, just as Tara and Gwen and Mary and every other woman she knew did. Self-defense classes: an unfortunate by-product of being female and living in the city. Of being female and living on this planet, she thought ruefully as she opened the unlocked outer door, peering through the glass first to make sure there was no sinister male form lurking in the shadows inside. She'd actually joined the class with her friends as research for her third novel, because the policewoman in the story had to get physical a couple of times. Now, Jill was grateful for the training, however rudimentary.

She was just about to unlock the inner door when she remembered the mailbox. She glanced over at the shiny row of brass-fronted compartments next to the intercom, debating. Mail usually meant bills, and she only checked the box every other day or, so. But Mary, her agent, had said something on the phone this morning about a new paperback contract for *The Mind of Alice Lanyon*. A larger advance, which was nice. The amazing amount of money people were willing to pay her for writing always thrilled her. She was very comfortable now, as her accountant and her broker and Mary Daley were quick to remind her. God bless the *Times* bestseller list, she thought, switching from the door key to the tiny one for the mailbox. And God bless the reading public in twelve—thirteen?—countries.

The contract was there, in a large manila envelope with the agency's logo on the sticker above her name and address. The contract, and something else: a square, pink envelope. A greeting card, she thought, wondering what occasion she'd overlooked. A belated Christmas or New Year's thing? Her birthday was in June, so it couldn't be that. Her name and address were neatly typed on the front, and there was no return address.

With a shrug, she carried the mail through the inner door and down the long hallway, past the staircase to the tiny elevator at the back of the building. She rode up the seven flights, emerging in the little foyer at the top of the stairs outside her door.

The last of the late afternoon sunlight shone weakly through the large front window as she came inside. She dropped the bag and the mail on the big, heavy mahogany coffee table and went immediately into her office at the back of the apartment, next to her bedroom. Once the smaller of two bedrooms, the tiny space was now dominated by a desk, on top of which rested her computer. Next to the desk was a small table holding her laser printer, and in the corner stood a three-drawer metal filing cabinet. The walls and bookshelves were her only concessions to vanity: framed cover art for her four novels, and first editions of all her books in several languages. Her Edgar award, received from the Mystery Writers of America three years ago for *Darkness*—that year's Best First Mystery by an American Author—had place of pride on the shelf next to the little back window above the desk. On the filing cabinet was her telephone with the built-in answering machine. Two messages, she noticed, hitting the playback button.

"Hi." Nate's rich baritone filled the room. "I'll be working on something this afternoon, so don't call between three and five. Call after five, unless you want a recording. Just stopped for a sandwich with Doug, and he says nine-thirty is fine. I hope this whole match-making thing works. You and your bright ideas! Bang on the floor and tell Tara nine-thirty, dessert and coffee, or whatever you're planning. The eligible bachelor will join us then.

17

He even promised to put on a clean shirt. See you about seven, and I'll be starving, so feed me or *I'll* run off with Tara. Love ya. Bye."

She grinned down at the machine as the second message began. Already planning the evening ahead in her mind, she didn't hear the first part of it. But as the unfamiliar voice continued, she stared down, her mind suddenly, completely blank. What? she thought. What did he—she?—say?

Slowly, she reached out to push the playback button again. There was a whirring sound as the tape rewound, then Nate's voice.

"Hi. I'll be working on—" She pressed the fast-forward mechanism, and Nate's deep voice sped up until it was a long, sustained whine. When his message was over, she removed her finger and listened.

It was a rasping, high-pitched whisper, so high and—what?—*singsongy*, if there was such a word, that she couldn't determine the gender of the speaker. But it was the brief giggle at the end of the message that sent a chill through her.

"Hello, Jillian. Did you get my card? Beautiful, isn't it? I'll be in touch real soon. Bye." Then the giggle, and then the click of the receiver being replaced.

It was an automatic reaction, she later determined, but it was a mistake. In one swift move, she lunged forward and hit the erase button. There was another low whirr as the messages were destroyed, and the tape was once again pristine. She stood there, shuddering, clutching the edge of the desk.

Brian Marshall, she thought. But it can't be: he's—

She stopped in mid-thought. He's what? Gone. In Cleveland, last she'd heard. Or was it Cincinnati? She couldn't remember, couldn't think clearly.

18

No, she thought. It can't be Brian: it's too absurd. There's probably an explanation; somebody's idea of a joke. . . .

The card. She hadn't even opened it.

She switched on the lamp on the desk next to the computer, then the overhead light in the office. She walked slowly back into the living room and stood staring at the bag and the envelopes on the table. Twilight had fallen, and the apartment was in shadows. She moved around the room, pausing to turn on every lamp and wall switch she passed. Tara won't be home yet, she thought, or I'd can her and get her up here right now. She didn't stop at the coffee table, but continued back past the dining area into the kitchen. Click. The yellow and white tiles and appliances came to gleaming life. The bathroom across from the kitchen. Click. White tiles and fixtures, frosted-glass shower doors above the bathtub. Then the bedroom. Click, click. The overhead light and the bedside lamp went on, filling the cozy blue room with cheerful, safe illumination.

When every light in the apartment was on, she walked back into the main room. Her shoes made a loud, hollow, reassuring tattoo on the polished wood floor as she passed the dinner table, then the Oriental carpet muffled all sound. She stood above the coffee table, staring down at the bright neon-pink envelope.

Dinner, she thought irrelevantly. I have to make dinner.

Slowly, she sat on the couch facing the picture window, reached down, picked up the envelope, and tore it open.

It was a large, heart-shaped pink card, with a design of cardboard lace around the border. In the center of the heart, in blood-red embossed letters, was the word "Valentine. . ." The ellipsis indicated a further message

19

inside. She opened the card. The same red script read: ". . . Be Mine!"

There was something else, neatly typed in capitals below the greeting card company's cheery message. She read the five words over and over again, her eyes slowly widening in incomprehension. After the incomprehension came disbelief, and then, at last, the first, faint thrill of horror.

I'M WATCHING YOU.
LOVE,
VALENTINE

The windows. Her gaze flew from the card to the big picture window that took up most of the front wall. The shade was up, the curtains open. It gaped darkly at her, and through it she could see the lights in the windows of the building across Barrow Street and, beyond it, the taller buildings farther uptown. Windows, thousands of them. She was vulnerable, naked; she was being watched. She'd actually jumped up and taken a step toward the window when a new consideration struck her, She stopped, thinking, and her gaze dropped Once more to the card in her hand.

She blinked.

Then, all alone in her brightly lit apartment, Jillian Talbot burst into laughter. Oh, for Heaven's sake! she thought as wave after wave of relief washed over her. Oh, Nate, how utterly tasteless! It was Nate, obviously: the only person she ever allowed to read a work-in-progress. And that is what this was.

It was the end of the first chapter of her new novel, as yet untitled. Only it wasn't a valentine card, just an ordinary sheet of white paper in an envelope slipped under the heroine's door. And the message in the story read: "I'M GOING TO KILL YOU." The telephone message—the high-pitched, almost girlish whisper—was Nate's own embellishment. And a good one, too, she admitted: I would never have recognized his voice, not in a million years. I'm going to kill him, she decided, echoing her own prose.

Still chuckling, she dropped the card on the coffee table and went into the kitchen to boil water for the pasta.

She didn't bother about the window.

The little cardboard sign taped to the door of the East Village studio read:

NATHANIEL LEVIN
ARTIST

It was his little joke, he supposed. It was the first thing he'd done a year and a half ago, his first official act after walking into the large, empty storefront on First Avenue between Fifth and Sixth streets, dropping his duffel bag and his easel in the center of the room, and telling the aging hippie landlady that he'd take it. Evening ("Call me Eve") Blanchard—whose real first name, he'd later learned, was Selma—had been delighted, so much so that she threw in the tiny apartment directly above it for less than he'd expected. In truth, she later confided over a Welcome to the Neighborhood gift of hash brownies and cheap red wine (neither of which he touched), she'd begun to despair of ever renting the space.

Not surprising, he thought, glancing around the big, brightly lit room with the front windows now covered by the permanently lowered—and permanently locked—metal gates. It was hardly an inviting place, and the two rooms and kitchenette upstairs were, all together, not much bigger than a walk-in closet. He didn't even want to

21

think about the apartment on the third floor, or the hairy young couple who lived there: he occasionally passed them on the stairs, and that was enough. But he was *here,* he told himself again, putting down the palette knife and reaching for a medium brush. New York, exactly where he wanted to be. The East Village; the center, the hub of the art world. And *this,* he thought, smiling, was as *downtown* as the Downtown Art Scene got.

He wiped the perspiration from his forehead, took a swig from the large bottle of Evian next to the glass palette, and reached over to aim the little electric fan more directly at himself as he painted. He wore only paint-spattered jeans and sandals; his denim shirt had been discarded three hours ago, when he'd begun. Why is it always so hot in here? he wondered for the hundredth time. Even now, in January. It's snowing outside, for crying out loud! Then he looked around at the gate-covered glass and up at the long tubes of industrial daylight, and shrugged. He pushed his thick, wavy black hair out of his eyes, stretched his tall, lanky frame, and went doggedly back to work.

Just finish this one, he thought. He looked over at the canvases stacked against the wall, counting them in his mind. The show, his second in New York, would consist of twelve paintings, and ten were completed. This one was the fourth of the Four Seasons series *Summer.* The vivid patches of red, orange, yellow and white were beginning to feel hot; perhaps an other reason for the warmth of the room. When it was finished to his satisfaction—well, not really: he was never completely satisfied—he would tackle the big one, the one he'd been saving for last. The Four Seasons would join the Seven Ages of Man and the final panel, *Life,* for the showing, which he was calling "Conditions." Henry Jason was expecting a lot of coverage at his SoHo gallery, more than they'd gotten for the first Nathaniel Levin show last March. Jason believed in him, and Jason was one of the movers and shakers. He was on his way.

Hell, he thought with a wry smile, adding more white heat to the upper left corner of the canvas, I'm even selling now! Money, never a primary consideration for him, was certainly nicer than the alternative. He was in New York; he was succeeding in the art world; and he had an interesting new circle of friends. And, most of all, Jill.

Jill. As he worked, he remembered the night they'd met, almost a year ago now. The crowded, noisy dance club on Seventh Avenue South, the hot spot of the moment. She was wearing a short, tight red dress. She sat at a tiny table near the strobe-lit dance floor, smiling around at the room as her friend, Tara Summers, danced with her date. Jill was alone: he'd ascertained that immediately. She was sort of nodding her head in time to the deafening music bursting from the sound system as she sipped her drink. He later learned that Tara had coerced her into coming. Tara—a television actress, as it turned out—was apparently on a one-woman campaign to find boyfriends for both of them. But he wouldn't find that out that night: all he knew was that she was briefly alone at the table, and that she was beautiful.

He'd edged his way through the crowd to stand beside her chair. He was preparing to ask her to dance when fate intervened. A boisterous man bumped into him, and his drink spilled on the front of his shirt. The man was loudly apologizing when he heard the soft giggle, and a cocktail napkin hovered in front of his face. He looked down to see her holding it up.

"Here," she said with a lovely smile. "I think you could use this."

23

They both laughed as he wiped his shirt.

"Thanks. It sure is crowded in here.'

"Yes. And they all have drinks in their hands."

"Dangerous."

"Apparently."

This got them both laughing again. He leaned down, extending his hand. "Nathaniel Levin. Nate to my friends. I owe you one."

Still grinning, she took his hand briefly in hers. "Jillian Talbot. Jill to my friends."

He stared. "Not Jillian Talbot, the author!"

Her eyes widened as she blushed. Then she laughed again, a low, musical sound. "Guilty, officer."

He smiled, his face a picture of surprise. "I just read your new book! It's terrific! I mean, no kidding!" Then he reddened. "Oh, God, that sounds like such a line—"

And they were both laughing again.

"I'm glad you enjoyed it," she said. "So, what do you, um, do . . . ?"

"I'm an artist. A painter. Would you like to dance? I mean, well, it *would* help me dry my shirt. . . ."

"Oh, all right. I don't want you to catch a cold. . . ."

They laughed as he led her out onto the packed dance floor, and as they danced, and later, as she introduced him to Tara Summers and her date. They'd sat close together at the tiny table, and he'd finally gotten up the courage to invite her to his very first show at the Henry Jason Gallery on Spring Street. He was careful to invite her friends as well.

She had come to the opening party at the gallery. That, he supposed now, was his first official date with Jill.

Jill . . .

Omigod, *Jill!* He glanced swiftly down at his wristwatch: twenty to seven. He was supposed to be there in twenty minutes. He looked back at the canvas and back at his watch, commanding himself to put down the brush and move.

He was out the side door to the hallway, up the stairs, and in the shower when the phone rang. Dripping, he lunged out of the cramped bathroom into the cramped living room/bedroom and retrieved the phone from under the pillows of the unmade Castro convertible, where he'd last stashed it.

"Nathaniel Levin Studio," he gasped into the receiver.

"Hello, Nathaniel Levin Studio," came the crisp, humorous reply. "This is the office of Jillian Talbot, Author. We have a date for dinner, remember? Or has your Muse ensnared you for the evening?"

"No, honey, I just lost track of the time. I'm on my way."

"It's okay if you want to work, Nate. But I *did* finally get Tara to agree to—"

"Good. Doug will arrive on schedule for her inspection, or I'll know why. I'm on my way."

"You already said that—oh! Pick up some Pinot Grigio on your way over, but just one bottle; I'm not drinking these days."

"Right. I'm on my way."

"Stop saying that! Besides, haste will not avail you. You're in the doghouse, my friend."

"Huh?"

"There's the little matter of a certain greeting card and a certain *sinister* phone message—oh, never mind. But I did *not* appreciate your sick, deviant sense of humor, especially if it was aimed at my new novel." He heard her laughing as she tried to be severe.

"What? What the hell are you—"

"Forget it. I'll scream at you later. You're on your way,

25

remember?"

"Uh, yeah. I'm on my way."

He replaced the receiver and stood for a moment, staring down at it. Then, with a shrug, he jumped back into the shower.

Seven minutes later he emerged from the entrance next to the gated storefront in a thick fisherman's sweater and black jeans under his favorite bomber jacket. He donned a scarf and driving gloves, then pulled his gleaming black motorcycle helmet over his head. The roar of the powerful engine briefly startled the other residents of the block, not one of whom, he was convinced, spoke English. Ukrainian, mostly—if Ukrainian was a language. He glanced around at the Russian—oops, *Ukrainian*—restaurants and markets that made up the rest of his neighborhood, chuckled, and took off up First Avenue in the direction of Ninth Street.

Four minutes later—after much bobbing and weaving and dodging taxis and crosstown buses in the freezing winter streets—he leaped from the Honda in front of her building, locked it securely, chained both wheels, and dashed down to the corner of Hudson. He bought wine at the liquor store, along with a pricey brandy for dessert—or the Dating Game, as he'd come to think of it. Then, taking a deep breath, he sprinted back down the block to arrive on her doorstep at the stroke of seven.

He pushed open the door and reached for the buzzer, unaware that he had been watched from the moment his motorcycle had roared into the street, oblivious of the eyes that studied him as he went inside and the door swung shut behind him.

"Well, if that isn't the damnedest thing," Nate said.

"Yes," Jill whispered.

The two of them were sitting in the living room, staring down at the bright pink envelope. After a moment of silence, he reached down and picked it up. He held it rather gingerly as he inspected it, front and back.

"New York postmark," he said. "Dated yesterday. American Greeting Company—God, Jill, it's two weeks to Valentine's Day. There must be a zillion of these things in every card shop and drugstore in America."

"Yes," she repeated. She leaned back against the couch and took a deep breath, willing herself to think clearly. Joke, she told herself. It's obviously a joke. Lighten up, Talbot. But, if not Nate, then who . . . ? She watched as he removed the card and studied it.

"'I'm watching you,'" he read, and his dark brows came together as he frowned. "You don't suppose Tara—"

"Of course not!" she cried. "This is New York, Nate. A violent crime is committed against a woman about once every twenty minutes. Maybe an extremely stupid *man* would think this was amusing, but no woman would even consider it."

He raised his hands in defense. "All right, all right. It's just that you said the voice on the answering machine might have been a woman—"

"It might have been *anyone,*" she said.

Then, as the import of her words registered, they looked at each other, eyes widening. There was a long pause.

"Oh, God," she whispered. "John Hinckley."

"Now, Jill, let's not jump to anything," he said quickly. "It's just some kind of—I don't know, but it's just a card."

"What about the phone message?" she asked, leaning closer and taking his hand in hers.

He squeezed. "You didn't recognize the voice?"

"No. Whoever it was went to a lot of trouble to disguise it. God, I shouldn't have erased it!"

Nate leaned forward, and she noticed that he was studying her face as he spoke. "I think I read somewhere that nine times out of ten you know these people. Any ideas?"

She lowered her gaze to the card on the table, shaking her head. "No. Not really. At first. . ." She shook her head again. "No."

"Come on, Jill," he insisted. "At first, what?"

She took a breath and looked up at him. "At first, I thought it might be my stepfather."

She watched as his eyes widened again. Then the doorbell rang.

In one swift move, Jill snatched up the card from the coffee table, thrust it in the drawer of the end table next to the couch, and headed for the dining area. "That'll be Tara. Answer it, will you? And not a word about any of this."

Nate nodded and went to the door as she cleared the dinner plates and glasses from the table and hurried into the kitchen. The plates went into the dishwasher and the glasses into the sink as she heard the light laugh that always announced her downstairs neighbor's rather theatrical arrivals.

"Nate, darling! I'm here, as instructed. How nice of you to provide me with my very first blind date! Is he here yet? Do I look all right? And where on earth is our very own *femme des lettres*? Oh, don't look so perplexed, dear; they're just rhetorical questions."

Jill was already laughing as she came out of the kitchen to greet Tara Summers, taking in the stunning sight: the revealing white dress and the long, long, tawny mane of hair that was the envy of every housewife in America Monday to Friday afternoon from one-thirty to two o'clock. Jill had met the actress in the elevator shortly after

28

both had moved here, and they had instantly liked one another. Now Jill considered her neighbor to be one of her closest friends.

"Hello, Tara," she said. "My, for someone with an unmentionable disease whose husband just left her for another woman, I must say you're looking very well."

"Oh, please!" the actress shrieked as Nate led her over to the couch. "I've told you a thousand times not to watch that trash. Besides, that disease is no longer unmentionable. Not on daytime TV, at any rate. Hell, half the time we're not even wearing any clothes. . . ."

Jill laughed again as she sank onto the couch beside her friend. She was still laughing a few minutes later, when Doug Baron joined them.

Doug was a tall, dark, handsome type with an easy grin and a quiet disposition that immediately attracted Tara's attention. Nate had met him a couple of weeks earlier at the gallery where he would soon be showing his new paintings, and they had become pals. Tonight was the first time Jill was meeting him, and she wasn't sure what she thought of him. She took in the string tie and snakeskin boots, the ponytail and the two-day growth of beard and the earring and all the other accoutrements of the hip, downtown scene she'd never quite warmed up to. *What is it?* she wondered. *There's something rather* intense *about the way he looks at everyone. . . .*

"So, you're a photographer," she said, handing him coffee and brandy. "What sort of pictures do you take?"

"Oh, all kinds," he drawled in his slow, vaguely Southern accent. "Landscapes, cityscapes—I just did a series of portraits—"

"Nude portraits, or so he told me," Nate informed the women, grinning.

"Oh, dear," Tara muttered. "You're not one of *those*

29

photographers, are you?"

Everyone laughed. Jill watched the handsome man with the deep brown eyes, waiting for his reply.

"No," he said, smiling around at them all. "Most of my models were men, and I don't use that 'I'm a photographer' line to get women out of their clothes." He turned to the actress next to him on the couch. "Actually, I haven't been dating lately, period. I'm a widower, you see, and I haven't really thought much about . . ." He trailed off with a shrug and a little smile.

Jill immediately relaxed. A widower: that explained the faraway quality that had initially disturbed her. She glanced over at Nate. He caught her eye, communicating that this was as much a surprise to him as it was to the two women. Then she watched, amused, as Tara immediately transformed herself from the soignée actress to the role she'd played two years ago in summer stock, Maria von Trapp in *The Sound of Music*.

From then on, everything went smoothly. Jill served the pecan pie and ice cream, and the brandy and coffee were steadily poured. Nate told some of his favorite awful jokes, and Tara became such a perfect combination of girl-next-door and nurturing maternal type that Jill half expected her to break out in a rousing chorus of "The Lonely Goatherd." By the end of the evening, Doug and a delighted Tara had made a date for dinner, Nate had indicated with elaborate hand signals that he would spend the night, and she had completely forgotten about the card in the end table drawer.

At last their friends were dispatched, Tara to her apartment directly below Jill's and Doug to wherever it was that he lived. It was snowing again outside, and she and Nate lingered on the couch, holding hands and watching the gentle flurries outside and discussing the romantic possibilities between Doug and Tara. After a while, they got up and went into her bedroom. As usual, she left a light on in the living room.

She did not lower the shade on the front window.

He watched as Jillian Talbot stood up, took Nate by the hand, and led him away toward the bedroom at the back of the apartment. Then he lowered the binoculars, switched on the lamp next to the armchair he'd pulled over to the window, and opened the fresh pack of Marlboros.

He'd just arrived back here, having run through the snow to the little bodega around the corner for the cigarettes. A calculated risk: she'd only been out of his sight for a few minutes. He sat back in the chair, inhaled the cigarette smoke, and thought about his luck.

This room—directly across the street, directly facing her apartment—had been available. He'd noticed the sign in the window of the front door that first day he'd arrived two weeks ago, when he'd located her building and studied the immediate area, looking for just such an opportunity.

And that, he reminded himself, was not his only break. She was remarkably easy to follow. He learned in the first three days of surveillance that she went almost everywhere on foot, keeping mostly to the neighborhood. And taxis, despite his initial misgivings, were relatively easy to tail. He'd followed her to two bookstore signings, her publisher, her agent's office, Nate's East Village apartment, and—just yesterday morning—a midtown television studio. And all the time, she'd had no idea that he was there.

Today, however, his luck had almost changed. Twice. She'd turned around, just as he thought she was going to cross the street and enter her building, and spotted him. But that was the lesser of his two miscalculations. The first had been a few minutes earlier, when she'd emerged from her favorite coffee-house and slipped on the ice, and he had reached out and touched her.

He had made physical contact.

Dumb, he told himself, taking a long drag on the Marlboro. If she had actually fallen, if the situation had been only slightly different, it could have been a bad mistake.

It had been all right, he supposed. But then he had watched her enter her apartment building, had seen her with the little pink envelope. Later, she and Nate had sat on the couch, studying the card and talking until Tara Summers had arrived. He would give a great deal to have heard that conversation. He knew what he would do about that. The lock on the door in her lobby would be a cinch. He was sure he could handle her apartment door as well. If not, there was always the fire escape at the back of her building, to the back window. In New York City, listening devices were amazingly easy to come by. Tomorrow, or the next day . . .

He looked back through the falling snow at the window across the way. She and Nate were definitely in for the night. He crushed out the cigarette, stood up, and took off his jacket, shirt, boots, and jeans. He switched off the dim lamp and threw himself down on the little bed in the corner.

He would not sleep much tonight. He would lie awake, as he did every night, thinking about the three dead women. And about Jillian Talbot.

It was now Friday, January 30. Two weeks, he thought. Two weeks to go until Saturday, February 14.

Valentine's Day.

CHAPTER 2

SATURDAY, JANUARY 31

"WHAT IS IT, JILL?" TARA ASKED. "WHAT'S WRONG?"

Jill looked up from her menu. "What do you mean?"

"Oh, come on!" the actress cried, leaning forward and placing her elbows squarely on the table. "All afternoon you've been very nervous. I know you don't like public appearances, but this is more than that. What's the matter?"

Jill shook her head and smiled weakly. She didn't know how to bring up the subject without sounding like a lunatic, or, at the very least, an alarmist. But her friend was right: she was nervous.

Yesterday had gone all right—well, almost. There had been that moment at the store. She'd written for most of the day, only going out briefly to the nearest supermarket. She'd found herself constantly looking around and behind her, all the way to the store and back. At one point, while she was debating with herself between chicken cutlets and a small roasting chicken, she glanced over at the tall, dark-haired young man in the leather coat who seemed to have materialized a few feet away, apparently making a similar decision. She stood quite still, clutching her two choices tightly, watching surreptitiously as he began to edge toward her. He was looking down into the freezer, but she was suddenly, keenly aware of his proximity. She looked around: there was no one else in sight here at the back of the store. The man came closer, closer. She could feel the heat emanating from his body, and she realized with a swift, awful certainty that she could not will herself to move. Then, when his arm inevitably brushed against hers, she nearly gasped aloud. The young man looked up, smiled, and moved away, his attention once more dropping to the frozen food. Only then did she relax, and her grip on the two plastic-wrapped packages loosened. She'd recognized the smile immediately; she used it herself every day. Polite, but essentially empty, disinterested. When the pretty, extremely pregnant young woman arrived at his side, removed the fryer parts from his hand, and pointed down at a large roaster, he grunted with displeasure, and Jill actually giggled. The woman smiled over at her and rolled her eyes. Men, her eyes said: leave it to them, and we'd live on nothing but deep-fried foods. Jill nodded and pushed her cart away, trying to bring her inane giggling under control. Several people glanced over at her as she strolled down the aisle, laughing all the way, toward the checkout counter.

She was at the cash register when she realized that she'd dropped both packages of chicken in the cart. Too disconcerted to explain her mistake to the girl who was already ringing them up, she ended up with b oth. Oh, well, she told herself as she hurried home, I can freeze one. . . .

She ate dinner, spoke briefly with Nate on the phone, and went back into her office. For a long time she sat staring at the computer screen. Then, on an impulse, she began to type, her fingers moving swiftly across the keyboard. When she was finished, she read back over what she'd written. It was a vivid, paranoid scene in which her heroine—the stalking victim—silently freaked out in the frozen-food section of her local supermarket, certain that the innocent stranger beside her was her anonymous tormentor.

This afternoon Tara had accompanied Jill to Murder Ink, the mystery bookstore on Broadway. The publisher sent a limousine for them, and they picked up Mary Daley on the way. Jill spent much of the ride rigid on the backseat between her agent and her other friend, staring at the back of the driver's head, wondering if he was a legitimate chauffeur. She briefly imagined a scenario of the real driver on some hazy warehouse floor, bound and gagged in his undershirt and shorts, while this man, in stolen livery, savored his closeness to his prey. The three women alighted in front of the bookstore, and Jill practically ran inside.

The crowd waiting for her was predominantly female, but she noticed quite a few men as well. Her male readership had been growing with each successive title. This should have cheered her, the all-important crossing of the gender line that most writers would cherish. But she found herself glancing sharply up from the little table at the back of the shop, searching the face of every man who arrived before her with a book to be autographed.

Mary and Tara stood at either side of her behind the table, and the actress caused almost as much of a stir as the author. The proprietor of the store was pleased: two celebrities for the price of one. The crowd remained steady for longer than the allotted hour, and afterward Jill lingered to sign the contents of several cartons of *The Mind of Alice Lanyon,* to be shipped to fans and collectors all over America. A very pleasant afternoon, really. But all the while she smiled at everyone, the fans and the bookstore staff and her two friends, she wondered how they would react if they knew how she was feeling, and why.

Now she and Tara were here at Carmine's, the enormous, popular Italian restaurant on Broadway and Ninety-first Street, two blocks south of the bookstore. Mary had rushed off to another engagement after the signing, and

Jill had dismissed the chauffeur and asked the people in the bookstore to recommend a nice place in the neighborhood for dinner. The cleaning woman, Mrs. Price, was in Jill's apartment on Saturdays from five to seven, and she didn't like having people underfoot while she worked, so Jill always dined in restaurants on Saturday. She looked around the cavernous interior of the dining room, realizing that she now felt more comfortable in large crowds than she ever had before.

Tara was still studying her closely, she noticed.

"You tell me what's going on with you," the actress warned, "or no dessert!"

They laughed together as the waiter arrived with their dinner. Seeing the size of the platter of ravioli he lowered between them, Jill wondered if no dessert was really a punishment. Her smile faded as she looked up to meet her friend's penetrating gaze. She took a long, deep breath, preparing herself.

Then she told Tara about the valentine.

He'd been in luck: the deadbolt on her apartment door was unlocked. The little lock in the doorknob had been easier than the main entrance downstairs. The elevator had been a risk, but here he was, actually inside the apartment he'd been observing from across the street for the last two weeks.

He stood in the center of the large, beautifully furnished living room, gazing slowly around him, taking in every detail. A big, enclosed, hollow space with an opening on the room: that is what he was seeking. He'd already placed the tiny chip inside the receiver of the phone in the office. Now it was a matter of concealing the little unidirectional microphone and its attendant activating mechanism somewhere in this room. He dropped his gaze to the equipment that fit so easily in the palm of his right hand, marveling yet again at the progress of modern science. The two bugs and the listening devices—the sound-activated tape recorder and headphones that now waited in his room across the street—had been remarkably simple to obtain. A reasonably intelligent, motivated fifteen-year-old could purchase all of this from any one of hundreds of establishments in Manhattan alone.

A big, hollow space . . . not the breakfront: the glass cabinets on top and wood shelves below were completely enclosed, soundproof. That was the problem with the drawers in the room as well. This left the furniture . . . the couch. There was a gap, perhaps three inches, between the bottom of the seat and the floor. Yes . . .
Carefully, he tilted the couch until it was lying on its back, the four short legs sticking out toward him. The underside, viewed from this angle, was hollow, the stuffed undercushion and solid-looking metal rib frame several inches above the opening at the bottom. The side and front panels just above the legs were wood. Perfect. He reached in the inside pocket of his leather coat and produced a roll of thick plastic tape.

Three minutes later, all was in place. He set the couch back in its original upright position, careful to match the feet to the indentations in the carpet. He spent the next five minutes moving swiftly through the apartment, searching, his sneakered feet making no sound on the floor. Not that it mattered: he knew she was signing at a bookstore uptown this afternoon, and that Tara Summers was with her. He'd watched from his window as the two women had been handed into the big black limousine nearly an hour ago. His search was a luxury he felt he could afford: she'd be out at least a couple of hours. And he had to ascertain one thing, to know beyond a doubt one particular detail of her life.

No, he decided at last. She didn't have a weapon. No gun, no Mace, no alarm system worth a damn, either on the doors or the windows. Perhaps she kept Mace, or even a gun, in her purse, but he doubted it. And what was the point of the deadbolt on the front door if she wasn't going to use it? She was completely vulnerable.

Getting to her would be a snap.

He took one more quick look around, to assure himself that everything, every single thing, was as he had found it. As she had left it. He was about to leave as he had come— he'd use the stairs this time—when he gave in to the final pang of curiosity. With a quick glance at his watch, he moved silently over to the little end table. He'd seen it there, in his first search for places to conceal the microphone.

He reached down into the drawer and picked up the bright pink envelope. He pulled out the card and opened it. Yes, he thought, nodding his head slowly. Yes . . .

He had just put the envelope back where he'd found it and pushed the drawer closed when he suddenly became aware of the sounds from outside, from the other side of the apartment door. He reached swiftly up with his left hand to pull the black ski mask down over his face, the right hand dropping automatically into his coat pocket and closing around the switchblade.

As he listened, the elevator door rumbled open. This sound was followed by the slap of solid, flat shoes on the uncarpeted foyer and the sudden, loud jingle of keys at the lock.

"My God, Jill, that is just Creep City!"

"You're telling *me*?" Jill pushed her plate away, the ravioli barely touched, and reached for her water glass. She watched in faint amusement as Tara continued to shovel in the rich food while she talked. Tara could eat under any circumstances, even these. Excitement, anger, fear; they had the odd effect of whetting, rather than dulling, her appetite. Actors, Jill thought.

"Two things," Tara muttered, scooping up a ravioli. "First, weapons. Second, police. Definitely. Now, wait a minute"—she held up her hand, cutting off Jill's automatic protest—"I know what you're going to say. You have a can of Mace in your purse, and you don't want to bother the cops with anything so trivial, yadda yadda. Sure." She finally put down her busy fork and leaned forward, looking directly into Jill's eyes. "You've seen me on *Tomorrow's Children,* right? You know the gal who plays Clarissa, Betty Hanes—with the big boobs and all that red hair? Well, this happened to her!" She nodded once, as if that explained everything, and reached for the fork. Jill's hand beat her to it.

"What?" Jill said, clamping down on the fork before Tara could once more fill her mouth. "What happened to her?"

"*This.* Same song, second verse." Tara leaned back in her chair. "Anonymous notes. Phone calls in the middle of the night. Someone kept sending her messages, like, 'I want you, and if I can't have you, I'm going to kill you.' Then, one day, she went back to her dressing room after a taping and found her street clothes slashed to ribbons." She leaned forward, dropping her voice to a whisper. "And her undies were gone!"

Jill's hand flew to her mouth. "Oh, my God!"

"Yeah," Tara said. "Cute, huh? Well, for the next few days, we had these police officers all over the studio. They escorted her to and from work, staked out her apartment, the whole bit. Unfortunately, nothing happened. And

39

they finally dropped it. It wasn't their fault, really. I mean, this is New York, and the cops have lots to do. So, Betty hired this guy, this private eye. Nobody else knew about it. We were told he was a new associate producer. Two days later he caught someone in her dressing room, stealing more undies."

"Wow," Jill whispered. "What did they do to him?"

Tara registered confusion. "Him who?"

"The guy who stole her undies."

Once again, Tara leaned forward. "My dear, it wasn't a guy. It was the prop girl, of all things."

Jill shook her head in disbelief. "I've never heard of that. I know quite a few lesbians, and none of them would ever—"

"Oh, she wasn't a lesbian." Tara waved her hand dismissively and reached again for her fork. "You see, Betty was dating one of the cameramen on the show. Before her, he'd been with the prop girl, and she got pregnant. So he dropped her and took up with poor Betty, who knew nothing about any of it. Prince Charming, right? The girl was trying to freak Betty off of the show so she could get back with him. That's when we *knew* she was crazy! But, hey, she does a great job with the props."

"You mean she's still *there*?" Jill's eyes widened.

Tara speared another ravioli. "Sure. Betty didn't press charges. Gave the cameraman a black eye, though. In front of the entire company! He was canned, and the girl got a raise. She just had the baby, a little girl, and she and Betty are pals. Now she's dating one of the writers—the prop girl, not Betty." She smiled and popped the pasta into her mouth.

The story, bizarre though it was, bordered on the ridiculous. Jill restrained herself from laughing. "So, what's your point?"

40

The fork clattered down onto Tara's plate, and her smile disappeared. "My *point* is this: don't screw around. Okay, it's just a weirdo card, and maybe you'll never hear from—whoever—again. But you don't know that. You say you're nervous? You're *right* to be nervous! Betty was lucky. Her wacko wasn't really a wacko, just a mixed-up, flaky girl who was pregnant and desperate. But that didn't stop Betty from replacing the Mace in her purse." She glanced around at the nearby tables and leaned forward, lowering her voice. "Now she carries a little friend around in there. It answers to the name Lady Wesson."

Jill shut her eyes and turned her face away. "I can't do that. That's not an option; it's not the kind of person I am."

"Yeah," Tara said, nodding sagely. "That's what Betty said. At first."

"How about you?" Jill cried. Then, as the waiter arrived with dessert menus, she, too, leaned forward to whisper. "Could you ever do that?"

A slow smile came to Tara's lips. She reached back, unhooked her shoulder bag from the back of her chair, and held it out.

"Care to look in there?" she said.

Jill stared.

"Okay," her friend said, putting the bag back on her chair. "I guess we'll wait on that. But at least tell the police. So they have it on record."

"You have a *gun*?" Jill was still assimilating this. "Has—has anything like that ever happened to you?"

Before Tara could answer, the waiter handed them the menus. Then he held out a small notepad and pen. "Ms. Summers, I don't want to bother you, but I'm your biggest fan. Could I have your autograph?"

The actress produced a smile that could light New York

41

City, signed the pad, and handed it back. The waiter thanked her and hurried away. The two women watched him go. Then Jill watched as her friend sat back and grinned across the table.

"Hey," Tara said, "you never know."

Gloria Price came into Jillian Talbot's apartment and took off her plaid winter coat, the one Lou had surprised her with last Christmas. It was a combination Christmas/thirtieth-anniversary present, not merely attractive but surprisingly warm as well. She loved wearing it, because of the warmth and because of what it represented. She smiled to herself, thinking, now that both kids have kids of their own, Lou finds reasons to spoil me. I'm his surrogate child. And he's mine.

That's why she was here today. They both had nine-to-five jobs, and on Saturday afternoons she cleaned apartments in several neighborhood buildings for extra cash. Lou was retiring next year, and they were moving to Florida. She was saving up for his new golf clubs.

She glanced over at the coat closet next to the front door. Then, with a shrug, she dropped the coat onto the couch and headed for the kitchen. Florida, she thought, chuckling. I won't need the beautiful coat much longer: next Christmas, he should buy me a bathing suit!

This was her favorite of the apartments she cleaned. It was certainly the most attractive, and she liked Jillian Talbot. The other two "professional women" whose places she did were nags, and that was a fact. But Jill Talbot was always cheerful, always friendly, and she was wise enough to leave the cleaning decisions to a woman who'd been cleaning since before Jill was born. She paid the best, too. And now Gloria had signed copies of all her books. Good books, Gloria thought: a little scary for her taste, but fun.

She reached in the utility closet next to the refrigerator for the vacuum cleaner, then rummaged under the sink for furniture polish and glass cleaner. She was about to go into the bedroom when she glanced at the microwave oven above the range, glanced at her watch, and made a decision. She took a mug from the rack near the sink, filled it with tap water, and opened the overhead cabinet containing the instant coffee.

She had slammed the microwave door shut and was removing her hand from the control panel when she stopped, arrested by a faint sound from the living room behind her. She stood still a moment, listening. She glanced at her watch again. Perhaps Jill had finished dinner early, and was returning. . . .

She turned around and went over to the pass-through, peering out into the dim living room. The sun was about to set, and little light came through the windows from the gray afternoon outside. Some instinct made her reach over and flip on the kitchen light switch. The ceiling globe came on, and with a small buzzing sound the fluorescent lighting under the cabinets winked to attention. Oh, well, she thought. Get to work. Just as the microwave alarm rang, she turned back to the oven and reached in for the steaming mug.

The second time Gloria Price heard a sound from the living room behind her, she knew she was not imagining things. It was a small, distinct click.

"Jill, is that you?" she called.

Silence.

She cocked her head, and her eyebrows came together in what Lou described as her "computer mode." She set the mug down on the counter, turned around again, and walked out into the darkened living room.

It was early evening when the two women stepped out of the cab and hurried into the brightly lit foyer. Jill was ready with her door key, but Tara turned immediately to her mailbox.

"Ah! Letter from my kid brother!" Tara announced with a smile, looking up just in time to see Jill reach out for her own mailbox but then draw her hand back, hesitating. Her smile faded.

Both women stood there, silently regarding the little brass square immediately next to Tara's. Bracing herself, ignoring the sudden chill that ran through her, Jill inserted the key in the box, opened it, and stuck her hand inside.

The envelope was not pink this time, but white. They stared down at it for a moment, noting the stamp and the postmark and the neatly typed name and address, and the lack of a return address. Then Tara snatched it from Jill and tore it open.

It was a home-made card, folded white construction paper. On the cover was the outline of a heart crudely drawn with a pink crayon. Inside the heart, perfectly centered, was the typed message:

ROSES ARE RED,
VIOLETS ARE BLUE,
SUGAR IS SWEET . . .

Tara opened the card and held it up so both of them could see the rest.

. . . AND I'M STILL WATCHING YOU.
LOVE,
VALENTINE

They rode up in the elevator in complete silence.

44

Tara was still holding the card and envelope, and there was no question of her getting off at the sixth floor and going into her own apartment. Jill closed her eyes as they ascended, trying to assess how she felt. There was no fear now: the shock had only been the first time. She wasn't shaking. She wasn't even angry. She was merely feeling . . . what? She cast around for the right word as the elevator stopped at her foyer. She walked up to her door and reached out to insert the key in the lock, and the word came to her. *Distaste.*

The door flew open.

With a small cry, Jill dropped her keys and stepped backward, colliding with Tara, whose hand was already inside her shoulder bag.

Gloria Price stood before them in a loud plaid winter coat, gaping, obviously as surprised to see them as they were to see her.

"Oh!" she cried, raising a gloved hand to her heart. "Oh, dear, you gave me a fright! I didn't hear the elevator."

Gloria hurried home through the chill evening, and she knew her shaking was not from the cold. That creepy feeling that had come over her in the kitchen had set her nerves on end, and she'd rushed through her duties, giving the apartment only a perfunctory cleaning. And all the while she'd switched on lights and glanced over her shoulder, unable to shake the mood. Then, as she was making a swift getaway, she'd thrown open the door and found the two women standing there, and she'd nearly jumped out of her skin.

She shivered again as she turned quickly toward her home on Bedford, glad that she'd decided not to tell Jill about the apartment door. Jill always left the deadbolt unlocked on Saturday afternoons. Gloria didn't have a key for it, did not want a key for it. But that was no excuse. She should always lock the deadbolt once she was inside, to prevent exactly what had happened. She'd obviously left the door ajar. Because that is what she'd heard from the kitchen: the distinct click of the front door closing.

They sat in silence for a long time. Finally, Tara went into the kitchen and emerged a few minutes later with chamomile tea. Jill looked up, smiling weakly as her friend handed her a mug.

"The police," Tara said. "Tomorrow."

Jill nodded. She took a sip of warm, sweet tea. Then she got up and went into the office to call Nate.

"The police. Tomorrow."
He watched as Jillian Talbot nodded and accepted the tea that was held out to her. The other woman sat. After a moment, Jillian Talbot got up from the couch and disappeared into the back of the apartment. Then the other tape machine, the one on the table next to him, came to life. He dropped the one set of headphones and reached for the other. There was the clicking sound of electronic dialing, followed by two rings, then:

"Nathaniel Levin Studio."

"Hi, it's me."

"Howdy. I was just about to call you. I'm going over to the gallery. Henry wants to set up some things, and then he and his new boyfriend are taking the soon-to-be-famous artist out to dinner."

"Oh. That's nice. Umm, Nate—"

"You don't remember his name, do you?"

"Whose name?"

"The new boyfriend."

46

"Uh, John, I think. Listen, Nate—"

Pause. The recorder hissed.

"What is it, Jill? What—"

"I got another one. Another valentine. In the mail." Long pause. An expulsion of breath, followed by Nate's muttered "Jesus." His voice was perceptibly lower now, low and angry. "Is Tara with you?"

"Yeah, she's here."

"Okay. Let me call Henry and cancel. Five minutes." Click. Nate had obviously thrown down the phone. Another click as Jillian Talbot replaced her receiver, and the machine stopped. He reached for the other headset.

Jillian Talbot came back into the front room. The two women sat there, the card and the envelope on the table in front of them, until the Honda roared to a stop in the street outside and Nate joined them. He watched them for a while through the binoculars. Everybody paced and talked and picked up the two envelopes and put them down again. Finally, Tara Summers went downstairs. It wasn't until after she'd left that Jillian Talbot at last went into her lover's arms, leaned against him, and wept.

He removed the headset, leaned back in the armchair and closed his eyes. At least all the machinery was working. After what he'd gone through to get it in place . . .

He frowned, remembering the tense moments in the front closet when the strange woman had come into the apartment and gone into the kitchen. The slow, agonizing move from the closet to the front door. It had taken several seconds to open it without making a sound. He'd heard the deafening click behind him as he'd dashed for the stairs. Well, he'd made it back here undetected, and listened as the cleaning woman had moved around with the vacuum cleaner. The sound was clear, and he could

47

hear her in all but the two back rooms. Good.

So. Two cards, and now Jillian Talbot was going to the police. Hmmm . . .

He gazed across the street at the two tiny figures embracing on the couch. Deep in thought, he slowly reached for a cigarette.

CHAPTER 3

SUNDAY, FEBRUARY 1

THE SIXTH PRECINCT IS A LONG, LOW, BEIGE BRICK building on Tenth Street between Bleecker and Hudson, exactly three blocks north of Jillian's home. It was constructed in a period of urban American architectural history when designers seemed to think that no style at all was its own form of artistic statement, particularly in public buildings. It has thick, functional walls and high, useless windows and a roof, and that's about it. A small blacktop drive along one side provides parking for several blue-and-white sedans. The station house stands out on the quaint, tree-lined Village street, nestled between long rows of elegant townhouses and lovely red brick apartment buildings like a minibus among Rolls-Royces. Jill looked up at the bland edifice before her, frowning. She'd been here several times in the recent past, researching her last novel. But the friendly detective who had served so patiently as her advisor was now retired: she no longer knew anyone here. Besides, she told herself again, the whole thing is just so silly. Had Nate not been with her, even now stepping forward and opening the glass door, she would have turned around and gone home. But Nate *was* here, regarding her steadily as he held the door for her, so she braced herself and went inside.

Nate did all the talking at the front desk, and a pretty, bored young woman listened, glancing occasionally from him to Jill and back again with what Jill could only interpret as polite skepticism. When he was through, the young woman nodded once and waved them over to the row of beige chairs along one beige wall that served as the waiting area. And wait they did, for nearly forty minutes, during which time Jill observed the steady comings and goings, the NYPD business-as-usual she always saw in movies and on television shows, and had never truly believed. A wino was brought in, booked, and sent to a holding cell somewhere at the back of the building. Two young hookers in miniskirts and mesh stockings were brought in and booked, and they, too, disappeared. Then came a very tall young black man in a miniskirt and mesh stockings and an enormous blond wig. He bore a remarkable resemblance to Tina Turner, and he insisted in a loud, high-pitched lisp that the arresting officers address him as Veronica. Nate brought Jill some terrible coffee from a nearby vending machine, and they waited some more.

At last they were approached by a small, stocky Hispanic man in a dark uniform, his curly black hair and impressive black mustache emphasizing the roundness of his friendly face. He introduced himself as Sergeant Escalera and led them to a tiny, partitioned cubicle at the front of the room. There was only space for one chair next to the sergeant's cluttered little desk, and Jill sank into it, purse on knees, wondering where to begin. Nate stood rigidly beside her, half in and half out of the cubicle, and dropped a hand onto her shoulder. They watched as the sergeant squeezed his fleshy frame into the chair behind the desk and reached for a blank report form.

49

She stated her name, address, telephone number, gender, age, Social Security number, and occupation. This last caused Sergeant Escalera to glance up, smiling briefly, before looking back down at the myriad tiny instructions on the paper. When he asked her the nature of her complaint, she paused, wondering what to call it, what word to use. Nate leaned forward and supplied one: harassment. Jill looked up at him and blinked, then turned back to the officer, shrugged, and nodded. Harassment.

They showed him the two valentine cards, and Jill told him about the telephone message. He sat back in his chair, his head resting against the thin partition, and listened politely. He leaned forward twice to scribble something on the form, and at one point he held up a hand to interrupt them and called out to someone in the main room, reminding him to tell someone named McCoy that he was to get in touch with someone named Peewee by four o'clock if he wanted help with the collar. A raucous, laughing voice behind Jill called back that Peewee was crazier than something-or-other, and so was McCoy, and, besides, the collar was already going down. She sat, staring at the purse on her knees, waiting for Sergeant Escalera to return his attention to her.

When he did, his dark features formed into an apologetic smile, and he explained in a low, reasonable voice that there wasn't really anything they could do at this point. He went on to say, after glancing surreptitiously at his watch, that no overt threat had in fact been made, and that, unpleasant as they were, the greeting cards were—well, greeting cards. He asked her if there was anyone, anyone at all, that she thought might be doing this, and even suggested that perhaps one of his men could pay that person a visit and tell them to stop. He glanced over, then, at the large, muscular, capable-looking young man beside her, who immediately picked up his cue and said no, that wouldn't be necessary, that *he* would do it. Pen poised, the sergeant nodded to him and looked back at Jill, waiting for the names of any suspects.

She could not think of any. Actually, she could think of only one, but she wasn't going to report that. Not yet.

Clutching her purse tightly, she rose to her feet, preparing to thank the friendly sergeant for his help. At that moment, however, there was a shout from the room behind her, and the sound of running footsteps, followed by several voices, raised and tense. The sergeant jumped up from his chair and rushed past them out of the cubicle, tossing back a brief good-bye as he went.

Nate took her by the hand, and they came out of the tiny office into pandemonium. People in uniforms and people in street clothes were running this way and that, calling to each other. The sergeant had gone to join the young woman at the main desk, who held a headset up to one ear as she shouted instructions to various people hurrying by. They stood aside at the main door as several officers rushed by them and out of the station. As she and Nate finally made their way out to the sidewalk, the sirens began. Three police cars came screeching out of the drive at the side of the building and took off down Tenth Street, their red fights flashing.

Jill and Nate stood in front of the station for several moments, communicating in silence what both were thinking. There was a fire, or a murder, or an armed robbery in progress, or some other earthshaking, life-threatening event. One of the endless trials and tribulations of city life, one of many that would occur on that day alone in New York. They both gazed mutely down at the envelopes in her hand. With a sigh, Jill put

51

the envelopes in her purse, and they walked away down Hudson Street toward home.

He stared at the photograph on the inside of the back cover of the paperback. Then he got a beer from the tiny fridge in the corner of the room and settled down in the armchair at the window with his new purchase.

He'd followed them to the Sixth Precinct on Tenth Street about an hour ago. Then, deciding that they'd probably be there for a while, he left them there and went over to Partners & Crime Bookshop a couple of blocks away. There he had bought three paperbacks and a shiny new hardcover: the complete works of Jillian Talbot. He'd come back here to wait for her return.

He'd never been much of a reader, and his life of late had provided no time for books. But now it was time, he'd decided; time to get to know Jillian Talbot better. He looked down at her four published suspense novels.

The cover of her first novel, *Darkness,* showed an attractive, terrified young woman staring out from the doorway of an attractive, suburban-type house. In the otherwise empty front lawn in the foreground lay a discarded Raggedy Ann doll. The copy proclaimed the book to be an Edgar Award winner, and a quote from a newspaper review read, "A mother's greatest fear . . . a modern masterpiece of suspense."

He turned to page one and began. For the next two hours he only glanced up from the book once, when he heard the motorcycle start up and roar away down the street. Then he saw the lights go on in the apartment across the way. Jillian Talbot was home, and Nate was no longer with her. He watched her moving about for a few moments, then returned his attention to her novel.

The attractive suburban housewife's seven-year-old

daughter had vanished in the very first paragraph. The first sentence, actually: *"At the moment that her daughter disappeared, Lauri O'Connell was in the utility room, adding fabric softener to the rinse cycle. The most mundane, everyday thing, she would later think: even as we do these, we are never safe. . . ."* What followed were three hundred twenty-seven pages of sheer suspense. He'd never read such a book before, but even he admitted that this was addicting. Not until the final moment of the story, after Lauri had overpowered the shell-shocked Vietnam vet/school custodian, and the police had finally arrived to drive her and her drugged-but-otherwise-okay child away, did he put the paperback down and reach for his binoculars. Moments later, the tape recorder on the table next to him sprang into action.

"You've reached the home and office of Dr. Dorothy Philbin. I'm not able to come to the phone now, but if you leave a message, I'll get back to you as soon as possible. Please wait for the beep."

Beep.

"Hello, Dr. Philbin, this is Jillian Talbot. I'm sorry to be calling you on a Sunday, but I—I was wondering if I could make an appointment. Umm, this week, if you have any openings. I—I'll explain when I talk to you. My number is . . ."

She left her number and hung up. She was reaching again for the receiver when she stopped herself. No, she thought, don't call Nate. He's busy.

Nate. Smiling, she relaxed back into her chair. This wasn't the longest relationship she'd ever had; not yet, at any rate. But it was the most complete, the most satisfying. From the moment they'd met, she'd been acutely aware of that amazing combination of sexual attractiveness, artistic

53

brilliance, humor, and tenderness that seemed to define the man. Her women friends were forever stressing the vast differences between the genders and decrying their men's roughness, their lack of attentiveness, their frequent moods, their covert attraction to other females: their insistence on doing "man" things. Jill shook her head, counting off all the so-called usual behavior patterns of adult males, and marveling again that Nate didn't seem to fit any of them. Today had been a perfect example: the strong, masculine presence she'd felt at her side throughout her unpleasant ordeal at the police station—

The police station. The memory sent Nate from her mind, replacing him with harsh reality. She sat in the little office at the back of the apartment, staring out the window above her desk as the shadows lengthened and twilight fell. She thought for a long time about the greeting cards and about her trip to the Sixth Precinct. Then, with a glance at her watch, she picked up the phone again and dialed.

"Hello."

"Hi, Tara, it's Jill."

"Hey, babe. What's shakin'?"

"Well, I've been thinking. A lot. You know your friend on the show, the one you told me about in the restaurant yesterday?"

"Yeah, Betty."

"Betty. Right. I want you to do something for me. . . ."

He listened to their conversation. Then, when they'd hung up and the machine stopped, he put down the headset, went to get another beer, lit a Marlboro, and reached for her second novel. This one was called *The Widower,* and the cover art was an extreme closeup of the face of a pretty blond woman, her eyes wide, her mouth

54

open in a scream. The copy on the back began:

The worst day of Heather Morgan's life was the day she said, "I do."

Until now . . .

He thought briefly about the phone calls he'd just heard. Then he opened the second book and began. He read long into the night.

Soon, he thought as he read. Soon . . .

CHAPTER 4

TUESDAY, FEBRUARY 3

"I DON'T UNDERSTAND," BARNEY FLECK SAID. "I don't understand what it is you want me to do."

Jillian stared at the unusually tall, gray-haired, fiftyish man behind the enormous desk in front of her. He'd been so friendly, so downright jovial ten minutes ago, when she'd first come into the surprisingly modern office in the big gray building on Twenty-fifth Street. He'd poked his large head out the door to the waiting room where she'd sat for some five minutes, watching the efficient-looking, middle-aged secretary working at her computer. When she'd first seen him, Jillian had wondered whether, perhaps, she had made a mistake in coming here. Barney Fleck ("Rhymes with 'tec'," he'd laughingly told her) had ushered her into his office, waving her into a leather armchair facing the big, cluttered desk, and gotten right down to business.

"What can I do for you, Ms. Talbot?"

She'd told him what he could do for her, but apparently he had not understood her.

"I want you to find him," she repeated, enunciating her words as if clarity of diction would make up for her apparent lack of clarity of meaning. "I want you to find Brian Marshall. He and my mother were divorced sixteen years ago, and he moved to Cleveland. At least, I seem to remember that it was Cleveland. It might have been Cincinnati—I always get those two cities mixed up. I guess it comes from being an arrogant New Yorker."

He laughed again, his hearty basso profundo unsettling the papers on the desk. "Yeah, I know what you mean. I have that *New Yorker* map of the United States permanently fixed in my brain. You know, New York on the east coast and L.A. on the west coast, and everything between them comes under the general heading of 'Kansas.' Well, if it really is one of those two places, I guess I can find him. I just don't understand exactly what you think your step-father has to do with all this."

She thought a moment before replying, finally deciding that complete honesty would be the best course of action. "I guess you could say that I was the reason for their divorce. My father died when I was seven. Lung cancer. Five years later my mother met Brian Marshall. He was a big, handsome Irishman, very friendly—at first. A friend of hers introduced them at a party. He was divorced from his first wife, and there was a child somewhere, a boy. He paid child support, or whatever. Anyway, six months later she married him. She was very happy, I remember. But then we began to see the problems."

"What problems?" the detective asked.

She sighed. "Well, he drank. A *lot*. Turns out, that's what ended the first marriage—I didn't find that ou until later, when I made it my business to find the first Mrs. Marshall and speak with her. He—he got violent with her, and she was afraid for their son. She told me something else: once, shortly after he married my mother, she actually called Mom and told her all about it. Mom hung up on her. Well, she lived to regret it, I suppose. You see, when I was seventeen years old, Brian Marshall tried to—he tried to rape me."

"I see," the detective replied, watching her closely. After a moment, she continued. "I can't say that it came as a great surprise. I became aware very early that he—he looked at me strangely. I can't explain it exactly, but even at fourteen, I knew that wasn't the way grown men were supposed to look at children. I made sure I was never alone with him. Until—well, one day this thing happened." She bit her lip, recalling the struggle on the kitchen floor of the Central Park West apartment: the torn blouse and the castiron skillet and the blood streaming down his face. Finally, she blinked it away and said, "Brian Marshall is the only person I know who's ever gotten—violent—with me. I want you to find out where he is, and what he's doing, and whether or not he could have done this." She waved her hand at the two envelopes that lay atop the pile on his desk.

Barney Fleck picked them up and studied them again. "Yes, I see. When was the last time you saw him?"

"Shortly after the—the incident. Mother threw him out, and she divorced him as soon as she could. I was going to press charges, but she convinced me not to. I've always regretted that: it is my greatest regret. Well, I went away to college, and he left New York. I seem to remember Cleveland being mentioned."

"Can't you ask your mother where he is?"

She bit her lip again before replying. "No, that would not be convenient."

He raised his large gray eyebrows. "That's a strange choice of words."

57

She sighed, remembering her promise to be frank with this man. "My mother has Alzheimer's disease. She's in a rest home on Long Island. She doesn't remember where he went. She probably doesn't even remember who he is." With a swift gesture, she brushed tears away. "I'm sorry."

He stood up and came around the desk, his eyes twinkling. "S'okay. In my line of work, I see a lot of it You just go on home and worry about writing books. Give me a couple of days, and I'll see what I can find out for you."

"Thank you." She smiled at him and rose to leave. His voice stopped her.

"Ms. Talbot—"

"Yes?"

"You didn't make a mistake in coming here."

She stared. "Excuse me?"

"That's what you were thinking, when you first saw me. I guess I don't look much like what you were expecting. And Verna outside doesn't look much like Della Street."

It was the first of several times that he would surprise her with his perception. She smiled as she buttoned her coat. "Betty Hanes assures me that you're the best person around for—for this particular problem—"

He shrugged. "I guess it's by way of being a specialty of mine. I was a cop for twenty years. Now I do it privately. I'm good at it."

She regarded him a moment, curious. "So why did you leave the police force?"

He laughed again. "You try being a New York cop for twenty years! Besides, my wife had a say in the matter."

Jill nodded and turned toward the door. His voice halted her again. "And, Ms. Talbot—"

"Yes?"

"Be careful. Whether or not it's this Brian Marshall—

whoever it is—he's not a very savory customer, if you know what I mean. He'll probably pull some other shit, begging your pardon. Just watch out, okay?"

"Yes," she said. "Yes, I'll do that."

He watched her come out of the building on West Twenty-fifth Street and turn east. At the corner of Seventh Avenue she hailed a cab. He let her go: he already knew her next destination, thanks to her telephone. She'd be there about an hour, he calculated, and then she was going home to get ready for dinner with Nate. Besides, there was something else he wanted to do.

He flagged down a cab at the same corner and gave the driver an address on Spring Street in SoHo.

She got out of the taxi and stood on the sidewalk in front of the pretty, three-story townhouse on East Tenth Street. Here you are, she told herself, right on time. Now just go inside.

It had been four years since she'd been to this house, to the lovely, cream-and-cocoa little office in the basement. After the publication of *Darkness,* and after her mother had gone to Port Jefferson, she'd moved to the Village and thrown herself into writing novels and cultivating a new group of friends. Tara Summers; Mary Daley; Gwen and Mike Feldman, the husband-wife mystery writing team who were also Mary's clients. By the time she'd met Nate ten months ago, she'd all but forgotten about the three years of weekly visits here. Her anxieties about ever being published, her guilt about her mother's growing illness and what she would inevitably have to do about it, her memories of her stepfather: these had gradually receded, been placed in some remote storeroom at the back of her mind.

Now she was here again. She looked up and down the busy, affluent Village street, watching couples walking hand-in-hand. There were people walking dogs, and attractive children with book bags and lunch-boxes hurrying home from school. Daily life, she mused. Normality. And here I am again, after all this time, with two greeting cards in my purse and a dreadful sense of doom.

With a long sigh, she pushed open the little wrought-iron gate and descended the five steps to the familiar oak door.

"And over here, on this wall, I want to put the big piece. So you go around the room and end here."
Henry Jason followed him through the gallery, nodding. "Yes, *Life*. That should be the final image—at least, I suppose it should. I haven't seen it yet, Nate."

The artist grinned. "You will, and soon. I finished it at about three o'clock this morning."

The small, dapper gallery proprietor in the impeccable blue Brooks Brothers suit grinned. "Marvelous! Congratulations, Nate. Let's see: two weeks. This"—he waved an arm, indicating the garish paintings of male nudes that currently weighed down the white walls of the little gallery on Spring Street—"will be out of here a week from Thursday, thank God! I happen to think she's a very talented painter, but we can't *give* the damn things away. Anyway, you can install yours on Friday, um, the thirteenth. I hope you're not superstitious! I'll send the truck to your studio. Now, if you'll just finish your text, I can come over and set prices, and we can make up the catalog."

"Oh, yeah . . ."

"We don't have much time, Nate. The invitations go

out tomorrow. If we want the *Times* and the *New Yorker* and *ArtNews,* we have to get on this. I need your catalog copy."

"Okay, okay. I'll get on it right away."

"Terrific! Now, why don't I take you down the street and ply you with liquor."

It was a familiar running gag, and he knew Henry was kidding, but he nonetheless suppressed a shudder. "Well, um—"

"Hi, guys."

The two men turned around to see Doug Baron coming through the door.

Dr. Dorothy Philbin let Jill in to the small reception area at the front of the basement and led her back to the main office.

"Sorry to be so informal," the doctor said over her shoulder as she led the way. "My receptionist got married the other day, and she's on a two-week honeymoon in Hawaii. The girl who was supposed to stand in for her just came down with the flu, so I'm here alone until further notice. I'm going crazy—but I guess an analyst shouldn't use that expression."

They laughed together as she waved Jill onto a couch and sat behind her desk. Jill brought Dr. Philbin up to date on her life: her new apartment, her novels, Nate, her friend Tara. Then she produced the cards from her purse and briefly described the events of the last few days. When she was finished, the doctor leaned forward.

"So, how are you feeling now, Jill?" she asked.

Jill stared at the handsome, sixtyish woman in the beautiful Chanel suit. The afternoon light slanting through the venetian blinds on the back windows gleamed on her silver hair and on the rope of pearls around her neck. The last time Jill had been here, the doctor's hair had been darker.

"How I'm feeling," Jill murmured. "I'm not really sure. I thought I knew; I thought it would be easy to talk about. But I don't seem to know how to describe it."

The doctor smiled. "That must seem strange to a writer."

"Yes, it does. And it's not just this." She indicated the cards on the table between them. "It's—it's a lot of things."

"First, tell me about this. What do you make of it?"

Jill glanced at the cards and leaned back on the couch. "Well, Nate said the other night that nine times out of ten we know the people responsible. . . ."

"Yes," Dr. Philbin encouraged. "That's correct."

"I think it might be Brian Marshall."

"Your stepfather? Why would he want to do this?"

Jill shook her head absently. "I don't know. I think he blamed me for the divorce, and he—he has a history of violence against women. I just don't know anyone else like that."

The doctor consulted her new notes. "So you've hired this detective."

"Yes. We went to the police, but . . ." Jill shrugged.

"I know," the doctor said. "I've had some experience with this. A client of mine was being hounded by her ex-husband. It's the price of freedom in America, Jill. The laws are such that the police are really unable to intervene unless a specific crime has been committed." She smiled ruefully. "Of course, your average lawbook and your average stalking victim will have two different definitions of the word *specific*." She looked down at the valentine cards. "*This* is a crime. You feel violated. You're afraid for your safety. You're angry, or you should be. You don't

62

know whom to trust. The police, and this detective, and even your friends—even Nate—may have a tendency to patronize you. Don't let them. You are not hysterical, and you are *not* imagining things: the threat against you is very real. I've seen too many people in your situation who are actually embarrassed. They feel they've somehow brought the unwanted attention upon themselves. Well, as my charming fifteen-year-old grandson would say, that's bullshit. You haven't done anything wrong. This 'Valentine' person is the only one responsible. Don't ever forget that."

There was a brief silence in the doctor's office. Then, Jill smiled weakly over at the other woman.

"Thank you," she said.

"You're welcome. Now, you said you were disturbed by several things. What else is happening?"

Jill listed them in her mind, then began with the easiest. "Well, I'm working on a new novel—about a stalker, of all things. I should have done some research: the man who's terrorizing the actress in my story is a complete stranger."

Dr. Philbin raised her eyebrows. "That happens, too, especially with celebrities. You're a celebrity, Jill. It may not be your stepfather. Have you thought about that?"

"Yes," Jill said, "I have. But that's not the point. It's about the book itself. It's just that—well, under the circumstances, I don't know if I want to continue with it."

The doctor shrugged. "Then don't. Write something else."

Jill stared at her, then burst into laughter. "You make it sound so easy!"

"It *is* easy. I've gotten to know you rather well, Jill. You're perfectly capable of making decisions—once you decide to decide."

The two women laughed together.

" 'Decide to decide,' " Jill said. "I like that. I guess it is an easy decision, when I consider the other things. . ."

"What other things?"

Jill took a long, deep breath. "Well, Nate. He—he wants to get married."

"Oh? When did this happen?"

"A few weeks ago. Right in the middle of the new hardcover and the new paperback and all these public appearances and talk shows, he, like, *proposed.*"

"I see. And what did you say?"

Jill smiled, remembering. He had surprised her with an early Christmas present, tickets to a hit Broadway show she'd wanted to see. He took her to dinner at Sardi's, and after the show they went dancing. But it was in the theater, in their perfect seats in the center of the tenth row that he must have purchased months in advance, just as the lights were dimming and the overture was about to begin, that he had suddenly turned to her, slipping a small black box from his jacket pocket and holding it out to her. Inside the box was a tiny, beautiful diamond engagement ring.

"Marry me," he'd whispered.

She had turned to stare at him just as the cymbals crashed, the downbeat that began the overture. It was the second time a man had proposed to her, and she had wisely refused Ted, the corporate tax lawyer. But she knew, even then, that this was different. It *felt* different.

Now, in Dr. Philbin's office, Jill grinned. "I told him I couldn't even *think* about it at the moment, but that I'd give it my full attention in the near future. He was actually satisfied with that: one of many reasons I'm in love with him. He still has the ring. I think he carries it around with him."

"Well, that certainly tells you how he feels about it.

How about you, Jill? You just said you're in love with him. Are you certain of that?"

Jill laughed. "I fell in love with him the second time I ever saw him. We met at a nightclub my friend Tara had dragged me to, and I liked him. He told me he was a painter, and he invited us to the opening party of his first show. So, we went. Tara had vague ideas of finding another artistic type for herself, and I was intrigued by him.

"I think I fell in love with his talent first. The show was a series of portraits, but they weren't realistic. He was obviously less interested in details of facial features than he was in the essence of each model, and he conveyed it all with color. This one was happy, this one was angry, this one melancholy: it was all in the colors and the brushstrokes. It was amazing, and I told him so. That was the second time I saw him blush. All these people crowded around him, patrons and critics and so on. They actually backed him into a corner. He stood there pressed against the wall, completely terrified. Then he turned his head and looked right over the heads of the crowd, at me. And he smiled and winked. That's when I realized how much we had in common, artistically speaking, I hate the whole publicity thing, and so does he. The work—the *doing* of it—is the important part, not what comes afterward. Suddenly, out of the crowd, my hand was grabbed and I was pulled toward the front door. He was escaping from his own party, and he took me with him. We went to a bar at the end of the block and talked for hours. I didn't get home until nearly four in the morning. The next day I read this big, glowing review of his show in the *Times*. A couple of days later, he called and asked me out, to Lincoln Center. He'd apparently found Tara and grilled her, and she'd told him I love the ballet. So he took me to the Met." She laughed again. "He was obviously bored to tears, but he sat there so patiently, smiling through the whole thing. I took him to dinner after the performance, and back to my apartment for coffee. Then we—well, we've been together ever since. He thought he was getting his revenge for the ballet a few months ago, when I took him to a Mets game at Shea Stadium. The Mets in exchange for the Met. But I blew it by confessing that I love the Mets. I love baseball, period. Now he's threatening to take me to a wrestling match: I should have kept my mouth shut!"

Dr. Philbin smiled. "So, do you want to marry him?" Jill shrugged, uttering a small, bemused laugh. "I honestly don't know. Tara thinks I'm crazy, of course. She hasn't had much luck in the romance department, which is weird when you consider how nice she is, not to mention gorgeous. She has that famous 'all-the-good-ones-are-married-or-gay' philosophy about men, and she may be right. Nate just introduced her to a friend of his—apparently a widower and apparently not gay—and they're having dinner together tomorrow night, so maybe she'll get lucky. Anyway, she thinks I should grab Nate."

The doctor smiled. "And what do you think?"

Jill was silent a moment, considering. At last she said, "I think I'd better think about it. 'Decide to decide.' I may not have much time."

Dr. Philbin noticed the sudden change in Jill's tone. She leaned forward, studying her client's face.

Jill met her gaze and nodded. "I haven't told him. I haven't told anyone, not even Tara." Then, for the first time in the three weeks she'd known about it, she spoke the words aloud.

"I'm pregnant."

The two men walked out of the gallery and headed down Spring Street toward the little pub at the end of the block. Henry Jason was all set to join them until a last-minute phone call from a hysterical agent had sent him back to his office with a grim scowl.

"This could take hours," he'd muttered, waving to them as he went. "Next time, boys."

A chilling wind whipped down the little Village street, causing them to huddle in their coats and hurry the last few steps to the inviting dark warmth of the pub. They straddled barstools, greeting the familiar bartender and the familiar lush on the farthest stool—the only other patron at this hour—and calling for draft beers. Two foam-topped mugs materialized before them. They relaxed in their seats, and Doug lit a Marlboro and exhaled a stream of smoke.

"So," Doug said, "when do I get a preview of 'Conditions?'"

"Oh, drop by anytime. In fact, Thursday Jill is coming over to my place to see the paintings. She's contributing the catalog copy. Don't tell Henry—he thinks I do it myself. Why don't you join us?"

Doug thought a moment. "Can I bring a date?"

"Sure! We'll all have dinner, and then I'll give you a private showing. I hope you like Ukrainian food."

"I'm not sure I know what Ukrainians eat, but, hell, I'll try anything once. Let me see how Tara and I hit it off tomorrow night. If everything's cool, I'll ask her about Thursday."

He studied Doug Baron's face, smiling at the calm expression that so obviously concealed a fit of first-date jitters. The cigarette in Doug's hand was trembling slightly. "Hey, Tara's a nice woman. You'll be fine."

Doug smiled and nodded. "I know. I just have to get

used to this. It's—it's been a while."

"I'm sorry, Doug," he said quietly. "About your wife. I didn't know till you mentioned it the other night."

"Yeah," the photographer whispered. "It's been three years now. Anyway, *you* didn't have much trouble finding the perfect woman."

"You'd be surprised. But you're right: Jill is pretty wonderful."

Doug Baron nodded slowly, not meeting the other man's gaze.

"She sure is, Nate," he murmured. "I'm really looking forward to seeing her again."

He picked up the mug in front of him, drained it, and lit another Marlboro.

The phone was ringing when Jill came into the apartment. She dropped her purse and the bag of groceries on the kitchen counter and hurried into the office before the machine clicked on. She hesitated a moment before picking up the receiver, as she had found herself doing for the last several days. Then, bracing herself, she answered.

"Hello," she whispered.

"Hello again, Jill, it's Dr. Philbin. I was reading over your file after you left my office, and I think—I think I may have found something. I'd like to talk about it with you."

Jill was confused. "What do you mean?"

There was a slight pause on the line. Then the doctor cleared her throat and said, "Well, I'd rather not discuss it on the phone, but—it's about something you told me during a session a few years ago. Let's see . . . ." Another pause, and Jill could hear pages rustling. "Are you free Friday afternoon? One o'clock? I have an opening then."

"Yes, that would be fine. But, please, what is this

about?"

She could almost hear the doctor thinking, choosing her words with care. "It's about—I mean, it might be about these cards, about what's been happening to you."

"You have an idea?"

"I—I think I might. Friday, then. One o'clock."

"Dr. Philbin," she cried before the woman could hang up. "Please, what is it? What have you found?"

Another pause. Her heart was racing: she felt as if she could scream. Then, at last, the voice. "Well, the only reason it caught my eye was the fact that you mentioned Valentine's Day. It's something you told me about, something that happened to you in college. Do you remember a young man in Hartley College, a young man named, umm, Victor Dimorta?"

She stared blankly down at her computer for several moments before the name registered. Then her eyes widened.

"Oh," she said. "Oh, my God!"

The moment the two women hung up, he reached up slowly to remove the headphones. He'd arrived back here from Spring Street just in time to catch the call. He crushed out his Marlboro and rubbed his stinging eyes. He gazed out the window from his armchair, watching as Jillian Talbot came back into the living room and sat down on the couch. She was facing him: he could see her expression clearly. Yes, he thought. She's thinking. Remembering. The plot thickens. . . .

EARTH, WIND, AND FIRE

SIXTEEN YEARS AGO

THEY CALLED THEMSELVES EARTH, WIND, AND FIRE after their favorite rock group, but the other students simply referred to them, collectively, as the Elements. Their real names were Sharon Williams, Belinda Rosenberg, and Cass MacFarland, and they were the three prettiest—and richest—young women in the tiny college on the outskirts of Burlington, Vermont. When they inducted the shy, introverted English major into the club, they assigned her the name of the fourth element. This was a great joke for them, as she had never learned to swim and was deathly afraid of water.

There was nothing they enjoyed as much as a great joke, preferably at the expense of others. But they were the prettiest, and therefore the most popular. The other girls were respectful, the boys attentive, the professors indulgent. They ruled the campus, three little martinets made powerful by their formidable intelligence, their biting wit, and their facility with lip gloss and blow-dryers. She knew they were not very nice. But after her relatively lonely childhood in New York, her bookish lack of popularity in high school, and her all-too-recent confrontation with her drunken stepfather on the kitchen floor, she felt a sudden need to be part of a group—any group. She had never lived away from home before, and the attention of these three, sarcastic as it was, was comforting. She soon learned that their true interest in her was due to her excellent knowledge of math, and her willingness to "help" them with their calculus homework, the bane of their existence. This, of course, translated into her actually doing the homework for them, but she

71

considered it a small price to pay. She was accepted by them; she was in a clique; she was Somebody.

It didn't last very long.

She remembered that first meeting, at the beginning of the second semester of her freshman year. A chilly day in the first week of February. The three senior girls—blonde, brunette, and redhead—sitting at the best table in front of the large glass wall and the dramatic view of the snow-carpeted campus, in their tight jeans and form-fitting sweaters with fur coats draped dramatically around them, smoking cigarettes, laughing and calling out as she came so tentatively into the cafeteria, clutching her tray.

"Oh, Jill! Jill Talbot!" This from platinum Sharon. "Come sit with us, honey. We want to talk to you."

"Yeah," added Belinda the brunette. "A sort of proposition."

Sly glances all around.

She'd felt profound surprise, followed immediately by a rush of warmth, of happiness, as everyone in the room turned to watch her step forward to join the Most Important Table. Redheaded Cass—the only nice one, really, when she was away from the others—merely smiled as Jill approached, letting her fellow empresses do all the talking. They grinned, made room for her, and offered her her very first—and last—cigarette.

When the coughing fit had run its course, amid much raucous laughter and slaps on her back, Sharon/Earth plucked the cigarette from her shaking fingers, crushed it out in a dish of Jell-O, and said, "How'd you like to be a member of our little sorority?"

"Oh, yes!—umm—yes, I'd like that," she'd stammered when she'd found her voice, trying mightily not to sound too eager or—worse—too uncool.

"Faboo!" cried Belinda.

"You're gonna love us, kid," added Sharon. "And you'll be one of us. And you know what that means—right, girls?"

"*Too! Too! Very! Very!*" the three shouted in perfect unison.

"That's our watchcry," the blonde explained, "because that's what we are. Stick with us, and that's what you'll be, too!" Then, lowering her voice, she continued. "So, we take it that you wish to apply for membership with the Elements?"

"Uh, sure," she whispered again, still recovering from the thrill, from the overwhelming glamour of it all.

"Faboo!" Belinda repeated before leaning forward and lowering her voice. "But, you know, there is one thing. In order to become a member, you have to pass a little—test."

"An initiation," Sharon said.

"Yeah," said Belinda as Cass smiled on. "An initiation."

Thus, it had begun. . . .

At eighteen, Jill felt that she was a late starter in the development department. She was too tall, too thin, too flat-chested. Her hair was fairly long then, down past her shoulders, but to her it was dull and lifeless. Everything about her seemed wrong: a graceless conglomeration of sharp angles and plain features. She would stand before the mirror, staring at her face and figure, trying to will them through sheer concentration into some more interesting, more pleasing mold. The fact that she was the only one who held this opinion did not occur to her. Her first semester at Hartley College was a protracted millennium of fear and uncertainty: she sat in the classrooms and wandered the campus, oblivious of the appreciative looks of the men and the envious looks of the

73

women, never suspecting that her presumed mousiness existed only in her own imagination. She didn't know that she was beautiful.

She missed New York City. She wrote long letters to her mother, who was still recovering from her recent divorce from Brian Marshall, and to her high school girlfriends at other colleges around the country. She missed the ballet classes she'd taken once a week for four years, and she lamented the fact that she hadn't chosen a college that offered them. But her favorite high school English teacher, Mrs. Worth, had assured her that Hartley was the right place for anyone with her facility for writing. She had never entertained any serious aspiration to a career in dance: she wasn't really that good at it. She'd known for a long time that she was destined to be a writer. So here she was at Hartley. The first semester dragged on, highlighted only by her two English classes, world literature and creative writing. She kept mostly to herself, and she was not invited by any cliques, to say nothing of the various sororities and societies that made up the campus social scene. The only group she joined was the English Club, an unofficial gathering of the brightest students who read a current book a week and came together on Friday evenings to discuss it. She would sit in the campus coffee shop with five or six others, her fellow misfits, listening as they droned on about Robert Stone and Toni Morrison and John Updike and Nadine Gordimer, acutely aware that everyone else was at parties and sporting events or roaming in herds through the nearby mall.

When that fall semester finally ended, she got on the train and went home for the intercession. Christmas was a drab and rather sad time that year: her mother was still not feeling well and her few New York friends were busy elsewhere. She sat in her bedroom those first two weeks of January, writing depressing poems and short stories. Toward the end of the holiday, she realized with genuine surprise that she was looking forward to going back to Vermont. The isolation of the college suddenly seemed more inviting, more appealing than the isolation of the apartment on Central Park West.

The second semester began more promisingly than the first. Once she returned to the college, Jill realized that she was tired of being alone, and she began to take more notice of the activity around her. She forced herself to interact more with her classmates, and she made an effort to sit with them in the library and the cafeteria instead of seeking out the only empty table in the place. Some of the other students were friendly, and she got along well enough. But it was in this time that her attention was first drawn to the Elements, the three beautiful women who ruled the place.

She would watch them from a distance, studying their dress and makeup and mannerisms, trying to analyze just exactly what it was that made them so popular. She noticed that the dark-haired one, Belinda Rosenberg, had her hair cut attractively short in the latest fashion. One day in the cafeteria, she even went over to their table by the window, introduced herself, and asked Belinda where she got her hair done. Belinda told her—in exchange for a little "help" with the calculus homework she was hastily completing over lunch, minutes before it was due. The following Saturday, Jill went to the salon at the mall and had her own hair cut in Belinda's style.

By that first week of February, when the Elements called her over to their table, she was only too eager to join them.

"He is *such* a creep!" Belinda exclaimed.

"Totally!" agreed Sharon, the blond ringleader. "Always leering at us. I swear, he stares at every woman on this campus as if she wasn't wearing any clothes. He's a complete gross-out." She paused for dramatic effect, then added, with a gleam in her eye, "And *we* are going to do something about it!"

Jill looked up from a calculus problem to stare at her new friends, wondering what they had in mind. It was now the second week of her tenure as an Element, and she was already beginning to wonder if joining them had been a mistake. She didn't like the gleam in Sharon's eye any more than she liked the general air of conspiratorial mischief that permeated Belinda's dorm room. And two weeks of doing their math homework was beginning to wear. Had she been any other kind of girl—more poised, more sure of herself—she would have gotten up from her seat at the foot of Belinda's bed and left the three of them to their own devices. Instead, she smiled half-heartedly around at them and waited for instructions.

The boy they were talking about, Victor Dimorta, was all they said he was, and more. She herself had recently had a run-in with him, dodging his clumsy, foul-breath advances in a suddenly empty classroom a few days before. The tall, skinny, pale young man with the acne scars pockmarking his face and the limp, greasy brown hair had attempted to engage her in conversation. When she'd smiled at him and edged toward the door, he'd taken her involuntary kindness as encouragement and tried to kiss her. The rough feel of his strong hands on her arms still sent a shiver through her. She pushed him away and ran down the hall, her pounding footsteps eventually drowning out his desperate, rather angry cries.

"Wait a minute! I just want to talk to you. I didn't mean to scare you. Jill? *Jill.*"

76

Now, in Belinda's bedroom, they were planning their revenge for that and several similar infractions.

"Okay, here's the plan," Sharon said as her fellow Elements watched her face in anticipation. "Belinda, this room will be perfect. I want candles, incense, red lightbulbs in the lamps—we are talking complete and total whorehouse, dig?"

"Faboo!"

"Okay. Cass, you're in charge of the video. I want this place totally bugged. You'll be in that closet over there, filming."

"Do you really think—?" the essentially good-hearted redhead began.

"*Don't* interrupt me!" came the quick retort. "You film. Period! B'lin, you set the stage."

"Sure," Belinda said. "And what are *you* contributing, Sharon?"

The beautiful blond girl slowly smiled. "My dear, *I* am the bait! And we, ladies, are going to take care of Mr. Victor Dimorta—Mr. Victory Over Death!!—once and for all! That's what his name means in Italian, you know. 'Victory over death.' Can you believe? Fifty million gorgeous, sexy Italian men in the world, and we get the only dud! But we are going to fix his wagon, make no mistake!"

There was silence in the room as the other three contemplated this. Then, swallowing hard and at last finding her voice, Jill whispered, "What about me?"

Sharon turned at last to the shrinking violet at the foot of the bed.

"Oh, my dear!" she said, a wicked smile brightening her lovely face. "*You* are the most important—forgive the pun—Element! I most definitely have big plans for you. *Most* definitely!"

77

It was a valentine card, all pink and lacy white. She was charged with delivering it to his desk during creative writing class. The three senior girls didn't have any classes with him, as he, like Jill, was a freshman. That, she would later decide, was one of the reasons they had been so eager to have her "join" their group. That, and the calculus.

But there was more. The day before she gave him the card, she was to stage a little one-act play for his benefit. The Elements had chosen another freshman girl from the class for this purpose. The girl—her name was Tammy, of all things—was only too happy to go along with it, as it afforded her the vicarious thrill of hanging out with the coolest women on campus. Jill and Tammy were summoned to Belinda's room and instructed by the older girls, repeating the lines over and over until everyone was satisfied that they would play the scene perfectly.

The day before Valentine's Day, Jill and Tammy had carefully positioned themselves a couple of rows in front of Victor in the classroom, pretending they weren't aware of his presence. Before the professor arrived and class began, they went into the routine.

"Oh, yes!" Jill cried as Victor slid into his seat. "Can you believe it? Victor Dimorta! Sharon Williams has the hots for him! For days now, she's hardly talked about anything else!"

"Wow!" Tammy gushed, suppressing a conspiratorial giggle. "I think he's dreamy! But, of course, Sharon is the most beautiful woman on campus. I bet he likes her: all the guys do."

"They sure do!" Jill agreed. "But she only likes him!" She leaned toward Tammy then, as instructed, careful to keep her whisper perfectly audible. "She said she's going to give him a big surprise for Valentine's Day!"

The other girl's eyes widened. "Oh? What? Tell, tell!"

"Shhh!" Jill admonished, giggling. "I'm not sure what it is, but she says he's going to love it!"

The two girls laughed together some more as the professor came in. Moments later, Jill turned around for a glimpse at Victor Dimorta. He was staring right at her, grinning from ear to ear. She blushed and looked away.

The next day—Valentine's Day—she walked right up to him at his desk and handed him the envelope. She blushed again as he grinned at her and tore it open. Inside the card, under the syrupy poem from the card company, was a brief, succinct message in Sharon's elegant hand: *Simmonds Hall, Room 407, 11:00 tonight. Just you 'n' me, Victor. Be there. Sharon.* Jill hadn't seen the card until that moment, and she only got a brief glimpse before he quickly closed it and returned it to the envelope. Noticing the triumphant gleam in his eye, she hurried away.

She didn't know that it was actually she, Jill, of whom Victor dreamed, for whom he longed, with whom he was obsessed. If she'd known that, she would never have delivered the message. She would never have approached him at all.

The hierarchy of students on any college campus is well defined. It is simply a matter of descending order: seniors, juniors, sophomores, freshmen. The fact that Jill had not immediately stopped to question why the three most powerful senior girls would want her in their clique illustrated how much she longed to be part of a group. But later, when she finally got around to analyzing it, the harsh reality became clear.

Jill was being groomed for the role of slave. The three women had been looking around for a likely candidate, and their eyes had fallen on her, the quiet, rather dull freshman girl who envied them enough to stare at them in the cafeteria and emulate their hairstyles. What fun, they must have thought. What a laugh it will be to have a plebe, a gofer, our very own lackey. An errand girl to do our homework. Our message delivering. Our bidding. . .

Their bidding, as it turned out, was to ensnare their prospective victims, the lower forms of life who would provide momentary amusement by serving as the butts of their jokes. They'd obviously performed similar pranks in the past, but their plan for Victor Dimorta was certainly their most elaborate. Jill would later wonder if they were actually planning to go as far as they did with this one. She doubted it: even these three, callous and cavalier as they were, would never have deliberately endangered themselves.

Later, when she thought about the Elements at all—less and less in her remaining years at Hartley College—she tried to understand them. She knew from her experience with her stepfather that some people are simply evil, and that trying to justify or even analyze their actions was an exercise in futility. But this did not seem to apply to Sharon and Belinda and Cass. She began to think, rather, that they were a living example of the harmful side-effects of boredom. As a group, anyway: individually, the three women were seemingly quite different from each other.

Sharon Williams was the evil one, Jill decided, if any of the three could be described that way. Twenty-one years of being rich and privileged and beautiful had taken their toll. She was a rich blonde from southern California, where everyone seemed to be rich and blond. Jill imagined that her high school years had been one long party, going to dance clubs and windsurfing and rollerblading with the children of movie stars. Her parents would probably be overeager and overindulgent; some powerful, attractive couple who spent entirely too much time and effort and money on their little darling. It wasn't difficult to figure out who ran the Williams household.

Belinda Rosenberg was the go-alonger. The third of four Rosenberg children, she would not have had the exclusive attention of her father, a surgeon specializing in heart ailments, and her mother, who was active in her synagogue in Buffalo and the president of two charitable organizations. Belinda would have grown up in the shadows of the two older siblings. She was the type who always found a Sharon Williams to attach herself to, and she would cheerfully allow her friend to be the leader.

Of the three, Cass MacFarland was the enigma. Jill knew the lovely Scottish redhead had grown up in some nice town in New Jersey, but she knew little else. Cass never mentioned her parents, though Jill knew they were around somewhere: she would later see all three women's parents, briefly, at their graduation. She had an older brother, whom she obviously adored, as she always seemed to be on the phone with him or writing long letters to him. She was very quiet, Jill noticed, almost unusually so. The single time Jill and Cass had been alone together, at the table in the cafeteria, Cass had barely spoken. Jill had asked her about the brother, but the other girl had merely shrugged and murmured something about his no longer being connected to the family. Jill often wondered why Cass tolerated her friends when she seemed somehow kinder, more considerate than they. But perhaps she only imagined this because she and Cass had something in common: both of them wanted to be writers. Even then, in college, Cass was already working on a novel. This made her, in Jill's eyes, the most glamorous of the three.

For whatever reason, or complexity of reasons, Jill voluntarily became an Element. She followed the three

81

women around the campus, reflected in the outer edge of their spotlight. She went to dorm parties to which she would never otherwise have been invited. She sat at the Power Table. She did their homework, which soon extended from mere calculus to other subjects as well. And when they sent her to deliver the fateful message to Victor Dimorta, she trotted dutifully off, never once considering the potential consequence of what she was doing.

Afterward, when the damage was done, she would briefly try to justify her own actions, convincing herself that she had not really been involved. She hadn't even been in Belinda's room that night . . .

She had been in Tammy's room, 408, directly across the hall from Belinda's room. The two girls had listened as best they could, giggling together until the awful noises from across the hall had checked their laughter. Tammy had burst into tears and shrunk into a corner, useless. It had been she, Jill, who had called Campus Security.

She had waited several minutes then, until she finally worked up the courage to unlock Tammy's door and step out into the hall. Sharon was there, naked to the waist, scratched and bleeding, surrounded by several other women from neighboring rooms. Jill had looked beyond her, through the open door to Belinda's room. Cass and another student were kneeling over Belinda, who lay on the floor, moaning as she clutched her bloody nose. But what Jill remembered most about that terrible moment was the sight of the blood on the white wall behind Belinda. And the music: as she stared at the bizarre tableau before her, she heard the low, provocative voice of Sarah Vaughan singing "My Funny Valentine." It emanated from the sound system beside the small television on the other side of the room.

Whenever she thought about it later, she always associated the incident with the song. And whenever she heard the song, she shuddered involuntarily, even after the incident was forgotten.

Later, in the dean of students' office, during the college's official investigation, she would hear the so-called complete story of what happened that night. She was merely a witness, an accessory, and she had received no censure for that. In fact, the dean—a lean, handsome man in his forties whom she had later observed going into Sharon's room after hours—hadn't punished anyone.

Except Victor Dimorta.

Sharon had told the "official" story. Victor had been bothering them all for weeks, she announced to the dean and the two other college higher-ups who sat in on the hearing. That night, he'd tricked his way into Belinda's room with a box of candy. When the three women had asked him to leave, he'd gone ballistic, tearing at their clothes as he removed his own, assaulting them physically. Belinda was not at the hearing: she was in the infirmary with a broken nose and a sprained ankle, the result of being thrown across the room and crashing into the wall. Cass had been shoved down onto the floor of the closet (no one mentioned that she'd been in there all the time, recording the incident), and Sharon had escaped down the hall, half-clad, with only superficial scratches on her face and arms. Victor had run from the room after the attack. He'd fled into the elevator, stark naked, only to be wrestled to the floor in the lobby of the girls' dorm building and taken into custody by three security guards. The physical evidence, including the broken chairs and lamps, together with Sharon's steady, clear-eyed recounting of the virtual forced entry and assault, had caused the dean to dismiss the whole thing as being over

83

and done with.

Almost.

Jill couldn't remember now exactly what had possessed her to do what she did next. She certainly didn't owe Victor any favors, and she wasn't even very clear on what had transpired in Belinda's room, But she knew one thing for certain: she was through with the Elements. She was through with standing by and knowingly abetting cruel mischief, with doing other people's homework, with being a doormat in exchange for the illusion of acceptance. She realized with a little shock that she didn't need these people. She was better than they, and there was only one way to resign from their dreary company. It forced its way up from the pit of her stomach, astonishing everyone, herself most of all. She'd been sitting on the couch against the back wall of the dean's office, listening to Sharon's elaborate lies. Then, suddenly, she was on her feet.

"No!" she cried, and everyone else in the room immediately turned to stare at her. Slowly, as if in a trance, she brought up her arm and pointed at the beautiful blond girl in the chair across the desk from the dean. "She's lying! That isn't what happened. They tricked him, the three of them. It was one of their stupid practical jokes. They got him there that night so they could humiliate him, just like they humiliate everybody! Victor was invited to that room by *her*." She stabbed her finger in Sharon's direction. "I know: I delivered the note myself. Cass and Belinda were in the closet, watching. The whole thing was planned!"

The shocked silence that followed lasted mere seconds. Then Sharon Williams jumped up from her chair, whirling to face Jill.

"Bitch!" she shrieked. "Liar! She's lying through her teeth, the nasty little dyke! Everybody knows why she's

84

been hanging around us! *Dyke*!"

The dean was immediately on his feet, raising an imperious hand to silence Sharon, who sank back into her seat. Then he stood clutching the desk in front of him, leaning toward the dark-haired freshman girl who stood, fists clenched at her sides, at the back of the room.

"That will be enough out of you, Ms. . . ."—he glanced down at the report on his desk, then up at her—"Ms. Talbot. I don't know what you're trying to pull, but one more outburst like that and I'll have you suspended! Do you understand me, young lady?"

Slowly—ever so slowly—Jill shifted her frosty, contemptuous gaze from Sharon Williams to the dean. For a long moment, she stared directly into his eyes. When at last she spoke, her voice was the merest whisper, but he heard it clearly.

"Shame on you," she said, and then she turned around and marched out of his office.

Victor Dimorta was not present to hear her brave confession: he had been sent home, expelled, the day before.

She'd never had any more to do with the Elements. Two days later she'd gone into the cafeteria before them and deliberately sat at their table in front of the picture window, calmly eating her lunch. A few minutes later, Sharon Williams arrived. The older girl banged her tray down on the table across from her, leaned forward, and began to shout.

"Just what the fuck do you think you're doing? You get away from our table, you *traitor*!"

Jill had looked calmly up from her meal. As everyone in the room watched, she delivered her final words to the blond girl.

"This is my table now. *You* go away. And if you or your creepy friends come near me again, I'll call your parents and tell them what really happened. They may be interested to know what kind of daughters they have. Now get lost!"

Two fraternity boys at the next table began it, but soon the whole room joined in. One by one, every student present began to applaud. The hand-clapping was supplemented by hoots and whistles, and it soon evolved into a steady, rhythmic pounding of fists on tables. Then came the chant, rising in volume until it flooded the cafeteria with sound.

"*Jill! Jill! Jill! Jill! . . .*"

Sharon stared around at them all, incredulous. Then, with a last contemptuous glance at her former acolyte, she barged out of the room.

The Elements graduated at the end of the semester, and Jill was never bothered again. Only once, weeks later, did any of them so much as speak to her. Cass MacFarland stopped her outside a classroom and apologized for her participation in the prank, telling Jill that she admired her for doing the right thing, and for standing up to Sharon.

From that day in the cafeteria until her own graduation three years later, Jill remained one of the most popular people on campus. She joined a sorority and became president of the English Club, and on Friday nights she went to parties and sports events when she wasn't leading a herd through the mall. She became romantically involved with another student, who was her first lover. This relationship, though pleasant, was never very serious for either of them, and she went out with several other men as well. But she was always acutely aware of other people's feelings: she kept a sharp eye out for the loners and the shy types, the students on the outside looking in, and she always invited them to join her and her friends at the table by the window.

And, as time went on, she forgot about the incident. She conveniently suppressed her memories of the alleged joke, the terrified screams, her brief glimpse of the broken furniture and the blood on the wall of Belinda's room. She blocked out all recollection of her part, small as it was, in the events that had resulted in the expulsion of a boy whose only crime, as far as she could see, was his unattractiveness.

JILL

CHAPTER 5

WEDNESDAY, FEBRUARY 4

HE CAME AWAKE SLOWLY, AND THE FIRST THING HE felt was the cold. He sat up on the lumpy mattress, rubbing his eyes with his fists, and for a long moment he couldn't place where he was. Then, looking around the small, bare room, he remembered.

He stood up, pulling the rough brown blanket from the mattress and wrapping it around him as he made his bleary way over to the window. Snow: a swirling mist that all but obscured the room beyond the picture window across the street. He stuck his right arm out of the folds of the blanket and switched on the mike. After a moment he heard the faint sound of running water—the bathroom, he reasoned—and the high-pitched whistle of a teakettle. Then the faraway but distinct slap of bare feet on wood, and the whistle faded and stopped.

"Good morning," he said aloud. "Good morning, Jillian Talbot."

Taking his cue from her, he reached over to the portable gas stove on the table and turned it on. The tin pot on the ring was filled with water: he did that every night now, before going to bed. He picked up the little jar of instant coffee and spooned some into the white mug with the I ♥ NY logo that he had bought at a souvenir shop on Seventh Avenue. While he waited for the water to boil, he sat in the armchair in front of the window, lit a Marlboro, picked up his binoculars, and peered through the snow at the building facing him.

It was snowing again. She took her mug of decaffeinated

coffee over to the front window and stood gazing down at the street, thankful that there had been no nausea this morning. Ten o'clock: just about time to call Barney Fleck with the new information. She had told Nate about Victor Dimorta at dinner last night, but he was skeptical, muttering something about its being so long ago. When she'd added that she would mention it to the detective and talk to Dr. Philbin on Friday, he merely shrugged. He didn't seem to be impressed by what little she remembered.

She paused in her reverie long enough to go into the office and call Barney Fleck. He was on the other line, but Verna Poole, the efficient secretary, cheerfully informed her that he already had two calls out on her behalf. He was expecting some answers anytime now, and he would contact her as soon as he had them. She thanked the woman and hung up. Then she went over to one of the bookshelves and took down the large faux-leather maroon volume with the title, *Passages*, and the year embossed in gold on the cover. She came back into the living room and sat on the couch, opening the first of her four college yearbooks and scanning the pages. And there they were, smiling ingenuously for the photographer, all frosty lips and big hair and bare shoulders. Earth, Wind, and Fire . . .

She gazed down at the pretty faces, remembering.

The phone rang. Jill glanced down at her watch, surprised to find that it was now nearly eleven. She hurried into the office.

"Hello."

"Ms. Talbot, this is Barney Fleck—"

"Yes, I've been expecting your call. Listen, there's a new—"

"Hold on a minute!" the detective cried. "I've got some

90

information for you. Don't you want to hear—"

"Yes, of course, Mr. Fleck, but—"

"Barney."

"Barney. Right. But I think I may have been a little premature about—"

"Whoa! Now, just hold on, Ms. Talbot."

"Jill."

His hearty laugh caused the receiver in her hand to vibrate. "Okay, *Jill.* Don't talk, just listen. I have the information you wanted about your ex-stepfather, Brian Marshall. I tracked him down through his first wife, the one you said was in New Jersey. I got ahold of her, and she put me in touch with him—in a manner of speakin'."

The pause after this compelled her to interject. "What do you mean, 'in a manner of speaking'? He's—he's not dead, is he?"

"No," Barney replied. "Not exactly—but he might as well be, far as you're concerned. He's in a sort of hotel outside Cleveland. A big, gray, concrete hotel, with bars on the windows."

She stared out the back window above her writing desk, assimilating this. "Oh."

"Yeah, seems he got married again, if you can believe it. The first wife gave me the number. Rich lady in Cleveland. Teenage daughter. 'Bout a year ago, he—well, let's just say he likes 'em young, but I guess you know that."

She swallowed, thinking of the charges she was going to press, dropped at her mother's request.

"Yes, Barney. I'm here."

"Charming fellow, this Brian Marshall. The girl was fifteen at the time of the incident. Marshall got loaded one night, and came at her in her bedroom. She struggled, and Marshall beat her up. Broke her nose and two ribs. She's

91

okay now, according to her mom. Anyway, she divorced him, and he's doin' three to five in the state pen. So I called the warden there. I had to fax a copy of my license to them before they'd talk to me, but then I explained your situation, and the warden's secretary told me what I wanted to know. Seems he got in a fight a couple of weeks ago, and he's in solitary until further notice. No privileges, including mail privileges. There's no way those cards came from him."

Jill thought a moment. "Could he have bribed someone to mail them? A guard, or another prisoner . . . ?"

Barney Fleck's loud laugh erupted in the receiver. "Honey, it's a cinch *you've* never been inside! He's in *solitary*: he's in a dark little room, with food shoved through the door three times a day. Once every three days, they hose him down. That's it. He's a 'short eyes,' a child molester. The guards hate him, and so do the other felons. Besides, the postmarks on the two cards are from New York, not Ohio. He's not Valentine."

She took a long, deep breath, resigning herself to the seemingly irrefutable fact. "Okay. Thank you for finding out so quickly."

"Hey, it's my pleasure—and it's your nickel. Now, what's all this new information you have for me? Do you still need my services?"

She was silent a moment, remembering that cold night in Vermont sixteen years ago: the screams, the crashing sounds, the incongruously beautiful music, and the blood on the wall of Belinda Rosenberg's dorm room . . .

"Yes," she said at last. "Yes, I still need your services."

"Wait a sec," Barney said. "Let me get a pen. . . ."

He brought a mug of coffee with him down the stairs from his apartment, and entered the dark studio on the

92

ground floor. He groped for the switch on the wall beside the door with his free hand, and the rows of long halogen tubes on the ceiling hummed, flooding the cavernous room with brilliant light. The twelve brightly colored paintings appeared before his eyes, and for several moments he stood in the doorway staring, a slow sigh escaping from his lips.

It was eleven o'clock. He'd slept late this morning, and he had things to do today. But he spent that quiet last hour of the morning moving slowly around the studio, spending long contemplative minutes before each panel, absorbed in thought. With the exception of Jill, these paintings were currently the most important things in his life. Soon the show would open at Henry's gallery, and whatever followed, whether praise or damnation—or, more likely, something in between the two—it would be another step on his road. The journey he'd planned for years now, at the end of which was his eventual recognition and acceptance as an important artist. If he became rich or famous, or both, that would be very pleasant, too. But it wasn't his main concern. Respect: that was the word that summed up his principal goal.

He arrived at last before the final painting in the series, the big canvas he'd completed just two nights ago. *Life*. And life it was, he mused, staring at the bold, powerful splashes of bright color that swept across the surface of the canvas. It almost appeared to move, to vibrate. He nodded slowly to himself: he had very nearly captured the image in his mind, the wild, pulsating motion he saw on the streets of this city every day. The energy that was everywhere, in every living thing. At the same time, however, a small part of him mourned the fact that the image in his mind would not—could not—ever fully be captured by him with acrylics and brushes and canvas stretched on frames.

Oh, well, he told himself as he gazed at his newest creation, I came as close as I could. I can't ask for more than that. Michelangelo, Monet, Picasso: they could do it. Not I; not yet. But someday . . .

He smiled at his own hubris. Then, feeling a need to celebrate this accomplishment before him, he immediately thought of Jill. Yes, he decided. Yes. We're having dinner tonight, and I know just what to give her. . . .

With that, he ran back upstairs for his coat. Then he went out into the snowy daylight, smiling. Thinking of Jill, he didn't even feel the cold.

A valentine card, Jill thought. The three girls had sent her to deliver Victor Dimorta a valentine card. It amazed her, now, that she hadn't thought of it before. Why hadn't she? Then, in a rush of memory, she knew.

Even now, try as she might, she could not form a clear mental picture of Victor Dimorta's face. He had been tall, she remembered, and pale and lanky. And rather greasy: greasy brown hair; shiny, acne-scarred face; oily hands. Other than that, nothing. A blank. She couldn't remember his eyes, or his voice, or anything else about him. She had blocked the whole thing out.

This reminded her of her other mental block, the traumatic incident with her stepfather. She went into the office and over to the telephone.

It was just after one o'clock now, Jill noticed, and Dr. Philbin was probably in a session with a patient. There was no receptionist for the time being: she wasn't surprised when she got the doctor's answering machine. Jill waited for the beep and left her message.

Coming back into the living room, she looked down at the yearbook on the coffee table. She smiled, remembering her triumph with the three senior girls and the new self-confidence born of it. She searched the yearbook for any photographs of Victor Dimorta, but found none. Then she closed the book, returned it to the shelf in her office, and called Nate. He wasn't in, so she left a message on his machine reminding him about dinner tonight. Her second attempt at cooking for him, she thought. I'll roast that chicken I bought by mistake the other day. . . .

The chicken could feed three, at least: that's what gave her the idea. She went into her office and called her agent. The phone was answered on the second ring.

"Mary Daley."

"Hi, Mare, it's Jill."

"Jill! This is so weird: I was just about to call you! ESP time. How's my favorite client?"

"Okay, I guess. Listen—"

"You guess? What the hell does that mean?"

"Well, I—"

"You're not sick, are you?"

"No, I'm fine. Listen, I know it's short notice, but how'd you like to come over for dinner with Nate and me tonight?"

There was a pause on the line, followed by the suspicious Irish lilt. "Is this a McDonald's thing or a Chinese takeout thing?"

Jill laughed in spite of her trepidation, happy for a sane friend. "Neither. I'm roasting a chicken."

"I *beg* your pardon?" Now both women were laughing.

"Didn't know I could cook, did you? Just ask Nate. I made dinner for him the other night, and it was so successful I decided to repeat my triumph. Are you free?"

"I'm free, but am I *game*? Oh, well, sure, why not. I gotta see this with my own eyes. My bestselling author goes domestic. And we can kill two birds—chickens?—

95

with one stone. I was about to call you because I just got an advance copy of the *New York* magazine article. It's running in two weeks, and if all goes well you're on the cover. How do you like that, cover girl?"

Jill blinked. She had to think a moment before she remembered it. The interview and photo session here in the apartment had been a mere three weeks ago, just after the new year. But now it seemed long ago. She'd smiled for the camera and given light, witty replies to the journalist's list of stock questions. She barely remembered what she'd said.

"Oh, wow!" she said. "That's terrific! Bring it with you. Come on over after work. We'll have Bloody Marys and wait for Nate to arrive. There's—there's something I want to discuss with you."

"Something *is* wrong, isn't it?" Mary said.

Jill was choosing an answer when the intercom buzzer sounded from the living room. "I have to go. Just come over when you close. I'll tell you all about it then."

"Okay. . . ." Mary's voice indicated that it was anything but okay.

Jill hung up quickly, before her friend could say more. She hurried to the speaker next to the front door. "Yes?"

It was a young man's voice, with a definite Hispanic accent. "Delivery for Jillian Talbot."

She felt a sudden stab of fear, and it took her a moment to catch her breath and reply. "A delivery from whom?"

There was a pause, accompanied by a rustling of paper. "Uh, Nate. The order form says, 'To Ms. Jillian Talbot, from Nate.' "

Relief. She let out her breath, felt her pulse returning to normal. Even so, the self-defense class kicked in: don't ever buzz strangers into your building. Go to them. "Okay, I'm coming down."

Two minutes later she was peering through the locked glass entry door at a tall, skinny, reasonably attractive Hispanic boy, perhaps seventeen. Under his open, snow-flecked leather coat he was wearing a green T-shirt with a faded logo, *Posies*, on his left breast. He held a large, long white box in his arms. His eyes were closed, and he swayed slightly in time to the music flooding into his ears from the headphones of the Walkman clipped to his belt. She smiled at the sight of him; a perfectly normal boy doing a perfectly normal thing. She opened the door.

"Hi," he said, jerking the headphones from his ears. The tinny, muffled sound of Gloria Estefan filled the foyer. He handed her the box and extended a small clipboard and pen. "Sign here, please."

She signed, thanked him, and closed the door. Back in her apartment, she placed the box on the coffee table and leaned down, untying the green ribbon at the center. She lifted the lid and found a dozen long-stemmed red American Beauties nestled in green tissue paper, a tiny envelope lying on top of the stems. Oh, Nate! she thought, staring down. She set the envelope aside on the table and reached down to gather the flowers up into her arms. So lovely, she thought, so lovely!

As she bent her head to bury her nose in the petals, something rather large and rather heavy came loose from its hiding place among the stems. It brushed against her just below her breast before dropping like a stone to land with a soft thud at her feet. She moved the bouquet aside and looked down.

It took a moment to register. When the message made its way from her eyes to her brain, she threw her hands in the air and jumped backward, tumbling back across the couch behind her, gagging. The roses, no longer held, sailed slowly down to crash, a dozen silent, blood-red

97

explosions on the carpet.

Dr. Philbin said good-bye to her last client of the day, closed and locked the basement entrance door behind him, and headed upstairs to her kitchen for a long-overdue cup of coffee. As she waited for the water to boil, she looked at her watch twice. She had plenty of time to relax before dinner with her daughter and grandson.

Taking her mug in hand, she wandered back downstairs into the office to check her answering machine. Three messages, she noticed. Her daughter, confirming dinner at six o'clock. Mrs. Schwartz, canceling her appointment for tomorrow afternoon: something about visiting relatives. Then came the final message. She sank into her leather-padded desk chair, sipping the strong, hot coffee as she listened.

"Dr. Philbin, it's Jill Talbot. I've been thinking about what you said, about, you know, Victor Dimorta. I think you may be onto something, but—well, I've got a problem with it. I think maybe we should do what we did about my stepfather, when I couldn't really remember everything that happened. I think maybe you should hypnotize me. . . ."

The sign above the door of the shabby little shop on Fourteenth Street was festooned with crudely painted daisies with the name, *Posies*, splashed across the center in looping green letters. It stood on the teeming, snowy block among discount electronic stores and cheap clothing outlets. Several rather bedraggled-looking floral arrangements crouched dimly on the other side of the grimy plate-glass window. Barney Fleck reached forward to open the glass door for her, and the two of them entered. The cheerful clanging of a little bell attached to the top of the door announced their arrival.

Inside, the temperature matched the cold outside, and it took a few seconds for their eyes to adjust to the darkness. They were alone in the dingy, ill-lit room, with droopy flowers standing everywhere and more, slightly brighter ones behind the glass of the refrigerator that ran along the back wall. A pile of white boxes like the one Jill had received stood next to several cellophane-wrapped baskets on a shelf beside the front door. An ancient cash register peeked out from a riot of blooms on the crowded work table next to the curtained entrance to a back room. After a moment the curtain moved aside, and a small, plump, frowzy-looking Hispanic woman in a dark green smock came in. Her black hair was worn in a bun on top of her head, and her gold loop earrings glistened. She stopped short, her eyes taking in the sight of the lovely young woman and the big middle-aged man in the center of the room. Then she summoned a smile to her overpainted face and came over to them.

"Good afternoon," she said. "May I help you?"

Jill winced, nearly recoiling from the smell of gin. Then, as agreed, she let Barney do the talking. She turned to look at him, noticing that his right hand was buried in the pocket of his overcoat.

"I hope so," the detective said, smiling pleasantly and stepping forward to place his bulk between the two women. "This lady's name is Jillian Talbot. About two hours ago she received some flowers from this shop."

"Oh, *sí*—yes. Talbot. That's right. A dozen red Beauties. My very best, no?" The woman paused, her smile fading as she noticed the grim expressions of the two people facing her. "Is—is something wrong? You get the flowers, no? My Niño, he delivered them, yes? I—"

"Yes, yes." Barney held up his large left hand to cut off

99

her babbling. "The flowers were delivered. We just want to know who ordered them, and how." He smiled again to reassure her.

Even so, the woman was clearly puzzled. She looked from one to the other of them, frowning. Then, apparently seeing no reason not to tell them, she turned to the table and picked up a thick, battered receipt book. She flipped back a few pages until she found it.

"Ah, yes. Here." She thrust the book toward Barney, who removed his right hand from his pocket and took it.

Jill stood next to him, reading. The yellow carbon copy of the receipt that had been given to the customer had the date and the order, 1 DOZ. RED ABR, in block letters. Under that, in the same hand, were her own name and address and the message for the front of the envelope, TO MS. JILLIAN TALBOT, FROM NATE. The price was written below this, and the instruction, DELIVER ASAP. The word PAID was circled at the bottom.

Barney handed the book to the woman and said, "Was this a phone order, or was the customer actually in the shop?"

The florist blinked. "He was here. He pay cash for the roses. Why do you—"

"So, it was a man," Barney said, more to Jill than to the other woman. Smiling again, he asked, "Could you describe this man to us?"

"Describe?" The woman watched them now, her voice taking on an indignant tone. "What is this about? What you mean, *describe?* He say, 'From Nate.' Nate!" For the first time, she turned to Jill and addressed her directly. "Don't you know what Nate looks like?"

Jill saw Barney's right hand slide back into the pocket. Quickly, she pulled her wallet from her purse and rummaged through the plastic photo section in the center.

She slid a recent picture from its sheath and held it up.

The florist stared, then squinted as she leaned forward to study the snapshot. "Who is that?"

"That's Nate," Jill said.

"No," the woman said, shaking her head until her gold hoops slapped her face. "That is not the man who was here."

"I'm not surprised," Jill muttered, returning the wallet to the purse.

Barney, his hand still deep in his pocket, leaned toward the woman. "Tell us about the man who bought the roses."

"Ay!" the woman cried, now more fearful than outraged. "I run a nice shop, the best flowers in the Village! You tell *me* what this is all *about!*" She looked wildly around as if for help, but they were the only three people in the shop. Her son, Niño, was obviously out delivering flowers.

"It's about *this!*" Barney yanked his hand dramatically from his pocket. He clutched a clear plastic Ziploc bag, which he held up in front of the woman's face. She emitted a piercing scream and fell back against the counter, overturning a vase of lilies. The water splashed down onto the floor as she cowered against the table, grasping it for support.

"Madre de Dios!"

The face and paws of the enormous dead rat were pressed against the plastic. Its clouded eyes bulged, staring, its mouth open as if to scream. The dull gray fur was matted with dried blood, and the long silver tail was coiled nearly twice around the circumference of the bag. That was the only way Barney could fit it in when he'd picked it up from the floor of Jill's living room.

The florist was completely sober now. Certain that she was alone with two crazy people, she slumped against the work table and burst into tears.

"Stop it!" Jill cried to the detective, pushing him and the ghastly object away from the woman. "She's obviously not involved."

"I had to be sure," he said, retreating to the other side of the room. He slipped the bag back into his pocket.

Jill approached the weeping florist, took her gently by the arms, and lowered her into the folding metal chair beside the worktable. She knelt before the woman and took her hands in hers.

"Listen to me," she said as softly as possible. "I'm sorry if we frightened you. That—that thing was in the flowers your son delivered to me. It fell out when I opened the box." The woman opened her mouth to protest, but Jill pressed on. "Don't worry; I don't think you or your son had anything to do with it. I'm not holding you responsible. But you see, Mrs. . . ."—she glanced at the name tag on the smock—". . . Mrs. Sanchez, someone has been playing some very nasty tricks on me. A man. You're a woman, Mrs. Sanchez; you know how crazy some men can be. This man is bothering me because he—he wants me, you understand? He's crazy." She tapped her own forehead. "*Loco en—umm—cabeza.* I am very frightened." She pointed to Barney. "That man is a private detective. Please, please help us."

Mrs. Sanchez stared at Jill a moment, then glanced over at Barney. With surprising dignity, she rose to her feet. She reached down to pull Jill up from her kneeling position.

"He was tall," she said to the detective. "Nearly as tall as you, but not big. Skinny. Long blond hair, down to shoulders. Dirty hair. He smell bad. Filthy jeans; dirty plaid shirt; an old gray coat with holes in it, and stains like dirt. He have—" She held her hands up to her chin,

102

searching for the word.

"A beard?" Jill prompted.

"*Sí*—yes, a beard. Like he don't shave in three, four days. His eyes were blue, very pale, and funny-looking, like he was on drugs. When he come in the shop I get scared. I think he is a bum, or a thief, yes? He maybe hold me up. But he ask for a dozen red long-stem Beauties, and he pull out a hundred-dollar bill. So I take the order. He takes paper from his pocket with the name and address." She turned to Jill. "Yours. He asks for an enclosure card, and I give him one. He takes a pen and writes something, and puts the card in the envelope. I don't see what he write. He ask me write 'To Ms. Jillian Talbot, from Nate' on the envelope, and I do. I give him change. He leave. That's all."

Barney came back over. "What happened then?"

"I fill the order and make up the box."

"And you put it—where?"

She pointed at the shelf next to the door. "There."

"How long was it there before Niño delivered it?"

"I don't know, maybe an hour."

"And in that time were you ever out of this room?"

"No—yes! Yes, I go in back to make a—a cup of tea."

With a twist, Jill thought.

Barney grunted. "How many times?"

"*Cómo*—?"

"How many times in that hour did you go in back to make a cup of tea?"

"Once. No, twice. Twice."

"And at either time did anyone come into the shop?"

Mrs. Sanchez stared at him. Then she sank slowly down onto the chair. "*Dios mío*! I forgot all about it!"

Jill knelt once more before the woman.

"You forgot what?" she whispered.

103

The woman pointed past Jill's shoulder at the top of the front door. "The bell. The second time I was in back, I heard the bell. But when I come back through the curtain, nobody is there. I think maybe they start to come in, then change their mind, you know?"

After a moment of silence, Barney said, "Just out of curiosity, did Niño leave with packages to deliver just before the man came into the shop?"

The florist watched him, her eyes widening. Then, apparently speechless, she nodded.

The detective grunted again. "Gave him plenty of time. . . ."

As the two women watched, Barney went out through the door to the street. He turned around and slowly pushed the door partly open. The bell remained silent. Moving carefully, he reached his arms through the door and picked up the nearest box awaiting delivery on the shelf. He pulled the box open as far as its green ribbon would allow and put one large hand in among the stems. Then he closed the box, replaced it on the shelf, and withdrew his arms through the opening. The bell tinkled once as the door snapped shut. He stood on the sidewalk, looking in at them. He executed a small bow.

The florist buried her face in her hands for a moment. Then she raised her head and looked at Jill.

"I think I'd like a cup of tea," she said. "A cup of *real* tea."

Jill grinned at her, murmured her thanks, and hurried out of the shop.

He stood on the other side of Fourteenth Street, watching Jillian Talbot come out of the flower shop to join the detective, Barney Fleck. He wondered what had been said inside; he hadn't dared to get any closer than this. That detective was no fool.

A chill wind whipped down the wide street, and he huddled in his leather coat. He watched the two take off at a fast pace, heading west, the private eye talking and gesturing with his hands, the woman listening as she struggled to keep up with him.

Keeping distance and crowds between himself and them, he followed.

"He was watching," Barney said.

"What?"

"He staked out that flower shop. He knew her every move, right down to her frequent trips behind the curtain. How close the boxes were to the door before Niño delivered them. He knew everything."

"What are you talking about?" Jill stopped, out of breath, and put her hand on Barney's arm to stop him in his tracks. They stood on the corner of Eighth Avenue and Fourteenth Street, the only stationary objects in the milling throng.

Barney grasped her arms. "Your friend. Valentine. He chose that florist very carefully."

Jill pulled the tiny envelope from her purse and read the card again. A shaky hand, block capitals, written with Mrs. Sanchez's blue ballpoint pen.

I'M GETTING CLOSER TO YOU.
LOVE,
VALENTINE

"Okay," she conceded. "But she said he has blond hair and a beard. And his eyes were blue. I don't remember Victor Dimorta very clearly, but I definitely remember dark hair and dark eyes."

105

Barney rolled his eyes. "My God, Jill, give me fifty bucks and about an hour, and I could pass for an Afro-American. So could you, for that matter. Besides, we don't know it's Dimorta."

She stared at him a moment, aware of the people passing by. She drew closer to whisper. "You're right. But I want you to check him out anyway."

"Of course. You just be careful."

"I will," she promised him. "Now I have to go make dinner. I have people coming over."

"Okay. But I'm seeing you home. No arguments."

Barney stepped out into the street and hailed a cab. Just before she stepped into the car, Jill turned to him again.

"Why a rat?" she asked.

He grimaced. "I don't know. Unless it was some sort of message. Maybe Valentine thinks you're a rat."

She shuddered as he held the door for her.

He watched them go. Then he pulled the crumpled sheet of paper from his pocket, the one on which he'd scrawled the name of the bar in Chelsea some four blocks from here, and the name of the man he was to ask for there. He checked his cash: yes, he had enough.

Several times in the past two weeks, after Jillian Talbot was safely in bed for the night, he'd left the little room on Barrow Street and wandered around the Village and Chelsea, stopping at every seedy tavern he found. In each, he would position himself at the end of a bar, nursing beers and listening to the conversations around him. On his fourth expedition, he'd gotten lucky.

He was on his second Budweiser in the dark grotto near the meat-packing district on West Street, just about to give up and find another likely spot, when the fight had begun. Two big, leather-jacketed men, one white, one

Hispanic, had exchanged words. The argument—something about a woman named Rosa—had escalated in volume, and soon every biker, dockworker, and minor felon in the place had gathered around to watch.

The first blow came from the Hispanic guy, sending the white man crashing into the jukebox. He came back with an uppercut that knocked the first guy to the floor. The other patrons shouted and clapped, and the bartender pulled his baseball bat out from under the bar. The Hispanic man came up from the sawdust, his nose streaming blood, and the next thing everyone heard was the click of his switchblade.

The sudden hushed silence in the room was disrupted by the second click. The big white man was holding an enormous semiautomatic, aimed at the Hispanic's heart. There was a long pause, which seemed longer than it actually was: sheer drama. Then, with a wide grin, the Hispanic sheathed his knife, returned it to his pocket, mumbled some sort of apology to the white man regarding the woman named Rosa, and left the bar.

He'd smiled, coming forward from the shadows. The weapon had already disappeared back inside the white man's leather jacket by the time he'd arrived beside him at the bar. The jukebox went back to its repertoire of heavy metal, the conversations began again, the dart game was resumed, and the bat disappeared behind the bar. He sidled right up to the victor, slapped him on the back, and called for two more beers.

In the next hour he'd bought two more Buds for himself and seven Heinekens for his new friend, Hatch, a biker with a gang called the Dead. Hatch and the Hispanic—also one of the Dead—were both sleeping with Rosa, a waitress at a nearby diner. Hatch didn't mind that, but he objected to Pedro calling her a whore. By the time the two Buds and seven Heinekens had been appropriately supplemented with four shots of tequila each, Hatch had supplied him with the vital information.

Now, on Fourteenth Street, he turned and headed toward Chelsea. He was to ask a bartender named Mick for a regular named Flash.

It was time to get a gun.

CHAPTER 6

WEDNESDAY, FEBRUARY 4
(CONTINUED)

THE CHICKEN WAS IN THE OVEN, AND THE WILD RICE had just been added to the boiling water on the stove. The salad was in a large bowl near the sink, waiting to be dressed. The two women leaned against opposite counters in the cheerful yellow-and-white kitchen, sipping Bloody Marys. Well, Mary had the real thing: Jill was drinking straight tomato juice.

Mary had handed over the advance copy of the *New York* interview as she arrived, and watched as her client dropped it absently on the coffee table without so much as opening the envelope. Now Jill launched into her monologue, watching Mary's face as she spoke. The agent was a tall woman, with wavy, shoulder-length brown hair and a large, attractive, friendly face. Her most arresting features were her eyes: deep, dark green, sparkling with intelligence and an innate humor. They gave anyone looking at her the impression that she would, at any moment, break into a dazzling smile.

She was not smiling now. On the contrary, her usual merry disposition was nowhere in evidence. The color drained from her face as she listened, frowning slightly and occasionally shaking her head in disbelief.

When Mary was up to speed on the cards and the roses and the analyst and the private detective, Jill paused for a moment. Then she delivered what she thought would be, for Mary, her most devastating news.

"So, all things considered, I've decided to stop writing the book."

Far from being devastated, Mary seemed relieved. "Of course, Jill. I was about to suggest that myself. You can't go on with it. Not now, anyway. It would be too—I don't know, *ghoulish.*"

"Yeah," Jill agreed. She looked at her friend and shook her head, thinking how crazy it seemed even to be discussing things like this. She'd been living with it for several days now, and yet the strangeness—the cold, macabre *reality* of it—struck constantly fresh, as if for the first time.

"Maybe you should take a break," Mary said. "Just not write anything for a while. You're certainly doing okay, and it's not like you're on a deadline for the next one. I can tell Bill—"

"No!" Jill interjected. "Please. I—I don't want everybody knowing about this—this situation." She shuddered at the thought of the projected conversation between her agent and her editor. "Besides, I want to keep working. At least I'll have that. He's not going to take *that* away from me, whoever he is! I have other ideas for books: I'll just pick one of them. Please don't say anything to Bill."

She was aware of the shrillness of her voice, and that, to Mary, she must sound desperate. With a tremendous effort, she forced herself to smile at her friend.

"So, we're going to have my home-cooked dinner, and

we are not going to let this nonsense ruin it for us."

Mary watched her for a moment. Then she, too, smiled. "All right. But—and this is the last I'll say on the subject—you might want to consider going away somewhere. You know, a little vacation. At least for a while."

Jill shrugged. "Where would I go in the middle of February?"

"Well, I have an idea. . . ."

Jill listened as Mary told her the idea, wondering why she hadn't thought of it herself. By the time Nate joined them, they were deep in conversation. When the buzzer sounded, Jill raised a finger to her lips, indicating to her friend that none of this would be mentioned, even to Nate. As she went to let him in, she stored the idea away for future reference, in case escape became necessary.

Nate was holding one hand behind his back, grinning that lopsided grin she loved so much, as she opened the door. He leaned forward to kiss her tenderly on the lips. Then, he whipped his hand around and thrust it toward her.

She stared, stifling the involuntary cry that welled up inside her. Then, with a deep breath and a smile she managed to pull from thin air, she reached shakily out to accept his gift.

One dozen red, long-stemmed American Beauties.

He watched as Tara walked into the crowded little restaurant on Bleecker Street. She glanced around for a moment before she spotted him. He rose from the table in the corner and waved, then stared as the tall, beautiful blonde in the wooly white coat broke into a dazzling grin and sailed across the room toward him. He quickly adjusted his brown turtleneck and straightened his brand-new Harris tweed jacket as she came up to him.

"Good evening," he said, moving around the table to hold out her chair.

Still grinning, she shrugged. The white coat fell to the chair behind her, and it was all he could do to suppress a gasp. She was wearing a long-sleeved, knee-length midnight-blue sequined sheath with a neckline that could only be described as dramatic. She sank slowly into her chair, and he sank quickly into his.

"You look lovely," he said.

The grin became a laugh.

"Oh, this old thing?" she said, raising a hand to her bare throat. The little white price tag attached to the cuff of the dress fluttered before his eyes. "Oops!" With another laugh and a wink, she brought up her other hand and removed it.

He laughed. It hadn't been a mistake, he knew. It was a deliberate, brilliant icebreaker. Leaning forward, he said, "I have a confession to make."

The soft glow of the candle in the center of the table danced in her deep blue eyes as she, too, leaned forward. "Oh?"

"I've owned this jacket for"—he glanced at his watch—"about two hours. Nate helped me pick it out. He also insisted I buy the aftershave. I've never bought aftershave in my life before that costs more than about two bucks a gallon."

She leaned even closer to him and sniffed. "Ah, yes. Well, that particular one probably cost more than the jacket. I approve."

He smiled over at her as he relaxed back in the chair, wondering why he'd been so nervous in the first place. As the waiter materialized beside them, he asked, "Do you like champagne?"

"My dear, I could bathe in it."

He nodded and ordered a bottle, noting her raised eyebrows as he pronounced *Möet* correctly, with the hard *t* most Americans got wrong.

"So," he said when the waiter had gone, "do all you New York women like expensive aftershaves?"

Tara laughed again. "I wouldn't know: I'm not a New York woman. I'm from a little town you've never heard of in Iowa, and I have what is apparently the world's only *functional* family. My father owns a furniture showroom, and Mom is a retired registered nurse. I'm twenty-seven years old, and I have one brother, Gilbert, twenty-four. He's in law school. I majored in drama at Northwestern; I moved to New York five years ago; and I am now appearing in a popular daytime soap opera you've never seen and don't want to see. I like chocolate ice cream, fuzzy slippers, and long walks on the beach. I hate mushrooms, popular daytime soap operas, and insincere people. The last book I read was—"

"Whoa!" he cried, laughing. "You sound like those centerfolds in *Playboy*!"

She laughed. "Have you ever taken pictures for them?"

"No," he said, smiling at her ingenuousness. "Photographers don't start out doing centerfolds for *Playboy*. They end up there—if they're lucky."

Tara nodded. "Yeah. I've done musicals in summer stock, but my dream is to star in a new musical on Broadway, one that Stephen Sondheim writes just for me. What's your dream?"

"To have dinner with a beautiful actress."

She laughed and glanced over at the entrance to the restaurant.

"Well, what do you know?!" she cried. "There's Stephen Sondheim—and he's coming this way! Just look

112

at all that sheet music under his arm!"

They were still laughing when the waiter arrived with the bottle and the ice bucket. As he poured, Tara once again leaned forward.

"So, Douglas Baron, photographer, tell me all about yourself."

Jill's surprising culinary skills had been remarked on at length, and now the three of them were in the living room with the remains of dessert and a pot of coffee. Nate and Mary had brandy.

"Aren't you going to join us?" Mary asked her, indicating the bottle.

Before she could reply, Nate jumped in. "Jill's on the wagon. Has been for several weeks—not that she ever drank much to begin with. . . ."

She knew Nate didn't suspect, but she was keenly aware, without even looking, of Mary's raised eyebrow. Every woman on earth knew there were three reasons why a woman suddenly stops drinking. Mary knew Jill wasn't an alcoholic, and that she wasn't trying to lose weight, which left only one thing.

No, she decided. I won't tell them. Not yet.

She changed the subject. "How's Phil?"

Mary registered disbelief. Then, with another raised eyebrow, she said, "He's fine. He called today from San Francisco." She turned to Nate to explain what Jill already knew. "My husband is out there for several weeks, supervising the construction of an office building he designed for his firm. It's the biggest assignment he's ever had—and the longest we've been separated from each other in the three years we've been married. He won't be back till the end of next month." She turned back to Jill. "'How's Phil?' What the hell are you going on about? You

113

got those flowers with that awful thing in them not six hours ago, and you're asking how Phil is? What are your nerves made of, anyway?"

Jill looked quickly over at Nate, then lowered her eyes to the coffee table. "I thought we weren't going to mention that."

"Flowers?" Nate was saying. "What flowers? What 'awful thing'?"

With a withering glance at her agent and a long sigh, Jill told him. The flowers, the dead rat, her trip with Barney Fleck to the florist on Fourteenth Street. She was aware, even as she spoke, of the growing tension in the room, knowing what was going to happen next. It was why she hadn't told him in the first place.

"*Damn it!*" Nate cried, jumping up from the couch before she'd even finished her last sentence. "*Goddamn it!* Who the hell *is* this guy? What the hell does he *want*?!"

She shook her head, watching as he paced up and down the length of the room.

"Me," she said at last. "He wants me."

That stopped him in his tracks. "What do you mean?"

"I mean, he wants to scare me. I thought it was Brian Marshall, but now I think it might be this crazy guy from college. The one I told you about last night, Victor Dimorta." She paused for a moment, once more staring down at the coffee table. "Victory over death."

"Come again?" Mary said.

She explained. Her friend and her lover stared at her. Then she said, "I know this is stupid, but I don't know what to do. Nothing like this has ever happened to me. So I've asked my analyst to hypnotize me on Friday. I have this blank spot in my memory where Victor's face should be. Just like my stepfather: I knew he'd assaulted me, but I didn't remember the whole thing—hitting him with the

114

skillet—until the analyst put me under. Then I recalled the entire incident, and I remembered it when I woke up. I still remember it. Maybe the same will happen with Victor. Maybe I'll be able to describe him to Barney and the police, and maybe I'll remember why it is he might be doing this to me. *If* it's Victor."

There was silence in the room, but she noticed with relief that Nate had stopped pacing and resumed his seat beside her. He reached over and took her hand in his.

"Well, whoever it is," he said, "he'd better stay far away from me!" She heard it in his tone: the desperation, the outraged helplessness that can only ring so clearly in the voice of offended masculinity. Then his face drained of color. "My God, I can't believe I just brought you those roses. Oh, Jill, I'm sorry!"

Jill held her hand up to his lips. "It's okay, Nate. You didn't know."

Their hands clasped tightly together, Jill and Nate turned to stare at the new flowers in the vase on the dining table. She felt his other warm, gentle hand come up to stroke the back of her hair.

"I won't let anything happen to you," he whispered, still staring at the roses.

Mary Daley broke the tension with her patented hearty laugh. "And they said chivalry was dead!"

In a moment, they were all laughing. Then, to change the subject once and for all, Jill said, "I wonder how Tara and Doug are doing. . . ."

"I'm thirty-two," he said, watching the beautiful actress across from him. "Atlanta. Dad was a podiatrist, Mom a homemaker. Both gone. No siblings. Prep school, then NYU. Art major, specializing in photography. Stupid lab job for Kodak: two years. Assistant to Juan Vega: three years. Loaded cameras, developed, traveled with him to fashion shoots all over the world. Favorite spot. Australia, the northern coast, near the Great Barrier Reef. Favorite model: Stacy Green."

He paused after that, waiting for Tara's reaction.

"Stacy Green," she said, her eyes widening. "Stacy? The girl who—"

"Yes," he whispered, cutting her off before she could say more. Then, because something was expected, because he couldn't just leave it at that, he added, "She was my wife."

She stared. "Oh, gosh, I'm sorry."

"Yeah," he said, smiling bleakly over at her. "So. That's my life story, I guess. Well, almost: the last book I read was a biography of Richard Avedon."

Not for nothing is she a gainfully employed actress, he thought. Sensing instinctively that his murdered wife was not a topic for dinner table conversation, Tara dropped it immediately.

"Is there any more champagne?" she asked.

He checked. "No."

"Let's get another bottle. *My* treat."

Jill, in her rather desperate search for conversational subjects that did not include her predicament, turned now to Mary. "When are you going to start that book you're always threatening to write?"

Mary blushed and shrugged. "Oh, God, I don't know. I'm doing so well on the other side of the desk—"

"Oh, please!" Jill said, laughing. "Don't use that as an excuse. Yes, you're a wonderful agent, and I hope you'll always, be *my* agent. But that's not really what you intended to do with your life, remember? That speech you gave me at our first lunch together, right after you accepted me as a client and sold *Darkness* in a matter of minutes. Something about envying me, and about Emily Brontë . . . ?"

"What?" Nate, now stretched out on pillows on the floor between them, sat up. "What about Emily Brontë?"

Jill giggled and reached for her coffee mug. "Oh, she has this monologue—"

"Fink!" Mary cried, also giggling. "Okay, Nate, just for you. When I was, let's see, fifteen, my parents rented this summer house on Fire Island. I spent most of my time there sunbathing with these other girls I met, you know, trying to attract boys, or fishing with my dad and my two brothers. I hate fishing, but they still do it every chance they get. Anyway, there was this one week in August where it rained every day, so boy-watching and fishing were out. I looked around this house we were in for something to do, and I found all these old books on a shelf in the living room. Dusty, leatherbound things. Mom found me going through them, so she looked through them all and pulled one down and handed it to me. Told me to read it: it was her favorite. Well, I was just curious enough about my mom to wonder what could possibly be her favorite book. I'd never even *seen* her with a book, and she said, 'Try having three kids, and see how much time you get to read,' or something. So, I curled up in the windowseat and gave it a look.

"It was *Wuthering Heights*. I sat there for three rainy afternoons, lost on these moors with these incredibly real people. I think I married Phil because he looks a little like Laurence Olivier in the movie version. Cut to the chase: that day to this, I've wanted to do that. To write, to create something real on paper, with nothing but language and my own imagination. To make other people feel something of what I felt in that windowseat in that rented house that summer on Fire Island, when it rained."

117

Mary smiled and picked up her brandy. Nate stared, entranced. After an appropriate moment of silence, Jill clapped her hands.

"Brava!" she cried. "I just *love* that Emily Brontë speech!"

"You're making fun of me."

"Oh, no," Jill assured her friend. "I'm perfectly serious. I have the same story, only it was *Rebecca,* not *Wuthering Heights,* and it was my bedroom on Central Park West, and it wasn't raining that I remember. I was fourteen. And, yes, Nate looks a little like Laurence Olivier in the movie version—boy, that Olivier certainly had his pick of the best parts, didn't he? But you describe it much better than I could, Mary. I think you're a writer. And I think it's time you started writing."

She watched with genuine pleasure as Mary Daley, who was not given to blushing, did just that. Then she looked down at Nate, who lay at her feet looking up at her. She recognized the expression on his face: he was still thinking about the valentine cards and the roses. With a smile, she reached down to push a lock of black hair out of his eyes. "How about you, babe? When did you know you were going to be a painter?"

He sat up, the troubled look immediately evaporating. "I told you about that, Jill. Our first dinner together. Lincoln Center. Remember?"

Jill winked. "Of course I do, but Mary wasn't there. She told you about herself; now it's your turn to reciprocate." She turned to her friend, laughing. "I swear! Sometimes he can be such a clam!"

Nate shrugged. Leaning back so his head rested against Jill's legs, he said, "Monet. He's my favorite, I guess. Actually, I was big on English, too, until I took this course, history of art. It was pretty dull stuff, you know, slide shows and all that, until the day we got to the Impressionists. One of the slides was Monet's *Water Lilies, #2*." He sat forward, his body suddenly tense. "I wish I could explain it the way Mary did. From the moment I saw that painting, I was hooked. I read every book on Impressionism I could find. I would stare at the pictures for hours: Monet, Manet, Degas—God, *all* of them! These people didn't paint what was in front of them, they painted what they *felt* about what was in front of them! And I knew I had to do that, too. I became obsessed with it, with getting my feelings into the brush and onto the canvas." He smiled, and his body relaxed again. "I've been trying to do that ever since. Not to re-create, but to *describe*." He held out his right hand before him, staring at it. "With this."

Mary nodded. "You love it, don't you?"

Still facing Mary, he reached up absently and stroked Jill's calf. "It's my second-greatest love in the world."

Jill felt the warm blush wash over her face, aware that Mary was smiling at her over Nate's head. She leaned down to kiss his hair.

"So," Mary said, mimicking her friend's words of half an hour ago, "I wonder how Tara and—what was his name, Doug?—are doing. . . ."

He watched her go into the building. She turned to wave just before the inner door closed behind her. Then she was gone.

It wasn't snowing again tonight, and the brisk wind was making the bitter cold even colder. He turned up the collar of his coat before stepping out into the street. He crossed it and stood on the opposite sidewalk, looking up.

She had been nice; a perfect date, really. She had steered the conversation expertly away from the past—specifically *his* past—and embellished dinner and dessert with amusing chatter about her work in television and intelligent questions about photography. They'd actually laughed a great deal, and he'd mentioned Nate's invitation to go to his studio tomorrow night. She had readily accepted. She'd saved the best for last: when the evening was drawing to a close, and he was wondering if some sort of sexual overture might be expected, she yawned prettily and said something vague about an early-morning rehearsal. So, *that* pressure was off, too.

Yes, he thought now, a perfect date.

After a few moments, the lights came on in the picture window on the sixth floor. He nodded to himself, gazing up through the bare branches of the tree in front of her building at her lights, and the lights on the seventh floor directly above her.

Jillian Talbot is home, he thought, and Nate is probably with her.

Jillian Talbot . . .

He stood there for a long time, looking up at the lights, remembering, bracing himself for tomorrow night.

"Stacy Green?!" Mary cried.

"Oh, my God!" Jill added. She stared at Tara, now comfortably ensconced next to Nate on the floor with a snifter of brandy. She'd stopped at her apartment only long enough to get out of the lovely but uncomfortable blue sequin number Jill had helped her pick out. Now, in ripped jeans and her kid brother's college football jersey, she still managed to look stunning.

"Can you believe?!" the actress cried. "There I am in my fancy dress with my look-at-me hair, doing my best Michelle Pfeiffer imitation, and he hits me with that. I, like, wanted to just go home right then and there. Stacy

Green!"

The three women looked at each other, shaking their heads in disbelief.

"Who's Stacy Green?" Nate asked.

At that, they turned their incredulity on him.

"You're kidding, right?" Mary asked.

"Sorry," he said. "Never heard of her."

All three women started talking at once, so Nate raised a hand to stop them.

"Hey, it was Tara's date, so let her tell it."

"Okay," Tara said. "Stacy Green was this incredibly beautiful fashion model. You used to see her face everywhere. Short dark hair, big brown eyes—she looked kind of like Jill, come to think of it. Anyway, she was sort of the well-scrubbed, all-American girl, selling toothpaste and corn flakes and lemon-scented shampoo in those off moments when she wasn't on the cover of *Sports Illustrated*. Then, about three years ago, she was stabbed to death in her house in East Hampton. Like, nobody could believe it. And *then* this whole story started coming out, about drugs and wild parties and lovers in the Mafia. The all-American girl, right? And—as if it weren't already sordid enough—it turns out she was *married*. All the news I followed just said he was some famous photographer's assistant who'd only been married to her for about a year, and that he and Stacy were already estranged at the time of the murder. I don't remember if they ever mentioned the husband's name, but I can tell you now: it was your friend, Doug Baron!"

"Jesus!" Nate muttered. Then he looked quickly up at the actress. "I'm sorry, Tara. I had no idea. Was he—I mean, did they—"

"Oh, no," Tara said quickly. "He wasn't the one. He was miles away at the time. There was this big

121

investigation, and they finally arrested some sexy-looking Mafia hit man. One of her lovers, apparently. One of many, if you can believe the tabloids. The story was that he'd just found out she was also entertaining some industrialist, or something. And there was a big inquest, or pretrial hearing, or whatever they call it, and they let the hit man go. Lack of evidence, if I remember, and some buddies who swore he was with them at the time, blah blah blah. . . ." She trailed off, took a deep breath, and finished on a dramatic note. "So, nobody was ever tried for her murder!"

Nate stared. "God, how awful for him."

Jill turned to him now, finally able to ask what she'd been wondering for several minutes. "How did you manage to miss this, Nate?"

He shrugged. "Three years ago I was in art school in Chicago, learning to paint. *Trying* to paint. I vaguely remember something about some cover girl being killed, but that's all. I was becoming an artist: World War Three could have been declared, and none of the students in my school would have noticed."

There was nothing left for them all to do now but look around at each other, shaking their heads. At last, Nate broke the silence.

"Boy," he said, "I wonder how Doug feels about all that now."

Tara grinned. "Ask him yourself. He and I are coming to your place tomorrow night!"

Everyone stared at her.

"You *are?!*" Jill cried.

The actress smiled complacently. "Of course. I mean, it's not like he's an accused murderer or anything. He was never even a suspect. And how many handsome artists are out there, anyway? All the good ones are either—"

"Don't say it!" Jill warned, and everyone laughed.

"That's good," Nate said. "I'm glad you like him, Tara. I have a feeling you may be just what he needs."

He reached for Jill's hand when he said this. She took his hand in hers and squeezed, smiling. Forget that he's sexy, she thought. Forget that he's talented and passionate and funny. He's just a very nice man. A man she should hang on to, she supposed; a man who would always be kind and considerate and supportive. A man who would protect her from bad things, like—

She shuddered, squeezing Nate's hand harder. He looked over at her and winked. She winked back, forcing a smile. Then she let go of his strong hand, got up from the couch, and went over to the big picture window. She stared out through the dark glass at the snowflakes drifting down to the street before her, then beyond them to the myriad lighted windows of the enormous city, thinking:

Valentine.

EARTH

THREE YEARS AGO

SHE'D ALWAYS BEEN A PRETTY GIRL, AND SHE KNEW IT. It was this knowledge that most motivated and most informed her actions. This, and the feeling instilled in her long ago that she was very special. Now, at thirty-four, she was ready to show the world just how special she was.

It had taken several years and a few false starts, but now it was going to happen. Her new screenplay was the best she'd written so far, and she was certain that as soon as she got it into the right hands, every major actress in Hollywood would be clamoring for the lead role. That's why today was so important. She had a good feeling about this. About *him*.

She hummed under her breath as she stepped into her best faded, form-fitting jeans and pink T-shirt. Then she picked up the brush before the mirror and went to work on her long blond hair. A picnic, she thought. What a lovely idea. Neil had left the invitation in the form of a card on the pillow beside her. He'd just called to confirm it a little while ago, waking her from a deep, satisfied sleep. A picnic in the hills above the city. Be ready at noon, he said—and bring the script.

He must have crept out early this morning, she mused, while I was sleeping. A business meeting at his production company.

Production company! She went over to the desk under her bedroom window, picked up the bound screenplay next to the computer, and opened it to the title page.

DANGEROUS CURVES
by
Sharon Williams

She closed the cover and hugged the book to her, smiling. Looking out the window at the bright sunlight pouring down on Los Angeles, she thought about her luck. This script in her arms wasn't going to make the rounds of half the studios in Hollywood like the two she'd written before it. This one was going to be different. *He* would make it happen.

Sharon loved the movies. Some of her happiest memories were of herself as a child, and later a teenager, staring at screens in darkened rooms. Daddy and Mother knew a few movie people, and she'd gone to her share of premieres and awards ceremonies and parties at producers' houses. She'd always dreamed of a career in Hollywood; not as an actress—she had no talent for that, though she was certainly pretty enough—but as a writer. She was forever making up elaborate stories in her mind, and she always saw them as a series of scenes, with appropriate editing and camera angles. She wanted to create movies. Films.

But first, she'd had to learn about writing: she thanked her parents for that bit of wisdom, as for so much else. So she went to Hartley College, her mother's alma mater, because it had one of the best English departments in America. Four years in Vermont, then three at Berkeley, where she took every filmmaking and screenwriting course available.

Then, for the next five years, she'd allowed herself to become distracted: Europe, the Caribbean, Hawaii. On a whim, she'd taken off for Amsterdam shortly after leaving

Berkeley, with an idle rich boy she'd been seeing at the time. This had turned into a protracted grand tour of the world in which the scenery shifted as often as the jet-setting revelers around her. But Europe and the West Indies and all those other adventures were behind her now, as were the men she'd been with in those places.

And Shane, of course. She grimaced at the thought of her ex-husband: another two years wasted. By the time she'd met Shane, at a dinner party on one of her rare visits home, she'd decided it was time to slow down. Five years of roaming the world was enough for her. Besides, Daddy was beginning to complain about all the money she was going through.

There was a row of tall palms lining the street in front of her building. She gazed out of her third-story window at the closest one as it rustled slowly in the warm breeze, remembering.

Shane Lennox had been a mistake from the start. He was handsome and amusing—and the son of one of her father's business partners. They dated for several months, and the dates were always fun. Even so, she should never have married him. With her restless streak and her as-yet-unformed but definitely developing professional agenda, she'd known it was a mistake, even as she'd walked down the aisle on Daddy's arm. And her instincts had been right.

When she'd imagined being married, she'd always envisioned a big house somewhere fun like Malibu, or Pacific Palisades up the coast near her parents. Her husband would be rich, of course, as rich as she. Every day he'd go to his law firm or his corporate headquarters or his movie studio—yes, movie studio: she should have married someone in the business. And she'd be home creating brilliant screenplays. They'd meet other movie people for dinner at Spago, and they'd have beach parties on the weekends.

But Shane was working his way up the ladder in Daddy's real estate development firm, which meant a cramped little two-room dungeon in a complex here in town, near the office. It meant no more allowance from Daddy, and living on Shane's meager salary. Cooking and cleaning: two things she'd had to learn on her feet, never having done either before. Going to the supermarket and the dry cleaners, and department stores for his socks and underwear. Boring dinners in unfashionable restaurants with his prospective clients. And then the news that she was pregnant.

That's when Sharon threw in the towel and went home to her parents. She didn't want a baby. She didn't want to cook and clean. She didn't want to be married to Shane Lennox. She sobbed in her mother's arms, telling her that she'd made a terrible mistake.

And that was that. Daddy had fixed everything, as Daddy had always done. He arranged for the divorce, as well as the abortion. She'd been married to Shane for a grand total of fourteen months. She was thirty-one years old, and she was going to be a screenwriter.

So, three years ago she moved here, to a nice apartment complex in town. It was a mere eight blocks from where she'd lived with Shane—where Shane now lived with his second wife—but it was hers alone. She didn't have to share space with a man whose ideal wife was closer to a maid than a mate. Not that she felt any resentment toward Shane: he was actually a perfectly nice man; he just wasn't for her. A few months after the divorce, she'd talked Daddy and Mother into financing this one-bedroom co-op, a Mustang, and a computer—an investment in her career. They were so happy to see her excited about actual work that they readily obliged.

She got back in touch with her old friends from high school. She spent weekends at the beach, and every night she went out. Dinner, dancing, whatever: she dated a lot of guys, but nothing serious—she'd already gone that route, thank you! And every weekday, from ten till five, she wrote. Story ideas and scenarios at first, and finally she had attempted full screenplays. Her own growing dedication to the work surprised and delighted her. She realized with a sense of pride that she wasn't completely useless after all. She was indeed as talented as she'd always hoped to be.

Last year, she'd made her first movie deal: she'd sold a story idea to a small, independent production company, and they had assured her that she would do the screenplay if they ever actually made the film. With her first option check, she bought her mother a Cartier watch. It was one of the few times in her life she'd ever felt completely altruistic, and it was the only time she'd ever seen her mother cry.

Now, staring out at the sunny, palm-lined street, Sharon smiled. She rarely looked back at things she'd already done. Besides, there wasn't much about Shane Lennox that she chose to remember. But her memories of traveling were good ones, as were her infrequent recollections of high school and college. Hartley had been fun—what a queen bee she'd been there! She thought of her two pals there, Cass and Belinda, and the adventures and good times that had served to alleviate the boredom of long Vermont winters for a California girl. The handsome dean of students, who'd been so much fun, sexually speaking. Creeping into the men's dormitory with her friends and short-sheeting all the beds. And that creepy freshman—Vincent, or Victor, or whatever the hell his name was—that she and the girls had lured to his doom.

She spared a moment's thought for Cass and Belinda. They hadn't been in touch in years, and she wondered vaguely where they were now, and what they were doing. Perhaps she should give them a call sometime soon. . . .

Oh, well, she thought with an amused shake of her head, onward and upward.

She returned her gaze to her reflection in the mirror and smiled, still hugging her latest achievement to her chest. Now she had a script—a good script, a *great* script—and now she had Neil.

Neil. She dropped the script on the dresser and stretched luxuriously, remembering last night's activities and anticipating today's picnic. Lucky break, she thought.

If she hadn't gone to Patchoulie the other night, it would never have happened. . . .

Sharon Williams was easy. Every day, she worked in her apartment, and twice in the last week she'd made the rounds of studios and production offices in Burbank and Hollywood, pitching her ideas and screenplays. And every night, she went out dancing, sometimes with men but just as often alone. And always in the same club, Patchoulie, the "in" spot of the moment on Hollywood Boulevard.

He'd been watching her ever since he'd arrived in Los Angeles, two weeks ago. He'd checked into a quiet, inexpensive motel not too far from her place and rented a Mercedes. He'd used an alias for both, and paid cash.

Watching her routine had helped him develop the plan. On February 10, he took a shower and put his new Givenchy suit on his new body. He inserted his new tinted contact lenses, patted Halston cologne on his new face, and carefully combed his new hair. Then he got in his rented Mercedes and drove to Patchoulie. He sat at the end of the bar, ordered a drink, and waited.

She came in, all right—on the arm of a guy he'd already seen her with at the beach last weekend. A big, handsome, deeply tanned blond man in a "Hang Ten" shirt and jeans, a surfer. He'd overheard her call the man Derek. He watched them take a small table near the dance floor and order drinks. Several times in the next hour, they got up to dance. At one point they danced to a Neil Diamond song. He'd always liked Neil Diamond, and he took it as a good sign. He smiled to himself, thinking: Neil.

He monitored their actions closely. At regular intervals, Derek's hands would begin to rove over Sharon's body, and she'd slap them away. So, they were only casually seeing each other, he surmised. The fact that Derek repeated the groping every few minutes, despite her protests, told him that Derek was none too bright. He noted the surfer's frequent trips to the men's room, and his glittery eyes and swift, manic movements: Derek had obviously discovered Better Living Through Chemistry. He smiled to himself again and waited some more.

The third time Derek went to the men's room, he gave him a few moments and then followed him. As he arrived there, Derek was by the sinks, snorting coke from a tiny spoon on a chain around his neck. He feigned happy surprise at seeing the surfer and went into his act.

"Hey, man—Derek, isn't it?"

The blond man stared, sniffing. "Uh, yeah . . . ?"

He grinned. "You don't remember me, do you? We met a while back, at that party. You know, the beach. You were with—what's his name, your buddy, the other surfer . . . . ."

Derek blinked, trying to remember. "Uh, Ron?"

"Yeah, Ron, that's right. I'm Neil, remember? From the film production company?"

Derek grinned to cover the fact that he obviously didn't remember. "Uh, yeah, sure, how ya doin'?"

"Oh, fine. You know, still working like a dog, looking for new scripts to develop into films. . . ."

"Uh, new scripts?" Real quick, was Derek.

"Yeah, you know, new screenplays to develop into movies." Spell it out for him.

Derek's bright eyes widened. "Is that what you do?"

"Yeah, sure, like I was telling you and Ron—"

"Oh, wow!" Derek cried, wiping powder from his nose and clapping him on the back. "I can't *believe* this, man! Sure, I remember you—the party on the beach, with Ron! You're lookin' for screenplays! Yeah!" He held up the little vial in his hand. "Hey, you want a hit?"

He grinned, shaking his head. "No, thanks, I'm trying to quit."

Derek roared with laughter and took the other man by the arm. "Man, this is *unbelievable!* Come with me, uh, Neil—there's somebody you just gotta meet!"

As the big man hustled him out of the room, he pretended confusion. "Oh, yeah? Who?"

"My date, man! *Sharon!* She's—you're gonna freak, man!—she's a *screenwriter!*"

He freaked. "No kidding! That's amazing, Derek! That's—that's *unbelievable!*"

Sharon sat at the little table by the dance floor, staring at the star. The Oscar-winning actress had arrived a few minutes ago, just after Derek had taken off to powder his nose. Now she and her husband were joining a crowded table across the room, obviously movie people. God, Sharon thought, if I could just get up and go over there, introduce myself, tell her about the script—

"Hey, babe, you're not gonna believe this! Look who I

ran into!"

She turned her head and looked up at Derek, and at the tall, dark-haired stranger beside him. She smiled absently. "Hello."

"This is Neil," Derek said, pulling over another chair from a nearby table and signaling for the waitress. "Guess what? He's looking for screenplays!"

Sharon blinked, looking more closely at the man. "How do you do, Neil? I'm Sharon Williams."

The man named Neil smiled at her, then glanced over at Derek and the chair he'd produced. "May I?"

"Please do," Sharon replied, and Neil and Derek sat on either side of her. She turned her full attention on the new arrival. "So, you're in the movie business?"

The waitress arrived to take their order. By the time she arrived with fresh drinks, Sharon had all but forgotten that Derek was at the table with them.

". . . so I've only been in town a few weeks," Neil was telling her. "The film section of the company is new—we were strictly theatrical, you know, Broadway and so forth, but now we're branching out. And I'm the acquisitions department. I'm just settling in here, getting to know everybody in the industry—"

Sharon looked over at the movie star across the room. "Do you know her?"

He followed her gaze. "Uh, no—but if I had a property that was right for her, I could certainly get it to her people. . . ."

She laughed. "Well, what a small world this is! I've just completed a new screenplay that would be *perfect* for her, and I have several other things as well. Of course, a couple of them are already under option, but I'd love to show you some of my work."

"That would be great," Neil said, producing a small

132

notepad and a pen from his jacket pocket. "I'll call your agent tomorrow—"

"Oh, I'm not—currently—being represented," she said quickly, smiling and shrugging her shoulders in her very best "you-know-how-it-is" attitude. She rolled her eyes. "Agents! But I'll tell you what, Neil . . ."

Derek had wandered off to the men's room again. By the time he returned, she'd made the date to meet Neil here—minus Derek—in three days. Neil was apparently unavailable until then.

As he rose to leave, Neil clapped Derek on the back, shook Sharon's hand, and thanked them for the drink.

"I'm glad I ran into you again, Derek," he said. "Thanks to you, Sharon and I may be able to do some business." He looked directly into her eyes when he said that. "Good night, Sharon. It was nice meeting you."

She smiled. Yes, she thought as she watched him go, it was nice meeting *you!*

He spent the next three days watching her, and once he even called her to confirm their date. He followed her to the beach with Derek, and to a party at a house in Laurel Canyon, and to a restaurant where she had dinner with a group of people. Then, on the evening of February 13, the night before Valentine's Day, he put on his new Ralph Lauren suit and arrived at Patchoulie a few minutes before her. He managed to get the same table they'd been at three nights before. Just before she arrived, he patted the pocket of his jacket that held the valentine card he'd bought for her, and smiled.

It was so simple, really. . . .

She'd dressed with special care this evening. The red dress was provocative without being too much, and her hair was loose around her shoulders. She knew she looked good, and that knowledge was reinforced by the expression on Neil's face the moment he saw her. Good, she thought. It's working.

"Hello again," she murmured as she sank into the seat beside him.

"You look sensational," Neil said, smiling.

"Thank you. So do you. I hope you like to dance, Neil. I feel like dancing tonight."

"Sure, but, uh, where are your scripts?"

She smiled her best smile. "Back at my place. You can see them later. But first, may I have a drink?"

They ordered, and later they danced. He held her close on the dance floor, and she could feel the heat emanating from his body. She'd already decided how this was going to go: he was certainly attractive, and he was obviously interested in her—and his production company was looking for properties. This man had fallen out of Heaven and landed at her feet!

She smiled and pressed closer against him.

Three hours and several drinks later, he was in bed with her. He followed her in his car, and by the time she opened her apartment door they were half undressed.

They made love twice. Then, when he was certain she was asleep, he slipped out of her bed and stole away, carefully propping the valentine card on the pillow next to her. Inside the card he'd written a note that read: *Mr. Avnet has an early meeting, but he requests the pleasure of Ms. Williams's company on a Valentine's Day picnic. Be ready at noon. Bring this invitation—and your best screenplay. N.* His phony last name was the name of an actual entertainment mogul.

At nine o'clock that morning, he called her. She sleepily

accepted his invitation. He hung up and drove to a spot high in the hills above the city, an isolated country road beside a forest. He parked beside the road, took a shovel from the trunk of the Mercedes, and hiked up to the tiny clearing in the woods he'd discovered shortly after his arrival in Los Angeles. Among the trees near the clearing, he went to work. He dug a hole six feet by three feet, four feet deep. He propped the shovel against a nearby tree and walked back down the hill to his car.

He went back to his room, showered, and changed. Then he drove to a nearby mall. In the trendy gourmet shop he bought a basket filled with country paté and Cajun chicken sandwiches and strawberries and champagne. In the record store he bought a portable cassette player and one tape. In the sleep shop he bought a large blanket. His last stop was the candy store.

She took a last look at herself in the mirror: yes, she was ready. She'd thought about calling her parents, but then decided it could wait until after the picnic. Perhaps by then she'd have some news for them. If Neil liked the screenplay as much as she thought he would . . .

He drove up in his Mercedes just as she arrived on the sidewalk outside her building. When she got in beside him, he leaned over and kissed her. She handed him the valentine card.

"My invitation," she said, affecting a formal tone.

He laughed. "Thank you, ma'am." He took the card and put it in his pocket, and they were off. She sat with the screenplay on her lap, smiling over at him as they headed for the freeway.

It was a beautiful day, warm and cloudless, and it seemed to get better as they left the freeway and drove up the winding roads into the hills. She had no idea where they were going, but she relaxed in her seat and left the details to him. She asked about his early meeting at the production company, and he smiled and said it had gone well. He named a famous director and told her that they were working on a possible deal.

At last they arrived on a small road high in the hills. There were trees above them, and the city lay far below. A few more miles, and then he slowed and parked by the side of the road. They got out, and Neil reached into the backseat for a large basket and a blanket.

"My, you seem to have thought of everything," she said.

He grinned, took her by the hand, and led her up into the trees. A few minutes' walk and they emerged into a small clearing. The sun bore down on the almost perfect circle of bright green grass.

"Well, here we are," he said.

"Oh, Neil, it's lovely! How did you ever find this place?"

He winked and began laying out the blanket.

First, he served the champagne. Then he brought out the paté and the sandwiches and the strawberries. They ate together in the clearing, talking and laughing comfortably, more like lovers of long standing than new acquaintances. After lunch, they made love on the blanket. It was perfect, just the way he'd dreamed about it all through the years in prison.

Later, Sharon sat up on the blanket, adjusting her clothes. She turned her head and smiled down at the handsome man who lay beside her. His eyes were closed, his face to the sun, and there was the hint of a smile on his lips. For a moment she thought he was asleep. Then he opened his eyes and gazed up at her.

"Hello," she said.

"Hi."

She found their discarded glasses and poured the last of the sparkling wine. He sat up on the blanket and took his glass from her. They toasted.

"To *Dangerous Curves*," she said, laughing.

Neil laughed, too. "Are you referring to yourself?"

"No, darling, it's the title of the movie we're going to make together." She reached down beside her, picked up the manuscript, and held it out to him. He took it from her, glanced down at the title page for a moment, then set it aside on the blanket.

"Ah, yes," he said. "But first, *I've* got something for *you*."

"Oh?" There was a provocative lilt in her tone.

Sharon watched as he leaned over and reached into the wicker basket on the other side of the blanket. He rose to his knees and turned back to her. He was holding out a pink, heart-shaped candy box, and there was a small cassette recorder in his other hand. She smiled dreamily up at him, took the candy box, and looked down at the recorder.

"What's this?" she giggled.

"Background music," Neil said, leaning forward to kiss her. In the middle of the kiss, he pushed the play button. The soft piano intro reached her ears, followed a moment later by the low, clear voice of Sarah Vaughan.

"My Funny Valentine."

Sharon stared down at the device in his hand, then up at him. "Why, that's one of my favorites! How did you know?"

Neil continued to smile at her, but she noticed the subtle change that crept into it. The gleam, the sudden look of triumph in his eyes.

"You don't get it, do you?" he whispered. Then he put down the recorder, brought up his arm, and smashed his fist into her nose.

The candy box skittered away as Sharon's head flew back onto the blanket, and for a moment she couldn't see. Something had hit her, she thought, and something was trickling from her now, but nothing was registering. Then her vision cleared, and she looked up at the handsome face grinning down at her. She blinked as she became aware of the throbbing pain below her eyes.

"What . . . ?" she began, her speech slurred by pain and surprise. "Wha . . . happened . . . ?"

He leaned down and took the sides of her face gently in his hands. Gazing directly into her uncomprehending eyes, he said:

"I'm Victor Dimorta. Happy Valentine's Day!"

She stared up, unsure that she had heard him correctly. Victor? she thought as her mind began to function again. Did he say—

Then the music reached her ears again, and she remembered. Victor Dimorta. Victory over death. Hartley College.

Panic possessed her. *Victor Dimorta!* She shot up from the blanket raising her arms in automatic self-defense, opening her mouth and filling her lungs to scream.

His fist smashed into her mouth, and she fell back on the blanket. Oh, God! her mind said over and over. Oh, God! She attempted to get up again, but she didn't get far. This time he punched her in the stomach. She lay back on the blanket, the hot California sun bearing down on her, slowly becoming aware of the horrible pain. That, and the voice: the odd, high-pitched laughter from the figure above her. And the monologue that accompanied it as he struck her again.

". . . thought you were all so much better than me . . . ugly, creepy Victor . . . not so ugly now, am I! *Am* I, bitch? *Cunt!* You're gonna die now . . . die . . . and die . . . and die. . . ."

She tried once more to rise, but he was sitting on her chest now and she couldn't move. Through her panic and her fear and her pain, she felt the pressure as he took her arm in his powerful hands. She heard the snap as he broke it at the elbow. Then the pain flooded up through her and she fainted. She regained consciousness slowly, feeling the slap against her cheek as he coaxed her back into wakefulness. She couldn't move her arms, and the excruciating pain informed her that he had broken the other one. The laughter continued from somewhere above her, and the words.

". . . like that, Sharon? Miss high-and-mighty Sharon Williams? Does it *hurt*, bitch!? Like you hurt *me*?! Well, does it, Mother?"

The words swam away from her, and everything began to fade. Mother? she wondered as the pain and the fear were replaced by the last phase, hallucination. Did he say Mother? . . . whose mother? Oh, *Mother!* Daddy! . . . Help me . . . help me . . . please, God, somebody . . . help me . . . .

It took a long time for Sharon Williams to die: he made sure of that. When it was finally over he knelt above her, smiling down, allowing the exquisite, unutterable sense of victory to surge through him. Then he raised his arms above his head and howled his triumph to the sun.

One down, he told himself. Three to go.

Afterward, he carried her body into the trees, dumped it in the makeshift grave, threw the screenplay in after it, and filled the hole. He covered the turned earth with leaves and a large dead branch. He collected the shovel and the picnic things and the candy box and made his way back down to the car. An hour later, the picnic things were in a dumpster across town.

Two hours later, Victor Dimorta was on a plane to Pittsburgh.

JILL

CHAPTER 7

THURSDAY, FEBRUARY 5

JILL HAD TO WRITE AGAIN. THE NEED HAD BEEN building up in her for days now, ever since she'd discontinued work on the novel. It was most apparent to her now, in the early morning, when she had conditioned herself through long custom to go into the office and turn on the computer. Within an hour after breakfast, she was usually well into the day's output.

She hadn't eaten breakfast this morning. The queasiness in her stomach was really what had awakened her in the first place, a full half hour before her alarm went off. She sat on the couch in the living room clutching a throw pillow to her body, feeling the chills of nausea course slowly through her. This made her think of Dr. Chang, her obstetrician, and the pills she concealed in the drawer of her night table. If she kept them in the medicine cabinet in the bathroom, Nate might see them. . . .

Dumb, she told herself. This is the worst time to be so up in the air. The worst time not to have something to write, some regimen in the mornings, when work would be the best thing. For several reasons.

She tossed the pillow aside and stood up. Enough, she told herself Take the medicine and go into the office. Write something. Write *anything.*

Barney Fleck's first telephone call was placed at ten in the morning. He sat at his cluttered desk with a cheese Danish and a large plastic cup of Dunkin' Donuts coffee, courtesy of Verna in the outer office, who had a cinnamon donut and tea with lemon. Just like every morning in their eight years together. He lit one of the Viceroys he sometimes smoked when nobody was around and dialed the number Verna had magically produced for him from Vermont information.

"Hartley College," said a woman's voice on the other end of the line.

"Hello," he said. "My name is Barney Fleck. I'm a private investigator, and I'm looking for one of your former students. Whom do I talk to about that?"

"Well, let's see . . . you want admissions, down the hall. Let me connect you."

"Thanks." There was a click, followed by a second ring.

"Admissions. Ms. Cooper speaking. May I help you?"

He smiled. Everybody in places like Vermont was polite! Try getting a greeting like that from a New York college. . . .

But she couldn't help him. Not yet, anyway, It seems Hartley was a very small school, and they'd only introduced computers there about eight years ago. All records of students before that were in some file room somewhere. He gave her the name and the date of admission, and—when she asked what this was about—a cock-and-bull story about a recently deceased distant relative who'd mentioned the student in his will. She promised to call him back just as soon as she could get out of the office and find the file. He gave his phone number, hung up, and inhaled half the Danish in one bite.

Ms. Cooper called back an hour later. By this time, he was wadding notepaper from his desk drawer into balls and shooting at the wastepaper basket he'd placed on the other side of the room. This was his favorite time-killer when waiting for important information. And he had every intention of solving Jillian Talbot's problem as soon as possible.

"Mr. Fleck? I found the file, but there's not much here. The student was only here for one full semester and a month of the second. Then he—well, it appears he was expelled."

"Oh? Why?" he asked. Because he tried to rape three co-eds, he thought.

"I don't have that information. There's just a stamp across the record, TERMNATED. That usually means expulsion . . . oh, well, here's the address and phone number we had for him sixteen years ago . . . ."

Jill stared at the computer screen. It stared back.

She'd been sitting here for a full hour now, ever since staggering from the bathroom, where she'd been sick. Physically, she now felt better. The prescription medicine the obstetrician had given her was doing its job. But she wasn't; the screen was still blank.

How about the rape thing? she thought. A vague story was in her mind, based on an actual recent incident involving a jogger in Central Park. What if they hadn't caught the gang of teenage boys? What if they were still at large, knowing that their victim had managed to retain some incriminating evidence? What if they were tormenting her . . . ?

No. That was too close to her own situation.

Okay, how about the haunted house thing? Again, a story she'd heard once, about a house in upstate New York that seemed to have a mind of its own. No fewer than three sets of tenants had hastly vacated the place after about a month. . . .

No. She'd never dealt with the out-and-out supernatural, and she'd probably end up attaching some prosaic, earthbound solution to it. Dull, dull, dull. She admired Stephen King and Anne Rice and Dean Koontz enormously, but she knew she didn't think like them.

Oh, come *on,* she told herself, grateful that her stomach was feeling better but frustrated by her own lack of concentration. Come *on.* . . .

When the phone rang, Dr. Philbin almost didn't answer it. Then, remembering that she hadn't switched on the answering machine, she glanced at her watch, found that she had five minutes before her first client of the day was due to arrive, and picked up the receiver on her desk.

"Dr. Dorothy Philbin," she murmured.

"Umm, doctor? Umm . . ."

She leaned forward in her chair, immediately curious. A male voice, youngish, clearly nervous, or upset, or both. Now she heard ragged breathing.

"This is Dr. Philbin," she said. "Can I help you?" Dumb, she thought. What a dumb thing for an analyst to say. . . .

Another pause. Then the man said, "Umm, I'm having a little trouble, and I was wondering . . ."

She waited. "Yes?"

"Well, I—I'd like to talk to you if—"

"Excuse me, did someone refer you to me, Mr.—?"

"No, no, nothing like that. Umm, you see, I live near you, and I pass your building every day, and I noticed that brass thing on your door, and—well, I think I'd like to talk to someone. I've never done this, but . . ."

Oh, she thought. An immediate, pressing problem. Someone who has no experience with analysts.

"I see," she said. "Would you call this an emergency, Mr.—?"

Pause. Then, "I guess so." After that, she thought she heard the soft sound of weeping.

She glanced down at her schedule for today, noting the

red line she'd drawn through Mrs. Schwartz, who was entertaining relatives. "It happens that I have an opening at four o'clock this afternoon. Could you be here then?"

No pause this time, but the distinct sound of relief. "Oh, yes! Yes, that would be fine, Dr. Philbin."

She picked up her pen, "Okay. I need your name, address, and telephone number."

"Of course. It's Miller. Franklin Miller. 147 East Tenth Street, apartment 3B." He added a phone number.

This street, she thought, about two blocks east of here. "Very well. I'll see you at four, Mr. Miller."

"Thank you," the man said, and he hung up.

The computer screen was still blank.

With a long sigh, Jill switched off the machine, picked up a yellow legal pad and a pen, and went out into the living room. She threw herself down on the couch and began to scribble every idea she had in her head.

Jogger rape victim. No.

Haunted house. No.

Policewoman blackmail victim. No.

Prostitute/Mafia don/presidential assassinationconspiracy. NO!!!

Oh, God! What the hell was she going to write?!

Staring down at the coffee table, she slowly became aware of the manila envelope. Oh, yes, she remembered: the magazine interview. She dropped the pad and pen, picked up the envelope, and opened it. As she read the double-spaced, typewritten transcript, she shook her head in wonder, nearly laughing at the irony of it.

The projected title of the piece was "Ms. Mystery," and the subheading that would accompany the first, full-page photo read, "With her fourth novel, *The Mind of Alice Lanyon*, JILLIAN TALBOT renews her claim to the throne

146

as America's Queen of Suspense." The article that followed was similarly gushing.

"So, where does a nice New York girl come up with such violent ideas?"

"Well, I start by reading the New York newspapers . . . ."

"How does it feel to win an Edgar Award?"

"Very nice, thank you. . . ."

"Tell me about Nathaniel Levin, the hot new artist who is the current man in your life. . . ."

"Oh, he's wonderful . . . great artist . . . we both love to dance . . . we both love the Mets . . . and we both hate giving interviews . . . ."

(Laughter.)

"Oh, that's marvelous, Jill! Now. Your home is lovely. What made you choose Greenwich Village . . . ?"

She stared down at the words, wondering whom they were discussing. Who was this charming, carefree, talented woman the journalist so obviously admired, with the wonderful home and the wonderful lover and the marvelous sense of humor? Now it all seemed so macabre. She knew, even as she read the article, that her life would now be forever separated in her mind into two distinct categories: B.V. and A.V. Before Valentine and . . .

After. Oh, God, was there going to *be* an After Valentine? What if he's more than a nuisance? What if he's—

The dead rat, staring up from the carpet.

—dangerous?

"I love Greenwich Village. I think so many creative people live here because . . . ."

With a little cry of disgust, she tossed the article onto the coffee table. Enough of that, she thought. I *will* get through this! This creep—Victor Dimorta, or whoever the hell it is—will *not* prevail. I'm going to—

Then, unheralded, Mary's suggestion from last night crept into her mind.

Yes, she thought. Yesss . . .

With a sudden, overwhelming sense of confidence, and of relief, Jill went back into the office and picked up the phone.

Barney slammed down the phone in sheer frustration. Verna, in the adjacent office, probably winced at the sound before returning to her perusal of today's *New York Times*.

Damn! he thought. Now what?

He leaned down to the phone and pressed the intercom button. Ignoring the fact that the door between them was wide open, that they were separated by a mere twelve feet, he whispered, "Mrs. Poole, would you come in here, please? Bring your notebook."

He smiled, his frustration dissipating into wicked delight as he heard the rustle of the newspaper being slammed down, the creak as she vacated her chair, and the tapping of her shoes as she came into the room and stood on the other side of his desk, smiling. She did not have her notebook: the intercom was an old joke between them, and neither could remember now how it had begun.

"Yes, Barney?" she said.

He grinned. "Verna, I need the benefit of your excellent advice."

She returned the grin. "Shoot."

"It seems Victor Dimorta no longer resides at 7 Franklin Street, Mill City, Pennsylvania. All I get at the number the college gave me is a recording. 'The number you have dialed has been disconnected. . .' So I called Information for the area, and there are no Dimortas listed. Period. What should I do now?"

Verna straightened up, stared indulgently down at him for a moment, and reached down to pick up the paper with the Dimorta information.

"*You* are gonna go down and have lunch," she said in her most maternal tone. "The Argonaut. Take your time. Bring me back a turkey and Swiss on rye, lettuce, no tomato, Thousand Island dressing but not too much, and tea with lemon. You're buying. I'll get on this right away."

With a smile, she turned and went back into the outer office. When he passed her moments later on his way to the door, she was already speaking into her phone.

"Hello, I'd like the number of the Mill City Town Hall . . ."

Barney went down to the Greek diner on the corner where he had lunch more often than not. He sat at the counter and had the roast beef special, shooting the breeze with Mr. Colouris, the proprietor. They talked about football and politics, two subjects on which Mr. Colouris was the world's leading authority. When Barney had killed about an hour, he collected Verna's order and ambled back down the frozen sidewalk to his building and up to the fifth floor.

Verna was scribbling shorthand a mile a minute. Her notebook was in front of her, the phone to her ear, and she wrote as she listened. She didn't glance up as he placed the bag with her lunch on the desk, but she immediately reached into it and grabbed the tea.

"Uh-huh . . . uh-huh . . ." was her contribution to whatever conversation was taking place.

He went back into his office, removed his coat and gloves, and sat. He'd shot nearly fifty wadded pieces of paper into the trash can, making only about ten of them, when he heard Verna slam down her phone. She came into his office, flipping through several pages of her

149

notepad, rereading everything she'd just written. At last she looked up at him. Her face was white, he noticed, her eyes wide.

"You are not gonna *believe* this!" she whispered.

Thirty minutes later Jill greeted Barney Fleck at the door, hung his coat in the front closet, and waved him into a chair. She'd just made a pot of herbal tea, so she got two mugs and put them down on the coffee table. Then she sat on the couch across from him, pushing the useless yellow legal pad aside.

"So," she said. "What are you so excited about?"

Barney regarded her a moment, licked his lips, and began. "Well, it seems we may be on to something here. I mean about Victor Dimorta. Are you ready for this?—he murdered his parents. About two weeks after he was expelled from Hartley College. Did twelve years in prison. Then—and you're *not* gonna believe this; *I* don't believe it!—he was paroled. *Paroled*! 'Model prisoner,' no less! He's been out for four years now. And here's the punch line: not long after his release—about two months, to be exact—Mr. Victor Dimorta disappeared from the face of the earth! Hasn't been seen or heard from since. Do you *love* this?!"

"No," Jill murmured, staring, "I don't. I don't love this at all."

"Yeah," the detective agreed.

There was a pause as they simultaneously reached for their mugs and took long sips. Then she said, "Tell me about the murders."

Barney pulled a wrinkled sheaf of pages from his pocket. He studied them a moment, his brow furrowing as he apparently tried to make head or tail of someone else's handwriting. She glanced over at the pages. Shorthand.

The secretary, probably . . .

"Okay," he said at last. "Here goes. On February sixteenth of that year Victor was expelled from Hartley, and he returned to his home in a place called Mill City, Pennsylvania. Small town, despite the name, about seventy miles northeast of Pittsburgh. Paper mill, long since defunct. Kind of a ghost town. Anyway, the father"—he consulted his notes—"Joseph Dimorta, lost his job as foreman at the mill when the paper company relocated. Drank, messed with women, abused Mrs. D. and Victor. . . ."

She sat there, listening to the whole strange, disgusting yet somehow inevitable story. Despite his terrible home life, Victor was apparently brilliant in school, showing a distinct talent for English. His high school English teacher had told him about her alma mater, Hartley, and even spoken to one of her former professors there about him. Result: partial scholarship to Hartley. But only partial, which is where the story took a turn. It seems Victor didn't tell his parents about the college, but he had some money of his own, from his maternal grandmother. He ran away to Hartley. During the intercession, he stayed at an inexpensive motel near the campus, waiting tables in the motel's restaurant. One month into his second semester—well, Jill knew all about that. The parents were called by the authorities at the school, and the Dimortas actually drove to Vermont and collected Victor. When they got home (according to Victor's attorney), the father beat Victor within an inch of his life and locked him in an upstairs closet for three days. It was not the first time, either, the public defender claimed: Victor was used to that particular punishment.

Angela Dimorta was an ineffectual woman. She had allowed herself to be victimized by a bully, and she never

151

interfered with the mistreatment of Victor. This is what had signed her death warrant.

On the night of February 29, two weeks after his expulsion from Hartley, Victor Dimorta crept into the bedroom where his parents were sleeping and cut their throats with a large carving knife from the kitchen. Mrs. Dimorta died instantly, but Mr. Dimorta had obviously struggled. The next-door neighbor heard the commotion and called the police. Victor was arrested thirty minutes later: they found him crouching in his bedroom closet, sobbing. It was clear to everyone that Victor had acted as a result of years of physical and psychological abuse. His youth was considered, and the incident at Hartley College wasn't even mentioned. The case never came to trial: the prosecutor offered a plea bargain, and Victor received fifteen to thirty years on each of two counts of voluntary manslaughter, to be served concurrently. He was originally sent to the maximum-security section of the nearest state facility, but after three years of good behavior there he was transferred to its medium-security section, downgraded when the warden and a review board deemed him unlikely as a threat to society in general.

Just as he was completing his twelfth year of confinement, he came up for parole. He had an excellent record, having spent much time in various rehabilitation programs and even teaching English to the other inmates for several years, all of which helped to reduce the minimum time. His interviews with state authorities and a psychiatrist reviewing his case went very well, and the prison was overcrowded, not to mention the long waiting list, so parole was granted. He left the penitentiary and checked into a rooming house in Pittsburgh. With the help of the parole officer assigned to him, he got a job in the stockroom of a local department store. He met with the parole officer once a week for seven weeks.

Then he vanished.

"It wasn't just like he disappeared," Barney was saying, "but like he never even *existed!* He was just gone—poof! They searched like crazy, but . . ." He shrugged and leaned back in the chair.

Jill sat silently for a long time, digesting this. She noticed that her stomach was churning again, but she knew that for once the baby was not the cause.

"What now?" she said at last.

The large, friendly detective leaned forward again.

"Well," he said, "I've been thinkin'. . . ."

He sat in the window across the street from Jillian Talbot's apartment, listening. His eyes were tightly shut, and he was remembering. The hot tears burned his hot cheeks.

When he heard the detective's idea and saw Jillian Talbot rise and go into her office, he wiped his eyes and nodded slowly to himself.

Jill came out of the office and handed Barney the yearbook.

"All the names and addresses are in the last section at the back," she told him. "The entire graduating class. I don't know how up-to-date they are. . . ."

"S'okay," he said, smiling to reassure her. "Verna's a whiz at updating information with that computer of hers. I'll call you."

She nodded and saw him to the door. After he had gone, she went back to the couch and picked up the yellow legal pad. She sat staring at it for a long while. Then, with a sigh, she tossed it aside and went back into her office to call Nate.

Tenth Street in New York City is a relatively quiet thoroughfare, no more so than at four o'clock in the afternoon. It is a full hour before rush hour, and, as it is more residential than business-oriented, there are few people around. Almost anything can happen without anyone noticing.

When the doorbell rang, Dr. Dorothy Philbin was alone in her office. She had seen her three o'clock patient out some ten minutes ago, and she was reading over the notes she had just jotted down during the session and was contemplating going up to the kitchen for a cup of coffee. She had been a widow for four years now, so she lived alone. Lately she'd been thinking about selling this large, three-story townhouse and getting a small apartment uptown, closer to her daughter and grandchildren.

So much for a cup of coffee, she thought when she heard the bell. She rose from her leather chair, straightened her gray suit, and went out to open the front door. A tall, nervous young man stood on the doorstep, a man she'd never seen before.

"Mr. Miller?" she said.

"Yes, Dr. Philbin." He made a vague attempt at smiling, but he was clearly preoccupied. Distraught, she decided.

"Come in," she said. He went past her into the reception room, and she closed and locked the door and led him back into the main office. He stood in the middle of the room as she walked by him on her way to the desk.

"Now," she began, "what seems to be the—"

They were her final words. She never saw the knife.

It was over in a matter of seconds. Then, he lowered her gently to the floor and slipped out the basement door to the street. In less than a minute he was at the corner. He turned onto Fifth Avenue and was gone.

Eleven of the twelve enormous paintings were lined up along the two side walls of the room. The largest, *Life,* dominated the entire back wall. It was before this one that the four of them were standing at nine o'clock that evening.

Jill regarded the picture, wondering what to make of it. The Seven Ages of Man were easy: Shakespeare had generously supplied the text for them some four hundred years ago. Nate had agreed that dividing the famous speech from *As You Like It* into seven successive paragraphs in the brochure was the sensible thing to do. The Four Seasons would each get a passage of appropriate poetry, again from Shakespeare. The unspoken agreement between artist and writer was that the quotes be uniform. The final painting would need something from the Bard on the subject of the human condition, but what . . . ? She stared at the vivid, swirling masses of bright color, and at the tiny core of pure white near the center. Is that God? she wondered. The human mind? The soul? She didn't want to ask him, and he may not be able to explain it to her, anyway. This dramatic panel was what he *felt* about life, obviously. He probably didn't have words for it.

"It's interesting," she said to him now. "I deal in words, you in images, and yet we're both doing the same thing. . . ."

Standing next to her before the panel, he squeezed her hand and leaned down to kiss her hair in answer.

"Do you two want to be alone?" Tara asked from behind them. "I mean, if all this raw creativity makes you just want to tear each other's clothes off, or something, I'm sure Doug and I can amuse ourselves elsewhere."

Everyone laughed. Well, everyone but Doug Baron, Jill noticed as she turned from the painting to face the others. She wondered about him again. All through dinner at the

Ukrainian restaurant down the street, she'd constantly caught him looking at her, felt his eyes on her. Tara is the one he should be looking at, she thought. She remembered her friend's words from the night before: Tara had mentioned that his dead wife, the fashion model, bore a passing resemblance to her. She wondered if that explained his frequent furtive glances. . . .

It leaped into her mind all of a sudden, and she would never know what had made her think of it. She whirled around to once again confront the big, final painting in the series. She looked at the bright, vibrant assortment of colors, and then her eyes traveled to the small, almost discreet spot of white pulsating in the center. Was it enlightenment? Hope? Immortality?

Then, thinking of her own private relationship with the artist who had created it, she knew what it was. And before she was aware of it, she spoke Miranda's words from *The Tempest*.

"O wonder!
How many goodly creatures are there here!
How beauteous mankind is! O brave new world,
That has such people in't!"

There was silence in the room as everyone regarded the painting. The quiet was broken by Doug Baron's reverential whisper.

"Yes," he said. "*Yes!*"

He turned to stare quite openly at Jill.

TWO YEARS AGO

WHEN VICTOR DIMORTA ARRIVED IN BUFFALO ON January 25, he discovered that Belinda Rosenberg no longer lived at her old address. He called every Rosenberg in the Buffalo phone book until he got her mother. He told her he was an old friend of Belinda's from Hartley College, in town on business. The mother told him about Colorado.

Forty-eight hours later, January 27, he was in the woods near her hillside home above Boulder, watching Belinda Rosenberg Kessler through binoculars.

On January 27, Belinda came home from the ski lodge early to make a special dinner. She stopped at the supermarket downtown to get all the ingredients for her husband's favorite meal: sirloin steak, baked potatoes, sour cream, salad, and New York cheesecake from the gourmet counter. She even remembered tortilla chips and salsa, and the blue cheese for the salad dressing.

She smiled to herself as she loaded her cart, wondering what her mother would make of Jake's favorite meal. Leah Rosenberg, though by no means Orthodox, had kept at least loosely to the rules when it came to food. Jacob Kessler, three generations removed from the last Orthodox Kessler, was only reminded of such things at weddings and funerals. He, like both his parents, was a self-described "Jewish atheist," and his favorite joke was his Conservative paternal grandmother's definition of Reform Jews

157

("Catholics!"). Belinda, a Reform Jew, always laughed at that.

She went down the street to the liquor store for the two bottles she'd had the proprietor put aside, her husband's favorite burgundy. As an afterthought, she added a bottle of Perrier-Jouët to her purchase. Yes, she thought as she loaded the back of the station wagon. A glass of champagne in lieu of cocktails. With chips and salsa, no less. Oh, well, it's what he likes. . . .

She drove up the hill and turned into the driveway. The house was situated on a cliff that afforded a lovely view of the city, separated from its nearest clifftop neighbors by thick groves of evergreens. The stone-and-wood structure was predominantly glass: large picture windows and sliding doors leading out to the wraparound veranda. She smiled again as she took the bags from the back of the car and went inside. She loved this house. She'd loved it from the moment she'd first seen it ten years ago.

Romeo was stretched out on the living room couch, and Juliet was asleep on the shag carpet nearby. As Belinda came in with the bags and headed for the kitchen, the male Siamese hopped down from the couch and followed her. She put the bags down on the counter and turned on the oven just as the wall phone next to the refrigerator began to ring. She wriggled out of her coat as she answered it.

It was her sister, Jessica, calling from Buffalo. Belinda's parents had already called earlier in the day to tell her to expect a package in the mail. She accepted Jessie's congratulations and spent the next fifteen minutes catching up on family news. As she hung up the phone and turned to unpack the grocery bags, she thought she saw something, some slight movement, in the trees outside the kitchen window. No, she decided, just the wind.

Besides, it was nearly too dark to see anything out there.

She looked at the kitchen clock: quarter to six. Get a move on, she thought.

When the steak came out of the bag, Romeo leaped up onto the counter and rubbed against her arm. She laughed as she placed the meat in the fridge and turned to stroke him.

"Sorry, darling, not for you."

With a low growl of indignation, he turned his back on her, jumped down, and went over to the corner. A moment later, Belinda heard the small crunching sounds as he attacked his Cat Chow in frustration. Romeo and Jake, she thought: my men are addicted to steak. Juliet, like Belinda, preferred fish.

The phone rang again. It was Toni, her best friend, whom she'd just left at the lodge an hour ago. Yes, she'd gotten everything for dinner. No, Jake wasn't home yet. Yes, she'd see Toni tomorrow. Toni congratulated her again. Belinda thanked her friend and hung up.

She quickly made the salad and the dressing, putting them in the fridge with the meat and the cheesecake and the champagne. She wrapped two potatoes in foil and placed them in the oven. She had a little trouble uncorking the burgundy, as she'd never quite gotten the hang of corkscrews. She set the open bottle on the counter to breathe, patted Romeo on the head as he ate, and went down the hall to the bedroom.

After a brief, hot shower, she stood naked before the bathroom mirror, applying fresh makeup. She regarded herself critically as she worked, thinking, not bad for thirty-five. Her dark hair looked just as it had in college, thick and glossy, and not a speck of gray. Her figure was similarly intact: her breasts and thighs were as firm as ever, and her stomach as flat, thanks to all the skiing. She winked at her own reflection, and laughed again. Her large brown eyes had always been her best asset.

Yes, she thought as she sprayed herself with Jake's favorite cologne. I'll do.

The heat was on: good. She could wear Jake's favorite dress, the midnight-blue silk with the short hemline and the low neckline. Where were the blue heels . . . ? She found them, fastened a single gold strand around her neck, and went out to set the table in the dining room. They would eat there this evening, not on the veranda, which she would have preferred. It was cold outside now, but at least it probably wouldn't snow. The darkening sky above Boulder was clear.

Back in the kitchen, she noticed that Juliet had awakened and joined her brother on the counter. A stern look from Belinda was all it took to send them both leaping to the floor. They knew better than that. She smiled as she thought this: she and Jake had decided at the outset not to have children, and Romeo and Juliet were obviously filling the void.

She was putting the salsa and chips in the functional but rather hideous Mexican ceramic bowls that had been a wedding gift from a distant cousin, when the phone rang again.

"Hello."

"Hi, honey."

"Jake! Darling, where are you? I was just getting—"

"Listen, I'm up to my eyeballs here, and I don't know how late I'm going to be. We're waiting to hear from New York about those Fremont contracts, you know, the new client I told you about? Then I have to draw up the new—"

"Whoa! Give me a bottom line here: are you coming home for dinner?"

"Oh, gosh, I'm sitting here with sandwiches. Ellie just went out for more coffee for everybody. I told you I might be late tonight. You weren't holding dinner for me, were you?"

Belinda stared down at the salsa. "No. I—I'm just about to throw something together for myself. You do the contracts, or whatever, and I'll see you when you get home."

"Okay, honey. Don't wait up. Love—"

And he was gone.

She replaced the receiver. She stood at the counter, looking down at the food. She wasn't sure how long she'd been standing there when she felt one of the cats rubbing against her leg. With a little shake of her head, she took the potatoes out of the oven, put them in the refrigerator with the salsa, recorked the burgundy, and went back to her bedroom to take off the dress.

In her bathrobe, she reheated a baked potato and ate it with a little of the salad. She took another shower, washing her hair and scrubbing the makeup from her face. She made a cup of tea, got into bed, and read for a while. At ten o'clock, she picked up the remote from the night table, clicked on the bedroom television, and watched the news. When it was over, she turned off the television, switched off the bedside lamp, and lay for a long time staring up at the ceiling.

Jake arrived home just after eleven. She could tell from the way he dropped his clothes on his way to the bathroom that he was exhausted. He climbed in beside her, kissed her on the forehead, and immediately fell asleep. She lay there, watching him sleep for a while before returning her attention to the ceiling. Her husband's even breathing was the only sound she heard as she silently wept.

161

January 27: their tenth anniversary.

He wasn't able to follow his established pattern with Belinda Rosenberg Kessler, and this was frustrating for him. He would have preferred to approach her romantically, as he had approached Sharon Williams. He also had an idea, a fantasy that had first developed in prison, of sending cards and gifts in the days leading up to it, and signing them "Valentine." And, when he finally decided on his means, he knew the idea of a candy box was out: there wouldn't be any time. But at least he could use the music. . . .

The husband worked in a big law firm downtown, racking up an impressive number of billable hours six days a week. The law firm widow had turned to Colorado's chief form of solace: skiing. She was a fanatic. Almost every day, she strapped her skis to the roof of her station wagon and took off for several hours of blissful schussing and slaloming. She was usually in the company of her best friend, another enthusiast named Toni Stanton, who happened to be a swinging single.

One look at Toni, and Victor knew he had his opportunity. She was tall and slender, athletic-looking, very pretty. She had blue-gray eyes and curly, dark blond hair. If he couldn't romance Belinda, at least Toni would provide a roundabout way of achieving the same purpose. Whenever the two women were at the lodge, Toni spent as much time on the prowl as she did skiing.

Victor had never skied in his life, but he learned in record time. He laid down a considerable amount to engage the best pro on the premises. Three hours a day for a solid week, the former Olympic bronze medalist worked exclusively with Victor, and the result was impressive.

He called himself Leonard this time, and he gave

himself an Italian last name, Vaneti, because it sounded good: many famous skiers, like racing-car drivers, were Italian, and he figured he might as well use his own nationality. When the pro asked him why he had to become an expert so fast, he grinned and pointed at his crotch, and the two men shared a lascivious laugh.

Getting the pro to introduce him to Toni was a breeze. Getting Toni to introduce him to Belinda was inevitable.

The first thing he noticed about the second Element when he saw her up close was that her pretty nose was slightly crooked. Remembering why, he grinned as he shook her hand.

"B'lin, this is Leonard Vaneti. Len, meet my best friend, Belinda Kessler."

"How do you do?" the tall, handsome man said. Then he grinned and shook her hand. She had just come into the lobby of the ski lodge, and she was a few minutes late. She had expected to find Toni alone and restless, looking pointedly at her watch as she usually did under the circumstances. But no; Toni was sitting near the fireplace with the handsome stranger, and they were laughing together. When Belinda came in, Toni jumped up and grabbed the man's hand, pulling him across the room. She was wearing her tightest sweater, Belinda noticed, and more makeup than she usually bothered with at the lodge. So, this was the mystery man Toni had been hinting about for the last three days.

"Hello, Mr. Vaneti," Belinda said as they shook hands.

"Len," he said.

She smiled. "Belinda."

Toni pointed toward the dining room off the lobby. "I thought we'd have lunch before we hit the snow. How does that sound?"

"Fine," Belinda murmured. The two women always had lunch here before skiing: Toni's announcement was by way of including Len in today's schedule. Well, why not? she thought as the three headed for the restaurant. He looks like a nice guy, and some of Toni's recent dates had been downright unbearable. Good old Toni, always searching. She thanked Heaven for Jake, despite his preoccupation with the law firm and his tendency to forget things like birthdays and anniversaries. At least he loved her, and he came home every night. She couldn't imagine being on her own, looking for Mr. Right—or, as Toni was so fond of saying, Mr. Right Now.

Len held their chairs for them as they were seated at the table by the window. Belinda smiled again: this room, with its large glass wall affording a panoramic view of the slopes and the Rockies rising majestically behind them, always reminded her of the cafeteria at Hartley. For that matter, Toni had always rather reminded her of Sharon Williams. I'm always following the leader, Belinda thought as she ordered *salade Niçoise* and coffee.

"So, Len," she said after they'd ordered, "do you live here in Boulder?"

"No, I'm from L.A. I'm a freelance photographer. Magazine stuff, mostly. I'm getting together some shots for a piece on winter sports. Well, that's what I'm *supposed* to be doing. . . ." He smiled, glancing over at Toni.

Toni beamed. "Can I help it if I'm a femme fatale? You should have seen him the other day, B'lin. Franz was giving him pointers on skiing, and he was wobbling all over the place with this camera around his neck, Finally Franz suggested that maybe he'd do better to lose the camera. I, being a good neighbor, went over and offered to hold it. And you won't *believe* what he said when he saw me!"

Belinda, who'd heard similar stories before, smiled. "Try me."

"He said, 'Franz, who is this gorgeous creature?' And Franz said, 'This is Toni Stanton, the woman you've been staring at for the last week!' I mean, how's *that* for meeting cute?"

" 'Meeting cute'?" Len asked.

"Sure," Toni explained. "That's what they call it in the movies. Like Cary Grant and Audrey Hepburn in *Charade*—who met at a ski lodge, incidentally. With that awful little boy who kept shooting them with his water pistol. They admitted that they both wanted to murder him, and that's what they had in common. Meeting cute."

Everyone laughed as lunch arrived before them. Belinda decided that she liked Len. He was obviously intelligent, and he seemed to be very interested in Toni. Something in their shyness with each other told Belinda that the two of them hadn't yet become intimate. But knowing Toni, she knew it was simply a matter of time.

When they told her about their tentative plan to ski together next Thursday, and invited her to join them, she almost said no. It was Valentine's Day, and she figured they would probably want to be alone together. Besides, she really should think of something to do with Jake. . . .

Later that afternoon, in the ladies' room, Toni talked her into it.

"Oh, please come with us, B'lin. He's very nice, and all that, but he's kind of quiet with me. Lunch today was the most relaxed I've seen him: I think a third party is just what the doctor ordered, at least until—well, you know . . . ."

Belinda knew. She also knew that her husband would be working on Valentine's Day. So she'd be the "third party" for Toni and her new man, then go home and try the steak dinner again.

"Okay," she said.

At home that night, after dinner, she told her husband about Toni's new boyfriend and the plans for Thursday. Jake was slouched in his favorite armchair, reading— another contract or agreement, from the look of it. He uttered a small sound of acknowledgment, but she wasn't sure that he'd heard her.

The slope was known by the regulars at the lodge as Dead Man's Folly. It was the highest and the longest, and there were a couple of difficult passages, especially halfway down. At the end of his week's instruction, Franz had declared him ready for it. The two men skied down the slope twice, and Franz congratulated "Len" on his expert work. He'd never had a better student, he claimed, or a faster learner.

Victor booked a room at the lodge for the evening of Valentine's Day and made a reservation for dinner in the restaurant. He knew that he and Toni would not be having dinner there or spending the night, but the reservations were important. They would be joined by Belinda for lunch and skiing that day, and then Belinda was to discreetly disappear while he and Toni consummated their new relationship. That's what the women thought, anyway. . . .

When "Len" suggested Dead Man's Folly, Toni and Belinda readily agreed. And that is how he got them there after lunch on February 14. He waited while a group went up on the lift and skied down, then he led the women outside. He carefully inspected the other people around; nobody else was currently headed for their destination. No witnesses. Good.

It was a beautiful day, he noted with pleasure as the lift

carried them up the hill. The air was cold and crisp, and the sun bore down on the snow, making the lodge and the slopes stand out in sharp definition—a heightened realism, the phrase he'd learned in photography class in prison. A beautiful day to die.

The two women had done the trail many times before, so "Len" suggested that he should go between them. Toni first, wait two minutes, then "Len" would follow her tracks. Belinda, the best skier of the three, would follow two minutes behind him. The two-minute thing had been explained by the pro: a safeguard against faster followers crashing into slower preceders on this particular narrow, often treacherous slope.

Perfect.

Toni took off, and he waited two minutes. Then he flew smoothly down to the place that he'd chosen after his first two trips, halfway down the mountain and approximately thirty feet from a cliff edge. Over that edge was a nearly, vertical, three-hundred-foot drop into a ravine, a small canyon around the side of the mountain from the resort.

When he arrived at his chosen place, he braked, moved off the trail toward the cliff, removed his skis, lay down in the snow, and waited.

She stood at the top of the hill, counting off two minutes on her watch. As she waited, she thought about Jake.

He hadn't forgotten their anniversary, after all. The morning after the missed dinner, he'd announced over breakfast that as soon as he could get away from the office, maybe as early as March, they were going on a two-week vacation. His plan had been to spend a week with her family in Buffalo, then a week with his folks in New York City. But Belinda had now come up with a better idea:

three days in Buffalo, three days in New York—and a week in Puerto Rico, just the two of them. Neither of them had ever been there, and Jake had often mentioned a longheld desire to see the Caribbean.

She gazed down at the endless fields of snow, thinking, Puerto Rico. Yes. Swimming and scuba diving and getting tans. Dancing to salsa bands every evening on tropical verandas. Rich Hispanic food and exotic, fruity drinks. They could even try windsurfing. Best of all, they would be together, blissfully alone. No families, no friends, and no law firm. Heaven!

Her two minutes had passed, she noticed. Shaking away thoughts of palm trees and lying naked with her husband under a slow ceiling fan, she lowered her goggles over her face, planted her poles and shoved off. As she glided down the first part of the slope, the familiar thrill suffused her. This was the reason she so enjoyed skiing, this rush as she gained momentum on her way down. She giggled as the wind flew by her, thinking, We can water ski in Puerto Rico. . . .

Then, as she came around the steep curve nearly halfway down the slope, she saw something dark off to the side, at the edge of her field of vision.

Someone—Len!—was lying in the snow several yards from the trail.

When Belinda came along, he cried out in pain to get her attention. She immediately braked and came over to him. He lay still, listening to the approaching crunching sounds as she moved awkwardly, crablike, toward him on her skis. He breathed deeply, evenly, enjoying the thrill of anticipation that filled him as he waited. She arrived beside him, leaned over, and asked him if he was hurt.

He looked up into her face, now a mask of concern. Then, to her obvious surprise, he smiled. He reached

168

slowly into the pocket of his down jacket, pulled out the tiny cassette player, and pressed the play button.

Sarah Vaughan.

"My Funny Valentine."

She stared down, confused, not getting it at all. In a flash, he was on his feet beside her. Even as he did so, he regretted the need for haste. He would have preferred to draw this out, to savor it, but there was no time.

"I'm Victor Dimorta," he said. "Happy Valentine's Day!"

If there had ever been a moment—and there hadn't—when he had considered sparing Belinda Rosenberg, now Kessler, her next action would have changed his mind in any case. She slowly raised her gaze to stare at his face, and her voice when she spoke rang with genuine puzzlement.

"Who?"

He returned her stare, feeling his exhilaration transform into dangerous rage. It filled him, surging through his chest, hot against his cold face. He flushed with indignation.

She didn't remember him.

He knew the importance of speed in this enterprise, but his next action was so swift and sudden that it even surprised him. He raised his fist and sent it crashing into her nose, breaking it for a second time. With a small sound more like a sigh than a cry, she fell flat on her back. Her dark hair tumbled out the sides of her parka and the blood began to trickle from her nostrils as she continued to stare up at him, her confusion turning slowly to pain.

Victor Dimorta stared down at her, laughing. "Yeah, you remember *that*, don't you, bitch!" Then he leaned down and shouted into her startled face. "*Victor Dimorta, you miserable little turd! Hartley College! Valentine's Day! You and the others, the Elements. You got me expelled,* asshole!"

Then, controlling the rage that threatened to overtake him, he took a deep breath, leaned farther down, and kissed her on the lips.

"You're going to die now, Belinda," he whispered softly, caressingly, like a lover. "Happy Valentine's Day!"

It happened so fast that Belinda's panicked mind barely had time to register the fact that these were her final moments on earth. He was shouting, and then he kissed her, and then he was whispering. Then, in a flash, she was being lifted up in his amazingly powerful arms. And all the while, the beautiful voice continued to sing "My Funny Valentine."

My funny valentine . . .

Victor Dimorta.

Oh, God! Victor Dimorta!

There was one last second of lucidity, of sanity, as she stared up into his smiling face, so unlike Victor Dimorta's face.

"My husband," she whispered as he carried her over to the edge.

He continued to smile.

"Tough luck, bitch," he said, and then he released her.

And his face was gone, his arms were gone, and she was moving, or something, and she could hear a great whistling of wind rushing past her, and she was freezing, *freezing,* and she was—

Falling! Oh, my God, I'm *falling!* But it can't be, I *can't* be falling I can't be falling oh please God don't let me fall I have to be okay I have to live I have to live I have to go to Puerto Rico with my—

He watched as her body smashed into a ledge some fifty feet below him. Then she bounced off and out into the air before plunging down. She fell and fell, landing at last in a snowdrift far below him and tumbling down the rest of the way into the little ravine beside the mountain. After that, she disappeared into the trees.

And that was the end of Belinda Rosenberg Kessler.

He smiled as he looked down, thinking:

Two.

Then he moved. In seconds, he smoothed down all telltale tracks in the snow, reattached his skis, and followed her trail up several yards. He came down, veering toward the cliff, stopping just short of the edge. He nearly fell over himself, but the danger produced a pleasant thrill. Then he took off the skis, tiptoed back to the trail—being sure to cover these last tracks—put on the skis again, and made it down the slope in no time flat. He and Toni waited at the bottom for Belinda to join them.

Fifteen minutes later, when she had not made an appearance, Toni ran to find the pro. He took off on the lift, then radioed down that there appeared to have been an accident. A group was quickly dispatched around the side of the mountain.

It took them nearly an hour to find her.

He spent the rest of that afternoon comforting Toni as she sobbed, and he remained inconspicuously in the background when the police and the paramedics and the dazed husband arrived. When the reporters showed up, he and Toni made brief statements. His greatest challenge that day was to keep a straight face, to look appropriately horrified and saddened when all he could feel was a tremendous sense of elation. Finally, Toni took Jacob Kessler by the arm and led him away. As they left, she called to Len over her shoulder that she was going to drive Jake home, and that she'd call him later at his hotel. He nodded and waved.

Then he went back to his hotel, packed, and headed for the airport.

CHAPTER 8

Friday, February 6

Jill was feeling better today. Nate had brought her home in a cab from his place late last night, and he had stayed over. He'd left her sleeping early this morning. The note on the bathroom mirror informed her that the framer was arriving at his studio early, and he would call her later. The slight dizziness she'd felt on rising had dissipated in the shower, and now she was ready for what she must do. In fact, she realized as she went into the kitchen to put on the water for tea, she was looking forward to it.

Elaine Williams stood up from the bed and made her way over to the bureau on the other side of her spacious bedroom. Accompanied by the sounds of the surf below and her own beating heart, she picked up the silver-framed photograph of her husband, Walter, and her daughter, Sharon, and kissed both images.

That done, she dropped her gauzy nightgown to the floor and proceeded into her marble-lined, gold-fixtured bathroom. She reached into the shower and turned on the hot water. Every day began with a shower: the prescription pills that were now her only means of sleeping left her groggy and disoriented, and there was another reason as well. Hydrotherapy, she thought, as she did every day of her life. Comfort: a temporary balm.

She was just stepping into the scalding shower when the

low, discreet knock came at her bedroom door. Jenny, the new maid, came cautiously into the bedroom.

"Good morning, madam," she whispered to the older woman who stood naked in the bathroom doorway. "Are you ready for breakfast?"

"Yes, thank you, Jenny," Elaine replied, turning her attention back to the shower.

Fifteen minutes later, dressed now in the blue caftan her late husband had so loved, she was seated at the glass-topped, wrought-iron table on the redwood sundeck of her immense Pacific Palisades home. She rang the tiny silver bell and waited patiently for the shy little maid to bring her usual coffee and toast. No more hearty breakfasts for her: the very act of eating was now a chore.

Jenny was placing the silver coffee service and toast rack before her when the phone rang in the living room. She poured a cup and waited as the maid went to answer. Moments later, the girl arrived once again beside her chair.

"A call for you, madam," Jenny whispered. "From New York."

Elaine glanced at the diamond-studded Cartier watch she always wore, a gift from her daughter. Nine o'clock, she thought. New York. Who on earth . . . ?

"Very well, Jenny," she said at last. The little maid trotted dutifully over to get the extension from the cabinet in the sideboard near the table, plugged it in, and placed it next to her mistress. With a nod from Elaine, she vanished back into the house.

Elaine regarded the telephone for several seconds. Then, with a sigh, she raised the receiver to her ear.

"Hello," she said.

She listened to the hearty male voice on the other end of the line. Then, when his words came through to her, assaulting her consciousness, she involuntarily opened her tightly clenched hand, sending the receiver crashing to the sundeck with a loud thud.

The deep blue water of the wind-whipped Pacific gradually appeared before her eyes. She looked out at the water, and at the white gulls dancing against it, searching for their own breakfast. Then, as her other senses once again became active, she heard the muffled voice of the man on the telephone.

"Hello? Hello?"

With a long, ragged sigh, Elaine reached down and picked up the receiver. Then she took another deep, painful breath and began to speak.

Jill came out of her building at twelve-thirty, gasping at the sudden assault of freezing air. Her first, instinctive act was a quick search of the street in both directions. Neighbors coming and going, warmly bundled small children playing with a ball, tradespeople: okay. She tightened the wool scarf around her neck, buttoned the top button of her heavy wool coat, and set off in the direction of Fifth Avenue.

She had reached the corner of Sixth Avenue and Tenth Street, glancing surreptitiously around and behind her several times, before she remembered about Gwen. She'd called the unlisted number from home yesterday, but all she'd gotten was a beep that indicated a message machine. She'd left her brief message—"Hi, folks, it's Jill. I'm thinking about taking you up on your offer. I'll call you tomorrow morning, so somebody stay near the phone. 'Bye."—and hung up.

Gwen and Mike Feldman were writer friends, introduced to her at a Mystery Writers of America reception three years ago by Mary Daley, their mutual agent. She'd read the clever mystery novels they wrote together under the name G. M. Feldman, and they turned out to be fans of hers as well. She was immediately attracted to their normality and their mutual sense of amusement at the world. Gwen was a small, friendly Earth Mother-type who had begun to despair of ever finding Mr. Right. Then her three married younger sisters had talked her into going on a Caribbean singles cruise. There she had met the big, bearded fellow writer, whose buddies had put *him* up to the trip. Now they were thinking about having children. This possibility had necessitated fresh income to supplement their modestly successful mysteries, so a few months ago they had bought a defunct summer camp on the eastern tip of Long Island and converted it into a writers' colony. This week was their first in business, and they had asked Jill to come. She had begged off at first, but now she had changed her mind.

Looking down at the watch on her gloved hand, she realized that morning was technically over. She'd better call immediately. If she waited until she got home, she might miss them again.

She walked over to the open-air phone booth on the opposite comer. Placing her bag on the little shelf below the phone, she spent several moments fishing for her wallet. I have entirely too much stuff in here, she thought, smiling at the wadded tissues and bank receipts and other odds and ends that kept coming to hand. She finally located the wallet and extracted her Calling Card. Locating her little address book took a further thirty seconds. She found the number and placed the call.

It was answered on the second ring, and the first thing she heard was the familiar, friendly voice saying, "This better be Jill."

"Hello, Gwen."

"Oh, thank God! I've got to go into the village for supplies, but I didn't want to miss you. What's up?"

"Well, I'm glad you waited. I know there's only the one phone there. Listen, do you and Mike have room for one more, or are you all booked up?"

Gwen Feldman's laugh reverberated down the line, answering Jill's question. "Honey, so far we only have two guests here. Barbara Benson is working on her new romance thing, and Jeff Monk is doing his new horror thing. Some grand opening, huh? We're expecting two more in the next few days, but that still leaves eight guest cabins empty. You can have your pick."

"Great. I'd love to see the place."

"Oh, Mike and the local handyman—wait till you meet *him:* he's about a thousand years old!—they've been hammering and moving furniture and so forth, and I've been busy with brooms and bed linens. Don't ever go into the guest house business, Jill. You'll go nuts. So, when were you thinking of coming out?"

Jill thought a moment. "Sometime in the next few days, I guess."

"Fine. You can come today, if you want. We're all ready. There's a typewriter and legal pads in every cabin, but you can bring your own stuff if you want. Mike put those things for computers in every cabin, you know, those electric things. . . ."

"Surge protectors. I have a laptop: I guess I'll bring that."

"Great! How's your new one coming? You're not stuck, are you? I mean, we've braced ourselves to have the place full of people with writer's block—"

"No, nothing like that. I just want to—to get out of town for a while."

"Sure, Jill. Will Nate be with you?"

"Uh, no, he won't. He's getting ready for a show. His opening is in two weeks. I'm on my own. As a matter of fact—" She paused, wondering how to phrase her next request.

"What, Jill? Is something wrong? You two aren't—"

"Oh, no. But I—I just want to get away for a while. I'm not telling anyone where I'm going. Not anyone."

There was a pause, When Gwen spoke again, her voice was low and serious, "Jill, something *is* wrong, isn't it?"

"Yes," Jill said, thinking, There's nothing for it but to tell the truth. "Yes, something is wrong. I—I'll tell you all about it when I get there. Now, what I need from you are directions."

"That's easy. Just take the train to Cutchogue. I'll pick you up at the station."

"No, I'm renting a car, and I don't know that part of Long Island."

"Okay," Gwen said. "It's pretty simple, really. . . ."

Jill fished an old bank receipt and a pen from her purse. As she was uncapping the pen, there was a loud thud nearby. A car pulling out of the nearest parking space had bumped into a passing taxi. The two drivers got out of their cars and started a loud argument, only half of which was in English. She pressed the receiver to her ear, repeating all of Gwen's words to be sure she got them right.

"Expressway to Riverhead . . . Twenty-five to Cutchogue . . . then northeast on main road to Peconic . . . Peconic Writing Colony. Okay, got it."

"Come on out anytime, Jill. We'll be waiting for you."

"Great. And remember, *nobody* knows where I'm going, okay?"

"Gotcha."

They exchanged good-byes and Jill hung up. She put

the pen and the hastily scrawled directions in her purse and glanced at her watch. Five minutes to one. She grabbed the bag and turned to leave the booth, nearly colliding with the back of a large man who stood just behind her, apparently waiting for the phone.

"Sorry," she murmured, already hurrying away down Tenth Street. She didn't want to be late for Dr. Philbin.

"S'okay," the voice behind her said.

Jacob Kessler came out of his ten o'clock meeting and went back down the dull, industrial gray corridor to his office. More a cubicle than an office, he thought, removing his navy blue blazer and loosening the tie that was biting into his throat. He rubbed the painful area just below his Adam's apple and dropped wearily into his padded leather executive chair. Eleven o'clock, he mused. It's only eleven o'clock in the morning: why am I always so tired?

Then, as he did every morning for the past two years, he remembered.

Oh, he thought. Yeah . . .

He buzzed the secretary he shared with three other minor partners in the firm and asked her for coffee. When she brought it in and placed it by his elbow a few moments later, he smiled rather distractedly and thanked her. Then he picked up the four little sheets of telephone messages that had accumulated on his blotter while he'd been down the hall holding the hand of a nervous client who was involved in a messy corporate takeover. Not even *his* client, he thought with mild disgust: he'd acted on behalf of a tardy senior partner, Wiseman. Idiot. Probably in some hotel room downtown with a hooker, nursing last night's hangover.

Oh, hell, he told himself. Just get on with it. With these

messages. With the next appointment. With your life.

It's Friday, he thought, turning his head to stare out at the beautiful vista on the other side of the glass wall beside his desk. TGIF. You have a date tonight.

Another date. Another infrequent attempt to get out and meet people, meaning women. Set up by a well-meaning friend. This one's name was Janice something. Very pretty, he'd been assured. Very nice. A divorcée who taught aerobics at the well-meaning friend's gym. Dinner and a movie tonight. The new Woody Allen comedy.

He looked out at the sun-washed city and up at the imposing, snow-capped mountains that ringed it. Woody Allen would inevitably remind him of New York, which was good. Lovely as it was, he didn't much care for Boulder. Especially now.

She had loved Boulder. She had loved everything about Colorado. She had particularly loved skiing.

Wincing at the sharp stab of pain the memory brought him, Jacob lowered his gaze once more to the telephone messages. Boring client . . . nice client. . . dumb client . . . New York. Who the hell was calling from New York? He looked at the name: it meant nothing to him. Underneath it, in the secretary's neat hand, was the phrase, "It's about your wife."

He stared down at the four words, slowing pushing the other messages off to the side of the desk.

Then he reached for the phone.

Jill waited several moments before trying the bell again. Nothing. She knocked on the heavy oak door, softly at first and then with greater volume. No answer. The blinds in both basement windows were closed.

She stared at the door for a moment, then checked her watch. One o'clock. One o'clock Friday: isn't that what the doctor had said on the phone? Yes, no mistake. So, where was she . . . ?

She climbed the steps to street level, then ascended the stairway to the front door of the house itself. Two buzzers, the lower one marked PHILBIN. She rang, waited, and rang again. Then she knocked. Nothing. The upper buzzer read CASTAING. The tenant on the third floor. She rang that buzzer, waited, and rang it again. Nothing there, either.

An emergency, she thought. After all, she *is* a doctor, and they always have emergencies. Even clinical psychologists—*especially* clinical psychologists. But it wasn't like the woman to simply rush off without so much as leaving a note on the door, or—more likely—calling her patients and canceling. Perhaps she did call, Jill mused. I didn't check my machine this morning. There's probably a message waiting for me at home.

Shaking her head more in wonder than exasperation, Jill went down the steps and headed for home. I'll call her later, she thought as she went. Reschedule. . . .

When she arrived back at her apartment, she went immediately to the machine in her office. Three messages. The first was from Nate, asking what she wanted to do tonight and telling her to call him at his place. The second was Tara, calling from the studio where she was taping *Tomorrow's Children.* With much breathless giggling, Tara was informing her that Doug Baron had called and asked for another date, and that she'd call later with all the glorious details.

Jill smiled as she listened to her friend, but her smile faded when she heard the next message.

"Jill, it's Barney Fleck. Call me at my office the minute you hear this. I have—I have some more information for you. 'Bye."

It occurred to her briefly, as she picked up the receiver

180

and dialed Barney's number, that none of the messages had been from Dr. Philbin. Oh, well, she told herself, I'll try calling her office again later this afternoon. I'm sure there's some logical explanation for the whole thing.

What happened to Jillian Talbot in the following twenty-four hours made her completely forget about Dr. Philbin and the missed appointment.

Elaine Williams and Jacob Kessler had never met, had never so much as heard of each other, and yet they were now doing the exact same thing. She stood at the rail of her sundeck overlooking the Pacific, and he at the picture window of his office in Boulder, Colorado. Both of them were gazing out at majestic views, not seeing them. They were both thinking about the telephone calls they'd received earlier today, and both were remembering the pain they had recently suffered. Alone and silent, they wept.

Barney had more notes with him, this time in his own illegible handwriting. He sat across from her in her living room, just as he had yesterday. She leaned back against the cushions on the couch, listening.

"Sharon Williams was trying to break into the movie business. You know, screenplays. She'd actually sold a story idea to one of the studios, but the picture was never made. Three years ago, she disappeared. Walked out of her apartment in L.A. and vanished. Never seen again. I spoke to her mother. The family is very rich, and they offered a big reward. The L.A. police got hundreds of tips—you know, sightings, confessions, the whole bit—but none of them led to anything. One of her friends told the cops that Sharon was very popular with the men, that she'd been dating a couple of guys, and maybe she'd run off with one of them. Apparently, the boyfriends were found and questioned, but they didn't know anything, either. The father, Walter Williams, became obsessed. Every time there was the slightest lead, he'd follow it up personally. Flew all over the country, and twice to Europe. Nothing. He'd been in ill health even before his daughter took off, and this didn't help. Six months after her disappearance, he died of a massive heart attack. On a plane to . . ."—Barney consulted his notes—". . . Atlanta. Somebody there claimed to have seen her. Sharon is still missing."

Jill curled her legs up under her, suddenly cold, and clutched her coffee mug tightly in both hands. She wondered how she had managed to miss this apparently national news. Then she remembered that Nate had confessed he'd never heard about Stacy Green, the fashion model who'd been married to Doug Baron, and that had been front-page headline stuff. When she was writing, she often went for days, even weeks, without any interruption from the outside world. After a moment of silence, she whispered, "And the others?"

She was getting to know Barney well, she thought as she watched him. His big, friendly face was the proverbial open book. He was worried. For me, she told herself. He's worried for me. . . .

Barney cleared his throat, took a sip of coffee, and continued. "Yeah, well, it's pretty strange. Belinda Rosenberg—or, I should say, Belinda Kessler—is dead."

Jill looked up sharply. "Dead?"

"Yeah. Two years ago. But it wasn't anything like—well, you know, what we were thinking. It was an accident. A skiing accident, at one of those fancy lodges in Colorado. She fell off a cliff while she and a couple of friends were trying to do some famous slope called Dead

Man's something-or-other. It was stupid of her, her husband said, because they weren't that good, they shouldn't have tried it in the first place. The trail had a nasty section about halfway down, where it was just a few yards from a sheer cliff face. She apparently hit a patch of ice on the snow and lost control. She fell about three hundred feet. The friends didn't even find out about it until they reached the bottom. That's what her husband told me—and we were lucky to find him. Belinda married him and moved to Boulder four years after she graduated, and Verna called all the Rosenbergs in Buffalo until she found Belinda's parents. The husband was upset, of course, so I didn't press him for details. The ski resort is very famous, and they managed to keep publicity to a minimum. It didn't get much play in the news."

"How awful," Jill whispered, guilt flooding through her. She actually blushed: someone she'd known had died in a senseless accident, and all she could feet was relief. She must not allow this ordeal to make her become self-absorbed. To cover her embarrassment, she pressed on. "You didn't—you didn't tell any of these people, you know, why we were asking about—"

"Of course not," Barney assured her. "I just said an old classmate from Hartley was thinking of having a party, a sort of reunion thing, and had asked me to locate everyone. They accepted that."

She nodded. "Okay. What about Cass MacFarland?"

Barney put down his notes and leaned back in his chair. "Ah. There I hit a dead end. I have no idea. The address in the yearbook was in Montclair, New Jersey, but she's not there anymore. Verna tried their town hall, but all she found out was that both the parents and Cassandra had moved away. She was married for a while, but she was divorced before she left town. No forwarding. Same with

183

her ex-husband." He leaned forward. "You don't remember anyone else who might know, do you? Friends or relatives?"

Jill thought about it for a moment, then shook her head. "No. She mentioned an older brother a couple of times, but I don't think she ever told me his name or where he lived. He was estranged from the parents, I seem to recall. He'd run away from home, or something like that. I don't remember anyone else. . . ."

"Hmmm," the detective said.

He's a big one for grunting, Jill thought, remembering the little noises he'd made throughout their interview with Mrs. Sanchez in the flower shop. She imagined she could almost hear his mind working.

"So," she said at last. "Where does that put me?"

He grimaced. "Square one, I'm afraid. One of your three friends is dead, but it was accidental. Another disappeared—for any one of a thousand reasons, I suppose. And the third simply moved: she could be anywhere. We have no reason to think this idiot who's so interested in you is Victor Dimorta, and we *know* it's not your stepfather." He leaned forward, studying her face. "Any other ideas? Anything at all? An ex-boyfriend, a fan at one of your public appearances, some writer who's jealous of your success? No matter how wild it is."

Jill shrugged. "I only had two steady boyfriends before Nate. One, an editor I worked with, turned out to be gay—he and his lover just bought a house in Westchester. The other one is now married, and they're expecting their second child. Both relationships ended amicably, and neither man is even remotely wacko material. I've never noticed any particular fans: I don't do that many signings. And if any other writer is jealous of me, I have no idea who it could be. Sorry."

After a moment, Barney grunted again. "Okay, so we're flying blind. We don't know who he is or what he'll do next. I suggest you may want to leave New York for a while. Think about it. If you hear from him again, you're leaving, understand?"

"I've already considered that possibility," Jill told him. "In fact, that's what I'm planning."

"Where will you go?"

She smiled. "Never mind now. If it comes to that, I'll let you know." She continued to smile even as she told the lie. She wasn't going to tell him or anyone else in her orbit where she was going. It might be dangerous—for them as well as for her.

Barney nodded and rose from his seat. He pulled a card from his jacket pocket and handed it to her. "Fair enough. In the meantime, my home number is on the back of this card. Anytime, day or night, you call me. Okay?"

"Okay," she said.

He watched as Jillian handed Barney Fleck his coat. Then the detective left the apartment across the street, and she was once again alone.

Okay, he thought. What now? He would have to come up with an idea of some kind. It was imperative that she know what she was dealing with—and with whom.

He could call her. . . .

No.

Nate? Or Tara?

No.

The detective . . . ?

No! That would be dangerous. That detective could ruin the whole thing. And the plan couldn't be ruined. Not now. He'd worked too long and too hard.

And he didn't have much time. . . .

He sat in the armchair by the window for the rest of the afternoon, thinking. The next time he became aware of his surroundings and looked out the window, it was already evening, and Nate was arriving across the street on his motorcycle.

The restaurant on the ground floor of Jill's apartment building was a genuine, old-fashioned Greenwich Village pub, complete with cross-beams and long oak bar and leaded glass windows. For many years it had been the famous Blue Mill Tavern, but it was now under new ownership. A bit brighter, a bit more trendy, perhaps, but still a lovely place to enjoy a good meal surrounded by the attractive, uppermiddle-class artists and writers and performers and businesspeople who are the main population of this part of town.

Despite her apparent composure, Jill was not having a good time. They had come out of the building and walked the few short steps to the restaurant entrance. The bartender waved a greeting, and the waitress, who also recognized them as regular customers, immediately showed them to their favorite table in the corner. Jill was having ginger ale, and she watched Nate playing with the swizzle stick in his whisky sour. She looked from his hands up to his face, wondering for the thousandth time whether she should just say yes to his proposal. She wondered if she should tell him about the baby. Of course, if he knew about it he might insist on marriage. Either that or disappear: men could be unpredictable about these things, or so she'd been told. She'd never been in this position before.

No, she decided. He wouldn't disappear. In their ten months together, he'd proved himself to be a gentleman. And he loved her: she was certain of that. He never mentioned the women he'd presumably been involved with before her, but he'd told her several times that he'd never loved a woman as he loved her. Thinking of her own earlier affairs, she realized that they had that, among so many other things, in common.

Then she thought of the other, more immediate problem she was keeping from him. It had been Mary who'd spilled the beans to him about the roses. Jill had decided not to tell him for a very good reason. He would become angry and worried—which he had done—and this was not good for him. Not now. He was an artist getting ready for his second show. She'd seen the paintings: this collection could put him on the map, artistically speaking. The last thing he needed in his life right now was any kind of distraction. She knew that from her own experience. Writing and publishing were time-consuming enough without—

Writing. Another problem, as if she needed one. She wasn't writing anything. She was going to have to start all over again. . . .

Oh, damn you! she thought as she reached for her soda. Damn you, Valentine! Whoever you are. Damn you and your stupid, nasty pranks.

But they weren't pranks. She knew that now: whatever doubts she'd entertained before had vanished forever the moment she'd looked down to see the dead rat on her living room floor. She remembered her certainty as she'd stared down, filled with dread, at the vapid magazine article. This person was serious.

So, she'd come to one decision. Only one, she thought ruefully, counting the number of other decisions she would have to make in the very near future. Sometime in the next few days she would disappear temporarily. A week, maybe ten days. She'd have to be back in time for

187

Nate's opening: nothing was going to keep her from that. But she would get away for a while to think about all this. The baby. The possibility of marriage. A new novel. Valentine. Everything.

She nearly smiled. What had Dr. Philbin said? Decide to decide. . . .

She looked up at Nate again. He was watching her, a quizzical expression on his face. She smiled at him, thinking, I'm not going to tell him where I'm going, or even *that* I'm going. I'm not going to tell anyone.

"Hello?" Nate said, grinning. "Anybody home?"

"Yes," she said, grinning back. "I'm here."

For the rest of the meal, she concentrated exclusively on him. She pushed the dark thoughts from her mind. She barely paid attention to her food. And she did not even notice the lone man who sat with his back to them two tables away.

He finished his coffee, paid the bill, and went out of the restaurant. Jillian and Nate had already left several minutes before, so he had no need for caution. He crossed the street and went up to his room across from her apartment. He removed the curly blond wig, the mustache, and the thick, nonprescription glasses and dropped them on the table next to the recorder.

They were in the living room, and Tara had joined them. He listened as the actress told them about her date next Tuesday evening. Then Tara went back downstairs to her home on the sixth floor, and Jillian and Nate had a brief conversation alone. He asked her if she was feeling okay, and she said yes. She mentioned the missed appointment with the analyst, and then he told her that he had to be up early tomorrow, something about framing his paintings. He offered to stay the night if she wanted

188

him to, but she shook her head and said no, that he should be at his studio in the morning when the framer arrived. They kissed, and then Nate left. A few minutes later the roar of his motorcycle filled the street for a moment, then quickly faded as he rode away.

Jillian Talbot was alone for the night.

He sat in the armchair, watching her, his new plan slowly forming in his mind.

Yes, he thought. Yes.

He knew what he was going to do next.

The music was coming from somewhere far away, and at first she couldn't place it. Lush chords from a jazz combo, the lonely wail of a saxophone, and a woman singing in a low, achingly beautiful voice. It made her sad, this song, but it also made her feel uneasy.

The other three were dancing, swirling slowly around a large, dimly lit room as the music washed over them. They were in long, flowing, identically designed but differently colored chiffon gowns: pale blue for the blonde, pale pink for the brunette, and pale yellow for the redhead. Overhead spotlights shone straight down, forming pools of bright white light in the darkness. The graceful, pastel-shaded forms of the women moved sinuously in time to the music, gliding in and out of her view as they danced from light to shadow, light to shadow. She had not joined them on the floor, but was seated instead on a hard metal chair at a large round table before a wall of glass. She turned from watching the women to gaze out over the snowy moonlit landscape stretching endlessly away from her on the other side of the windows.

Where was she? What was happening to her? And why did the singer's plaintive voice fill her with dread? She knew this place and this music and these young women, if only she could think. If only she could concentrate. But there was something

189

wrong with her. She couldn't move. She sat heavily in the hard metal chair, aware of her bloated stomach and the pressure inside. The baby: that was it! The baby was kicking her, squirming around in her womb, a beautiful nucleus of life at her very center. She smiled despite the discomfort and the rising panic. My baby, she thought. Our baby. Nate's and mine . . .

Nate. Where was he? She turned from the view and looked swiftly around the room, searching frantically for her lover. Her future husband. Nate, she thought, opening her mouth and trying to form words. Nate! Where are you?

But no sound would come. It stuck in her throat, frozen there by her own mounting terror. And even if she could cry out, she knew she would never be heard over the music. It seemed to be getting louder, coming closer, filling her ears and her mind and her very soul until she could not move. Something was about to happen, she was certain of it. Something awful.

The sudden, horrible knowledge struck her so forcefully that for a moment she thought she had been slapped across the face. In one swift, violent flash, she knew.

Hartley College.

Sharon Williams. Belinda Rosenberg. Cass MacFarland.

And the waves of music crashed against her, transforming from vague noise into distinct melody.

Sarah Vaughan.

"My Funny Valentine."

Valentine . . .

VALENTINE!

She opened her eyes and stared into utter blackness. The dark room swirled around her, as the dancers had done. She was hot, very hot, and her hair and her nightgown were drenched with perspiration. Her mouth was dry, her throat parched. But she was awake, she realized, and it had only been a dream.

Slowly, slowly, the whirling movement receded as her eyes adjusted to the darkness, and wave after wave of relief flooded through her. She was in her bedroom in her apartment on Barrow Street in Greenwich Village, New York, New York, United States of—

Then she became aware of the music.

It was coming from beyond the closed bedroom door, from the living room. From the stereo in the living room. That magnificent voice; that soft, insinuating melody . . .

Sarah Vaughan.

"My Funny Valentine."

The reality of it smashed into her, assaulting every sense. There was a swift jab of pain, a lurch of sheer terror just below her left breast, and for a moment she could not see anything. She held her breath, transfixed, unable to move, as the sharp, nauseating terror flowed down through every inch of her body.

Her first thought was to scream. But even as she opened her mouth and filled her lungs, some modicum of common sense, some primitive instinct of survival, took over. She brought her hand swiftly up and clamped it over her mouth before any sound escaped. In the same instant, the survival voice deep inside her began to bark instructions.

Get out of the bed.

Before she knew she had moved she was lying on the carpet, the bed between her and the bedroom door. She pressed herself down into the soft pile, listening.

The music. The hum of the refrigerator on the other side of the wall. Soft hissing from the radiator. Distant traffic through the closed window. Nothing else.

He's not in the bedroom. He's somewhere else in the

191

apartment.

Telephone.

She lay on the floor, silently cursing herself. The only phone in the apartment was in the next room, her office. Now, too late, she realized the practicality, the sheer common sense of bedroom telephones.

Weapon.

She reached cautiously over to the wall next to the bedside table beside her and unplugged the lamp. It was a large, heavy brass affair, and its mate was on the matching table on the other side of the bed. She rose to her feet and quietly removed the blue parchment shade. She unscrewed the lightbulb and swiftly wrapped the cord around the base. Picking up the lamp by the neck, she raised the weighted base above her head as she crept over to the closet door on the other side of the room. In one swift, violent move, she threw it open.

Empty.

She moved silently across the carpet to the bedroom door and pressed her ear against the wood, listening. Sarah Vaughan continued to sing softly.

Nothing else.

She grasped the doorknob with her free hand, turned it, and yanked the door open. The heavy lamp was poised, ready to smash down on anything beyond the door.

The hallway was empty.

The office door across the way was open, as was the bathroom door next to it. She turned her head and peered down the hall toward the living room. She could see a dim light, a soft, flickering glow emanating from the other side of the couch. From the coffee table. A candle. It illuminated the room enough for her to see that it, too, was empty. She craned her neck and glanced quickly around the corner into the kitchen. Empty. Leaning forward, she surveyed the office. Empty. There was a closet in that room, but it was stuffed floor-to-ceiling with filing cabinets and summer clothes. Too crowded to afford room for a human body.

Holding the lamp above her, she stepped silently out into the hallway and crept over to the bathroom. She planted herself in the doorway and reached over to switch on the light.

Empty.

From where she now stood she could see the entire apartment.

Empty.

The song came to an end, and a moment later it began again. He had recorded it on a cassette tape, over and over. She could see the tiny green lights of the home entertainment center glowing in the dimly lit living room.

Slowly, inevitably, her gaze traveled over to rest on the last possibility.

The closet next to the front door.

Move!

She stepped quickly into the office, closed the door, and locked it. She was already across the room, reaching for the telephone, when she became aware of how cold she suddenly felt. Her gaze rose from the phone to the window above her desk.

It was wide open. A small, perfectly round hole had been cut in the glass just above the lock in the frame at the bottom.

She leaned forward, peering out onto the fire escape. Her gaze traveled down, down as far as she could see. The fire escape was empty.

The receiver was now in her left hand, and she was fumbling with the buttons of the dial, trying to remember the sequence of the numbers as she held the lamp aloft in her right hand. No use: she couldn't think of anything. She dropped the receiver and fell immediately to her knees, throwing aside the rug in the center of the floor. Tara's bedroom was directly below this room. Oh, please, God! She brought the brass lamp up in both hands and smashed it down to the floor. Three quick raps, then three slow, then another three quick. Again. And again. She beat out the tattoo over and over, staring all the while at the closed, locked office door, expecting at any moment the sharp, heavy pounding of his fists on the other side. . . .

Count to ten.

One, two, three, four—

Then, mercifully, it came, resounding through the entire apartment. Pound, pound, pound on the front door, followed by the loud, threatening shout of a seriously angry female cop.

"*Open up! Police!*"

She wasn't aware of the fact that she had moved. The office door was open, and she was running, and she was now at the front door, staring at the closed door to the closet not six feet away. The pounding came again.

"*Police! Open the door!*"

Still brandishing the lamp, Jill reached out for the doorknob, shouting, "Tara, it's me! Don't shoot!"

She threw the door open. Her friend stood in the doorway in her bright Chinese kimono, legs apart, arms rigid in front of her, the .22 caliber Lady Wesson aimed at Jill's heart.

They stared at each other for a moment, Tara with the gun and Jill with the lamp. Then, in a flash, the actress was at her side, aiming her weapon toward the interior of the living room. Jill raised a finger to her lips and pointed at the closet door. Tara nodded. Jill went cautiously over to the closet, reached for the doorknob, and glanced back at her friend. Her feet planted, arms rigid, aiming at the center of the door, Tara nodded again. Stepping aside, out of the line of fire, Jill turned the knob, threw the door open, and dropped to the floor.

Nothing.

She slowly rose to her feet, still clutching the brass lamp, and peered into the closet.

Empty.

She turned back to her friend. Tara slowly exhaled and lowered the gun. Jill leaned back against the closet door, dropping the lamp to the floor beside her.

"He's gone," she said.

The song had come to an end, but now it began again, and the smooth, soft voice of Sarah Vaughan suddenly filled the room. Tara whirled around, instinctively bringing up the gun.

"What the hell—?"

"No!" Jill cried, and Tara once again lowered her weapon.

In the same instant, both women turned toward the source of the light. The tall red candle glowed, set in its own wax on the surface of the coffee table. Jill stepped forward, Tara right behind her. Silently, they stared down at the candle, and at the envelope next to it. On top of the envelope rested a small, flat black velvet box, six inches by four. A jewelry box, Jill thought, already reaching out her hand.

She pulled the envelope out from under the box and tore it open. It was another store-bought valentine, this one from Hallmark. Two tiny children with enormous eyes cuddled on the front. The boy was handing the girl a heart-shaped card. The scripted legend read:

"FOR YOU . . ."

As Tara peered over her shoulder, she opened the card. The printed words were:

"WITH ALL MY HEART!"

Underneath this, in the now familiar typescript, was the usual signature:

LOVE,
VALENTINE

She dropped the card and the envelope on the table and picked up the jewelry box. Without hesitating, without thinking, she snapped it open. She stood rigid, staring down at the large, gaudy diamond ring that winked up at her.

It was attached to a severed human finger.

The box clattered down, spilling its obscene contents out onto the table. The first, involuntary thrill of horror came up through her, only to fade as quickly as it had begun. Tara gasped and stepped backward, away from it. Jill did not. She leaned down, inspecting the object more closely. She slowly reached down, picked it up, and held it next to the candle.

It was fake, of course, and a crude imitation at that. One of a million allegedly humorous vulgarities on sale at every novelty shop and amusement park in America. It was somewhat larger than life, for one thing, and the ring with the bit of glass in it was painted a dull, improbable copper color. The bright red, two-inch fingernail was too thick, almost as thick as the rubber finger itself. And the jagged, bloody wound at the base was nowhere near the color of actual blood.

Filled with contempt, with a loathing she had never felt before, she tossed the disgusting thing down onto the table. It actually bounced, landing silently on the Oriental carpet. The two women stared down.

Jill regarded the finger for a long time, thinking, He was here. He was in my house. In my home. While I slept in the next room, he came in here and did this insane, this unspeakable thing. He could just as easily have murdered me.

No, she realized. He doesn't want to murder me.

Not yet.

He's waiting for Valentine's Day.

Belinda died on a ski slope, but it wasn't an accident. Sharon had disappeared, and Cass had moved away to parts unknown. Yet, standing there, she knew that all three women were dead. She was certain of it, as certain as she had ever been of anything.

And now, she thought, it's my turn.

She looked over at Tara, who stood shivering in her thin silk kimono, clutching her arms to her body. She summoned a smile for her friend, walked into her bedroom, and came back with her warmest blanket. Handing it to Tara as she passed, she proceeded to the picture window. The first, faint light of dawn slowly filled the dark sky as she stared out at the street, the opposite buildings, and the enormous cityscape beyond them. Windows. Thousands and thousands of windows.

The loathing had vanished, replaced by something else she'd only experienced once before, on the kitchen floor of the apartment on Central Park West, when she'd reached up and grasped the heavy iron skillet and brought it down on her stepfather's head. Rage. Blind, naked, prehistoric fury.

Staring out at the city, she slowly filled her lungs. The shout that emanated from her crashed into the window and came back at her, smashing into her face, echoing through the room as if it were uttered not by her but to her.

"You're dead, Victor!" she cried. "Do you understand me? *You're dead!*"

Tara came up behind her and gently placed her hands on her shoulders. Then, Jillian Talbot reached for the cord and slowly, ceremoniously closed the curtains.

"What are you going to do?" Tara asked.

She turned around to confront her friend, noting Tara's look of surprise when she saw the dangerous expression on her face.

"I'm going to stop this," she said. "I'm going to stop it right *now!*"

CHAPTER 9

SATURDAY, FEBRUARY 7

JANE FLECK WAS AWAKENED BY THE SOFT RINGING OF the telephone on the night table beside her. She rolled over on her side and fumbled for it, nearly knocking it off the table in the process. She glanced at the luminous dial of the alarm clock next to the phone: six-thirty.

"Hello?"

"Hello, umm, Mrs. Fleck? My name is Jill Talbot. I'm a client of your husband's, and I'm terribly sorry to disturb you at this hour, but it's important that I speak to him."

"Oh, yes. One moment."

She reached over to nudge the giant, still form in the bed beside her.

"Hmmm?"

"Phone for you. Jill Talbot. Wake up." She deliberately rubbed the cold receiver against his neck. That and the name of the caller was all it took. He was off the bed and around it in an instant, reaching for the receiver. He stood beside his wife in the dark bedroom of their Cobble Hill apartment, naked and shivering, listening to the voice on the other end of the line.

Jane opened one eye to watch him. His face was immediately drawn, tense. She knew that look: bad news. The series of short grunts he emitted only confirmed her suspicion. Finally, she heard him say, "Okay. Stay there with your friend. Don't go back into your apartment till I get there. Give me twenty minutes."

She closed the eye and drifted, only half listening as he went over to the closet and dressed. She was nearly asleep again when she heard the odd sounds, the little series of metallic clicks from the other side of the room. When she looked over and saw what it was, she immediately sat up in the bed.

"What?" she said. "What is it?" She watched, fearful, as he checked that his gun was loaded, placed it in his shoulder holster, and quickly put on his coat.

"Nothing. Go back to sleep." He came over, leaned down, and kissed her cheek. "Back in a while."

With that, he was gone. She lay back in the bed, listening as the apartment door closed behind him.

Twenty minutes later, having given up on the idea of sleep, she got out of the bed and shuffled nervously into the kitchen to make coffee.

Jill sat in Tara's living room, piecing everything together. She had learned so much in the last half hour that her brain was numb, threatening to shut down from the overwhelming reality of it. She was trying desperately to concentrate.

What now? she wondered.

Well, that, at least, was decided. She'd told Barney Fleck on the phone, and nobody was going to talk her out of it.

And then, what?

No. She wouldn't think about that. She'd just do what had to be done now, and cross that bridge when she came to it.

Those bridges. Plural.

Right.

She looked at her watch again. Where was Barney . . . ?

Tara watched her friend. She'd been sitting quite still for a while now, staring down at the coffee table, an unreadable expression on her face. Now and then she glanced at her watch or sipped from the mug of chamomile tea Tara had given her when they'd first come downstairs to phone the detective. That had been right after Jill had performed what Tara, the actress, could only describe as her "mad scene."

She had shouted her threat to this Victor person, this Valentine, and closed the curtains. Then, she'd suddenly started babbling almost incoherently, something about him knowing more than he could just from watching. He always knew when others were with her and when she was alone. He knew when Nate stayed over, and when he didn't. He knew everything she was doing, even before she did it.

With that last statement, her eyes had grown very wide, and she'd glanced wildly around the room. Then, before Tara could grasp what was happening, she'd rushed from the living room into her office. By the time Tara arrived in the doorway, the receiver of the telephone was in two pieces. She'd gone to stand next to Jill, who silently pointed down at the little metal thing inside the mouthpiece. She did not remove it: instead, she'd screwed the mouthpiece back onto the receiver and replaced it in its cradle.

Then she'd gone nuts. She raised a finger to her lips, instructing Tara to remain silent, and began—very quietly—to trash the room. Every stick of furniture was overturned and inspected. The closet, the filing cabinets, the bookshelves, even the framed cover art on the walls. She'd grabbed a pen and a pad of paper and scribbled furiously, then ripped off the page and handed it to Tara. It read, *Bugs! You take bdrm & bath. Look EVERYWHERE!!!* The last word was capitalized and underlined twice.

Tara had nodded and gone immediately into the bedroom. She quickly, quietly checked the bedside tables, the vanity, and the closet. She then attacked the bedframe and mattresses, silently thanking God for her kid brother's teenage phase as an electronics geek. Years ago, he'd bored her and their parents endlessly with his nonstop monologues on the subject. Now, thanks to him, she knew that what they were looking for was of considerable size. The tiny devices you saw in the movies and on television were only good for a few hours—unless they were being operated from the next room. Anything that remained active for weeks, relaying transmissions a decent distance, would involve not only a microphone but an electronic gadget for activation and some sort of battery or power pack. It would definitely be bigger than a thimble. Her brother's words—only half heard at the time—came back clearly to her, and she made a mental note to call him.

She'd finished with the bed and gone into the bathroom. Jill had done the kitchen, opening every cabinet and fixture, even the oven, and progressed to the living room. Tara was removing the porcelain lid of the tank behind the toilet and peering down inside when she felt the hand on her arm. She'd replaced the lid and followed Jill out to the living room.

The couch was lying on its back. Jill had knelt at the bottom and pointed. There, taped to the inside above the legs, was the object of their search. Tara had stared, the rage growing inside her as she knew it was growing in Jill. Without a word, the two women had left the apartment and come downstairs. Tara had closed her own front curtains as Jill had called Mr. Fleck, and now they were waiting.

The buzzer sounded, and Tara went over to let him in downstairs. A few minutes later, she opened her apartment door and saw the detective for the first time since the incident with Betty Hanes at the television studio. She'd forgotten how big he was. Amazed and comforted by the sheer size of the man, she stepped aside and watched as he went immediately over to Jill.

"I want to see," he said.

Without a word, Jill stood up and led him out.

Ten minutes later, Jill and the detective were back in Tara's living room. She noticed that Jill was now fully dressed, and she had her coat and purse with her. Tara sat across from them, listening to their conversation.

"Okay," the detective said, "we'll leave them in place, and active. We don't want him to know you've found them. But how are you going to keep up the charade?"

"That's simple," Jill said, her voice curiously flat. "I'm not going back there. Not for a while, anyway."

"Where will you go?"

Jill looked up at him, then over at Tara. She shook her head. "Never mind. I'll be with friends. I'll be perfectly safe, but I don't want any of you to—to have that information. Not now. I'll be in touch with both of you." She turned to the detective. "It's okay. My agent gave me the idea, and I remember our conversation clearly. Neither of us mentioned our friends' last name, or where they were. Even if he was listening, he wouldn't be able to put it together. I called them once from the apartment, but they weren't home. I left a brief message, again revealing nothing specific. Yesterday, when I called them back, I did so from a pay phone on the street. Otherwise, I haven't mentioned it—not in the apartment, certainly."

"What about with Nate?" Tara asked.

Jill shook her head again. "No. I—I haven't even told him. I'm just going away for a few days, maybe ten. Until after Valentine's Day."

Tara and Barney stared at her. She turned again to the detective beside her on the couch.

"Do you have your notes from yesterday?" she asked him.

He nodded and pulled them from a coat pocket.

"When you spoke to the relatives," Jill continued, "did they mention dates, or at least times of the year?"

Tara watched as Barney Fleck read over the pages and his eyes suddenly widened.

"Shit," he muttered. "Sharon Williams disappeared three years ago, in early February. That's what Mrs. Williams said, 'early February.' Belinda's husband mentioned a holiday. He said it was two years ago, and something about a 'holiday ski trip.' He didn't say which one, though. . . ."

"Call him back," Jill said. "I'm willing to bet it was Valentine's Day. And I think—I think he killed Cass on

203

Valentine's Day last year. Of course, we have no way of tracing her. But I see a pattern here. The cards, the flowers, the jewelry box. He's paying us all back for that Valentine's Day in college. My God, it's so sick!" She shuddered. "He must have listened to me in my bedroom. In my bathroom. . ."

"I don't think so," the detective said quickly. "I'm no expert, but I don't think that mike would pick up much more than the living room."

Tara noticed that Jill took little comfort from that. Then she watched as Jill reached into her purse and produced a checkbook and a pen.

"On second thought," Jill said as she wrote, "don't call Belinda's husband back. Don't approach Mrs. Williams with this. Not yet. For now, I want you to concentrate on Victor. Can you go to that town in Pennsylvania, what's it called, Mill City?"

"Yeah," Barney said. "Monday or Tuesday. But it's quite a drive—"

"Don't drive," Jill interjected. "Fly to Pittsburgh, then rent a car. Ask around the town. Go to his house. The local newspaper. Whatever. I want a picture of him. There must have been pictures in the papers after he killed his parents. The prison will have pictures."

"He killed his *parents*?" Tara stared, amazed at the snippets of information being tossed back and forth between her friend and the detective. This was the first she was hearing of any of it. An icy knot began to form in the pit of her stomach.

"Later," was all Jill said. "Now, I'm getting the hell out of here." She tore out a check and handed it to Barney. "That should cover expenses, and then some. There's a Sergeant Escalera at the Sixth Precinct. If you find anything in Mill City, you should tell him about it."

Barney nodded. "I know him."

"Good," Jill said, rising. "That check should also fix the window in my office. I want you to get someone to put bars on the back windows as well, and a good alarm system. Can you handle all that?"

The detective nodded again. "But how will I get in touch with you?"

"I'll call you at your office on Thursday. You should be back from Pennsylvania by then." She handed her apartment keys to Tara. "I'll get in touch with you, too. And Nate. Gloria Price lives on Bedford Street. Her husband, Louis, is listed in the phone book. Call her and tell her I won't need her to come in for a couple of weeks. Now, I'm going to catch a cab."

"I'll go with you," Barney offered. "He may be watching the building, and we don't want him following you to—wherever you're going."

Jill smiled. "Oh, he won't. I'm not leaving, as far as he's concerned. You go on home now."

The detective rose. Tara walked him to the door. He turned around in the doorway and looked back at Jill.

"You take care of yourself," he said.

Jill nodded. "You too."

As soon as Tara shut the door, Jill picked up her coat. "I'll take the back way, if you don't mind."

Tara shrugged. "Sure. I have about a million questions, but I'll save 'em for later." Then, her decision made, she said, "Let me help you with that."

Jill smiled as Tara took the coat from her and stood behind her, helping her into it. "Thanks."

They embraced. Then Tara went into the bedroom at the back of her apartment, opened the window, and watched as her friend climbed out onto the fire escape. She handed Jill her purse.

"Please be careful," she said.

Jill grinned. "Have a nice time Tuesday night."

Tara had to think a moment. "Oh, yeah. Doug. I'm sure I will."

"I'm sure you will, too. I'll call you. 'Bye."

"Good-bye."

It occurred to Tara again just how bizarre the whole thing was as she watched Jillian Talbot, the renowned author of four bestselling novels, climbing down the back of her own building and sneaking away like a thief in the night. Tara, who had never been particularly religious, closed her eyes and murmured a prayer for her friend.

Jill descended the fire escape to the second floor, then lowered the ladder to the ground and climbed down.

Escape, she thought, over and over as she made her way quickly down the narrow alley between buildings to Hudson Street. She stopped instinctively and peered both ways before stepping out of the dark alley into the bright morning sunlight. There were only three people in sight, two women and a little boy. She walked straight out into the street and held up her hand to the oncoming traffic. Twenty seconds later she was in the backseat of a cab moving swiftly north, away from her apartment. Away from Greenwich Village. Away from her lover and her friends.

Away from Valentine.

She leaned heavily back against the cool leather seat and closed her eyes.

Barney came out of Jill's building the conventional way and stood for several moments, looking up at the buildings across the street. Yes, he calculated, his gaze moving swiftly along the edifices. Two buildings. The top

206

front rooms of the red brick one, and the top corner apartment of the big gray one. Four windows—eight, if you count the ones directly below them. No, the angle would be too low. He'd noticed from her apartment that the buildings behind these two were several blocks north, too far away. And her side windows were too small. It had to be one of these two buildings, here in front of him. Nothing else would suffice.

Realizing that he might be observed, he turned and walked quickly away, toward his car on Bedford around the corner. But he'd be back, he decided. Within the hour . . .

The cab took Jill to a car rental agency on Thirty-ninth Street. Half an hour later she was at the wheel of a red Chevette, moving north and east toward the Queensboro Bridge. She could feel herself relaxing more and more with every mile she put between herself and her home. By the time she reached the Long Island Expressway, she'd actually begun to sing softly to herself. She stopped abruptly when she realized what it was she'd been singing.

"My Funny Valentine."

Andrea Skinner was worried about her mother. Yesterday she'd left two messages, one in the afternoon and one in the evening, but Mom had not called her back. This was odd: she rarely had to wait more than an hour to receive a reply to a phone message, to say nothing of a whole day. As far as Andrea knew, her mother was supposed to be home.

Now she stood at the top of the steps at nine o'clock on a Saturday morning, ringing her mother's buzzer and getting no response. She shook her head, silently cursing her mother's stubbornness, not to mention her stinginess.

Sally's honeymoon in Hawaii had been planned for months. When Sally's friend, the replacement receptionist, called in sick, she should have called a temp agency to get someone to handle the phones. But temporary people charged twice as much as regular employees. Dorothy Philbin had always been frugal: she'd rather do without than pay an inflated salary.

So now Andrea had come all the way down to Greenwich Village, simply because her mother didn't have anyone to answer the phone. What a bore, Andrea thought as she produced her own key to her mother's house and let herself in.

The living room and the kitchen were empty, so she immediately went up to the second floor. Mom's bedroom, the bathroom, the guest room: nothing, anywhere. With a little sigh of impatience, she came back downstairs. Of course, it was Saturday, and her mother did not see patients on the weekend. Perhaps she'd gone out somewhere, or she could be working in her office. Nodding to herself, Andrea walked back the way she'd come.

Her first instinctive, almost clairvoyant perception that something was wrong occurred in the kitchen, just before she opened the door to the basement. She paused for a moment, listening, straining her ears for any sound. The house was entirely too still, too quiet.

Then she opened the door to the basement stairway and flicked on the stair light, and she immediately knew her instinct had been right. The strong, sickly sweet odor of decay rushed through the open door, emanating from the darkness below her. For a full ten seconds she was unable to move. Surprised, terrified, and hoping against hope, she slowly descended the stairs. At the bottom she waited a moment, wincing at the vile smell, before reaching over and switching on the office light.

Several minutes later, when she regained consciousness, she discovered that she was lying at the base of the stairs, and that her hands and coat were stuck to the carpet. Her mother lay on the floor five feet away from her, in front of her desk. She was on her back, clad in her gray suit, staring sightlessly up at the ceiling with dull, glazed eyes. There was a jagged, gaping hole where her throat had been, and small black insects were swarming over her. Roaches, and something gray and furry running from the light, away from the body toward the darker reaches of the room.

When Andrea Skinner looked down and realized that her hands and coat were adhering to a roach-infested pool of her mother's dried blood, she began to whimper. By the time she had torn herself and her clothes from the carpet and scrabbled furiously up the steps toward the kitchen, she had begun to scream.

Clothes, Jill thought as she drove. I'm going to need clothes, and makeup and toiletries. I forgot my laptop. I'll have to use a typewriter, or Gwen's legal pads and a pen, if I actually get over this block and write anything. No big deal: I've done it before. I'll stop somewhere for the other things. After I stop for lunch at the rest home in Port Jefferson. . . .

A quick stab of guilt coursed through her as she realized that she hadn't visited her mother in more than a month. Oh, well, she decided, that can be amended right now, today. I'll have lunch with her in that nice dining room, and I'll bring flowers and chocolate for her and her new friends, Mrs. Davis and Mrs.—Mrs.—Mrs. whatever-her-name-is.

Oh, God, Jill, *think!* Don't fall apart.

Not now.

Not yet . . .

The landlady was useless, Barney decided as he followed her up the narrow stairs to the seventh floor. She must be about ninety, and her eyesight was apparently poor, judging from the way she squinted at everything through her thick glasses. She'd only seen the young man once, two weeks ago, and she couldn't remember his name. Something foreign, she thought. He'd paid her cash for three weeks. No, there hadn't been any written contract, or anything like that. Unofficial income, she'd murmured proudly, to supplement her meager Social Security benefits. She'd actually winked at Barney when she'd admitted that.

She'd only agreed to take him up to the room after he'd shown her his detective's license and made up a quick story about a worried wife and kids in Brooklyn, and that he'd traced the errant husband to this street. He just wanted to see her tenant, he assured her. He probably wasn't the person he was looking for, but . . .

She'd pursed her lips and nodded then, muttering something about the inconstancy of the male gender, and the sorry lot of wives and children. He could tell, even as he followed her up the stairs, that she was half hoping her tenant was the guilty party. She'd give him a piece of her mind, no doubt.

When they reached the landing on the sixth floor, he stopped her. She was fairly gasping for breath by this point, so he turned his need to go to the door alone into an act of kindness.

"You wait here," he said, smiling. "I'll just knock on his door. If he doesn't answer, I'll have a little peek inside. That's all." He grinned as he reached out and gently removed the key ring from her withered hand.

"I don't know—" she began feebly, but he was already up the last flight of stairs. He glanced briefly down at her as he positioned himself before the door. She was muttering to herself, not even looking up the stairs in his direction. Thank God, he thought as he reached up and removed his weapon from the shoulder holster.

He didn't knock, of course. He carefully slid the key into the lock and turned it. Then, in one swift, surprisingly graceful move, he pushed the door open, dropped to his knees in the doorway, and aimed directly into the room.

He stared.

Empty.

Then he rose to his feet, slowly lowering the gun. The old woman was calling up from the flight below, but he paid no attention to her. His gaze moved around the tiny, drab space. There was an old, ratty armchair near the window, a sagging wood table beside it. On the table was a battered ashtray. In the corner were piled two bare, dirty striped mattresses. He went quickly over to the closet door and threw it open. Two or three rusting wire hangers. That was all.

He walked over to the window and looked out. Jill Talbot's picture window was directly across from him. If her curtains were opened, he'd be able to see most of her apartment perfectly.

Valentine has been here, he told himself.

The landlady's irritated, irritating cries reached him as he stood in the center of the room and slowly inhaled through his nose.

He nodded to himself.

Cigarette smoke.

The room had been vacated recently. Very recently.

He left the room. Locking the door behind him, he rejoined the woman, who waited at the bottom of the stairs. As they descended, he thought, I'll pay Escalera a call today. There might be fingerprints in that room. . . .

Then he thought, where are you? Where are you, Valentine?

His next thought stopped him in his tracks. He stood on the staircase, watching the landlady moving away from him down the stairs.

Where are you, Jill Talbot?

Jill Talbot was on the expressway, heading east.

She reached down and patted the pocket of her coat. She could feel the unreal, bizarre but oddly reassuring bulk through the wool: the solid, comforting weight of the gift Tara had slipped into the pocket when she'd helped her put the coat on. Keeping her left hand firmly on the wheel, she reached down with her right hand and transferred the heavy, loaded Lady Wesson from her pocket to her purse.

A gun, she thought. I've never so much as touched a gun in my life. But Mike knows all about them: he's going to give me a lesson.

A lesson. How to shoot. Maim. Cripple. *Kill* another human being.

Oh, Jill, what have you become?

Please, God, help me get through this. Just get me to Port Jefferson, to Mother. Then a shopping mall, for the things I'll need, and straight on to Peconic. To Gwen and Mike Feldman.

To safety . . .

MONDAY, FEBRUARY 9

VICTOR DIMORTA SAT IN A LITTLE BOOTH AT THE BACK

212

of the drab Greek diner, making plans.

His original plan had gone awry, he grudgingly admitted to himself. He'd known all along that there was every chance that Jillian Talbot would take off, but he hadn't expected her to do it so abruptly. Oh, well, it was the price he'd paid. The price for making this last one so elaborate.

This last one . . .

He remembered what he now thought of as his first one: February 29, sixteen years ago. Mother and Father. But it hadn't begun there, he knew. He thought of all the events that had led up to it, and of the catalytic event that had immediately preceded it: the prank played on him by the four girls in college. Yes, that night in the house in Mill City had been a long time coming. Eighteen years.

Eighteen years of Joseph ("Big Joe") Dimorta, the burly, scowling second-generation American who never tired of telling his skinny, soft son how he'd worked his way up from pulp mixer to lineman to head honcho. Who earned his nickname driving eighteen-wheelers and wielding paper bales that normally took two men to haul. Who never looked at Victor without an expression of naked contempt. Big Joe used his booming voice and mighty fists in a never-ending battle to make the boy a man.

Victor remembered the first time he'd gone to the hospital. His nose, his left arm, and two ribs. His mother told the admitting nurse that he'd fallen down the stairs. The nurse probably didn't believe her, but she didn't say anything. Nobody said anything, ever: the doctors, the cops, the teachers at school. And, least of all, Mother.

Mother. She was so small, he remembered. A small, dark-complectioned Italian woman who had, like her husband, been raised by immigrants who had themselves worked in the paper factory. It was considered a great thing when the quiet, plain, dutifully church-going front-office secretary had attracted the attention of the foreman, the best-paid and most respected man in Mill City.

Glancing around the nearly empty diner, Victor frowned at the memory. No sooner had Big Joe and Angela been married and blessed with their only child than the true reason for everyone's respectfulness became evident. The whole town was terrified of him. His temper, especially when drinking in the local tavern, was well known and feared by the people whose employment and only means of livelihood were determined entirely by him. Even his fellow foreman and presumed equal, Bob Wells, who lived two doors down from him on Franklin Street, took pains to stay in his good graces. And rumor had it that Joe's salary was augmented by under-the-table payoffs from the owners to keep the employees from unionizing—which ultimately involved three men being hospitalized, as Victor had been. All three swore that their attackers were Big Joe Dimorta and Bob Wells, but everyone, even the local sheriff, looked the other way.

If only, Victor now thought. If only Mother had been another kind of woman. If only she'd listened to her parents before marrying Big Joe: they—the only sane people in town, apparently—tried to talk her out of the marriage, and later disassociated themselves from her as a result of it. But she had married him. And, when she realized that her parents had been right, she remained as silent as everyone else in the town, retreating more and more into her perfect-wife-and-mother sham as a balm for the reality of her life. She was an active regular attendee of the little Catholic church in town. She even had framed pictures of Christ in nearly every room of her immaculate house, just to prove to everyone what a good and pious

214

woman she was. She quietly nursed her own wounds, physical and emotional, and learned that survival meant always obeying her husband, even when obedience meant closing her eyes to his brutality. By the time Victor was sixteen, two years after the factory shut down, she would occasionally strike Victor herself, especially when she'd had too much wine at dinner.

Then, in his senior year at the local public high school, Victor suffered the ultimate mortification at the hands of his parents. He'd always kept to himself and never invited other kids around, for obvious reasons. His exclusion from all youthful activities in the town had already garnered him the nickname "Victor Diweirdo." His one attempt to talk to a pretty girl in his class, who laughed at him and ran away, had resulted in a group of boys following him home from school, throwing rocks at him and calling him names. His father, hearing of this, had beaten him senseless—his second trip to the local emergency room and locked him in his bedroom closet overnight. But all of this might have been borne if it hadn't been for Angela Dimorta.

It was a Sunday afternoon. He remembered that, because his mother had been wearing her best dress and hat, having just returned from Sunday morning service and lunch with the priest. His father, who never accompanied them to church, was out somewhere with his buddies from the factory. Victor had begged off church that morning, claiming a cold. The truth was that, at seventeen, he already knew he didn't believe in God, and he was growing increasingly disgusted with the long, smarmy sermons he endured in God's house. He had stayed home alone that day, lying naked on his bed staring at the magazine he'd stolen from the back racks of Mr. Garvey's newsstand. So intent was he on the sight of Miss

215

October and the rhythmic, ever-increasing strokes of his right hand that he hadn't heard a sound until his bedroom door opened.

Angela Dimorta stood frozen in the doorway in her Sunday best, holding a glass of orange juice and a bottle of aspirin in her gloved hands, staring. The magazine fell to the bed as the glass and the aspirin bottle smashed on the floor. There was a long, charged moment as the two of them stared at each other in complete silence. Then, uttering a sharp cry of pure disgust, his mother turned around and marched down the hall to her room. Victor was out of the bed and fumbling frantically for his underpants when she returned, her husband's largest belt in her hands.

The first blow struck him on the side of the head, just behind his ear, knocking him to the floor. He made a groggy, painful attempt to rise, to protest, but the second, stronger impact of the heavy brass belt buckle sent him down again. His arms, his legs, his back: vicious lash after lash, seemingly without end. He lay on the wood floor, hearing the belt long after he ceased feeling it, as consciousness slowly seeped away.

A neighbor heard the sounds and called the police. When Victor woke up, he was in the hospital again. His mother soon joined him there, but not as a visitor. His father had come home that afternoon, roaring drunk, and Angela had told him what she had done, and why. Outraged by the unwanted police publicity, not to mention his wife's punishing their son for what was—to his way of thinking—the only remotely normal thing the boy had ever done, Big Joe turned on her. By the time he was through, Angela had a fractured jaw and two broken ribs.

The sheriff couldn't look the other way from that, and

Big Joe spent three days in the only cell in the Mill City police station. He came home and locked Victor in the closet for three days. Payback, he called it, for three days in jail, for Victor and his mother causing his imprisonment.

That was the turning point for Victor Dimorta. Always ostracized by the other children, he was now the public laughingstock, the kid with the crazy parents. He hated the world, Big Joe and Angela most of all. He sat in the closet for three days, only being let out to eat and go to the bathroom, and decided that he would get away from this. He would get out of Mill City and make something of himself. Once free of his parents, he would be accepted by society, by his peers. He didn't know how he would get away, but he would. There, in the dark, he swore it.

The answer was waiting for him upon his release from the closet. It was in the form of a letter addressed to him from a law firm in a nearby town. His maternal grandmother, who had legally disowned her daughter as a result of her marriage to the town bully, had died in the rest home where she'd been for eight years, and she'd left all her money to her only grandchild, some eighty-four thousand, to be inherited upon his majority. That was only six months away. His English teacher, impressed by his capability in her class, had helped him to get a partial scholarship to her alma mater, Hartley College.

The following spring, on his eighteenth birthday, he presented himself at the law firm. Near the end of June, he received a check from them. He deposited the bulk of it in a savings account, taking only five thousand with him. Then, in the first week of September, he slipped out of the house on Franklin Street in the middle of the night and made his way to the bus station. Eleven hours and two buses later, he was in Burlington, Vermont.

217

Now, in the diner in Greenwich Village, he signaled to the waitress and ordered food. Might as well eat, he thought, feeling the tightness that always gripped his stomach whenever he thought of college.

It should all have turned out some other way. He'd thought that getting away from his parents and Mill City would somehow magically transform him, turn him into an attractive, well-adjusted person. But he wasn't well-adjusted, he soon realized. He was shy, almost cripplingly so, and the slightest things made him angry. The other students at the college shunned him, and even the teachers mostly ignored his presence. The one bright spot in the whole place was a beautiful girl named Jillian Talbot.

He remembered that first day he saw her, sitting two desks away from him in English class in a yellow dress, her long, dark hair tied back with a yellow ribbon. She was quiet, almost as quiet as he, and like him she was something of an outsider. Whenever he saw her in that first semester, she was alone. He took to following her around, and he would watch her in the cafeteria or the library, wishing he could work up the courage to go over and speak to her. But, remembering the girl in Mill City who had laughed at him, he never did. He simply continued to adore her from a distance. At night, in his dorm room, he would lie awake making up elaborate fantasies in which they were married, running together on beaches and shopping in grocery stores and lying in bed, naked, making love. And when he slept, he dreamed of her.

After intercession, when classes reconvened, she had changed. No longer alone, she was now always in the company of three pretty senior girls, the ones who were called the Elements. He'd seen them around, and he'd sometimes substituted the blond one, Sharon, for Jillian in his masturbatory fantasies. He'd even tried going up to Sharon, and even the other two Elements, and speaking to them—as a sort of warmup to Jillian—but they all told him to get lost. But Sharon often looked at him in the hallways, he noticed, and there was always a gleam in her eye. He decided in private that she was attracted to him.

All of which led him into their trap.

One day, at the end of class, he steeled himself and went over to Jillian Talbot. He'd finally convinced himself to ask her for a date. She'd smiled and was polite at first, but when he'd tried to touch her she'd pulled away from him and fled, leaving him to shout down the hall after her receding form.

"Wait a minute! I just want to talk to you. I didn't mean to scare you. Jill? Jill!!"

A few days later, he'd overheard this same girl, the object of his adoration, telling another student that the blond senior, Sharon Williams, was hot for him, confirming his own secret suspicion. The next day, Valentine's Day, Jillian Talbot had smilingly handed him the card with Sharon's bold invitation.

"Simmonds Hall, Room 407, 11:00 tonight. Just you 'n' me, Victor. Be there. Sharon."

He would never, ever forget that night on the fourth floor of Simmonds Hall. He'd cut the rest of his classes that day, walking through the snow to the nearest candy store some three miles away. He'd bought the biggest, most expensive heart-shaped box of chocolates in the place. Then he'd gone back to his dorm and taken two showers. He hadn't been able to eat dinner that evening, he was so nervous. He put on his best shirt and pants, combed his hair for about an hour, and borrowed a bottle of Brüt cologne from his next-door neighbor. Then he made his way to Simmonds Hall, arriving outside the room at exactly eleven o'clock.

As soon as he knocked, the soft, sultry voice on the other side of the door told him to come in. He opened the door and walked into Heaven. The room was dark, sort of red-tinged, and there was a scent in the air like smoky perfume. A beautiful female voice was singing softly from the stereo, something about valentines. Sharon Williams was lying on the bed in black, lacy bra and panties, her long legs curled under her. He stood over the bed looking down at her, and she grinned and told him to take off his clothes.

He'd never done that before while a woman watched him—he'd never been with a woman—and he removed his clothes awkwardly, self-consciously. He had to put down the candy box, so he handed it to her. She tossed it aside. She watched as he took off his shirt, then socks and shoes, then his pants. When he stood before her wearing only his briefs, she sat up on the bed, reached out her hand, and groped him through the cotton material.

"Oh, what a big boy you are! Show me."

He was feeling more relaxed, more confident now, after her action and her remark, and he was about to burst out of the cotton briefs anyway. So he reached up, hooked his thumbs under the elastic at his waist, and slid the underpants down. They hit the floor as his erect penis sprang forward. Then he picked up the candy box and clutched it to his chest as he whispered to her in the dark.

"Happy Valentine's Day, Sharon."

Sharon stared, smiling. Slowly, slowly, she reached up to the wall behind her and switched on the overhead light.

He was blinded by the sudden assault of whiteness. When his vision cleared, all hell broke loose. The closet door burst open and two giggling women came tumbling out. One of them was holding up a movie camera, aimed at his manhood. The other had a microphone. Sharon jumped up from the bed, pulling on a bathrobe, her lovely face contorted with derisive laughter. At her instigation, the three of them began to sing along with the record.

Victor never really remembered exactly what happened next. He remembered being filled with a sudden rage such as he had never experienced before, not in all the years at home. He remembered smashing the record, and he remembered their screams of laughter turning to screams of fear. He knew he pushed one of them into the closet, the one with the video. And someone else hit the wall and started to bleed. And Sharon: he'd pulled her robe open and torn off her bra. Then he'd clawed at her with his nails, and she had fled from the room, screaming.

"Rape! Rape! Rape!!"

The word had filled him with sudden panic, replacing the rage, and he had stumbled down the hall to the open elevator. Downstairs, he was still clutching Sharon's bra when the three large, uniformed men had grabbed him and wrestled him to the ground. He'd looked up from the floor of the lobby to see about twenty people, mostly young women, staring down at his naked body. Many of them were laughing. And all he could hear was that song, over and over in his head . . .

Then Big Joe and Irrelevant Angela, the two people he hated most in the world, arrived in Burlington to take their runaway son home. His father had remained mostly silent the entire trip, his big hands gripping the steering wheel, as his wife raged from her seat beside him. All the way home.

"I can't believe you did this, Victor! Do you know how much you upset me? How you worried your father? What on

221

earth has gotten into you, you wicked creature? What will the neighbors think? We give you a good home and all our love, and look how you repay us!"

Then his father's terse shout, and the slap that sent her crashing into the passenger door. *"Shut the fuck up, you crazy bitch!"*

All the way home.

By the time the car arrived in bleak Mill City, Pennsylvania, Victor knew what he was going to do.

But he wouldn't think about that now.

The waitress brought his cheeseburger deluxe and coffee. He grinned as he thanked her. Blushing, she sidled away.

His memories of the weeks immediately following that February 29 were indistinct. He was in jail, and a lawyer kept arriving to talk to him, asking about his father and his mother and how many times he'd been in the hospital and locked in the bedroom closet. And somebody kept going on about a bargain, and voluntary manslaughter rather than second degree, and fifteen to thirty instead of life, consecutive. *Not* consecutive, his lawyer had continually shouted. No way consecutive! *Concurrent!* That's final, take it or leave it. And the phrases: "hot blood" and "severe abuse" and "emotional trauma." He didn't understand any of it, so he let the lawyer do the talking, and he agreed to the bargain he was offered because fifteen years, minimum, sounded better than life—not to mention Pennsylvania's death penalty, if there was a trial. These were options, the lawyer explained. So he did what he was told at the arraignment. The next thing he knew, he was in prison.

He remained there for twelve long, long years,

dreaming of the day when he'd be free. When he could find the Elements. He hated them now, more than he'd ever hated his parents. The whole thing was *their* fault, after all. If it hadn't been for them, none of this would have happened. He would never have been expelled. He would have stayed at the college studying English, and by now he'd be a world-famous author.

Like Jillian Talbot, Goddamn her soul to hell! Most of all, he hated Jillian Talbot.

He sat there in the prison, day after day, cursing them, cursing the very existence of the four young women he held responsible for his plight: earth, wind, fire, and water. Their own stupid joke gave him the idea for his justice.

But how would he accomplish it?

The answer arrived in his first days in the prison yard, and in the big communal shower room. He had never seen other men naked before, not even his father. He looked around the shower at the big, muscular convicts, then down at his own body. He realized that he had never thought about his personal appearance, what he presented to the outside world. Watching the men shower and work out in the yard and the gymnasium, he became aware for the first time that he was different from them. Very different. Victor Dimorta was ugly.

The answer was simple: he wouldn't be Victor Dimorta anymore. He would re-create himself, reinvent himself. Transform himself into something else. Someone else. He would become—

He grinned now, thinking of it.

—*Valentine.*

That's when he began his rebirth.

For the duration of his internment, Victor was a model prisoner. He never complained, he never got sick, and he kept a respectful distance from everyone, authorities and cons alike. He enrolled in every rehab course the prison offered: he painted, potted, sculpted, and photographed. He discovered his own brilliant talent, even greater than English. He submitted himself to one hour a week of elective psychiatric consultation. He taught illiterate inmates how to read and write. He joined a softball team and a basketball team. And every day for two hours, he worked out: Nautilus, freeweights, running, wrestling, calisthenics.

And every night, he dreamed about women. Four specific women. He allowed his hatred to fill him, consume him, until it became the most essential part of what he was. The obsession grew: he even found pictures in magazines of women who looked like them. He cut them out and taped them to the wall next to his bed. One in particular, a supermodel named Stacy Green, bore a striking resemblance to Jillian Talbot. Jillian was the Element to whom he'd been the most attracted. So he stared at pictures of Stacy Green, thinking of Jillian as he fondled himself.

And he did something else he'd never done before: he made friends. Most of the others liked him, especially the ones he patiently coaxed toward literacy. Two in particular, a guy about his age named Eric and an elderly lifer named Benny, became actual pals. He had long conversations and traded jokes and played beside them on teams, enjoying the newfound camaraderie that everyone else in the world took for granted. He learned how to fit in, how to get along, how to make people like him. This, too, was essential.

He never thought about his parents. He discarded their memory as useless, unconstructive, and potentially repressive. Big Joe and Angela Dimorta couldn't touch him, couldn't hurt him now. Not anymore. He relegated them to the past, to the oblivion they so richly deserved. The oblivion to which he, Victor, had sent them.

He was changing. Little by little, over the course of those twelve years, he evolved toward that new image he had formed in his head; that man who was not shy, skinny Victor Dimorta. Day by day he grew, becoming more strong, more controlled, more magnificent. And by the time he came up for parole, he knew that he was close, very close.

His parole was granted. On the day he walked out of the prison, he weighed fifty-five pounds more than he had on the day he walked in. He had a new body and a new personality. A new vitality. But there was still one more thing he needed, the most important part of his plan.

He went to Pittsburgh, where he met with his parole officer. This man—very nice, really—found him an inexpensive room and a stockroom job at McCrory's on Fourth Avenue. He went dutifully to work every day and dutifully back to his room every night.

During the next weeks, he reoriented himself to freedom, to living in the outside world. It felt new to him, this ability to move around unchecked and even unnoticed. He had the job and the rooming house, not to mention the parole officer, but beyond these there was an acute sensation of being unrestrained that he had never experienced before. With it came the realization: he had never been free before. Not in the past twelve years, certainly—but not in the eighteen years before it, either. He assimilated the feeling, making it a part of his new identity.

His new identity, he thought. Yes. It's time., Now.

One day, a month into his parole, he went to the Pittsburgh branch of his bank in Mill City. The eighty thousand he'd left there thirteen years before had nearly

225

doubled: he figured he could well afford what he was going to do now. He then went back to the prison to visit his friends, Eric and Benny. Sitting on the other side of the bulletproof glass panel from them had been odd, downright embarrassing, but he needed information that only Benny could supply. Benny had, in more than thirty years in prison, become a living encyclopedia of useful criminal information: he told Victor where to go and what to ask for. Victor thanked his friend, lied that he would visit again soon, and returned to Pittsburgh.

At the end of seven weeks of stockroom work, when the parole officer had relaxed surveillance and was looking the other way, Victor Dimorta left the rooming house one morning, walked two blocks west to Chatham Center, and entered the taxi waiting there for him. He was driven to a private clinic on the outskirts of the city.

Twelve weeks and three operations later, he was no longer Victor Dimorta.

He was Valentine.

He emerged from the clinic's post-op facility on August 23, three and a half years ago, and began what felt like his longest wait. He waited for months, living in a motel in a small town near Pittsburgh. In this time, he finally lost his virginity—with a vengeance. He employed the two prostitutes who worked out of the motel's bar and grill, and took them to his room. There, he asked them to teach him everything they knew, everything that pleased a woman. Every way to make her tremble at his touch. He spent entire weekends in bed with them, sometimes singly, sometimes both at the same time, until they both assured him that he was no longer merely having sex with them: he was making love to them, and extremely well, too.

He made frequent pilgrimages to his home in Mill City,

now an abandoned shell in a row of ramshackle houses on the hill above the dying town. He had to be careful approaching the house, because the state police were looking for him. Still, every few weeks he found himself there again, sleeping in his childhood bed and eating at the rotting table in the dusty dining room. In the years since, he'd been drawn back there again and again, often living there for weeks at a time, alone and unseen. It was his home, the only home he'd ever known. And now that his parents weren't there, it was perfect.

He spent a great deal of time inspecting himself in the full-length mirror inside the door of the upstairs bathroom. He would stand before it naked, drinking in this handsome, powerfully built new person he had become. This sexy, friendly animal who could excite women with his grin and satisfy them with his body.

He was Valentine.

And he was going to kill the four Elements. Every last fucking one of them.

On January 26, three years ago, the waiting was over. He flew to Los Angeles. He rented a room in a quiet part of town. He rented a Mercedes. He went to Rodeo Drive and bought a new wardrobe. Then he drove to Sharon Williams's apartment complex and began to watch her.

The waitress shuffled over with fresh coffee as he remembered the picnic in Los Angeles, and the second meeting, a year later in Boulder. He smiled.

The next one on his list, Cass MacFarland, was the most difficult of the four to find. She was not in Montclair, New Jersey, anymore. Taking a tip from the relocated Belinda, he'd decided to locate Cass in August, a full six months before Valentine's Day, and it was a good thing he did.

He went to Montclair and began his search. For three days, he checked out every place near her old home where he thought people might know her. He asked every neighbor on her street and came up empty. He asked bartenders and waitpeople in every restaurant and tavern in a two-mile radius. Nothing. Finally, on a hunch based on their major at Hartley, he went into the nearest bookstore to her childhood home.

Bingo. The middle-aged couple behind the counter knew Cassandra very well. They'd watched her grow from a girl to a woman. She'd always been one of their best customers. Read all the time, probably because she wanted to be a writer. She used to come in with her husband, before the divorce. She left Montclair then. Where did she go? he asked. Well, they didn't know where she'd moved to—but David would. David was her older brother, an actor who lived in New York City, and he and Cass were very close. So sad about his disinheritance, the wife observed. He's gay, you know. . . .

There were only two David MacFarlands in the Manhattan directory. He got him on the first try. He was an old friend of Cass's from Hartley, in town on business. How could he reach her?

The brother surprised him. Well, I can't just tell someone that on the phone, he said. But if you'll give me your name, I'll mention it to her the next time I call her. . . .

Victor slammed down the phone: he hadn't been expecting that. Cursing his luck, he left Montclair and went straight to the address on West Forty-fourth Street in New York.

David MacFarland was either a tall, lanky, handsome man with black hair or a slightly shorter, equally good-

228

looking blond with a mustache. The blond man was obviously ill, and he walked slowly, painfully, with the help of a cane. He watched them coming and going from the building a couple of times. They lived in the basement apartment of the four-story brownstone.

It was easy. He'd learned all about lock-picking from Benny, the old lifer. He'd studied fundamentals of electronics in one of his brownie-point courses. A quick trip to a shop on Broadway and he was all set.

He checked into a fleabag around the corner, went back to David MacFarland's building, and waited. That evening, the two men came up the steps to the street and hailed a cab. Both were holding brightly wrapped birthday gifts. Wherever they were going, he reasoned, they'd probably be a while. He waited until the cab turned the corner before bounding down the steps.

There was a deadbolt on the door. He stood there, frustrated and furious, casting his gaze around for some other means of entry. Then he laughed and put his picking device back in his pocket. The window next to the door was slightly open: someone had forgotten to close it.

The first thing he did was look for an address book, or anything in the apartment that might have the address, or even a phone number. The leatherbound Filofax he found in the bedroom obviously belonged to the roommate, and there were no MacFarlands listed. So, plan B. In ten minutes, the bug was in the phone receiver and he was in his room around the corner, setting up the tape machine. Then he went out for a steak dinner.

He spent the next three days exploring Wonderland, this beautiful, exciting city he'd read about and seen in movies. He went to museums and Rockefeller Center and the Empire State Building and Macy's. He saw his first Broadway musical. New York was such a perfect place to get lost in, to be anonymous in. He knew, before those three days had passed, that he was going to live here. He'd find a place—but first . . .

On the evening of the third day, he came back to the room and played the tape back. In the two previous days, he'd heard mundane conversations between the roommate, Rick—apparently the blond with the cane—and his mother, who called every day to be sure he was taking his medication. Then David, the tall one with the black hair, would get on with her and assure her that Rick was okay, that she needn't come to New York yet. He'd heard David talking to a woman who was apparently his theatrical agent. No calls this week, she said, whatever that meant. He'd heard calls from friends, men and women inviting them places and chatting aimlessly and always, always asking after Rick's health.

This evening, he got lucky. He recognized Cass MacFarland's voice immediately. She spoke to her brother, confirming an already-made plan for tomorrow. David was getting his car out of the garage on the corner at one o'clock, and the two men were driving to New Jersey to stay with her for a couple of days. How's the cabin? David asked. Cozy, she said. Take the Holland Tunnel; it's faster.

The next day, he checked out of the hotel, threw the tape recorder away, and went to Hertz Rent-a-Car. Then he parked near the garage on the corner near David's home and waited. At precisely one o'clock the two men appeared and went into the garage, emerging a few minutes later in a green Volvo.

He followed them through the tunnel and along miles and miles of the New Jersey Turnpike. They drove for nearly two hours. Just when he was beginning to think that New Jersey couldn't possibly continue much longer, the car ahead went onto an exit ramp.

The smaller, secondary highway led to a tiny town surrounded mostly by hills and forest. David turned right at the main intersection in the center of the village, and took off down a small road. Victor waited a while at the intersection: from now on, tailing them was going to be tricky.

He followed. The road went through the woods, and there were lots of curves. He caught a glimpse of the other car once, on a long stretch, far ahead of him. Then it turned on a curve and disappeared in the trees. He sped up a little.

After a few miles, he realized that the car was no longer in front of him. He stopped, turned around, and drove slowly back the way he'd come, scanning the few turnoffs, all of which had mailboxes. Long driveways, apparently: there were no houses visible from the road. The third turnoff on the left had a bright, shiny new mailbox, and the name neatly painted on it was C. MACFARLAND.

He ordered apple pie from the waitress, smiling. Smiling at the memory of his own ingenuity in tracing his third victim. Smiling at the glorious memory of his Valentine's Day liaison with her six months later.

Cass MacFarland was a pleasant surprise. In college, she had always been with the other girls, one part of the four-headed monster that was the Elements. Now, fifteen years later, she was a quiet, dignified, serious woman. She never spoke with her parents, she would tell him shortly into their brief relationship, and she'd lost contact with all her former friends. She'd been married for six years to a man she'd grown up with, a college instructor who'd eventually run away with one of his students. The only person she kept in constant touch with was her brother, whom she obviously adored. Her dark red hair and her easy smile had made this third task a pleasant one.

But first, he'd had to make initial contact. And the way he did that was clever, as clever as anything Valentine had ever done. He knew—and who would know better?—that people who isolated themselves from society were particularly susceptible to kindness.

There was a little restaurant in the town where she went by herself for dinner every Saturday night. He'd moved to New York by now, but he came out to this remote part of New Jersey every now and then in the following months, to keep an eye on her. He watched her alone in her cabin, and he noted the careful dress and makeup she affected on her Saturday-night trips into town.

He would watch through the window as she sat, always alone and always at the same table, chatting with the waitress and the busboy. Once or twice the proprietor, a portly, middle-aged man, joined her for dessert and coffee. Before leaving the restaurant, she would go up to the bar near the front for an afterdinner drink, and she would laugh and joke for half an hour with the bartender. Then, with smiling farewells for all of them, she would go out to her car and drive slowly back to her house in the woods.

He watched this routine every Saturday for six weeks. Other than that, she rarely left the house, except to go to the supermarket or the drugstore, and she would always linger there, talking with the checkout girls or the pharmacist. Once, he followed her to the town's tiny movie theater. She bought her ticket for the film, a romantic love story that had been highly praised, according to the posters outside. Then he watched through the glass front doors as she had a long conversation with the girl who sold the popcorn.

Cass MacFarland was lonely.

Meeting her in the restaurant was easy. One Saturday night, four weeks before Valentine's Day, he sat at the next table in the nearly empty dining room and struck up a conversation. By dessert, she'd invited him to join her.

I'm a writer, trying to write a novel, he said, but the city is too noisy. Friends said to try way out here on weekends. Amazing! she cried: *I'm* a writer, too! No kidding! he said. I'm staying at the little hotel down the street on weekends. Would you like to have dinner next Saturday night . . . ?

He'd added the new embellishments with Cass: the anonymous cards and flowers. He'd spent the three weeks before Valentine's Day—when he wasn't dating her— watching her in the cabin from the nearby forest. (After he'd smothered her, in retrospect he found that he derived more pleasure from watching her than from eventually killing her. He would remember this with Jillian.)

Cass was writing a novel, and she'd used her divorce settlement and part of her trust fund to buy this isolated cabin. The rest she'd given to her brother, she told him, to take care of his lover, who was dying. She had deliberately removed herself from the world to make a serious attempt at a book. She'd been attempting to write novels ever since her college days, but she had yet to complete one. Six years of trying to make a go of the relationship with the philanderer had put her further off course. Now, at thirty-six, she felt it was time to accomplish what she'd always set out to do. She'd smiled when she said this, adding that it was time for her to meet her true destiny.

Yes, he agreed. It was.

When the cards and the flowers appeared, she immediately figured it out. She told him about Victor Dimorta, the creepy freshman who had assaulted her and her girlfriends. She never once mentioned the prank that had gotten him to the room that night. She tried to contact her friends at old addresses, which is how she learned from Sharon's mother that Sharon had vanished two years ago. She never traced Belinda, and she never mentioned Jillian Talbot, giving him the odd impression that she did not consider Jillian to have been part of the practical joke. Even so, she was worried enough to buy a gun to protect herself, and she actually showed it to him.

Don't worry, he assured her. I'll be here with you on Valentine's Day.

And he was.

Every time he thought about the burning cabin in the woods, he became sexually aroused. He'd read about it in the papers back in New York. The photos of the ruined cabin. The devastated brother. The search for a tall, dark-haired man thought to have been dating her in the last three weeks of her life. He'd used the name he'd first given to Sharon Williams with Cass and at the hotel, and that was the name the hotel proprietor gave the police. The man who never was, he mused, smiling.

It was so brilliant, he reflected. Sharon Williams had been buried. Belinda Rosenberg had fallen to her death from a great height. Cass MacFarland had been immolated.

Earth.

Wind.

Fire.

And now, in the diner, he thought, it's your turn, Jillian Talbot. Water, the fourth element. You can run, but you can't hide. Not from me. Not from Valentine. I know how to find you.

But first, that detective. Barney Fleck, the big guy on West Twenty-fifth Street. He went to the police the other day, and they searched the building across from her. Yes, the detective . . .

He hummed his favorite tune to himself as he stood up and went over to the cashier. "My Funny Valentine." He caught a glimpse of his own image reflected on the mirror-paneled wall behind the girl at the cash register. Yes, he told himself again, that analyst had to go. Reconstructive surgery could only do so much. Jillian had been the least self-absorbed of the four Elements: sometimes, he thought she had been the only one of them who'd really *looked* at Victor Dimorta. If her memory were jogged, she'd see right through the minor alterations. She'd look at him and remember, and that must not happen. Not yet.

He smiled at the cashier and went back to the table to leave a large tip, happy with the world. He was thinking about her again.

She was going to be his masterpiece. He would do this one perfectly. And in his mind he spoke to her.

Are you frightened, Jillian? Are you afraid of Valentine? Have you ever felt such fear, such terror, in your whole stupid, privileged, lucky life?

My dear Jillian, the terror has just begun.

WATER

CHAPTER 10

TUESDAY, FEBRUARY 10

SHE WOKE TO THE SOUND OF BIRDS. THE SMALL, SOFT chirping noises slowly coaxed her from sleep, and it was several moments before she realized where she was. When she did, she stood up, yawned and stretched, and went over to the door of the little log cabin. Outside, the air was crisp and cold, and there was a swirling blanket of thick white mist hanging among the evergreen trees and above the still, gray water of the lake.

Jill took a long, deep breath: fresh, clean air, tinged with salt from Long Island Sound, which lay some four hundred yards in front of her, beyond the massive sand dunes on the other side of the retreat. The twelve cabins were nestled in the forest around the main house, the biggest structure nearest the lake, where Gwen and Mike lived. Her cabin, number 12, was the farthest one from the lake, back among the trees. It was the most isolated, and the most quiet.

The main room was long, with doors at either end. A barracks: that was the word. In her mind's eye, she saw the rows of bunk beds against the two longer walls, accommodating perhaps seven little boys or girls and one counselor. At present, there was just the one big, comfortable four-poster, an overstuffed armchair, a braided area rug, and a desk and chair against the wall under the window that, if opened, would face the lake. On one wall hung a large, old-fashioned pendulum clock that chimed the hours. Gwen's touches, of course. The windows were cabin-style, top-hinged wood things that had to be swung out and propped up with sticks to remain open. Now, in February, they were closed and latched. The bathroom in one corner was a recent innovation: the camp had utilized now-vanished latrines and shower houses, not to mention a mess hall with industrial sized kitchen that had also been torn down. She smiled, trying to imagine Mike and Seth, the ancient handyman who apparently came with the place, installing fixtures and septic tanks. They must have been busy for months.

The water in the tiny shower stall in the tiny bathroom was freezing—and that was from the tap labeled HOT. She washed quickly, shivering, wondering what could possibly emanate from the cold one. Well, she reasoned, it had to travel a long way from the central cistern, wherever that was. She dried her hair with her brand-new blow-dryer, put on new jeans and a new sweater and a new down coat, and headed down the hill through the trees along a well-worn path.

She passed several other log bunkhouses, now refashioned as guest cottages, and crossed the large clearing at the center of the complex that still housed a baseball diamond. Near home base stood the lone, denuded flagpole that had been saluted twice every day by a hundred little patriots in morning and evening rituals involving bugles. The trees pressed in around the clearing on three sides; she smiled as she walked by, imagining the number of lost, rotting baseballs that, even now, probably adorned the forest floor. The fourth edge of the clearing was lakefront, with the main building and the dock. The little paved road from the highway half a mile away came in from the forest near the shore, and there were parking spaces there. She could hear voices inside the big house as she approached it, and the enticing aroma of frying bacon wafted out to greet her. She smiled at that: this was her fourth day here, and so far there hadn't been a single incidence of morning sickness. She had apparently left that behind her, in the city. Along with so much else . . .

She stopped on the porch and looked out at the view. The lake was perhaps a hundred feet away. It was a medium-sized body of water, she supposed, but in the eyes of a city girl it was enormous. The thick, green forest ringed it all the way around, and here and there by the water were other small clearings with other buildings, six or seven lakeside summer homes for affluent New Yorkers, all of them now deserted. The farthest houses, on the other side, were so remote as to be barely visible. The dock directly in front of her was a solid-looking old wooden structure jutting twenty-five feet out into the water, with a diving board and a ladder at the end. The little strip of gray, muddy beach beside the dock was crowded with three rowboats and two canoes—another legacy from the summer camp. The morning sun peered down through the mist, highlighting the water. She sighed: beautiful.

The downstairs area of the large, two-story stone-and-redwood main house was mostly one big room, with a spacious kitchen at the back. The large space was an all-purpose gathering place; half hotel lobby, half dining room. Couches and easy chairs were gathered around an enormous coffee table, and there was a rocking chair in one corner, the mate of the three on the front porch next to the suspended porch swing. The dining area at the back of the room, close to the kitchen, housed the biggest mahogany dinner table she'd ever seen. It currently seated twelve, but Gwen had told her there were extra leaves to accommodate a grand total of eighteen, should the need arise. One side wall was of fitted flagstone, with an impressive fireplace that was constantly working in these winter months. Along the other side wall was the little wooden staircase leading to Gwen and Mike's apartment. This had obviously once been the home of the camp's proprietors.

There were three people in the room, a lone woman and a couple seated across from each other by the fire, and she heard banging and clattering from the kitchen: Gwen. The small, pretty, middle-aged woman in tweed was Barbara Benson, the romance writer who had been something of a national institution for nearly thirty years now. Her hair was wavy and slightly blue-tinged, and Jill noted the double ropes of pearls and the scent of lavender, both of which were trademarks. Barbara had published nearly sixty books so far, and she was probably fabulously wealthy. The same could be assumed of the small, dark-haired, goateed man across from her: Jeffrey Monk was a world-class horror novelist. He was rather intense-looking, and Jill noticed that he rarely spoke. The attractive, friendly woman next to him was his wife, Ruth, who always seemed to smile. She'd made an impression on Jill the evening she'd arrived here from New York, leaning over after dinner and confiding to Jill that she couldn't stand her husband's books. All three of them had gone out of their way to be friendly to Jill, which made her wonder if Gwen and Mike had, perhaps, told them something of her recent ordeal. Jill also knew that both writers, successful as they were, could easily afford to be anywhere else but here, and that their participation in the opening weeks of the colony was more for Gwen and Mike's sake than their own. Cachet, not to mention publicity: allirnportant for a business just getting under way. Jill understood that Barbara and Jeffrey were trying to help their young colleagues, and she immediately liked them for it.

"Good morning," she said to the three.

"Hello, dear," Barbara cooed. "Don't you look well rested! The peace and quiet here is just heavenly."

"Yes, isn't it?" Ruth chimed in. "I think we've found a cure for Jeff's insomnia."

The horror writer agreed, smiling.

"Come and get it!"

The cheerful voice that uttered this belonged to the cheerful little blond woman in the black-and-white polka-dotted granny dress who now bustled in from the kitchen with a heaping tray. She set the massive pile of scrambled eggs down on the long sideboard near the dinner table and trotted over to peck Jill's cheek. "Hello there!"

Jill grinned. Gwen Feldman was easily the most energetic person she knew, with the possible exception of her husband. As everyone rose and went to the sideboard, she asked, "Where's Mike?"

"At the train station," her hostess sang, handing out plates and checking for serving utensils in all the dishes: eggs, bacon, sausage, waffles, toast, fruit, hot and cold cereal. "I am happy to announce that we will soon have two new recruits joining us any moment. Craig Palmer, the mystery writer—you know him, don't you, Jill?—and Wendy Singer, who has that detective series about the woman veterinarian. And someone else called this morning to book a cottage for Thursday. We're turning into quite a little crowd! And speaking of that, the Valentine's Day party, originally scheduled for Valentine's Day, has become the Day Before Valentine's Day party, courtesy of Ms. Barbara Benson and Mr. and Mrs. Jeffrey

240

Monk, who will be leaving us on Saturday afternoon. So get your dancing shoes ready for Friday night. Mike will be at the turntable, playing his entire collection of big band records. Champagne, door prizes, and dancing till dawn. We've invited several of our new neighbors, too, so it's your only chance to meet some of the locals. I hope you all plan to attend. Now, let's eat."

Jill, following the strict instructions of Dr. Chang, abstained from the delicious-looking heavy foods and settled for half a grapefruit and a bowl of corn flakes. It was an effort, however: she noted again how strongly her appetite had returned the moment she'd left New York City. She got a cup and saucer, poured decaf from a pot at the end of the sideboard, and sat next to Gwen, who was at the head of the table.

They had barely begun the meal when they heard the approaching van, and in moments the door swung open and three people bustled in, laden with suitcases, laughing and chatting. The biggest of the three was Mike, in flannel shirt and overalls and stocking cap, his bushy black beard covering his face. He resembled nothing so much as Paul Bunyan.

"Here we are, folks!" he boomed, dropping several bags to the floor and instructing his charges to do the same. "We'll get all this stowed away later. But first, grub!"

They all headed for the sideboard. Jill knew the aristocratic, fiftyish Craig Palmer: they'd met on several occasions, having not only a mutual publisher but a mutual editor. The lovely young woman, Wendy Singer, was fairly familiar to her as well, from meetings of Sisters in Crime that Jill occasionally attended.

Craig and Wendy were introduced to the other celebrities at the table, and Mike dropped into the seat on the other side of the table from Jill, next to his wife. As he

241

dug into his breakfast, Jill leaned toward him and said, "Are we still on for today?"

"What? Oh, yeah, sure. How about three o'clock? I'll be finished with my chores by then. The range is on the other side of the baseball field, just inside the woods."

"Okay," Jill said. "Three o'clock."

Gwen frowned at the two of them. "Are you sure about this, Jill?"

"Oh, yes." Jill smiled to placate her peace-loving friend. "Your husband's going to show me how to defend myself."

Barney was on the highway again, heading northeast, away from Pittsburgh. The weather today was cold but remarkably clear, and the rental car was not as annoying as rental cars usually were. A couple more like this, he thought as he drove, and I might actually get to like automatic shifts.

He glanced down at the road map on the passenger seat with the route outlined in ink. Yes, take this highway to that exit, then Mill Road right into the town. He could ask there for directions to Franklin Street.

He yawned luxuriously, thankful for the fact that he'd stopped for a sandwich and coffee after leaving the prison. The early morning flight from New York had necessitated his being up at six A.M. It was now two-thirty. He'd left the roadside diner twenty-five minutes ago, but it already seemed to him that he'd been driving for hours.

The highway was fairly empty at this hour, and the flat, gray landscape of southwestern Pennsylvania in midwinter held no allure. He reached over to the seat next to him and moved the gas station map aside. Under it were the copies the warden's secretary had made of Victor Dimorta's mug shots. He looked at the photos again, a full-front and a profile. A long, thin, pockmarked face with a dull expression. Lank, greasy hair. Large, dark eyes that revealed nothing but a vague disinterest. A long, sharp, almost hawklike nose over a thin, straight line of a mouth. The prominence of the Adam's apple and the marked hollowness of the cheeks indicated that this eighteen year-old was underweight.

A thoroughly unremarkable young man, Barney thought. A kid you'd never notice; a kid who looked exactly like a hundred other kids you saw every day on the streets of New York. And yet, this particular run-of-the-mill, nondescript individual had just murdered his parents in their sleep mere hours before these pictures were taken.

He wondered what the kid looked like now.

It was the warden, a genial, almost fatherly man named Sanford, who had suggested that Barney talk to the stoolie. Now, Barney was grateful for the warden's intelligence.

When the small, elderly con had been brought into the office, he'd stood staring at the warden and at the enormous, gray-haired man who sat on the other side of the desk. He was not handcuffed, Barney had noted, making him realize that this old man had spent most of his adult life in this facility. He was not a security risk, and he had certain privileges. He was introduced to the detective merely as Ed.

For the apparent price of a pack of cigarettes, tossed to him by the warden, Ed told Barney what he knew about Victor Dimorta. Very quiet, he said, kept to himself. But he'd been liked and respected by everyone, especially the cons he'd taught to read and write. And he'd had a couple of particular friends, two guys who had since departed: well, one had left this prison and the other this earth. After his release, Victor came back to visit his buddies

243

once, and word went around the yard that he was planning to get a face-lift. That was all Ed knew.

Ed had been dismissed, and Barney had thanked the warden and left for Mill City.

A face-lift, he thought as he drove. Reconstructive surgery. This man is a blank: no face, no fingerprints.

There had been no fingerprints in the room across from Jillian's apartment. Barney knew Juan Escalera of the Sixth from the old days, and Juan had no objection to Barney's presence at the scene. In fact, the sergeant greeted him as an old friend, which he supposed he was.

The table, the ashtray, the doorknobs: all had been dusted, but only partial smudges appeared, nothing clear. The bathroom on the floor below his room—shared with the two elderly men in the rooms on that floor—had been cleaned the day before, and only one set of fingerprints had been found on the sink. They belonged to Mr. Abrams in 6A. The old men had only gotten brief glimpses of their tall, dark-haired upstairs neighbor.

Escalera had thanked everyone for their cooperation. Then, with a hearty handshake and a promise of dinner together real soon, the sergeant and his associates had gone back to work on another, more immediate problem: the clinical psychologist who had been murdered on Tenth Street. The press was having a field day with it. Barney had promised to call Escalera if he found anything interesting in Pennsylvania.

Now, as he drove toward Mill City, Barney wondered what he was going to do when he got there. Find the house, certainly. Talk to neighbors, local tradespeople, anyone who might have known the family. Anyone who might have known—or still knew—Victor Dimorta.

He had to see Victor's new face.

"Beginner's luck!" Mike cried as he retrieved the paper

target from the post in the trench at the other end of the clearing and brought it over. "Look at this!"

Jill stood on the wooden platform of the shooting range, clutching the small handgun as she stared down at the square of paper Mike held up for her inspection. She had fired four shots, all of them hitting within the second circle, two in the bull's-eye.

Mike grinned. "Are you sure you've never done this before?"

"Positive," she said. "Let me try again."

He nodded and went to post another target as she reloaded. When he was back beside her, she stood straight, feet apart, and extended her arms in front of her. Her right hand held the gun, her left hand clutched her right wrist, steadying it. She gazed down the length of her arm and the short barrel, and past them to the tiny white square some twenty feet away. She didn't see the paper: in her mind, she saw a tall, skinny, dark-haired phantom without a face. When she was ready, she squeezed the trigger.

"Bull's-eye!" Mike shouted.

Seven Franklin Street was a shabby little two-story wood structure, vaguely Victorian in design, its front porch sagging, the once-white paint peeling away. Even the FOR SALE sign sticking hopefully up from the dirt next to the porch steps was faded. It was virtually identical to the others in the row in which it stood on one side of the small road overlooking the valley that contained the rest of the town, such as it was. Beyond the little clump of buildings that covered an area of four square blocks below him, Barney saw the remains of the paper factory, a crumbling cement skeleton with broken rows of windows and empty smokestacks pointing up into the gray sky.

Gray, he thought: everything in this place is gray. The factory, the town, the sky, and this row of houses on this gray drive above the gray valley.

He turned from the depressing view and went back across the road and up the steps to the porch of number seven. The door was locked, the windows shuttered. He left the porch and circled the house. The tiny, fenced-in backyard—like the others in the row—was overgrown with weeds, its two trees dry and naked. The back door of the house was locked. A tiny, rock-lined strip of black earth along the back of the house next to the kitchen door bore witness to Angela Dimorta's long-ago attempt at flower gardening.

Back on the road, he noticed that two or three other houses on either side had cars parked in front of them, On a porch two houses away to the left sat an old woman in a rocking chair. She had knitting in her lap, and she was watching him with the steady gaze of one who has seen everything and found precious little of it to be of much interest. He smiled and waved to her. She nodded. He took this as encouragement and walked up the road to stand below her porch.

"Good afternoon," he said.

She nodded again, her knitting needles clacking. "You fixin' to buy the haunted house?"

He smiled. "Number seven? Why do you call it that?"

"Ev'body calls it that. Crazy kid lived there, killed his father and mother. 'Course, *they* were crazy, too . . . ."

"Did you know them?" he asked.

She eyed him. "Sure. My late husband and Big Joe Dimorta were the foremen at the paper plant."

Barney came up the steps to her. "What about the kid?"

"Victor?" She uttered a dry laugh. "He was always a strange one, even when he was little. Used to throw rocks at dogs, see if he could hit 'em. Got bit a couple of times, too." She chuckled again. "Bothered the girls in school— and the other boys beat him up, just like his daddy did. Big Joe used to whale on him and Angela somethin' fierce! Two doors away, and sometimes I had to put my hands over my ears. Victor ran away from home, off to some college, then got thrown out of there. I heard that had to do with botherin' girls, too. They didn't mention that at the arraignment."

"The arraignment?" Barney widened his eyes, the perfect audience.

"Yeah. After he killed 'em. Cut their throats while they were asleep. Went to prison, but he's out now. He broke his parole. Had all these state troopers here a few years ago, askin' questions. Oh, well, I'd think twice about buyin' that house, I was you."

"Why?"

For the first time, she stopped knitting. Her hands were still in her lap as she looked up at him, then down the street at Victor's house. "It's haunted. I've never seen him, but I think he comes back there. Every now and then, not much lately. The Olsens down the road, number five, they say so, too. We've all heard things, mostly at night. Voices. Music, sometimes. We've seen lights in the windows. Stuff like that."

"Have you reported this to the police?"

She went back to her knitting. "Nah. None of my business."

Barney watched her. "Aren't you afraid of him?"

"Of who? Victor?" The old woman laughed again. "Why would he want to kill *me*? I'm not his mother!"

Barney forced himself to smile at her witticism. He looked at his watch: four o'clock. He would have to wait for nightfall to do what he was going to do. "Anywhere around here to get something to eat?"

She jabbed a thumb in the direction of the main highway. "East, next exit. There's a real town there, with a mall. Lots of restaurants in the mall."

"Thanks. Who owns the house now? I mean, who's selling it?"

"Big Joe's sister."

He nodded. As he left her porch and walked back down the road, she called after him. "So, are you gonna buy it?"

"No, I don't think so." He grinned. "I wouldn't want to crowd him."

Her dry cackle followed him all the way to the car.

After Mike left the range, Jill remained for another hour, setting up her own targets, loading, and shooting. She was growing used to the feel of the weapon in her hand, and she was actually beginning to like the sense of power it conferred. As for her aim, the worst she'd done all afternoon was narrowly miss the target, and that had happened only twice. All her other shots were within the circles, nearly half of them in the center two.

When the sun began to set and the light faded in the little glen, she put the gun in her purse and went across the baseball field to the main house by the lake. Ruth Monk was the only person there, sitting near the fire with what Jill was flattered to see was a copy of her own new paperback, *Murder Me.* All the writers were probably in their cabins, hard at work. I'm the only one who doesn't have a project, she thought as she waved to Ruth, who held up the book and raised her eyebrows before going back to it. Jill smiled at the compliment and went over to the little table in the corner of the room that held the colony's only telephone. The cabins did not have phones, or televisions or radios, or any other form of distraction.

Newspapers were not allowed in the compound, and even modem hookups for personal computers were discouraged. Gwen and Mike had the only television, in their bedroom. This place was here so that people who were easily distracted could get some serious writing done.

The handmade sign sticking out of the wicker basket beside the instrument read:

5 MINUTES PER CALL ONLY!
LOCAL CALLS: $1.00.
NEW YORK CITY: $2.00.
LONG DISTANCE: SEE GWEN.

Jill dropped a five-dollar bill in the basket and placed two calls to New York City. Neither Tara nor Nate was home. She left a brief message on Tara's machine, wishing her the best on her date tonight. But when she heard Nate's deep voice on his machine, she immediately hung up, remembering their conversation from two nights ago.

She'd broken Gwen's rule and stayed on the phone with him for fifteen minutes, trying to explain that she hadn't meant to hurt him. She'd left town abruptly because she just wanted to get away for a while, and she hadn't asked him to come with her because he had a show coming up, and that's what he should be worrying about. Nate was actually somewhat mollified until he'd asked her where she was calling from and she'd refused to tell him. Then he'd started yelling again, and she had said a quick good-bye, promised to call him again soon, and hung up.

Now, she couldn't think of a suitable message to leave on his answering machine. She wasn't going to explain to him that she was hiding from someone who had broken into her apartment to give her another grisly gift, who had bugged her telephone and her living room, who had murdered two people and had probably murdered three others as well. If she told him any of these things, he'd insist on knowing where she was, and he'd come out here to hold her hand instead of being in New York getting ready for his opening, which is what he should be doing.

With a little grimace, Jill took the five-dollar bill out of the wicker basket and replaced it with two singles. She'd call Nate later. And she promised herself that, after this, she'd never withhold things from him again.

She went back to the kitchen and offered to help Gwen with dinner. Her offer was gratefully accepted.

The phone was ringing as Tara came into her apartment. She dropped the dry cleaning she'd just collected—the red dress she would wear to dinner tonight—and picked up the receiver.

"Hello."

"Hi, Tara, it's Doug."

"Hello there! I'm just getting ready for—"

"Umm, listen, Tara. I'm afraid I'm not going to be able to meet you tonight. Something—something's come up. Business. I'm sorry about this, but I promise I'll make it up to you."

"Oh, sure, that's okay. I understand."

"Thank you for being so nice about it. I—I'll call you in the next couple of days, okay?"

"That'll be fine. I'm sorry about tonight, too. Don't work too hard. 'Bye." She hung up quickly, hoping she hadn't sounded too disappointed, too desperate. She hadn't really been aware until this minute just how much she'd been looking forward to tonight.

She looked over at the plastic-covered red dress. Oh, well, she thought. Later. He'll call in the next day or so, and we'll try this again.

I hope.

After dinner, Jill helped Gwen load the dishwasher and straighten up the kitchen. Then the two women went out into the living room, got hot water for herbal tea from the pot on the sideboard, and sat together on a couch, away from the others. Barbara Benson and Craig Palmer were playing chess at a little table by the fire, and Jeffrey Monk was imparting to Wendy Singer some arcane information she needed for the mystery she was writing. Something about poisoned darts, if Jill had heard them properly. Ruth Monk was again reading Jill's novel, and Mike had retired for the night.

They sipped their peppermint tea in amicable silence. It was Gwen who began the conversation. With a glance over at the others, she turned to Jill and spoke in a low whisper.

"Are you pregnant?"

Jill turned her head sharply to stare at her friend. She thought about denying it, then realized the futility of lying. She nodded. "How did you know?"

Gwen laughed. "Oh, please! You've never met my three sisters. Seven babies between them in the last five years! I know all the early warning signs. You usually have wine with dinner, but you're suddenly not drinking alcohol. Or coffee, or eggs and bacon, or any of that stuff. You put your hands on your stomach; you're always touching yourself there. Never mind how I know. What are you going to do about it?"

"I'm not sure. I think I want it, but I want it to have two parents."

"Does Nate know?" Gwen asked.

Jill shook her head. "Not yet. It's one of the reasons I came out here—well, that's not true. There's only one real

251

reason I came out here. I told you and Mike about that. As for the baby, well . . . I don't know."

"Do you think Nate will marry you?"

"Yes. He's already asked me to marry him."

Gwen reached over to pat her friend's arm. "Well, then, what's the problem?"

Jill smiled. "You don't know him: you and Mike only met him once, at that party in New York a few months ago. He's—well, he's an artist. Very intense, very focused on his career. And now, with this new series he's done. . . ." She shrugged. "I just don't think now is the right time to broach the subject with him."

Gwen took Jill's hand in her own small, warm one and smiled her Earth Mother smile. "Darling, he's asked you to marry him. You obviously want to accept. The baby is just more good news—for both of you. Anytime is the right time."

Jill nodded. "You're right, of course. You're going to be a wonderful mother someday."

Her friend smiled. "And very soon, I hope. Oh, Jill, it's wonderful news! Tell Nate. I'm sure he'll be delighted."

"Yes," Jill said slowly, "I think so too, now that I think of it—now that I've decided to decide."

"Excuse me?"

Jill smiled. "Nothing. Yes, I think Nate will be happy. And he'll make a wonderful father."

Gwen nodded. "Well then, that's it. Darling, when you know it's right, that's all you have to know. Everything else is just not important."

Jill stared at her friend, thinking, Yes. That's true. When you know it's right. . . .

She decided, then and there, to have a long, honest talk with Nate as soon as she got back to New York City.

Barney sat in his car, waiting. He'd parked by the side of the road here, at the beginning of the long row of houses, over thirty minutes ago. He checked his watch: nearly eleven. There was a moon tonight, and the sky above western Pennsylvania was fairly clear. The moonlight shone down on the row of houses extending up the hill away from him, transforming them with its usual magic from shabby fossils into what they had once been: a line of respectable residences for the employees of the paper company. A few lights winked from the smaller houses in the valley below, the homes of the former factory workers who had lost their livelihood some twenty years ago. He wondered briefly what they did for a living now.

He'd taken the old woman's advice and made his way to the mall in the neighboring town. And what a culture shock that had been, he reflected. There, not three miles from this forgotten ghost town, was a bustling small city, with several other affluent towns nearby, populous enough to necessitate a rather large shopping center.

His first stop was a bank of pay phones. Using his Calling Card, he placed two calls. He told Jane that he'd be spending the night in Pennsylvania and flying back tomorrow or, at the latest, Thursday. She told him to keep warm, and he told her he loved her. Then he called his office and told Verna where he was and what he was doing. He instructed her to tell Jill Talbot that Victor Dimorta had apparently had plastic surgery. He also told her to suggest to Jill that she stay put wherever she was hiding until after Valentine's Day. Verna said she'd convey the message, and told him to keep warm. He told her he loved her, too.

He'd had a long, leisurely dinner in a steakhouse at the mall. Then he'd wandered into a housewares store that had a small hardware section and made two purchases.

253

After that, he'd gone to the multiplex cinema at one end of the center and sat through a really terrible horror movie.

Now, having killed enough time, he was back in Mill City, ready for action. He glanced up the road. The houses immediately flanking the Dimorta residence were obviously deserted, but lights still shone from the front windows of the old woman's house two doors away. He'd wait a little longer.

Presently, her living room light went off, and another light came on in her second-story front bedroom. He waited until that, too, was extinguished, then ten minutes more. Now the whole row of twelve houses was dark except for the occasional porch light.

Barney got out of the car. Gasping at the sudden assault of freezing air, he pulled his coat closed and buttoned it. Then, as silently as possible, he walked up the road toward number 7. Once there, he glanced up and down the hillside drive. A bitterly cold wind was blowing, causing the bare trees along the road to sway and rustle. He fancied he saw something, some movement in the bushes beside the porch of the house next door. As he stared, a thin, mangy-looking black cat slid out from the clump of dead bushes and crept away down the street. He was alone here, alone with a few sleeping neighbors and a starving cat.

Making his way carefully in the darkness, he went around to the backyard. The cheap padlock on the back door was visible in the moonlight. He pulled the newly acquired screwdriver from his coat pocket and set to work. Two minutes later, the door swung open.

He stepped inside the house, pulling the door closed behind him. Then he reached into his other coat pocket and produced his other purchase. Snapping on the

254

flashlight, he cast its bright beam about him. He was in the kitchen, a small, narrow room with gold-flecked white vinyl tiles and cheap-looking appliances: refrigerator, range, and a big, old-fashioned round washing machine with a wringer on top squatting in one corner. There was a wooden dinette set in another corner, and he tried to imagine the boy in the mug shots sitting there with a fierce-looking factory foreman and a silent woman who all but ignored his presence.

He moved forward through the swinging kitchen door and found himself in the large front room. A dining table stood just before him, and beyond it, a couch and two armchairs covered with sheets. He shone the torch across the surface of the table. It was not covered: the sheet that had once been used for that purpose was lying crumpled in a corner of the room. Two candles in porcelain holders stood on the table, and when he reached down to run his finger along the surface, it came away remarkably free of dust. A shiny brown stain on the lighter brown wood caught his attention. He leaned forward and sniffed: ketchup. Yes, he thought. The old woman was right. Someone had eaten at this table, and recently.

The living area was cramped and unappealing. He lifted the sheet on the couch and saw what he expected. Cheap, well-worn upholstery. The sheet on one armchair was no longer draped loosely over it, but fitted snugly in the seat area, as if someone had lately sat in it without bothering to remove the covering. A sheet-covered spinet piano crouched in a corner. There was one painting on the wall above the little table that had probably once held a television—a terrible portrait of Christ gazing mournfully out at the room, His eyes reflecting only His pain and suffering, and none of His benevolence. Barney shuddered and moved over to the stairs.

255

When he shone the flashlight slowly up the staircase, he saw what he had expected to see. The stairs were coated with dust, but there were footprints disturbing it on each tread. Nodding to himself, he ascended.

There was a short hallway at the top of the stairs, with one large door on the left and two smaller doors on the right. On the back wall in front of him was a window looking out over the barren backyard. In the faraway distance shone the lights of a nearby town. He looked around at the doors for a moment, guessing. Then he went over to the large door on the left and opened it.

Yes, he'd been right: the master bedroom. A large brass bedframe, its naked springs gleaming in the light from the torch. A bureau, a vanity table with a cracked round mirror on the wall above it, two closet doors. Another painting of Christ, this time on the cross at Calvary, His anguished face raised to Heaven. Dull green-and-yellow striped wallpaper.

So, this is where it happened, he thought. They were asleep in that bed when he crept silently into the room, the huge kitchen knife clutched and raised. The mattresses and pillows were gone, of course: they must have been ruined. He went over to the far side of the room, shining the light along the wall above the ornate brass frame. Several large patches of the striped wallpaper here were considerably lighter than the rest, as if someone had scrubbed them. He nodded to himself. Yes, there would have been blood everywhere.

He went out of the room and across the hall. The little door on his left opened into the tiny, white-tiled bathroom, the cheap, corroded plastic shower curtain black with mildew. The whole room stank of it. He quickly shut that door and turned his attention to the other one.

Yes. Here it was, at last. He pushed the door open and aimed the flashlight into the dark depths of the room, directly into the eyes of a pretty young woman. He took an involuntary step backward, staring.

A sudden, sharp wind rattled the panes of the window in the upstairs hallway behind him, and the entire house creaked and shuddered. He held his breath, listening. Was that a noise from downstairs? No, just the wind. This old wooden structure groaned under the slightest forces of nature. Shining the light before him, he stepped forward into Victor Dimorta's bedroom.

The pretty young woman stared invitingly out from the far wall of the little room, and she was flanked by many others. The entire wall had been covered with photographs, some poster-size and some obviously cut from fashion magazines. A few were regular eight-by-ten glossies. Blondes, brunettes, redheads; hundreds of them. Leaning in doorways, running on beaches, holding up wineglasses, displaying beautiful clothes. Not all were professional models: among the others, he saw several photos of the young women from the yearbook. Sharon Williams, Belinda Rosenberg, Cass MacFarland.

And Jill. There were more pictures of her than of the others. On closer inspection, he noticed that not all of them were actually Jill. Several were of another young woman—a professional model, obviously, who bore a remarkable resemblance to his client.

When he stepped forward to study the pictures more closely, he recoiled in distaste. Every single one of the photographs had been marred with a thick red felt-tipped pen. Each girl had a long, bold slash of red across her throat. Bright red Magic Marker drops rained down from some of the wounds.

Oh, Victor, he thought as he stared at the macabre

257

mural. Is this what you dream about?

He tore his gaze from the awful sight and played the light around the rest of the little room. A sagging chest of drawers. A little, boarded-up back window covered with lace curtains on a brass rod. A wooden desk and chair. Another picture of Jesus, this one more benign. He sat gazing lovingly down at a little girl on His lap, a fluffy lamb nestled at His feet. In the far corner beyond the desk was a closet door.

Barney stared at the door, thinking, Is that where he put you, Victor? Is that what he locked you in for three days after dragging your sorry ass back from Vermont? Did you sit there in the pitch dark for three days, making plans?

Another sudden gust rattled the house. He listened again: more creaking. One good storm, and this whole place just might come tumbling down. He stepped forward and opened the closet door.

At first, he thought the closet was empty. The only thing he initially saw in the light was the usual rod, from which hung two bare wire hangers. The little shelf above the rod was empty.

Then he looked down.

He stared, sinking slowly to his knees in the closet doorway. He leaned forward, playing the light slowly over the contents of the bottom of the closet. There must be a dozen of them, he thought. All different, yet the same. And all sick; so incredibly sick.

Oh, God, he thought. Jill!

That's when the hand grabbed him from behind. He felt his hair being pulled viciously back, and his head snapped back with it. A dark shape loomed over him, reaching down toward him. He felt the sudden, sharp pain under his chin, felt the warm gush flowing down, and

258

then his hair was released. He pitched forward into the closet, spewing blood as he fell. He rolled over on his back and shone the flashlight up into the face of the man who stood above him. He dropped the flashlight and reached into his coat, fumbling for the gun in his shoulder holster, aware that his throat was full of liquid. He began to choke as he tried to draw a breath, and a boot came out of the darkness to kick his hand away from his coat.

Then everything slowly faded and he was falling down, down, down through space and he thought, Oh, Jill . . . Verna . . . Jane . . .

The music was playing again, and the three women were dancing around the dark cafeteria. She was sitting at the round table by the windows, looking out at the snowy landscape, unable to turn her head and look back into the room. It was as though she knew what was about to happen to them.

Then the shadow fell upon the room, and the women behind her began to scream. She clutched her belly with both hands, silently shouting. Oh, my baby! My baby . . . !

She was sitting up in the large four-poster bed. Gradually, as reality crept into her fevered consciousness, she realized where she was. She was in Cabin 12 at Gwen and Mike's writing colony in Peconic, Long Island. She was many miles from her apartment in Greenwich Village. Nobody knew she was here.

Valentine didn't know she was here.

She stood up and went into the little bathroom. The freezing water from the tap in the sink flowed into her mouth, soothing her parched throat. She patted a little water on her face to cool off, switched off the bathroom light, and got back in the warm bed, thinking over and over to herself:

259

Valentine doesn't know where I am.

In moments, she was fast asleep. She slept on through that night, untroubled by any more dreams.

When he was finished in the back garden, Victor took the shovel into the kitchen and replaced it in the utility closet. Then he went upstairs to clean up the blood.

There were three dusty, moldy towels hanging on the rack in the bathroom. He put them in the sink and ran some cold, rusty water over them. Then he proceeded into his bedroom. He smiled as he worked, thinking, He never knew I was there. He didn't see me once all day; on the plane, at the car rental agency, outside the prison, on the road here, in the steakhouse. He had no idea I sat in the movie theater five rows behind him, munching popcorn, watching all those teenagers being hacked to death by the escaped mental patient. And he didn't see my car on the lower road, in the valley, as he waited in his car before coming in here.

He glanced over at his bedroom wall, thinking, he saw my pictures. He looked in the closet. He invaded my privacy. He came in here uninvited! He had to go, just like the doctor.

As he went back down to the first floor, he began to whistle. He checked around the place to make sure everything was once again neat and tidy, the way he liked it. Noticing a small stain on the dining room table, he used his sleeve to remove it. Then he let himself out the back way, carefully replacing the padlock on the kitchen door. He slipped around the house and away down the windblown street to the detective's car. He took the keys he'd found in the pants pocket and drove the car to the mall, parking it in the enormous lot. It would be days, maybe weeks, before anyone noticed it. Then, using shortcuts he remembered from childhood, he walked quickly back to his own rental car at the edge of Mill City.

Now, he thought. Back to New York. Back to Jillian Talbot. Four days. Four days till Valentine's Day . . .

As he drove away into the shadows of the night, he began to sing.

CHAPTER 11

THURSDAY, FEBRUARY 12

"HELLO?"

"Tara, it's Jill."

"Hi there!"

"Hi there, yourself. I wasn't expecting you to be home. I was going to leave a message on your machine. Why aren't you taping?"

"I've got a few days off. My character has gone to Lourdes."

"*Lourdes!* Oh yeah, the unmentionable disease."

"Right. How are you, Jill?"

"Oh, fine. It's very peaceful here—where I am. How was your date Tuesday?"

"Don't ask. Doug called and canceled. Work, or so he said."

" 'Or so he said'?"

"Yeah. I don't know, Jill. I get the feeling he's not really interested in me. Or afraid of me, or something. And something else: have you noticed the way he's always staring at you? Maybe you're the one he wants."

"Oh, Tara, don't be silly. You said yourself that I look kind of like his dead wife. if he's afraid of anyone, it's me."

"Hmmm. Well, let's see if he calls me again. What's

up?"

"I want you to do me a favor. I want you to keep an eye on Nate for me, make sure he's all right. He's getting ready for next week, and when he gets working like that, he sometimes forgets to eat and sleep, little things like that."

"Sure, Jill. I was going to call him, anyway. Maybe I'll take him out to lunch today."

"That would be great. I—I've got to tell you, I've made a decision. I'm going to marry him."

"Oh, Jill, that's terrific! And baby makes *three,* right?"

"How—how did you know?"

"Please, Jill! Mary and I both figured it out ages ago. At least, we suspected it. That's wonderful!"

"Yes, I'm beginning to think it is. Now, remember: if you take him to lunch, not a word about any of this. I want to tell him myself."

"You got it. Men are always the last to know, aren't they?"

"Yeah. Listen, I've got to check in with Barney Fleck, so—"

"Oh, he sent the security people Monday, and I let them into your place. You now have an alarm system."

"Great. Say hi to Nate for me."

"Haven't you spoken to him?"

"Not in a couple of days. It's hard to talk to him without telling him about—you know, everything that's been going on."

"I think you should tell him, Jill."

"I will—soon. Gotta go. 'Bye."

"Good-bye."

Tara waved to him from the table in the corner of the crowded restaurant on lower Broadway. He grinned,

262

taking in the sight of the potted palms and garish tropical murals that were the decor for this trendy West Indian place. Calypso music formed a background for the buzz of voices in the room. He made his way through the tables and dropped into the rattan chair across from hers at the bright yellow wicker table.

Tara took one look at him and began to laugh. "You have paint on your face."

He raised a hand to his cheek. "It's not paint, it's stain. I've been working on the frames for the paintings. Thank you for calling. I was going a little crazy."

"It's the fumes."

"Probably. How are you, Tara?"

"Oh, fine. Let's have piña coladas, okay?"

"Sure." He signaled to the waitress in the flower-print muumuu, and they ordered. "Have you seen Doug lately?"

"No," Tara said. "I was about to ask you the same question. He canceled our date the other night."

"Hmmm. Well, he mentioned a job the other day, some magazine layout, or something . . . ."

"Oh, don't worry, Nate. I'm sure he'll explain. That's not why I asked you here."

"Oh?"

The drinks arrived. He took a sip, wincing at the sweetness of the frothy coconut-and-pineapple concoction. Tara nearly drained hers.

"Yeah," she went on. "I'm afraid I'm going to meddle, but I think it's the right thing to do. I know you're busy getting ready for your show, but—well, it's about Jill."

He leaned forward, lowering his glass to the table. "What about her? Is she all right? Where the hell is she?"

Tara raised a hand to stop the barrage of questions. Then she told him.

263

He sat there in the rattan chair in the silly, chi-chi restaurant on lower Broadway, listening to the whole story. The break-in. The jewelry box. The bug on the phone. The listening device under the couch. The music on the stereo. Then she told him what she'd gleaned from Jill's conversation with the detective, Barney Fleck. Victor Dimorta killed his parents, and Jill thought he'd killed these three other girls she went to college with. The four of them had played some kind of practical joke on him, and he'd been systematically killing them. On Valentine's Day.

For a moment he couldn't move as the room whirled around him. Then he was on his feet leaning down, his hands clutching the edges of the wicker table. "Where is she, Tara?"

She shook her head. "I—I don't know. But Mary does. The other day, she said that Mary suggested it to her."

"Thanks for the drink, but I couldn't possibly eat now. I—I've got to call Mary."

"I thought you should know about this, Nate."

"Thanks. You did the right thing." He was already heading toward the door.

After lunch, Jill called Barney Fleck's office. The secretary answered on the second ring.

"Fleck Agency."

"Hello, Mrs. Poole, this is Jill Talbot. I was wondering if Mr. Fleck was back from Pennsylvania yet."

"No, Ms. Talbot, he's not. He said he might not be back until today. But he called Tuesday with some information for you. . . ."

She listened as the woman relayed Barney's message. Then Jill thanked her and hung up. She sat in the living room of the house by the lake, staring into the fire.

Plastic surgery. Victor Dimorta had a new face.

She actually smiled when she thought of the second part of Barney's message: stay put until after Valentine's Day.

Yes, Barney, she thought. I certainly will. Trust me. I'm not going *anywhere!*

The framer was in the studio downstairs, hammering and sanding. He put his free hand over his ear to block out the racket.

"Hello, Mary, it's Nate."

"Hi, Nate. How are you coming with the paintings?"

"Oh, fine, fine. Listen, Mary, I want to know where Jill is."

There was a pause on the other end of the line before the agent replied. "Gosh, Nate, she'd kill me! She said nobody was to—"

"I know what she said. But I think—well, I don't want to sound melodramatic, but I think she may be in danger."

Another pause. "You mean, this 'Valentine' guy."

"Yeah. He's done some other stuff, stuff she didn't tell us about." He told her, briefly, about the break-in and the listening devices.

"Oh, my God! I had no idea, Nate. That's awful!" There was a sudden, loud hammering from downstairs. In frustration, he reached over and slammed his apartment door. "Listen, I want you to tell me where she is. I'd just feel better if I was with her. I've got to put my pictures in the gallery tomorrow, but after that I can go to her. Is she far away?"

Mary didn't hesitate this time. "No. just a sec." He heard rustling papers. "She's with some friends of ours at a writers' colony on Long Island. Peconic Writing Colony.

It's way the hell out, at the end of the North Fork. You know where that is?"

He uttered a sigh of relief. "I can find it. Thanks, Mary."

"Nate, are the police in on this?"

"Oh, God, Mary. We went to the police. They couldn't do anything because he hadn't committed an actual crime."

"Well, if he broke into her apartment—"

"Yeah, I know. But then she took off, you see, without telling anyone anything."

"That sounds like Jill, all right. Actually, I'm glad she's there, Nate: the whole city seems to be going crazy. I've just been reading about that doctor who was murdered the other day, that psychologist."

"I haven't seen the papers in about a week."

"Well, it was right near her, in the Village. So, can you go out there tomorrow night?"

"Yeah, just as soon as I'm finished at the gallery."

"Okay. Say hello for me."

"I will, Mary. 'Bye."

He hung up, nearly shaking with relief. Okay, he told himself, calm down. Do your work. You'll be with her tomorrow night. He thought about finding the phone number of the Peconic Writing Colony and calling her, but immediately dismissed it. She'd argue again. He'd simply arrive there, and that was that.

Then he thought, bugs? Listening devices? What the hell . . . ?

Shaking his head in confusion, he went back down to the studio to see to the framing.

The new arrival joined them just before dinner.

Jill had been sitting in the comfortable armchair by the

266

fire all afternoon, gazing into the flames and exercising her most effective defense mechanism: she was formulating a new story.

The desire to work had come upon her suddenly, almost the moment she actually made the decision about Nate and the baby. She found it fascinating that her mind worked that way: solve one problem, and the others immediately seem clearer as well. Even Victor Dimorta was remote, so far removed from this peaceful, relaxing place. Now that she was certain of what the future held for her, everything seemed possible. She would accept Nate's proposal, and she would have the baby. She would talk with Barney Fleck soon, and together they'd do something about Valentine.

But now, she would start a new novel, and she knew just what kind of book it would be. It would be set in Nate's world, the East Village art scene. Nate had made a joke recently, an offhand remark about some artist who would be worth more dead than alive. She'd laughed at the time, but she'd also been aware of that little alarm bell that rang in her mind when ideas came along, and she'd filed it away in her memory. Thinking so much of Nate and his upcoming show had reminded her of it.

So . . . a young woman, a painter . . . her mentor a well-known artist . . . a mysterious accident . . . a series of other "accidents" . . .

She was just beginning to elaborate, to formulate the whole international conspiracy, when the door behind her was flung open and a blast of icy wind shot into the room. She clutched her arms to her, shivering, as she turned to look.

Mike Feldman marched in, carrying a medium-sized brown suitcase. He turned to call behind him.

"Right this way, and you'll be warm in no time!"

Then, in walked one of the most attractive men Jill Talbot had ever seen. He was tall, very tall and slender, with black hair and dark eyes. Dark brown, belted camel hair coat. A brown hat, one of those handsome things men wore in the forties.

This thought was immediately followed by a guilty twinge. Nate. Oh, well, Nate is really as good-looking as this guy. But he isn't here to defend himself. She silently berated herself for her disloyalty.

Mike clapped his hand on the man's shoulder and brought him over. "Jillian Talbot, meet Mr. Richard Farnum."

She smiled and extended her hand. "How do you do?"

He was staring at her, and now that she was closer to him she could see that his handsomeness, though considerable, was not exactly perfect. There was a tightness about his face, a rather haggard look, as if he hadn't been sleeping well lately. But the single most arresting thing about him was the expression in his large brown eyes: she looked into them and saw a stricken, soulful quality that filled her with an inexplicable sense of sadness. It also made him seem even more attractive than before, which further disconcerted her.

Then he smiled, and her brief impression of sorrow vanished in a dazzling display of laugh lines and even, white teeth.

"Hello," he said, taking her hands in his. "I'm honored to meet you, Ms. Talbot. I'm a big fan of yours."

She blushed, feeling the waves of warmth that seemed to emanate from him "Really?"

"Oh, yes. I've read all of your books."

"Oh." She continued to smile vacuously, never certain how to reply to that particular, and increasingly frequent, confession from strangers. "How nice," she finally offered, wincing at her own dullness.

He grinned again, and her awkwardness seemed to vanish.

Then Mike took each of them by the arm. "Come along, children. Cocktail time!"

Mike Feldman poured him a beer as he took off his hat, coat, and gloves. He stood there at the little bar in the corner near the kitchen, looking around him. Only with a conscious effort did he avoid openly staring at the woman who stood next to him.

When the three glasses were ready, he took the orange juice from the counter and handed it to her. She smiled, and their eyes met. Then he picked up one of the two draft beers, and the three of them clinked glasses across the bar.

"Mud in your eye!" Mike Feldman boomed.

"Cheers," she murmured.

"'Happy days," he whispered.

As they drank, he could feel her gaze on him, curious, questioning. He looked over at her and smiled again.

"So," she said, "what do you write, Mr. Farnum?"

"Richard," he corrected. "I'm a mystery writer—at least, that's the plan. I've just started my first story, and I want to see if I can finish it."

She laughed, nodding. "I know the feeling. Is it a detective story, or—?"

"Yes," he said. "My detective is a football player. A quarterback who kind of gets involved in—well, I guess you don't want to hear all that . . . ."

"Do you play football?" Mike asked as he led them over toward the fire.

"I did. You know, in high school." He continued to stand as Jillian Talbot returned to her former place in an armchair, and Mike dropped into a nearby chair. He looked around the big room, smiling. Pretty, he thought. Comfortable. Then he looked down at the beautiful woman. "Are you working on a new book, Ms. Talbot?"

She smiled up at him, and her dark hair glinted in the firelight. "It's Jill—Richard. And, as a matter of fact, I was just dreaming something up when you folks arrived."

He laughed as he once again surveyed the room. "Yeah, I guess it comes naturally, in a place as peaceful as this. It's so secluded here. Kind of amazing: a two-hour train ride, and New York could be on the next planet! I have trouble writing in the city."

She nodded, smiling again. She has a lovely smile, he thought.

"I know *that* feeling, too, Richard," she said. "Too many distractions."

Mike Feldman laughed. "That's the whole point behind this place. All the peace and quiet a writer needs. Except tomorrow night, of course. We're having a party here, but it's only a temporary distraction. I have a big collection of oldies: I hope you both like to dance."

"I sure do," he said. Then he turned to Jill. "May I look forward to a dance with you?"

"Why, yes," she said. "That would be lovely." She smiled when she said it. Yes, he thought: a lovely smile.

A dance, Jill thought. Yes. I've been so worried lately, so distracted. Gwen's party will be just the thing. Loosen up, Talbot. You're safe; you're with friends, nobody else knows where you are.

He doesn't know where you are. . . .

With a determined shrug and a smile for the new recruit, she forced that thought from her mind.

270

Tara was curled up on her couch in her beloved red kimono, discussing upcoming fashion ideas on the phone with the costume coordinator of *Tomorrow's Children,* when the intercom buzzer interrupted her.

"Hang on a sec, Enid. There's someone at my door." She put down the receiver and went over to the speaker. "Hello?" She let go of the talk button and pressed the one marked "Listen." At first she heard little, just sounds from the street outside the foyer and some breathing. Then, just as she was beginning to decide someone had accidentally pressed the wrong button, she heard the low, distinctive voice.

She blinked, a small thrill of anticipation coursing through her.

"Yes," she said. "Yes, of course." Then she pushed the buzzer that unlocked the lobby door.

Not for nothing was she an actress. She grabbed the phone, promised to call Enid back as soon as possible, hung up, and flew into her bedroom. The red kimono hit the floor. The doorbell rang just as she emerged from the bedroom in her best jeans and popcorn blouse and sandals. She pushed her beautiful hair over one shoulder à la Meryl Streep, took a deep breath, formed a dazzling smile on her lips, and opened the door.

Doug Baron stood before her in a leather coat, string tie, and jeans, holding out a dozen long-stemmed, red American Beauties. His expression of nervous anticipation disappeared the moment he saw her, replaced by a slow, appreciative smile.

"I lied to you," he said. "On the phone the other night. I wasn't really busy. I just . . . I just . . ." His brows came together in concentration as he searched for the words.

Tara Summers, actress, held the door wide and smiled some more.

"Won't you come in?" she whispered.

As Jill smiled and made more small talk with Richard Farnum, she found herself unaccountably thinking of Tara, and of Doug Baron. I've been so wrapped up in my own problems, she realized, that I've barely spared a thought for anyone else. I really must not let that happen. There are other people in the world.

She laughed politely at some small joke Richard made, thinking, I've got to call Nate. Maybe he can straighten Doug out. Maybe Nate and I can both play Cupid. . . .

Richard Farnum was staring at her. With a deep blush, she raised her glass of orange juice to her lips.

He watched as other people began to arrive in the building for dinner, and a small blond woman—presumably Gwen, the hostess, with whom he'd spoken on the phone when he made the reservation—emerged from the kitchen to set the table. Jill excused herself, got up from the couch, and went to help her. Their host stood, too, and prepared to take drink orders from the man and woman who had just come in. As he excused himself, Mike clapped him on the shoulder again.

"Well, Richard, I hope you can get your work done here."

"Oh, I'm sure I will," he said. "I intend to—to get my work done here."

He continued to smile, first at Mike Feldman, then at the beautiful woman setting the table with Mike's wife. And as he smiled, he was thinking.

So, Jillian Talbot. How nice to see you again. Up close and personal.

Instead of through binoculars.

272

CHAPTER 12

FRIDAY, FEBRUARY 13

THE SNOW BEGAN AT TWO O'CLOCK IN THE afternoon, and within ninety minutes everything was white. The heater in Cabin 12 wasn't doing its job fast enough, so Jill put on her coat and scarf and her new boots, picked up the yellow legal pad she'd been scribbling in for the last three hours, and made her way through the snowy forest and across the white open field to the main house.

The heating, recently installed by the ancient handyman and two local assistants, was apparently a universal problem. Almost everyone was here, settled at the card table and the dining table with legal pads and laptop computers. Barbara Benson and Wendy Singer had the card table by the fire, working across from each other in amicable proximity. Craig Palmer was on a couch across from Ruth Monk, the chess set on the coffee table between them. Only the horror writer was missing: apparently, the heater in the Monk cabin was working adequately.

Richard Farnum sat alone at the dining room table, working on a legal pad. He was wearing a chocolate brown turtleneck—the color of his eyes—and jeans and boots, and he was smoking a cigarette. The ashtray on the table in front of him was already crowded: he'd obviously been here for some time. He was the only one who looked up and smiled as she came into the room. She went over to take a place across from him.

"Hi," he whispered.

"Good afternoon," she whispered back, smiling.

"It's kind of like the public library in here. I was banished to this side of the room because of these." He indicated the pack of Marlboros and lighter at his elbow. "Hope it doesn't bother you."

She shook her head. "How's the quarterback doing?"

"What? Oh, yeah. The quarterback. He's okay—if you call being chased around by two guys with guns 'okay'."

They laughed together. She pointed at his notebook. "This is your conscience speaking: get back to work."

"Yes, ma'am." He winked and lowered his gaze to his writing.

It was difficult for her to concentrate at first, directly across the table from the handsome man who glanced up occasionally to watch her as she wrote. He did that last night, too, she remembered; all through dinner. But soon, as always when she was hammering out a new story, she fell completely into her own reality.

Her heroine would be called Tara. She hoped her friend would be pleased. Tara Winters, as opposed to Summers. Tara Winters would be a talented young painter, and she would have Nate's apartment and studio. . . . The mentor would be an eccentric older man, patterned after de Kooning, only not so famous. De Kooning has a place out here, she thought, in the Hamptons—no, I'll give my man a farm in Vermont, like that one near Hartley College. . . . Tara Winters is visiting him when he has the accident . . . accident . . . what sort of mysterious accident can you have in Vermont? Well, skiing, of course—

Skiing.

Jill dropped her pen on top of the legal pad, staring down. Skiing. Belinda Rosenberg had been skiing. He must have been there, too. He must have done something, found some way to trick her, to get her over to the edge of that cliff. He must be very clever. . . .

274

No! she commanded herself. I will not think about that. Not now. I will concentrate on the story.

Richard Farnum was staring at her. She glanced up at him, wondering if she'd spoken aloud, or made some sudden move. No, she was sure she had not done anything to attract attention. So why was he—

With a weak smile for him and a quick, despairing grimace down at the legal pad, she stood up and went over to the telephone. Dropping two singles in the wicker basket, she dialed.

"Fleck Agency."

"Hello, Mrs. Poole, it's Jill Talbot again. Has Barney returned yet?"

"No, Ms. Talbot, and, to tell you the truth, I'm a little worried. So is Jane, uh, Mrs. Fleck. She's called here several times. He told both of us he'd be back in New York by yesterday at the latest, and neither of us has heard from him in three days now."

"Do you have a number for him, some place he's staying?"

"No. He told me Tuesday that he'd stay at least one night, and that he'd find a motel somewhere. But I never heard from him after that. The last thing he said before he left was that he was going to Victor Dimorta's house in Mill City. So about an hour ago I called the police in Mill City and asked them to go to the house, Seven Franklin Street, and look around. To see if there's any—any sign that Barney was there. I'm waiting to hear back from them."

Jill sank into the chair next to the phone table, a chill creeping slowly up her spine.

"I see," she finally managed to say. Making an effort to keep her voice steady, she added, "I'm sure he's all right, Mrs. Poole. I'll call you later."

She slowly replaced the receiver, unable to shake the feeling of dread that had suddenly come over her. She looked around the room. Everyone was busy, either writing or playing chess. Only Richard Farnum was watching her from the dining table, a curious expression on his face. She looked quickly away from him, back down at the telephone, thinking:

Where are you, Barney Fleck?

Mill City only had two policemen, a sheriff and his deputy. The sheriff Verna spoke with was obviously an old-timer, dating back to the paper mill days. His assistant, he assured her, was a very bright young man. He'd send Fergus up to the old Dimorta house on the hill to have a look around.

One hour later, the sheriff called her back. Two things, he said. The padlock on the back door of the Dimorta house had recently been tampered with, and old Mrs. Wells two doors down remembered speaking to a man who fit the detective's description on Tuesday afternoon. He and Fergus were going to check all the motels in the area. At Verna's nervous request, he promised to check the hospitals, too. Then he asked her what type of car Barney Fleck was driving. A rental, she told him.

This memory gave Verna an idea. As soon as the sheriff had hung up, she called Hertz Rent-a-Car at the Pittsburgh airport. She told the woman who answered that she was Mrs. Barney Fleck, and she was looking for her husband, who had been missing for three days. The anguish in her voice was genuine, which probably caused the woman to bend the agency's rules and tell her.

The rental car had been found in a parking lot of the Sunny Acres Mall in Oakdale yesterday morning. No sign of Barney Fleck.

Verna quickly asked if Oakdale was anywhere near a place called Mill City. After consulting a state map, the woman came back on the line and said, yes, just a couple of miles from it, as a matter of fact.

She hung up and called the sheriff back. He listened to the news of the abandoned car in silence. She told him what she was going to do, and he agreed.

Then Verna called Jane Fleck. Yes, Jane would go with her. Charge it to the company.

Verna spent the next hour calling airlines. Everything was booked for the Valentine's Day weekend, but she finally found a little northeastern airline that could give them two seats on tonight's last flight. Nine P.M. She booked the seats, called Jane and told her, and went home to pack.

Jill finished her initial rough outline by six-thirty. The party would begin at eight, so she bundled herself up and trudged back through the snow to Cabin 12 to get ready. She'd bought one dress at the shopping center in Port Jefferson, after she'd left her mother at the rest home, but the inclement weather negated that idea. They were going to have to accept her in a flannel shirt, jeans, and boots. Judging from the amount of snow that continued to fall, that would probably be what everyone was wearing anyway.

Mike and Seth had apparently been at work, and the heater was now working. There was even hot water in the bathroom. She set water to boil for coffee on the little hot plate in the corner, shed her damp clothes, and got in the shower.

As she washed her hair, she thought about her mother. The scene in the greenhouse of the rest home overlooking Long Island Sound had been a sorry disappointment.

She'd gone there with some hope of seeing her mother improved, and of having lunch with her and her two friends. But when she arrived she was informed by the head nurse on duty that one friend had passed away and the other had been taken home to spend the rest of her time with her family. She'd found her mother in a chair in the greenhouse, looking out over the water. Her hair was quite white now, and she seemed so small and fragile, bundled in blankets and a wool coat Jill had given her one Christmas, years ago. Shivering with cold in the reasonably warm greenhouse, surrounded by rows of potted plants and artificial heating devices, one of them not three feet from her chair. Jill had been forced to remove her winter coat in the warm, humid room.

She'd sat in the wicker fan chair across from her mother, who looked up and smiled at her, but said nothing. Then, Jill had gone into a monologue: about Nate, about the pregnancy, about her career, and, finally, about Victor Dimorta. She talked it all out to the woman she had always gone to with her problems, knowing as she did that not one word of it was registering. Her mother continued to gaze out over the water beyond the glass walls of the greenhouse. At last, when Jill could think of nothing more to say, she rose from the chair and placed the box she'd brought with her, her mother's favorite candies, in her lap. Only then, as she was preparing to leave, did Mrs. Talbot finally look up at her with recognition.

"Oh, Jill, there you are," she'd said, smiling and reaching out to pat her daughter's hand. "Your father will be home soon: would you like to help me with dinner?"

She'd stared, the tears welling in her eyes. Then, forcing a smile, she'd replied, "Of course, Mother. I'll help you with dinner."

"Thank you, dear. I'm making beef Wellington, his favorite. Won't he be pleased?"

Assuring her mother that Daddy would be very, very pleased, she'd kissed her on the forehead and fled from the place. She hadn't stopped running until she'd reached her rental car in the parking lot outside. Then, she'd leaned against the steering wheel and wept.

The shopping center had been a blur, but she'd gone into Macy's and collected the clothing and toiletries she thought she'd need, and handed her credit card to the cashier. Then the long drive here. She'd stopped once, for gas, and arrived at the Peconic Writing Colony just as Gwen and Mike and the others were gathering for dinner.

That had been Saturday, she reflected as she came out of the shower. A mere six days ago. And in that six days, this restful, soothing place had helped her immeasurably. She couldn't do anything about her mother, she knew, but there were other possibilities. Infinite possibilities. There was Nate, dear Nate. And the baby. And her friends. And this strong new idea for a novel. Barney Fleck was incommunicado at the moment, but she was sure he'd surface soon with concrete news about Valentine, about Victor Dimorta. Barney and the police would find him; she was certain of it.

As she went out into the main room to make coffee, the clock above the desk chimed seven times. Lucky seven. It occurred to Jillian Talbot for the first time in several weeks that maybe, just maybe, everything was going to be all right.

The van Henry Jason had leased arrived at seven o'clock, mere minutes after he and the framer had finished wrapping the twelve newly framed paintings for moving. They loaded the pictures into the back as quickly as possible. Then he jumped on his motorcycle and followed the van down to the gallery on Spring Street.

Just put in the damn paintings, he told himself as he drove. Then you can get the hell out of here. Peconic . . .

"Oh, Nate, I'm so glad you're here!" Henry squealed as he entered the gallery. "There's been the most awful screw-up!"

Indeed there had. He stood staring around the room as the previous tenant, a young woman named Dina Lustig, rushed about the place, shouting orders to John, Henry's latest lover, and two assistants. Ms. Lustig's male nudes were still in place, only now being taken down for removal.

"What the hell?!" he shouted.

"My fault," Henry said. "Dina swears I told her *Friday* evening. I could have sworn I said Thursday! Last night, when she didn't show up, I—"

"Forget it," he muttered, already stepping forward to help. "Lets just get her stuff *out* and my stuff *in*."

"Right," the gallery owner said. "Wouldn't you know, it's Friday the thirteenth!"

Cursing silently to himself, he went to work.

Gwen had outdone herself in the short hour she'd had the big room to herself. With the obvious help of Mike and the elderly handyman, she had festooned the place with red and white streamers. There were heart-adorned white tablecloths and napkins, and clear plastic cups rimmed with valentines. Hors d'oeuvres and party food were laid out on the dining table. Heart-shaped red balloons, hundreds of them, floated against the ceiling around the mirror ball in the center. A hundred red candles, augmented by the crackling fireplace and the flashing mirror ball, provided the room's only light.

Jill cringed inwardly at the sight of the valentine-themed room, not because it was garish but because of the two cards it brought to mind. Then she braced herself: she had carefully avoided mentioning the particulars of her recent ordeal to Gwen and Mike. Gwen would never have dreamed of doing this had she known.

"How lovely!" Jill said as she joined her hostess in the already crowded room.

Gwen's hearty laughter transformed her face. "Oh, tell the truth, Jill. It's the tackiest thing you've ever seen! Just like the parties in the high school gym. We couldn't afford crystal and silver and caterers, so I just went to the other extreme. Everything you're looking at cost about fifty bucks, which is just in my budget. But we're all going to have a good, old-fashioned, high-school-gym time!"

Her friend's enthusiasm drove all thoughts of the past two weeks in New York from Jill's mind. She could feel herself relaxing.

"Of course we are!" she said, reaching over to squeeze Gwen's hand.

The other authors were there—all but the new one, she noticed. Several couples she'd never seen before milled among them, introducing themselves. There was quite a crowd around Barbara Benson and Jeffrey Monk, the most famous writers. Two local teenagers, obviously hired for the evening, were serving drinks on trays, and a third manned the bar in the corner. Mike's promised big band music played softly in the background.

"Coats go on the bed upstairs," Gwen said above the din. "Then I'll take you around, introduce you to everyone."

Jill nodded and headed for the stairs.

He stood naked before the full-length mirror on the

bathroom door of Cabin 5, listening. He heard the low rumble of voices and Benny Goodman music coming from the main house, through the trees and across the clearing. The party had begun.

As he dried off with the towel, he inspected himself. My face is pale, drawn, and I'm entirely too thin, he decided. Oh, well, I can't worry about that now. Now there's something I must do.

Jillian Talbot.

She doesn't recognize me, he thought. Not from the street that day, and not from outside the phone booth on Sixth Avenue, when I heard her talking to Gwen Feldman. And the address of this place, Peconic Writing Colony. She couldn't recognize me from the restaurant on the ground floor of her building: I was wearing that disguise, just to be safe.

So, here I am. With Jillian Talbot . . .

Thinking of her, and of what tonight would bring, he slowly began to dress. He put on his underpants, socks, white shirt, gray slacks, striped tie, and shoes. He donned his double-breasted navy blazer and his thick winter coat.

The Beretta went in his coat pocket.

Then he left Cabin 5 and walked through the mounting snow toward the lights of the main house.

Jill put down her ginger ale and inspected her watch: nine o'clock. Verna Poole wouldn't be in the office this late, she reasoned. With a sigh, she fished in her purse for her wallet. Drawing out Barney's card and two singles, she went over to the phone and dialed his home number in Brooklyn. No answer.

She was replacing the receiver, wondering if she should call Nate, when someone touched her elbow and asked her to dance. She turned around, already forming a polite smile and a polite refusal.

It was Richard Farnum, looking more handsome than usual in a double-breasted navy jacket and gray pants.

With a bright smile, she accepted.

He didn't get out of the gallery until nearly nine-thirty. He and the assistants carefully hung the big final painting, *Life,* on its own wall at the end of the exhibit. As soon as it was in place to everyone's satisfaction, he grabbed his coat and headed for the door.

"Don't forget," Henry Jason called after him. "The opening party is at seven o'clock next Wednesday. Seven o'clock!"

He nodded and ran out to his motorcycle. Five minutes later he ran into his own building and up to the second-floor apartment. He grabbed the things he'd need and threw them in his saddlebag. Then he ran back down to the street.

Nine-thirty, he thought as he strapped on his helmet. In this snow, I'm going to be slowed down. I should get a car. Williamsburg Bridge, Brooklyn-Queens Expressway, Long Island Expressway to Riverhead, Highway 25 to Cutchogue, Cutchogue to Peconic. . .

He started his engine and raced across Seventh Street to Second Avenue, then south toward Delancey Street.

She wondered where he'd learned the Lindy. He started with her, and soon he had everyone out in the middle of the floor, jumping and swinging as if they'd done it all their lives. Even Barbara Benson, who, judging from her age, had probably done it before, hopped around the room now with a succession of partners. Jill smiled as she danced, thinking of Gwen's comment about the high school gym. Tonight, everyone was having even more fun than that. They all danced to Mike's old 78s featuring Harry James and his band as the snow continued to fall outside.

At ten-thirty, Gwen clapped her hands, calling the room to order, and announced the sweetheart prizes. This involved all the women in the room writing their names on slips of paper and placing them in a bowl. Then, the men would each draw a name, and they got to kiss that woman and dance with her.

The names were drawn. The next thing Jill knew, Craig Palmer had arrived to kiss her on the cheek and lead her out to the floor. She glanced over to see Richard Farnum doing the same with a pretty young local woman. He winked over at her as he swept the woman into his arms.

After that, she had to stop to catch her breath. She threw herself down on the couch next to the telephone, looking at her watch. Ten forty-five. She'd pay the kitty later, she decided as she reached for the receiver and dialed.

She let it ring ten times. The machine wasn't on, she noticed. Oh, well, Nate must be out somewhere. I'll call him tomorrow. . . .

He watched her replace the receiver. Then he grabbed two heart-ringed plastic tumblers of champagne from a passing tray and made his way over to the couch. Sitting beside her, he held one glass out to her.

"No, thank you," she said. "I'm not drinking these days."

"Just one glass," he insisted. "For Valentine's Day."

She smiled and took it from him. They toasted, and she took a tiny sip before setting it down. "That's enough for me. Actually, I'm rather hungry."

"So am I," he said. With a smile, he reached for her

284

hand. After a moment, she placed her hand in his, and he led her across the room to the dinner table.

They dined on cold turkey and asparagus vinaigrette and salad. He washed his down with more champagne, she with more ginger ale. They laughed a great deal, and then she danced with him again.

As she moved slowly around the room in his arms, she thought of Nate. They had had evenings like this—they had *met* like this, at the dance club in the Village, when he'd spilled his drink and she'd offered him her napkin. And they would have many more together. It made her happy just to think of it. This man seems very nice, she thought, but Nate's the one for me.

I'm going to have his child. Our child. Funny; what seemed like such a problem such a short time ago now seems to be a blessing. And it *is* a blessing.

She smiled up at Richard Farnum, thinking, I love you, Nate.

He had to stop for gas in Ronkonkoma, and it seemed to take forever for the sleepy teenager to come out of the warm station office to fill up the tank. He threw a twenty at the kid and took off down the road, searching for the ramp that would lead him back onto the Long Island Expressway. At last he found it, and the motorcycle roared off again. Past Holbrook now, on his way to Manorville, then on to Riverhead.

He glanced at his watch as he drove: ten after eleven . . .

A few more people had arrived, and now the party was in full swing. Gwen announced that the dance contest would take place at midnight, the minute it was officially

285

Valentine's Day. First prize: a bottle of Dom Perignon. Second prize: a box of Godiva chocolates. Gwen, Mike, and Barbara Benson would be the judges. Everyone applauded.

Then Gwen came over to Jill. As she arrived by her side, Jill reached up to stifle a yawn.

Jill "I've just brought out the hot drinks," Gwen said, pointing at the urns on the bar. "You look like you could use a cup. So could I, for that matter."

Laughing, the two women made their way over to the bar, where Gwen poured decaf for both of them.

"I'm sorry, Gwen," Jill said. "It's a lovely party, really, but I'm suddenly exhausted."

"You mean you're not going to stick around for the contest?"

"Oh, I just couldn't. I'm going to get a good night's sleep and tackle my new story first thing tomorrow morning."

Gwen nodded. "Good for you. But I know someone who's going to be very disappointed." She jabbed her thumb across the room, indicating Richard Farnum.

"Yeah," Jill said, laughing. "He's very sweet—but he's not for me, thank you. I already have a dance partner."

Her friend smiled. "Yes, you do, don't you?"

He looked around the room, wondering where she could be. Then he saw her at the bar in the corner with Gwen Feldman. The two women were chatting together as they drank coffee. He excused himself from Mr. and Mrs. Monk and went over to join them.

"May I have a cup?" he asked, smiling.

"Of course," Gwen said, and she poured one for him.

"So," he said to Jillian Talbot, "are you going to be my partner for the dance contest?"

She smiled and shook her head. "Sorry. The truth is, my coach turned into a pumpkin about five minutes ago. I'm dead on my feet."

His eyebrows rose at her choice of words, but he quickly collected himself. "I guess I can't persuade you?"

"No, really. But thanks. I'm going to go back to my cabin in a few minutes."

Ah, he thought.

"I'll walk you there," he said. "In the dark, with the snow still falling. . . ."

"Oh, you don't have to do that," she said quickly. "Gwen issued flashlights to everyone whose cabin is far away, and mine is in my coat. I'll be fine."

"Please, I insist." He smiled his brightest smile.

That did the trick. He saw her hesitate a moment, then she capitulated. "Well, if you really want to . . . ."

"I really want to. Now, one more dance—for the road."

She glanced over at Gwen Feldman, who was smiling again.

"Oh, all right. One for the road. Thank you."

"My pleasure," he whispered, leading her out on the floor. As he took her hand in his, he glanced down at his watch: eleven thirty-five.

Twenty-five minutes, he thought.

Twenty-five minutes to Valentine's Day . . .

The Andrews Sisters belted out "Boogie Woogie Bugle Boy" as he whirled her around the floor, complete with lifts and dips and all the rest of it. The room began to spin around her, and she was aware that everyone else had stopped dancing to watch them. She grinned and gave herself over to it, allowing him to lead her through the paces. When the song ended, he kissed her on the cheek as the crowd around them burst into applause.

287

She smiled around at everyone, preparing to leave the dance floor, but she never made it. At that moment, Mike put on another record, and the room was suddenly bathed in the soft tones of an old favorite, "Dancing in the Dark." Richard took her in his arms and everyone around them began to dance as a low, smoky woman's voice began to sing.

Richard Farnum was holding her close, and she could feel the heat emanating from his body. She relaxed against him, resigning herself to the inevitability of one more dance. It wasn't bad, really: this song reminded her of her parents. Her father had played it on the record player in the living room on Central Park West when she was a little girl. Once, when they'd thought she was asleep, she'd tiptoed out of her bedroom and stood in the living room doorway, watching her mother and father dance slowly around the room to this very song.

The mirror ball was spinning, casting a million flickering spots of light around them. She closed her eyes and hummed along with the recording, remembering her parents and being a child, small and protected and safe. She leaned against the tall, dark, handsome man, thinking, Nate. Nate . . .

Jamesport and Mattituck had flown by him, mere blurs of light beside the highway. He'd almost missed the road in Cutchogue, turning right instead of left and traveling for several minutes before he saw the sign with the word, PECONIC, and an arrow pointing in the opposite direction. He'd squeezed the hand brake, nearly going into a skid on the snowy country road. Then he'd turned around and sped off the way he'd come.

Now the flat, open fields of Suffolk County had disappeared, and there was thick black forest on either side of the road. He slowed the bike, looking for signs. He was sure the map had indicated that the turnoff to Lake Peconic was on his left somewhere around here, before he came to the town itself. He peered ahead through the snowflakes.

And there it was. Two big wooden posts with a crossbar, the rustic-looking painted wood sign hanging down. Peconic Writing Colony.

The drive that led away from the road through the dense forest was piled high with snow. There was no way the bike would make it. He cut the engine and leaped from the motorcycle, pulling it off the road into the trees near the signpost. When he was several yards in, he lowered the kickstand. He quickly removed his helmet, chained the front tire, heaved the saddlebag from the seat and over his shoulder, and set off down the winding drive, slogging through foot-high piles of snow in the direction of the lake. As he made his way, placing each foot carefully before the other in the dark, his boots sinking before him, he looked down at his watch.

Eleven forty-five.

When "Dancing in the Dark" ended, she smiled and gently pulled away from him.

"Thank you," he said.

"Anytime," she replied.

Then Mike's booming voice filled the room. "And now, folks, let's get a jump on Valentine's Day!"

The music began again. She stood there for a moment, rooted to the spot, not believing her ears. Then, an instant later, she remembered that she hadn't told them that part of it. Mike and Gwen had only been given a rudimentary, sketchy version of her recent ordeal. She'd never mentioned Valentine's Day, or the song, the significance of it. It wasn't the Sarah Vaughan recording, but some woman was singing it, just the same.

"My Funny Valentine."

The momentary shock passed, and she became aware that Richard Farnum was watching her face closely.

"What?" he whispered. "What is it?"

She regained her composure enough to shake her head. "Nothing. It's nothing, really. I—I'm very tired. I think I'll go back to my cabin now. . . ."

"Sure," he said. "I'll take you. Wait here a minute. You have that white wool coat, the one you were wearing earlier today, right?"

She nodded. Then she watched as he made his way swiftly through the crowd and bounded up the stairs to Gwen and Mike's living quarters.

"Darling, are you all right? You look like you've seen a ghost!"

She turned in the direction of the voice. Gwen was now at her side, reaching out for her arm, a look of concern on her face.

"I'm okay," she assured her friend, forcing herself to smile. "Just tired, that's all. Richard's gone to get our coats. I hate to desert you like this, but—"

"Oh, don't worry. I understand. You go back to your cabin and get a good night's sleep. This is probably going to go on for a while: Mike hasn't made his way through *half* of his collection of old records yet, and he's not going to stop till he's played every last one of them!"

She found that she was laughing, laughing with Gwen as Richard arrived before her with their coats and the music once more crashed into her consciousness. Then he was helping her into her coat, and she was smiling rather foolishly around at everybody, and he was gently removing the flashlight from her hand.

290

"I'll take that," he said.

Gwen kissed her on the cheek. "Good night, darling. Sleep well."

And he was taking her by the arm and leading her across the floor, through the crowd and out onto the porch, into the cold, snowy night.

He kept his hand clamped firmly to her elbow, flashing the powerful beam ahead of them as they made their slow, steady way through the mounting snow-drifts toward the path at the edge of the woods. She seemed calmer now that they were outside, and she even giggled once or twice as they slogged across the open field.

"I hope Gwen has a lot of sleeping bags handy," she said, pointing. He looked in that direction, and they both laughed. The parking lot near the lake was covered, the van and the cars of the local guests nearly invisible.

"Oh, I'm sure everyone will manage," he said.

They made it to the edge of the field and plunged into the darkness of the forest, moving slowly, carefully up the path toward Cabin 12.

The strains of the song followed them.

"I'm sorry to be such a spoilsport," she said, peering forward into the beam from the torch to avoid running into the trees that loomed up at either side of the narrow path. "I hope you'll find a good partner for the contest."

"Oh, I think I've had enough dancing for one night," came the voice from the dark beside her. "Besides, I'm a little tired, too. I'll see you to your door, then I think I'll call it a night."

"Yes," she said. "That's probably best."

"Just a few more steps and we're there," he said.

He could hear the music ahead of him, and he saw the lights through the trees. A party, he thought. They're having some kind of party. He moved forward toward the parking lot at the end of the long, long driveway. He was at the edge of the forest now, looking out at the big main house and the snowy baseball field and the still, black lake.

Then he saw it, off to his left: the beam of a flashlight moving up the path through the trees. And he heard voices fairly close to him, a man's and a woman's.

Jill.

He stopped in the drive, clutching the helmet in his left hand, the saddlebag slung over his right shoulder. He looked at the house by the lake again, all lit up and shining in the snow. Everyone else is probably there, he thought. But Jill wasn't there: she was walking away through the woods somewhere on his left. Walking with a man . . .

He left the road and plunged into the trees, in the direction of the flashlight beam and the voices.

"Well, here we are," she said as they arrived at the door of Cabin 12. They stood together in the pool of light from the single bulb above the door. "Thank you for seeing me home."

"Of course." Richard Farnum smiled. "You don't happen to have anything warm to drink in there, do you?"

"No," she said. "Sorry. I just want to get to bed, really. Thanks again."

She unlocked her cabin door, aware that he was lingering. She got the distinct impression, without turning around, that he was watching her. Oh, dear, she thought fleetingly. I hope he's not going to be difficult . . .

She opened the door and stepped inside. Turning in the doorway, she saw that Richard was indeed still watching her.

"Well, good night," she said, and she smiled again.

They regarded each other a moment. Then he grinned.

"Good night," he said, raising his hand in a little salute. He reached forward with the other, offering her the flashlight.

"You'll probably need that to get back to your cabin," Jill said. "I'll get it from you tomorrow."

"Okay. 'Bye." He turned and started off down the path.

With a little sigh of relief, she shut the door.

He moved away down the snowy path, shining the torch before him. As he moved farther down into the forest, he glanced at his watch again.

Two minutes, he thought. Two minutes to Valentine's Day.

When he was sure he couldn't be seen from the cabin, he switched off the flashlight and stepped off the path into the trees.

She slowly removed her coat and dropped it at the foot of the bed. She yawned and stretched, thinking, I haven't danced that much in years. Tara belongs to that gym around the corner from us, and she's been after me to go with her. Maybe I should become a member. Especially now, with the baby coming . . .

Nodding to herself, she reached over to turn down the covers on the bed.

He watched the strange man move away down the path, the beam of the flashlight flickering ahead of him. When the man had disappeared among the trees, he stepped forward toward the light of the cabin. He wondered who the man was. . . .

Then he dismissed the thought. God, he told himself, this whole thing is making me paranoid. He's just some other writer who's staying here, who walked her to her door, for Heaven's sake! Stop panicking . . .

He arrived in the pool of light outside the cabin, smiling in anticipation of the surprise and delight he'd see on her face when she opened the door. Grinning, he reached up and knocked.

She froze, the quilted comforter clutched in her hand. Oh, God! her mind cried. How on earth—

Then she realized who was probably knocking on her door. He hadn't even made it more than a few yards down the path, and he'd decided to give his powers of seduction another try. With a grimace, she moved toward the door.

"Who is it?" she called, trying to sound surprised.

"Jill, open up. It's me, Nate."

She stared at the door. "What?"

"It's Nate, Jill. Remember me? Surprise!"

Then relief surged through her, followed immediately by a wave of purest joy.

"Nate!"

She threw open the door, and there he was. Grinning that lopsided grin, saddlebag over one shoulder, helmet in hand, soaked to the skin.

"Nate!" she cried again.

And he stepped forward into her arms.

He was pressed against the trunk of a large tree, some thirty yards away in the darkness of the forest. He stared in disbelief as the boyfriend, Nate, came out of the trees and into the pool of light outside the cabin.

What the *hell?* he thought. What the hell is *he* doing here?

Nate knocked on the door, and after a moment she

opened it. Shouting his name, she threw herself into her lover's arms.

I can't believe this! he thought. He's going to spoil everything!

Then, in the very next instant, he had another idea.

No, he thought slowly to himself. Perhaps not. Perhaps he won't spoil it, after all.

"Oh, Nate! Am I glad to see you!" She continued to embrace him in the doorway, the flecks of snow swirling in on the chill wind from outside. "How did you find me?"

He was laughing as he moved into the room. "Hang on a minute. I'm freezing!"

She let go of him and stepped backward, allowing him to get all the way into the cabin. He slammed the door behind him and shot the bolt. Then he took her in his arms again and kissed her.

When they paused for breath, she stepped back from him and looked up at his face. His hair was wet, hanging down into his eyes. She laughed, partly at the sight of him and partly at the warm, solid reality of him, and went into the bathroom to get a towel. When she came back, he was lowering his dripping saddlebag onto the desk beside the dripping crash helmet. She handed him the towel and he hung it around his neck, grinning.

"Whew!" he breathed. "You sure are one tough lady to find!"

She grinned. "I hope it was worth it. How did *you* find me, anyway?"

He laughed as he reached up to towel dry his hair. "Mary, of course. Well, Tara started it. She was worried about you—as well she should be. She told me all about the other night, before you took off without telling anyone where you were going. Jill, you should have said something."

Jill felt the hot blush rise to her cheeks. "I know, darling, but you were so busy with your show, and I thought—"

"Did you think *anything* was as important to me as you?" he cried.

"Well, I—I guess I wasn't thinking clearly. . . ."

He laughed. "*I'll* say! But, given your circumstances, that's understandable."

She stepped forward to embrace him again. "Oh, Nate, it was *awful!* But you're here now, and we're away from there, away from *him*." She buried her face in his chest.

He reached up to stroke her hair. "Yes, Jill, I'm here now, and everything's going to be okay." Then he reached up gently to pull her away from him. "But first, I have a surprise for you."

She smiled and took the wet towel from him. "A surprise? It's enough that you're *here!*"

He turned and leaned down, opening the saddlebag. "I know, but I came all the way out here, so . . ." He took something out of the saddlebag and put it down on the desk, but she couldn't see what it was because his body was blocking it. Then he reached down into the saddlebag again.

At that moment, the clock above the desk began to chime for midnight.

They both looked up at the clock.

Then she heard it. Coming from the desk behind him.

Sarah Vaughan.

"My Funny Valentine."

"What?" she began. "Nate, what on earth—"

Then Nate whirled around to face her, extending his hands. She looked down. He was holding out a bright

296

pink candy box.

Jill looked up into her lover's eyes. He was no longer smiling.

"Happy Valentine's Day!" he said.

CHAPTER 13

SATURDAY, FEBRUARY 14
Valentine's Day

DAVID MACFARLAND STOOD BEHIND THE TREE THIRTY yards from the cabin, staring at the door and the pool of light that flooded down on it. They were in there, Jillian Talbot and her boyfriend.

Her boyfriend.

He'd dismissed him as unlikely, as he'd dismissed his friend Doug Baron, the photographer. He'd even followed them around Spring Street that day, finding nothing suspicious about them.

The boyfriend. He'd been with her for months nearly a year . . .

Then, he thought of his own sister, Cass. *She'd* had a boyfriend, too, in the weeks just before . . . a man named Neil something . . .

Neil Avnet.

He'd never been able to trace Sharon Williams after she'd disappeared, but the other one, Belinda, on the ski slope. . . yes, there'd been a strange man there, too. He was quoted in the newspaper reports. Leonard something. Something Italian. Morelli . . . Vanelli . . . Vaneti.

Leonard Vaneti. Len, for short.

Oh, my God! he thought.

Len Vaneti.

Neil Avnet.

Valentine!

Then he was lurching forward, out from behind the tree, and crashing through the dense forest ahead of him, stumbling blindly in the direction of the light, of the cabin, the name screaming in his mind, over and over and over.

Nate Levin!

"What?" she said again, stupid, numb, her mind suddenly off, unable to function. "What—"

"Happy Valentine's Day!" he said again.

Instinctively, she stepped backward, away from him, away from the music and the heart-shaped candy box. "Nate!"

Then, in a long, awful moment, a slow smile came to his face. It was not a smile she'd ever seen, not in all the months they'd been together. It wasn't Nate's smile, it was nobody she knew. It was nothing human.

"I'm not Nate," he said, his dead voice belying the horrible smile. "There is no Nate. Nate Levin is an anagram, you stupid, evil bitch. My name is Victor Dimorta." Slowly, he raised the box again and held it out in front of her. "Happy Valentine's Day."

The shock coursed through her. She stared, fascinated, as the song continued and her death stepped smiling forward holding out a box of candy and she couldn't think couldn't breathe couldn't move couldn't move simply . . . could . . . not . . . move. . . .

Crash!

Something big and powerful smashed into the other side of the door inches behind him, as if someone had thrown himself against it. He gasped and whirled around toward the noise, and in that instant the spell was broken

298

and the survival voice deep inside her came rushing up into her brain.

Move.

She reached up with her arms and pushed with all her might, with a strength born of shock and pure adrenaline, sending him crashing forward into the door. He lost his balance and fell to his knees, the candy box flying from his outflung hands.

Weapon.

The gun was in her purse, her purse, her purse, where the hell was her *purse?*

On the table in the corner. She would have to get past him to get to it. She was already stepping forward in the direction of her purse when his hand clamped viciously down on her wrist.

And he was on his feet in front of her. He brought up his other hand in a fist, rearing back to strike.

Disable.

She yanked her wrist from his grasp and stepped backward. She kicked her right leg out behind her, straightening her knee as the instructor had taught her. Then she brought it forward with all her strength. Her boot made solid contact, directly between his legs.

His face contorted in a dreadful grimace of pain, and he fell heavily backward onto—

Her purse. So much for the gun.

Move.

She was running, running away from him, across the room and into the bolted back door.

Unbolt the door.

And she was reaching and she was yanking and she was pushing and then the door was open and she was falling out of the doorway into the snow, facedown in the snow and she was groping with her hands and she was on her knees and she was up, up and running, running, running through the blackness, through the dense forest behind the cabin where there was no path no light no anything only darkness and more darkness and the pounding of heavy feet behind her and run run run oh, God, *run*!

When David MacFarland came to, he was lying in deep snow in a pool of light outside the door of a cabin. Blood, apparently from his nose, was already frozen to his cheek and neck. His ungloved hands were numb, and there was a tearing pain in his chest and his arms. He heard faint music, big band music, coming from somewhere far away.

It took him a moment to remember. Then it came rushing back to him: he had thrown himself against the door. He'd smashed into it with such force that he'd been temporarily knocked out.

In the next instant, the rest came back.

Valentine!

And he was on his feet, ignoring the pain and the blood and the numbness, pounding his fists against the door. Then he stopped, listening.

There was other music, coming from inside. A woman's voice, softly singing "My Funny Valentine." Otherwise, nothing. Not even breathing. Nothing.

Without really thinking, acting on instinct, he ran around the side of the cabin toward the back, stopping at the wooden window just long enough to ascertain that it was locked. He raced to the rear side and saw the open door and the footprints leading away from the cabin, into the trees. A brief glance through the open back door told him that the cabin was empty.

Pulling the Beretta from his coat pocket, he plunged into the black forest.

She was running aimlessly now, through the endless

trunks of trees, caught up in her panic. Her body had become a machine, a fulcrum of perpetual motion born of her instinct to survive. Keep moving, the voice inside her repeated. Just keep moving.

So she kept moving through the forest, raising her hands to ward off the dark shapes that constantly loomed up in front of her. Falling in the snow and rising, always rising and moving on. She was aware of the sounds behind her, the crunching and the crashing and the panting. She knew he was mere yards, perhaps feet, behind her, and that he was gaining on her. Run, the voice inside her said. Run.

There was nobody in front of him: he was certain of it. David stopped to catch his breath. He would catch up with them, though; he had no doubt of that. It was the one purpose he now had on this earth.

He would find Valentine, and he would kill him.

He had made the silent promise over her coffin. Cass—dear Cass, who had remained beside him when everyone else was gone. Their parents had thrown him out when he was eighteen, when he had told them that he was gay. His high-school friends had shunned him, even the rest of the football team. He had been their first-string quarterback for two years, leading the school to an unprecedented number of victories. But that didn't matter to them: he was a homo, a queer, a faggot, and that was that. Only Cass had been loyal, had continued to love him.

And now he would avenge her.

He turned around in the snowy forest, moving off in the direction of the faint noises he could hear through the trees. Victor Dimorta was somewhere over there, and he must get to him. If he managed to save Jillian Talbot, too, that was good, but it was a secondary consideration. He knew only that he was going to kill.

Even as he ran through the dark woods, he smiled at the satisfaction his lover would have gotten from knowing the part he had inadvertently played. Richard Farnum, a name as familiar as his own, had been the name he'd used to get into this place. Now Richard Farnum—Rick—was gone.

As he ran, he remembered that final telephone call from Cass. She'd just received flowers, after the three valentine cards, and she'd finally figured it out. Victor Dimorta, she'd said: that's who's doing this. Then she'd told him about the prank that she and her friends had played. He'd offered to go there, to drive to her cabin in New Jersey to be with her, to protect her. Don't worry, she'd replied. I have a gun, and I know how to use it, and Neil Avnet, my new boyfriend, will be here in a few minutes. The date: February fourteenth.

Valentine's Day.

In the weeks after her death, he'd found out about Sharon Williams and Belinda Rosenberg. He'd left Rick in his mother's capable hands and traveled to Hartley College, where he'd demanded and been given the official records of the incident in the dorm room leading to Victor Dimorta's expulsion. Then he'd gone to Mill City, Pennsylvania, and learned the rest. The following days had been a blur of feverish activity: the call to Sharon's mother in California and the process of finding Belinda's family at their new address in Buffalo. Mrs. Williams told him about her daughter's disappearance in the middle of February, two years before. The middle of February, he'd thought. February fourteenth.

Valentine's Day.

Belinda's mother told him about the skiing accident the previous year, and the day on which it had occurred.

302

Valentine's Day.

According to the Hartley College file, there had been a fourth girl involved in the incident. The college registrar proudly informed him that this girl, Jillian Talbot, was now a noted mystery writer living in New York City. He'd thought, briefly, about calling her and warning her, when his new idea had been born.

Jillian Talbot was his key, he realized, his only possible access to Valentine. Cass and Belinda were dead, and Sharon Williams was probably dead, too. Jillian Talbot was the only one of the four who was still alive. But now, he knew, it was her turn. She was to meet the same fate as Cass and the other women.

Valentine's Day.

So, four weeks ago, he'd gone to Greenwich Village. To wait. To wait for Victor Dimorta to arrive. He'd followed the woman, and he'd bugged her apartment. He hadn't made his presence known to her, fearing that Victor Dimorta would get wind of it and vanish without revealing himself. He'd watched her in her home, suffering through the evil jokes: the cards and the flowers. He'd followed her to the police and the private detective, and still he had forced himself to remain silent. He felt, sometimes, that he could do anything, whatever it would take, to avenge his sister.

He tightened his grip on the Beretta. He could hear his quarry now, somewhere among the trees directly ahead of him. Taking a deep breath, he began to run again.

There were trees in front of her, and more trees, and more. And suddenly none. She stumbled out of the forest onto the road. The driveway, her panicked mind informed her. You're on the main road leading to the colony.

But which way?

303

She stopped for one precious moment, listening. Yes, the faint music was coming from her left. The main house. Go there, the survival voice ordered. Get to them. Get close enough, then scream. Scream your head off. They won't hear you from here, not with the music. Go *now!*

She turned in the direction of the party and began to run.

She didn't get three steps. In one sudden, chilling instant, her hair was grabbed from behind and she was being whirled around. Nate—Victor Dimorta—loomed up in front of her, a horrible grin, a rictus of death and destruction plastered to his suddenly ugly face. He drew back his fist and smashed it into her jaw.

She heard a crack and saw white light, and she was falling, falling backward into the snow, and floating out to some unknown destination. Then the darkness enveloped her, and she knew no more.

Victor Dimorta reached down and picked up the unconscious woman. Moving slowly, carefully in the deep snow, keeping to the shadows at the edge of the forest, he carried Jillian Talbot toward the lake.

Water. The fourth element.

He smiled as the snowflakes fell on him, flying into his face and instantly melting. He could hear the sounds behind him: someone was trying to chase him, but they were going the wrong way. They were obviously lost, disoriented in the dark woods. Ignoring the sounds, he pressed on.

He'd finally figured out the phone tap and the listening device Tara had told him about. It must have been the late detective, Fleck. He must have put them there without her permission, in a feeble attempt to catch Valentine.

He laughed. As if that idiot—as if *anyone*—could catch Valentine! He was too smart: hadn't he fooled all those women? Hadn't he fooled Jillian Talbot for *ten months?!* Hadn't he been clever enough to hire that street person, that drug addict, to go into the flower shop and order the roses? How could they catch him? He was invulnerable. Invincible. Invisible.

And Fleck was fertilizer. In Mother's flower garden.

Tara, the actress, had not once suspected the presence of a far greater performer. Mary Daley had liked him and trusted him, enough to reveal Jillian's hiding place. Dr. Philbin had fallen for his performance on the phone and let him into her office. And Doug Baron, Stacy Green's widower, had no idea that the man who had befriended him after the chance meeting at Henry Jason's gallery had only done so because of Stacy. To be near someone who had actually slept with the model who looked so much like Jillian, the dead model whose photographs he had defiled so many times on his prison cot. To savor his power, Valentine's power, over all of them.

Mother.

Father.

Sharon Williams.

Belinda Rosenberg.

Cass MacFarland.

And now, Jillian Talbot.

The enemies of Valentine.

He spared no thought for Dorothy Philbin or Barney Fleck. They were nothing to him, mere impediments. Stones in the road.

Smiling, he gazed down at the beautiful face of the unconscious woman. His love for her had long since turned to hatred. She was the last, and now she would go the way of all the rest of them. His vengeance would be

305

complete.

He suppressed his laughter. The music was growing louder, and the big main house loomed up on his left as he arrived at the edge of the lake. He would have to be very quiet now. Like when he made his way down the hall and into his parents' room that night. Quiet; oh so quiet . . .

Holding his breath, careful to make no sound, he headed for the dock.

She was floating through the air, borne up by powerful arms. Nate's arms. Nate had arrived to save her; he was here to protect her from—

No! her mind cried. Nate is not Nate. There is no Nate, he had said.

Nate is Valentine.

Nate is Victor Dimorta.

The shock brought her fully back to consciousness. Even so, the little voice that had not deserted her told her to remain still, to keep her eyes shut. The music was very close now: they must be near the house. If he puts me down, she thought, I can run. I can scream . . .

Then she became aware of the hollow sounds below her, the clomping of his boots on wood.

Oh, God! The dock!

He's going to throw me in the lake!

He burst out of the forest into wide-open space and doubled over, gasping for breath. He was sweating profusely, despite the freezing cold. As his breathing returned to normal, he strained his ears for any sounds that might indicate where they were. He could hear only the distant laughter and the music from the gramophone.

Then he stood up and looked around him. A snowy

field, a flagpole, a backstop. The baseball field! And there was the main house, down by the—

The lake.

He saw the tall, black shape emerge from the shadows by the lake and step out onto the dock. Even at this great distance, with the snow falling, he could see that the figure was carrying something in its arms. Someone: Jillian Talbot.

He began to run again.

The panic overtook her, forcing her to open her eyes, to stiffen in his arms. She had never learned to swim. Water terrified her. She was going to drown.

No! her mind cried even as she reached up with her nails to claw at his face. The nail of her index finger poked at his left eye, and the other drew blood from his cheek.

He uttered a hoarse, startled cry, and then she was falling through space and landing with a jolting thud on the dock. She scrambled to her knees, looking wildly around her. They were at the very end of the dock: the edge was mere inches from her. And Nate—*Victor*—was standing above her, his body between her and dry land.

But now she had made him bleed, and that had made him angry. She was rising to her feet when the blow came, and the pain of it was greater than any pain she'd ever experienced. With every ounce of his considerable strength, he smashed his fist into her stomach. She fell facedown on the dock, paralyzed with pain. After a moment her vision returned: she was staring down at the wood mere inches from her eyes. When she could move again, she rolled onto her side, her legs curled up under her, and her hands found their way to her stomach. Oh, my baby, she thought, my baby . . .

"You're going to die now, Jillian Talbot. Happy

Valentine's Day."

At first she thought she'd imagined the words, but she realized an instant later that they had been uttered from somewhere above her. The words were followed by the most awful sound she'd ever heard: the keening, high-pitched laughter of Victor Dimorta. Then the little voice inside her cut through her pain and shock, through his dreadful laughter, barking its last orders.

Get up.

She took a deep breath. Ignoring her broken jaw and her other, greater pain, she dragged herself up to her knees, facing him. Her feet hung over the edge of the dock behind her.

Speak.

She looked up into his eyes, the eyes of the man she had loved. But that man was gone now, replaced by this vile thing in human form. His gaze bored down into her: she could feel the waves of hatred emanating from him. From *it*. Whatever it was. And beyond him, beyond *it*, she saw the hazy, dark figure step silently out of the shadows onto the dock.

Speak!

On her knees, she reached out toward him with her arms in a bizarre parody of supplication.

"Vic—Victor," she slurred, trying desperately to enunciate despite the smashed jaw. "Victor, I told the dean what they did to you. I tried to help you. Please, please—don't—hurt—me."

He continued to stare down at her. The sounds came again, the high-pitched hyena snorts, the laughter of a small child. Behind him, at the other end of the dock, the dark figure raised its arm.

"Oh, *sure*, you tried to help me! When did *any* of you try to help me? You're dead, bitch!"

With that, he reached out his hands to push her backward into the lake. He must have moved swiftly, even violently, but to her fevered mind it seemed to take forever, as if he were moving at the wrong speed, in slow motion. She even had time to think one last rational thought: so this is it, this is death. She closed her eyes and flinched, steeling herself. She would fight him. She would not, *must* not die. Not like this, Not now. The hideous eyes stared down at her, and the large hands came closer, closer. She drew in a painful breath, forming her hands into fists.

The explosion that followed ripped through the darkness and resounded across the lake. It also ripped away most of Victor Dimorta's head.

At first it didn't register: her mind did not grasp what had happened. Then she opened her eyes and saw. She was staring up at him, at what remained of him, as the blood and bone and brain tissue rained down on her. She was raising her hands to cover herself from the onslaught when his body smashed into her chest, and then she was falling and falling and she heard a splash and she was freezing and she was—

Wet. She was in the water, *under* the water, and Victor's nearly headless torso was on top of her, weighing her down, pushing her down to the bottom of the lake. She struggled briefly, attempting to remove the heavy weight, but her mouth was full of water and she was swallowing it and there was nothing to breathe, only water and more water and still more water, and she was a little girl standing in the living room doorway watching her parents dance and she was laughing and everything was very bright and then it was dark and the cold was going away now going away going away and she was floating . . . floating . . . floating. . . .

309

He lowered his arm, and the Beretta fell heavily onto the dock beside him. He shut his eyes and held his breath, aware of the odd silence. The dock, the lake, the falling snow. And nothing else, not a sound anywhere, as if the world had suddenly come to a complete stop.

Cass, he thought. For you, Cass. This silence is for you.

Then the music reached him. It had continued throughout, he supposed, though he hadn't been aware of it; bizarre underscoring for the scene on the dock. He nearly laughed aloud: the devil was dead, his sister had been avenged, the world had been made right again—and all to the tune of "Chattanooga Choo-Choo."

And with the music came the rest. The startled cries from the house behind him. The slamming of the screen door and the approach of running footsteps. The sudden, almost electric shock as his sanity at last returned to him. And the other voice, the one that came up from somewhere deep inside him and rushed out through his lips.

"*No!*"

He ran. He threw himself forward, down the length of the dock, shouting the word again. "*No!*" Cass was gone, and nothing would bring her back, not even his love. "*No!*" Sharon Williams and Belinda Rosenberg Kessler, whom he had never known, had never met, but who had others who loved them as he loved Cass. "*No!*" Now this woman, Jillian Talbot, was in the lake ahead of him, a pregnant woman with a mother, and friends who loved her, and a life; a vital, purposeful life. "*No!*"

With that final cry he ran, and then he leaped, and he dived into the black, freezing water.

The numbness spread through him instantly as the cold assaulted his senses, but he barely noticed it. He stroked mightily with his arms and legs, forcing himself down deeper, deeper into the blackness. Some force, some power almost beyond him had taken control of his body. He stroked again, thinking, *No!* This woman will not die.

His outstretched hand made contact, grasping something soft and fleshy: the exposed brain of Victor Dimorta. With a shock of revulsion, he yanked his hand away and reached lower, to the shoulders. He shoved with all his strength, and the bleeding corpse fell aside, floating languorously off into the darkness. David reached down with his right hand, and it sank into mud. He felt blindly around the bottom of the lake until his hands at last discovered her. He pulled her up by the hair, tucked his arm under her chin, and pushed off with his legs from the lake floor. They shot swiftly up and broke the surface.

As he drew in an enormous gulp of air, he looked furiously around him, trying to orient himself, but he couldn't see anything in the snowy darkness. She was not moving, not breathing; she was dead weight against him. Just as he was beginning to panic, he heard the most wonderful sound he'd ever heard: the deafening splash as something large arrived in the water nearby. Massive, powerful arms reached out for him. Between them, he and Mike Feldman dragged her some twenty feet to the dock. David grasped the nearest piling and clung to it as the big man raised her body up, and other arms reached down for her.

Then Mike grabbed him and pushed him over to the ladder. He muttered something to Mike about the body in the lake, and he pointed over to where he had surfaced with Jill. Then he pulled himself up the rungs and fell forward, landing facedown on the dock. He heard shouting around him, and running footsteps, and the splashing underneath him as Mike climbed the ladder. He wasn't sure how long he lay there: he seemed to have lost

311

all sense of time passing. The soft snow continued to fall on him as gentle hands reached out to cover him with a blanket. Gradually, he became aware of the other sounds: a hundred sirens, filling the night.

The shrill wail of the sirens faded and died, followed almost immediately by the sounds of other feet arriving and pounding swiftly down the length of the dock. He pushed down with his hands and brought himself up to his knees in time to see several figures in bright orange drop to the dock around the still form of Jillian Talbot.

He heard muffled pounding and sharp voices barking instructions, but he couldn't see through the clutch of orange jackets. The gentle hands reached down to pull the blanket more securely around him, and he looked up into the kindly, concerned, beautiful face of Gwen Feldman.

"My God!" she whispered. "What on earth happened, Richard?"

He stared at her, thinking, Richard? Who's Richard—? Then he remembered. It was the only name these people knew him by. Richard, his lover, was dead.

His teeth were chattering so violently that for a moment he could not speak. He looked over at the orange jackets, then his gaze traveled down the length of the dock to where two more people in white uniforms were approaching, carrying a stretcher between them. Beyond them, on the porch of the main house and on the sloping hill above the dock, the other partygoers stood staring, an enormous, freeze-frame tableau accompanied by the incongruous music that continued, unheeded, from the gramophone in the empty room behind them.

"What happened, Richard?" Gwen said again.

He looked back at her and shrugged.

"Valentine," he whispered.

She stared. "Valentine? What are you talking about?"

He shook his head, unable to summon the will to explain. Then he looked over at the crowd on the dock a few feet away. Jillian Talbot was on the stretcher now, and several EMS people lifted her up and rushed away down the dock. One of them was holding a clear plastic mask over her nose and mouth. Just as they began to move, he saw what he had been waiting, hoping, praying to see.

Her eyes were open, and she was breathing.

Gwen and her husband helped him to his feet. As he began to move, a group of blue-uniformed men came past the stretcher toward him. He assumed they were there to arrest him. They stopped before him, and the one who was obviously in charge stepped forward. He was a large, beefy man in his fifties, with steel-gray hair and mustache. His eyes took in the sight of David in the blanket, shivering, and the man and woman who flanked him. Mike said something to him and pointed out at the water behind them. The man nodded grimly and turned to his subordinates.

"Wilson and Lopez, get these people into the house. The rest of you, come with me." Looking back over his shoulder, he called to a blue-clad figure on the shore. "Get that rowboat over here, the big one."

"If it doesn't float, we're going to need divers," one of the others said. He reached for his radio and began to talk into it.

David thought he meant the rowboat. What did that mean, he wondered, "if it doesn't float"? Why wouldn't the rowboat—

Then he realized what the cop meant. It. The body. Victor Dimorta: Valentine. They'll have to fish him out, what's left of him. He'd forgotten all about him. . . .

He drew the blanket tighter around his shivering body, and with the two officers followed Gwen and Mike down the dock. The little group passed a lone officer, a woman, kneeling beside the fallen Beretta, guarding it. He looked up toward the parking lot in time to see the paramedics load the stretcher into an ambulance. As it shrieked away, lights flashing, he moved his lips in silent prayer for Jillian Talbot. He continued to pray for her as they moved through the crowd of party guests and into the main house.

There was no music now. For the first time tonight, the ancient gramophone was silent. Mike went immediately to the hearth to rebuild the fire, and Gwen brought him a glass of brandy. Flanked by the two officers, David sat on a couch close to the roaring flames and waited to tell the story.

EPILOGUE

JUNE

SHE STOOD ON THE LITTLE STRIP OF BEACH BESIDE THE dock, gazing out over the lake, waiting. The thin blouse over her bathing suit was enough to ward off the slight, early morning chill of the surrounding forest. Even so, she hugged her arms to her as she remembered.

Gwen and Mike, now making breakfast for the guests in the house behind her, had told her she could stay there as long as she liked, and she was grateful for the isolation of the writing colony. The police had finished their business months ago, but the press was unrelenting. The story itself had been bad enough, but the appearance of the fluffy *New York* cover story two days after the initial nationwide headlines had further amplified the problem. Gwen had finally disconnected the single telephone in the compound, wondering aloud how so many reporters from all over America had managed to get the unlisted number. Now there was a new unlisted number, and they'd see how long that lasted. She smiled at the thought of Gwen: she had good friends.

Tara and Doug. He'd finally arrived to make up for the canceled date—shortly before Valentine's Day, wouldn't you know. Nearly four months ago. Doug had canceled their date because of Jill, because the sight of her had brought back painful memories. Cold feet. But subsequent events had proved to him—o all of them—ow tenuous life is, and how precious. So Doug called Tara. He didn't have to explain to her that he would no longer mourn his murdered wife.

315

Besides, there were other people to mourn.

Barney Fleck. The tears began as she thought of him. Mrs. Fleck and Verna Poole had descended on Mill City, Pennsylvania, with grim determination. And it had indeed been grim. They and the sheriff and his deputy had turned the Dimorta house upside-down. They had found traces of blood in an upstairs closet, in front of the paintings. She'd seen photo reproductions of a couple of the paintings in the newspapers: horrible, sick pictures of women in various stages of dismemberment. Okay, not women—*one* woman. Herself. In keeping with the fantasy, he'd signed them "Nate Levin." They were probably the last things Barney saw before he died.

The sharp-eyed young deputy had noticed the freshly turned earth in the back garden, and that's ow they found him. Barney was given a full police funeral in Brooklyn. She'd stood off to the side, wincing at her own fresh pain, watching Jane Fleck and Verna Poole and his family and friends. As the commissioner presented Jane with the American flag and the gunshots resounded through the cemetery, she prayed for Barney. And for Dr. Philbin. And for all the others, including her own unborn child.

It had been a boy, they informed her when she demanded to know. She had miscarried, they said, a direct result of the blow to her stomach and the sustained lack of oxygen in the freezing lake that had nearly killed her. Nate—Victor Dimorta—ad claimed one final victim. His son.

Nate—*no*! She couldn't, *wouldn't* think of him that way. His name had been Victor Dimorta. Valentine. He had murdered seven people. Eight, including the baby. They had left behind families and friends who could only mourn them: more victims. The only people who were happy about him were the Japanese businessmen who had

316

snapped up the final collection of paintings from Henry Jason's gallery for an undisclosed sum. *Life*, she thought: his final painting. She shook her head at the horrible irony of it.

As she waited, she thought about it all; the whole, strange story. The stupid practical joke perpetrated by three careless young women—okay, *four* careless young women—that had, in an odd way, started the whole thing. But no, it had truly begun eighteen years before that, the day Victor Dimorta was born.

Mary Daley had come out to visit her last weekend, with Tara and Doug. She announced that she was finally going to write a book, with Jill's permission: the biography of Victor Dimorta.

Yes, Jill had said, write it. If everyone could learn the whole story, maybe it would help. There were other Victor Dimortas in the world—and other Jill Talbots. Yes, she'd repeated, write the story.

She winced as she thought about that: writing. She'd been here at the writing colony for nearly four months now, recuperating and hiding from the world. But she would leave soon. She would go back to New York, to a new apartment. She was selling the apartment on Barrow Street as she had sold the one on Central Park West, and for the same reason. It was time to begin again. And it was time to write again. She would not use the idea she'd been forming, the thriller set in the art world, with all the borrowed facts from Nate.

Victor Dimorta, she told herself again. His name was Victor Dimorta.

It was going to take a long time, but she would do it. She would survive this, and she would be stronger for it. And it would begin right now, this morning. That's why she was here now, waiting.

As if on cue, David MacFarland arrived on the beach beside her. He had a T-shirt on over his bathing suit, and he looked surprisingly animated for someone out on bail. She'd paid it, as she was paying for his defense attorneys. The arraignment was next week, but the lawyers assured them that there was a good case for dropping charges, all things considered. David didn't care: he was willing to spend time in prison. He would do even that, he'd said, for Cass.

He came quietly down to stand next to her, leaning over to kiss her on the cheek.

"Good morning," he said as he pulled his shirt off over his head. "Ready for your first lesson?"

She smiled and dropped her blouse on the bank beside his shirt. "Yes, David, I'm ready."

He regarded her closely. "You're not afraid?"

"No, I'm not afraid." She looked out over the gray lake. Because she felt it, because she meant it, she added, "I'm not afraid of anything."

Smiling again and reaching for his hand, Jillian Talbot walked forward into the water.

ACKNOWLEDGMENTS

ANY NEW YORK RESIDENT WILL GLADLY TELL YOU that although Jill Talbot's building actually exists, it is only six stories high, in accordance with the regulations for Greenwich Village, which is a New York City landmark. The building facing hers, on the north side of Barrow Street, is only four stories high, which would make spying on her difficult (even if she *does* live on the roof!). There is no Mill City, Pennsylvania, no Hartley College, no Peconic Writing Colony, and no ski resort such as I have described in Boulder, Colorado.

I would like to thank the following people for their assistance in the preparation of this novel:

My colleagues at Murder Ink, my friends, and my family, for their unflagging encouragement and support.

Judith Albert, Renée Cyr, Terry Hall, Jennifer Jaffee, Steve Miller, Dr. Arlene Pack, Larry Pontillo, Sharon Ragan, Ann Romeo, and Elizabeth Ubell, who answered certain questions and provided legal and medical information. Any errors are my own, not theirs.

My agent, Stuart Krichevsky, for getting my work out there, and just for being my most enthusiastic fan.

My friends at Little, Brown and Company, particularly my editor, Fredrica. Friedman, for her brilliant guidance.

Most of all, I thank the people—friends, acquaintances, and even strangers—who have told their personal stories regarding the topic of this novel. Katie Couric's recent television documentary on the subject was most enlightening, as was the testimony of the people who came forward and talked to her. I have the greatest admiration and respect for Theresa Saldana, actress and survivor, and

Victims for Victims, the organization she founded in the wake of her own ordeal.

All of the characters and events in this novel are fictitious, but Jill Talbot's peril is, unfortunately, entirely plausible. I have seen the statistics, and they are unacceptable: stalking is one of the most prevalent—and potentially avoidable—major crimes in the world today. With newer, stronger laws than those we presently have, we may be able to do something about it.

Dear Reader:

I hope you enjoyed reading this Large Print book. If you are interested in reading other Beeler Large Print titles, ask your librarian or write to me at

> Thomas T. Beeler, *Publisher*
> Post Office Box 659
> Hampton Falls, New Hampshire 03844

You can also call me at 1-800-251-8726 and I will send you my latest catalogue.

Audrey Lesko and I choose the titles I publish in Large Print. Our aim is to provide good books by outstanding authors—books we both enjoyed reading and liked well enough to want to share. We warmly welcome any suggestions for new titles and authors.

Sincerely,